A VISIT FROM VOLTAIRE

A VISIT FROM
Voltaire

Dinah Lee Küng

Peter Halban
LONDON

FIRST PUBLISHED IN GREAT BRITAIN BY
PETER HALBAN PUBLISHERS LTD
22 Golden Square
London W1F 9JW
2003

A catalogue record for this book is available from the British Library.

ISBN 1870015 80 0

Typeset by
Computape Typesetting, Scarborough, North Yorkshire
Printed in Great Britain
by MPG Books Ltd, Bodmin, Cornwall

Monsieur V. says *merci*
To Helen, Mike, Nina, and Kadi
Katie, George and Martine
Dedicated to my husband, Peter

A Note from the Author

This book is part of that genre of fiction in which well-known persons, both living and dead, feature in the narrative. Only those persons given their real names exist. All others are fictional and any resemblance to persons living or dead is nothing more than a coincidence.

Contents

The Last Straw

"We're broke."

"No, we're not," I correct my husband. "We have $85,000 in the bank."

"We did yesterday," Peter says. "We don't now. I've just had a chat with our so-called contractor."

His haunted face glances in the direction of the gutted kitchen. The workers are enjoying their second coffee break of the morning – croissants, butter, jam, black coffee, and cigarettes.

"They're running 75% over his original estimate."

"This includes installing the kitchen and rebuilding the stairs to the third floor, right?"

Peter shakes his head. "Apparently not."

A burst of raucous French laughter from the kitchen makes us wince.

"Where'd he go after you talked to him?"

"The contractor? He left to look in on another job."

"Off to bankrupt someone else. Isn't there anything we can do?"

There is a long silence. Peter, hypnotized by sudden destitution only five years away from retirement, stares right through me. In Manhattan, I would suggest we sue the pants off the contractor. Now we've moved to Peter's country. This time I'm the foreigner, in a small village in the Jura mountains.

I bite back the word, "lawsuit," and wait to hear the Swiss solution.

"I'm taking the kids skiing."

"Peter, are you okay? Skiing? Now? Shouldn't we talk to a lawyer? Or an accountant? Isn't there some kind of contractors' tribunal we can appeal to before it's too late?" He isn't listening. "Where are you going? Are you all right?"

"I'm fine," he says. "I'm going skiing."

"But you promised to put up shelves this morning so I can unpack our books. We've waited six weeks for this stuff to arrive. You go back to work on Monday. And you can't leave me alone with those guys! What if they try to ask me something? I can hardly understand a word they say. Besides . . . besides . . . our kids don't ski!"

"You forget I was a ski instructor to pay my way through college. They're half-Swiss. It's time I taught them," he says with eerie resolution. "Are they upstairs? We'd better hurry before the rental place closes for lunch."

"Don't you think we should talk more about what the contractor said?"

I've seen this movie. The parched Legionnaire stumbles off into the desert without a drop of water, never to be seen again. The diver delirious with nitrogen pulls off his oxygen tank and drifts away. The space walker disconnects from the mother ship and spirals off into blackness. A Swiss facing financial ruin takes the ski lift to oblivion.

He summons the children.

"Peter, not right now, with these guys installing — "

"Oh, boy! Finally! Is the snow deep enough now? You said we had to wait a few more weeks. Theo, those are my gloves. Hey, Mama, we're going skiing! Mama? Don't you want to learn how to ski?" The eager faces of Alexander, Theo, and Eva-Marie glance up at me over the tumble of snow boots and parkas.

Ten minutes later, I stand abandoned in our empty living

room, surrounded by one hundred and forty-four cardboard boxes. An electric saw whines from the kitchen. I can just make out the carpenter shouting some vulgarities over Franco-Arab rap music from a radio. The gasman adds some salacious riposte. My French is only good enough to make out that the innuendoes are about me – this *New Yorkaise* who ordered a "wok" gas-burner.

Something the carpenter adds about my bottom inspires suggestive retorts from the tiling man from Ticino. I contemplate our new poverty and wonder which happy jokester will be the very last to be paid.

There is a restful silence that grows ominous, some grunting, and a change in tone. Worryingly serious discussion follows. Then footsteps.

"*Madame?*"

I follow the carpenter and the gasman to the kitchen where the work island stands on bricks smack in the center of the room, a granite cube blocking all passage.

"Oh, uh, no, not in the middle, put it here, *ici*," I stand an arm's reach from the sink.

"*Non.*" The lanky carpenter dolefully wags his head.

"*ICI!*" No, I mustn't shout. "*Ici*, here. Not there. *Pas là.*"

"*Non,*" squeaks the gasman. "*Regardez les règles.*"

The carpenter thrusts five pages of Swiss regulations into my hands. Flicking his cigarette butt on what would be a parquet floor if they weren't so many weeks behind schedule, he shifts his weight to the other hip and coolly points to the second page. I can just make out some tiny print to the effect that an *île* must be placed far enough from the counter to allow three full-grown men to pass. *Trois hommes.* At the same time.

"There must be some mistake," I insist. "That would mean —"

"*Ici,*" the gasman squeaks, swinging his legs from his perch on the island.

"Wait a minute." I flip back to the first page. "These are

restaurant regulations!"

The carpenter explains in slow, simple French, as if I were a backward child. Swiss kitchens are too small to have islands. Counters, *oui, les îles, non.* My kitchen is too big, too American. Hence he's resorted to the rules for installing professional cooking spaces, *comme pour l'Armée.*

Down in the village, the Protestant chapel and Catholic church bells ring out noon. All around me there is a clank of tools hitting the floor. The workers wave, *"Bon appetit,"* and file through the kitchen door like a circus act retreating from the ring. Out in the snow, I see the tiling man light up a cigarette and cellphone in one seamless gesture.

I return to the living room and savagely attack packing tape with a fruit knife. I wrench open the top of the first box and a whiff of mildew hits my nostrils. I peer into the box and pull off wads of the *Los Angeles Times.* Something's wrong here. We just moved from New York, not L.A.

"Wait a minute," I mutter, panicking. I'm staring at sixty-year-old paperbacks by John Masters and James Mitchener with yellowing, lurid covers.

Under *Bhowani Junction,* lie the *The Complete Works of Eugene O'Neill.* At the bottom of the box lie five-years' worth of *Theater Arts* magazines.

Where are my books? A vision of my late mother wagging a finger at me from her death bed, insisting no one ever throw out her *Theater Arts,* haunts me.

"A complete play in each issue. You couldn't find some of these plays in print anywhere else."

I know, Mother, I know.

Wildly, I rip open box after box. Our kitchenware is here and the toys already went upstairs. But the shippers have sent my parents' books from storage in L.A. and kept back at least half of the books belonging to Peter and me.

I'm whipped. I sit down, holding in my hand a flat package. Folding back a corner of brown paper wrapping, I unveil a framed black-and-white photo of a middle-aged Leonard Bernstein pointing a gun to his temple and smiling at the camera with chagrin.

A caption on the back reads, "The critics will shoot me. L.B., New York."

New York. Only weeks since our departure, it seems a lifetime ago. Through the whirlwind of open suitcases, sawdust, and drills, here is the great composer of *West Side Story*, pantomiming during rehearsal that he'd reached the end of his rope.

I know just how you feel, Lenny.

I unwrap eleven volumes of *The Story of Civilization* by Will and Ariel Durant – the glue of the spines crackling with age. My heart gives a turn when I see my mother's handwriting in the margins. She didn't just read, she chatted back in a torrent of comments down the margins of each page. She had a relationship with dead people going back centuries.

Here in these foreign mountains, so far from anything I regard as civilization, the finality of my emigration hits me. My mother will never see her books arranged in my first real home, bought after decades of overseas assignments and rented apartments.

I hoist the heavy tomes on to the new shelves – *The Age of Louis XIV, The Age of Voltaire, Rouss* —

Frantic pounding at the living-room door alerts me to Peter's panicked face hunting for me through the frosted window.

"What is it?"

His expensive ski suit is ripped open at the sleeve and covered up to his shoulders in clumps of snow. His drained expression freezes my heart.

"Eva-Marie's had an accident. Her ski caught in the underbrush at the side of the *piste*. She ricocheted off a tree. I found her lying in a snow drift with her leg facing the wrong way."

"What? Wha..?"

"I'm leaving the boys with you. The doctor's waiting for us at a clinic in Genolier. Wait – I have to warn you. Her face is pretty bad."

I rush out to the car and find my six-year-old lying across the back seat of the Subaru, her entire right leg enveloped up to her hip in an inflatable red casing. Her face is awash with blood, cuts and bruises. I feel faint at seeing a ghastly quarter-inch hole dug by a tree branch into the bridge of her perfectly-sculpted nose.

"I'm sorry, Mama."

Under all the congealing blood, she is sheet-white with pain and she hasn't even seen herself in a mirror yet. I'm dizzy with horror.

"It's not your fault, baby."

I want to throttle my husband, Mr. "I-was-a-ski-instructor," but he drives off too soon for that. I never learned to ski. I always disliked the clumsy equipment of skiing, and the social pretensions of *après-ski*. Now watching father and daughter race off to the hospital, there is no remaining doubt. I, who have just moved to a Swiss ski station, really hate skiing.

"I feel funny, Mama," says a forgotten voice at my side. Theo and his older brother Alexander are waiting in their ski suits just inside the kitchen door. Theo, who is asthmatic, has red-rimmed eyes.

"How's your breathing?"

"Not so good. I'm getting that rubber band feeling across my chest." My eight-year-old sounds apologetic, the classic middle child. We climb past broken planks to his attic bedroom. Sadly, I unpack his nebulizer, switch the voltage from 120 to 240 and place the mask over his small face. He greedily sucks in the aerated medicine, panting in the hope of relief. There is no question he's going into an asthma crisis. I take his pulse, feel his stomach, and fetch a saucepan for the inevitable vomit. The same damned, hateful routine I thought we had left behind in the polluted Manhattan air.

My husband returns with Eva-Marie in his arms around five that afternoon. Underneath fresh bandages, her face is still pale, but the drama of a leg-cast up to the hip is enhanced by painkillers and bravado. The fresh plaster has been wrapped with neon-pink protective tape.

"It's a spiral break of the tibia, from here to here." My eyes follow the tracing of my husband's finger. I start cutting up her brand-new school pants, the ones I bought at Gap in New York just days before our flight. I slash angrily all the way up to the crotch to accommodate the plastered limb.

"The village doctor is coming to check on both of them as soon as he can, a Dr. Claude," Peter says.

I marvel. A doctor who makes house calls? This is so far the only reason I can think of to live in Switzerland. We agree that Dr. Claude will first visit Eva-Marie and Peter on the second floor while I wait with Theo on the third.

The merciless snowfall starts up again, amassing on Theo's skylight, flake by flake. Soon the window pane is a square of pure white. I lay my head, eyes burning with the day's unshed tears, at the foot of Theo's bed. Even his rasping can't keep me from dozing off.

I'm awakened by a polite cough and faint tap at the open door. I look up to see a slender young man of medium height dressed in pants fastened below the knees – the kind that people wear for cross-country skiing – with heavy white socks finished off by soft leather shoes. He's wearing a long, padded coat, a hand-knitted scarf, and a woolly cap on his head.

His white flesh stretches across the bones like a drum skin. His aquiline nose has a slight aristocratic bump and is tinged with blue from the cold. He has a wide, smiling mouth and a strong, almost pointed, chin. What is that pleasant, almost spicy smell he carries in from the snow? I can't imagine anyone looking less like Dr. Rothberg, our sixty-year-old paediatrician back in New York. He always smelled like antiseptic hand wash.

I sit upright at attention. It's obvious our emergency call has interrupted this man's afternoon outing.

"*Merci, merci*, thanks for coming to us on a Saturday evening."

He brushes this aside. His hands are delicate, and adorned with two ornate rings. Doctors in America don't wear fussy rings, but on an evening like this, I'll take what I get.

"You've seen Eva-Marie? Will her leg really be all right?"

"I'm sure it will. A delightful little patient. The doctor who set the leg has done a very thorough – and if I might say so – colorful job."

I am relieved this man speaks good English. I was dreading a country doctor who sounded like Inspector Clouseau.

He darts to Theo's bedside and gently places long, thin fingers on the boy's forehead. Theo's face is flushed red, but his sweat is cold. I shift into "competent mother mode."

"Theo's had bronchial variant asthma since he was eighteen months old. I may have given him too much ventolin, but I haven't got on top of the wheezing yet."

"His pulse is very high, *Madame*."

"Yes, well, I probably started the medicine too late. We were all distracted by the broken leg. He must've caught a chill on the slope while waiting for Eva-Marie to be rescued."

The man ignores my despairing noises. Moving Theo's noisy nebulizer carefully out of his way, he reaches for a chair with a polite lifting of the eyebrows.

"Oh, yes, please," I say. Only then does he sit down, so European.

"The cold wind brought it on, *non?*"

"Well, in New York, his triggers were cold air, fatigue, and over-exercise. No problem with dust mites, or animals. They did allergy tests on him at Columbia Presbyterian Hospital."

"Any bleeding?"

"No." I recoil. "He's never coughed up blood."

"I beg your pardon, *Madame*. It's my poor English. It is so long I haven't spoken English. I ask myself, have you bled him?"

The room is softly lit. I hope my momentary confusion doesn't show. "Nooo," I say, "but I do have a bottle of ephedrine, just for emergencies. I brought it from New York."

"It's probably just as well. I was never terribly convinced by leeches, or the dried toads of my father's day. Such remedies supposedly cleanse the blood when combined with lots of liquids."

Peter warned me St-Cergue was rural, but leeches?

"Have you tried lemonade?" he goes on.

"You did say lemonade, didn't you?"

"*Oui, les citrons.*" He seems accustomed to a Doubting Thomas like me. "At the age of twenty-nine I caught smallpox during a house party at the Château des Maisons. The other guests fled in terror. Dr. Gervais rode out from Paris to attend me. I locked myself up and drank nothing, nothing you understand, but two hundred pints of lemonade and *voilà*, I was cured."

Those sharp brown eyes test my reaction. "Never underestimate lemonade."

"Lemonade."

"It can work miracles. If you'll pardon the expression."

"Doctor, would you excuse me?"

I leap over the broken planks and scattered nails to find Peter reading *And To Think That I Saw It On Mulberry Street* at Eva-Marie's bedside.

"Peter, please come upstairs and join us," I hiss. "I think you'll find this Dr. Claude is a total quack. A *careful* quack, I'll give him that. He's ruled out leeches and dried toads, but he's opting for the lemonade cure."

Peter glances up, uncomprehending.

"I've had it, Peter. We camp for weeks eating off a grocery store *hibachi*, sleeping with bats, and blasted by Arab hip hop. This morning we find out we're broke, that our kitchen has to look like an army canteen, that the shippers sent the wrong boxes — "

"What?"

"YES! and to round things off, two out of our three children are taken seriously ill. NOW we get a local doctor who prescribes lemonade for smallpox. Peter, I'm done! I'm cooked! Take me out of the oven! I want to go home!"

A thick-set man in sweater and dark pants emerges from our master bathroom, drying his hands with one of my brand new Bloomingdales towels.

This stranger smiles politely. "*Enchanté, Madame. Docteur Grégoire Claude. Je suis prêt pour Theodor.* Or we speak the English, if you prefer it." I shake Dr. Claude's moist hand and mutter, "Peter, who's the man upstairs?"

He shrugs, "The workers all left."

"Nobody, I guess."

I've lost my mind, that's all. The Swiss are so sensible. We'll deal with the small question of my sanity later.

A Real Nobody

The second Dr. Claude and I clamber up to the third floor.

Theo's rales — a sound like rolling pebbles rising from his small lungs — greet our ears before we even reach the landing. Dr. Claude runs me through the procedure: two vials of ventolin administered via the nebulizer every three hours throughout the night, extended to an interval of four hours if the gravelly sound subsides. If Theo starts to suck hard at his stomach or the muscles of his small neck start to flutter, I should give him the first dose of ephedrine and drive him immediately to a hospital.

As for our girl, I must bring her to the clinic for a check-up in three days. Her facial bandages will be changed, but no one can judge the damage to the nose until the swelling subsides in about ten days. He can recommend an ear, nose and throat man, and a plastic surgeon later.

My husband accompanies Dr. Claude to the kitchen for coffee. I march back up to the attic.

The pine chair next to Theo's bed sits empty. I nervously look around me, but see only packing cartons covered in a childish scrawl, "Theos Toy."

"People always underestimate lemonade."

I jump in shock. The voice came from under the low eaves at the back of the room.

I wheel around and there, leaning easily against the beams in the shadow, is that lemonade guy again. There is no way this weirdo is touching my child. I move protectively in front of Theo who lies, eyes closed, breathing noisily.

"What'd you say?"

"Calm yourself, *Madame*. Sometimes it is only the puniest who survives. For example, take me, born on this very day, November 21st, the runt of five children. 'He won't last an hour,' my nurse wept! and called the priest to baptize me still wet from my mother's loins. Then a week passed, then a month and – oh, I was always sick, but here I am."

"Are you?"

I'm playing for time. He's probably the village idiot, somebody who's used to this old house standing empty. If he came in through the upper back door that connects the second floor to the rising slope behind the house, he could have snuck up to the attic unobserved. It's just that he looks rather insubstantial in the dark. And where did he learn English?

"*Oui*. Here to reassure you. I survived tuberculosis contracted from my own mother, then – oh, let me see —" he ticks off diseases on his fingers with ghoulish delight, "dysentery, smallpox, *la grippe*, fever, colic, erysipelas, gout, apoplexy, inflammation of the lungs, scurvy, herpes, rheumatism, and strangury!"

"That all sounds," I hesitate for fear of offending a loony, "awfully uncomfortable."

"*Oui, oui*. I finished off with deafness, indigestion, dropsy, falling teeth, loss of voice, neuritis, blindness and paralysis."

"Um, you seem better now. Where do you live? In the village? I'll just go catch Dr. Claude to give you a lift home."

"Oh, he can't see me," the visitor says, as if this is a small thing hardly worth mentioning.

I fight off rising panic.

"Theo?" I nudge my son gently.

"Hmm?" He opens his eyes over his mask.

"Is there anybody over there, at the end of the room?"

Theo glances down the length of scattered boxes and toys. "Nope."

"Maybe the light is bad. Wait a minute." I shine his toy flashlight into the deeper recesses of the room. I play the beam across the wall. The visitor casts no shadow.

"I'm tired," Theo sighs, and closes his eyes.

"You demand of yourself, am I a creature of the imagination?" the Frenchman asks blithely. "No. *Cogito ergo sum*, as they say." He chuckles, "Although I once changed that to, 'I have a body and I think; I know no more.'"

He glances at me, "You catch the difference, I hope?"

"More like *Cogito, ergo non es*, I would say – I can think straight, therefore you don't exist, *Monsieur*. Am I having a nervous breakdown?"

"*Au contraire!* I am the real me! I apologize for being somewhat materially diminished by circumstances beyond my control, although I think I could still lift something, if I just concentrate . . ."

The visitor grimaces almost comically with the effort of focusing on one of Theo's Playmobil cannibals. His fingers reach out and miss entirely. With an enormous grunt, the Frenchman manages to coalesce his digits into something more solid and the second time, he succeeds in grasping the little plastic figure and lifting it an inch or two in the air.

"Erh! *Voilà!*"

The cannibal drops back on the table. He looks at it for a second and mutters, "*Zut*. It's a question of monads, I think. Leibniz would know. I'll have to practice more if I want to get anything done."

He has such a frustrated expression on his face, that I giggle despite myself.

"I trust you didn't appear in my son's room just to perform party tricks. Why are you here?"

"Well, it's my birthday," he suggests, brightening. "Are you throwing me a *fête*?"

"A birthday party?"

"Obviously, you summoned me," he says, slightly offended.

"Sorry, I did not."

"*Pardonnez-moi.*"

He turns impatient. "Perhaps, you needed someone to remind you of the fragility and resilience of childhood, the eternal and often unwarranted fears of parents throughout the centuries? So, look who you got! Death always stood at my elbow," he laughs, but there is a creepy echo that dies a second too late.

"Now you plan to stand at mine?"

"Well, I thought I might stay right here," he suggests. "I'm no longer alive, so I won't take up much space or food. Although I was never able to give up coffee. Do I smell some brewing downstairs?"

"You're joking."

"It might be entertaining to linger for a while, keep you company, help you settle in. I take it your life has changed greatly without warning?"

I'm mesmerized. This invisible lunatic is reading my mind and I answer him carefully, racing to understand this new madness.

"Well, last year I was a correspondent with twenty years of reporting in China behind me, wife of the International Red Cross delegate to the United Nations in New York – wait a minute — "

Why am I confiding in this guy? I should be screaming for help.

"And now?" He lightly brushes some cobwebs caught in his luxurious curls. I'm beginning to suspect this character of wearing some kind of hairpiece.

"Now, we're camping in a near-derelict house in the middle of a ski station in economic decline. The wiring won't be finished 'til Christmas."

"Ah, *bien*, I see workers haven't changed in two centuries."

The stranger's sympathy is frighteningly soothing to my nerves. I can't help continuing, "What's worse, my husband loves it. He's finally back in Switzerland, 'the best of all possible worlds'."

"Ah," that expressive mouth breaks into a broad, knowing smile. "I can imagine a woman who has traveled and experienced life as you describe could not imagine being very happy in this *petit* village, 'the best of all possible worlds'."

"I hold out little hope . . ."

"I made a flourishing life in exile, so to speak, dragged from the excitement of Paris, the social whirl of the Court —"

"Court? There isn't even a bookstore here —"

"*Madame*, life is always either *ennui* or whipped cream. I expect today you've seen more whipping than cream, that's all. You just need a friend. Reading nurtures the soul, but an enlightened friend brings it solace."

"Yes. Yes! Solace, solace! Good word! I could use some of that." My burst of despair surprises even me.

"Sadly, my name is not Solace, *Madame*. I have yet to introduce myself properly."

Where's my sense of humor? Remember the Woody Allen story when he ends up playing poker with the Devil? I could unpack the chess set . . . "You can skip the formalities. Let's cut to the chase. Just reverse the events of today, starting with the contractor's little announcement, in exchange for my soul. I'm ready to cut a deal. Let's say my people call your people."

The visitor laughs, but it sounds kind, not satanic. "Oh, *chère Madame*, I'm not the DEVIL – although the Jesuits do call me the Anti-Christ."

He stands up and puts one hand behind his back and thrusts a toe in front of him. He bows very slightly, a minimal gesture that bespeaks merely basic courtesy.

"François-Marie Arouet, Seigneur de Tournay et Ferney, at your service," he says. He sits back down, a quicksilver motion of his slight frame. "You know, I overheard you downstairs just now, when you referred to me as 'Nobody.' I hope you now stand corrected. You may apologize."

"Well, Mr. Arouet, I'm sorry."

"I should think so," he sniffs. "I'm the greatest playwright, philosopher and essayist ever."

"Ever? When exactly were you born?"

His eyes widen. "Surely you've heard of me? Born in 1694, I came of age between the reigns of Louis XIV and Louis XV. Oh, what a period of political mayhem and social dissolution! It is I who broke the shackles of the Catholic Church over Western thinking!"

Now I know he can't be my own hallucination. I was a Chinese Studies major who slept through European history class. I'll have to look him up.

"You gape at me, *Madame*? Everywhere I go, I defy that royal terror, the Keeper of the Seals. I've mastered the scientific theories of Newton, have won my place at last in the Académie Française and, I might add," his bright eyes glitter, "have had my luck with the ladies."

He takes off his woolen scarf. "By the way, are you married or widowed?"

"Married," I mumble.

"That never made any difference before. I can always fit in. I'm a tutor to kings and empresses, a millionaire financier, a benevolent landlord, and a gentleman-farmer."

"Is that all? You can't be the Devil. Even the Devil would've been more modest."

He ignores my sarcasm.

"*Non*. They call me the true king of my time, *La Lumière*, the light. But that's enough for now. I can see you are *énervée*."

"I've lost my mind," I mumble. "I am bantering with a transparent person."

"I leave you now to tend to your child. *Bonne nuit, chère Madame*."

With a sweeping bow, this Lord of Light goes out by Theo's door. At least he's got the good taste not to fade through walls.

I sit, waiting for the next ghost to appear. The Headless Horseman? My Great Aunt Nell? Why this particular vision? I have nothing in common with this guy except, perhaps, that I graduated from U.C. Berkeley in the seventies, a period of mayhem and dissolution, for sure. Is this house haunted? And after a day like today, do I really deserve a ghost with a major attitude?

The Price of Imagination

I bolt upright in bed. Harry Lime was right about Switzerland. It's quiet out there. Too quiet. My New Yorker's subconscious can't stand this tranquility. I miss the comforting clatter of the garbage truck on 80th Street.

I hear sniffles next door. Eva-Marie is crying through her bandages in the dark. Stupidly I assume that what upsets me – the broken leg, the facial wounds, and the painful, inconvenient months to come – are the cause of her sleeplessness.

As usual with my third child, I've got it all wrong.

"I don't want to grow old," she sobs. "Next February, I'll be seven, and that's so *old*. That's the limit. Six is best. After six, it's, it's . . ."

"What?"

"Over. Seven is the last time you have imagination."

I embrace her tightly, the edge of her plastered hip cutting into my side. I croon into her ear, "No, no, look at me, I'm forty-nine and I still have imagination."

She closes her eyes, wrinkling the bandages around her temples. "You're different."

I haven't forgotten Saturday night's departure from lucidity, but everything was back to normal on Sunday – no apparitions in kneebreeches – just hours of tedious unpacking. Having an imaginary friend at age four or even six is right on schedule. Having one at forty-nine is worrying. I fish for more reassuring examples.

"Well, then, take Theo. He's eight and — "

"Right! And he doesn't believe in anything anymore – not even unicorns!"

This diagnosis of Theo's senility strikes me as a tad premature. He spent most of the weekend before the asthma attack playing *I, Claudius*, his beloved "blankie" draped over one hairless, pudgy shoulder. I hold to one hard and fast rule: they must not watch the episode where Caligula disembowels his sister pregnant with his love child. The boys might find this too inspiring.

"Playing *I, Claudius* takes imagination, doesn't it?"

"No, Mama. That's acting. Roman senators were real. I mean imagining real magic things."

I sigh, recalling when a five-year-old Singaporean visited Alexander in Manhattan for a playdate. He marched into my bedroom at 3:58 pm, announcing it was time to watch *Batman*.

"We don't watch T.V. during playdates," I told the intruder firmly. "In this house, we play with our imagination."

The child shook his head. "My mother hasn't bought me one of those yet."

Peter and I immediately disconnected the kids' T.V. from the cable feed and bought Broadway musicals, old-fashioned swashbucklers, the old Robin Hood black-and-white series – anything with more acting and imagination than special effects. I'll have to order more. Can videos keep them speaking decent English for the next decade? Or will they start slipping into French with a backwoods Vaudois dialect? Given a few more years on this Swiss mountain, where will they fit in? Where will I?

"My leg hurts," says Eva-Marie.

I give her a painkiller and soon she falls asleep, stringy hair pasted to her cheeks. The garish pink cast is propped up on a doll bed at the foot of her mattress. I ache at the sight of those tiny toes, painted blue with washable marker. She won't be able to touch them until after Christmas.

I tiptoe downstairs across the ground floor of our Grit Palace, kicking aside scraps of wall trim. It's still too soon to say how well our Hong Kong furniture will go with a low-ceilinged stone farmhouse. Suzy Wong meets Heidi.

The silence is broken by the rustling of paper packaging. Oh, God, is the loony back? I creep across the dining room and peer into the kitchen, hoping it's something I can handle, like rats.

"Hi, Mama."

"Oh, Alexander." I take a deep breath. "You're up early."

"I want more reading time before the train leaves." He pours himself a second bowl of cereal.

"Alexander?"

"Hmm?"

"Who reigned in France between Louis XIV and Louis XV?"

He glances at me over a thick history book. "Louis XIV½."

"Your mother is not that stupid."

"The Moon King."

"Yuk, yuk. Okay, you don't know."

"I know," he says, putting the book down with feigned reluctance. "The Regent, Philippe, the Duke of Orleans, a nephew of the Sun King."

"Was that a period of mayhem and dissolution?"

"I'm not sure," my skinny pedant weighs this question. "Depends on what you call dissolution." He gives his eyebrows a lusty Groucho Marx twitch.

"Who are his teachers?" a French voice butts in.

"OmiGod!" I cry.

"Sit on something?" Alexander hardly glances up from his tome.

Our ghost saunters into the kitchen from the living room. I see he has been busy near the fireplace. On the coffee table sits one of my mother's porcelain coffee cups. Somehow, he has excavated this delicate vessel from a newspaper-wrapped jumble of jelly-jar glasses, cheap Hong Kong dinnerware, and kid-proof plastic cups.

"I spent Sunday warming up my physical capacities," he explains. "I've moved on from cannibals."

He seats himself unobtrusively next to Alexander who doesn't blink an eye. My child is already dressed in his jeans and sweater, and in a few minutes he'll head out into the pre-dawn chill. Gone are the days of the Jamaican nanny laying out his St. Boniface uniform in time for the private yellow bus service.

What do I smell? A trace of carnation?

"Alexander, do you smell something?"

"I took a bath last night. Theo didn't."

"My toilet water, *Madame*."

The ghost is not only freshly perfumed, he looks as perky as if he'd been up for hours. He's wearing a floppy red velvet cap over thick brown curls tied loosely at the nape of his thin neck with a black ribbon. His face is scraped clean of whiskers. His dressing gown of green brocade reaches below his stockinged knees. His rather bony feet are encased in needlepointed slippers. In a word, gorgeous.

"History student?" he asks casually, glancing at Alexander's book.

I nod, slowly. Are there any English-speaking shrinks closer to us than Geneva? This'll take more than one consultation, for sure.

Alexander goes upstairs to brush his teeth.

"History is often just a list of those who have accommodated themselves with the property of other people," the phantom quips. "Or a picture of human crimes and misfortunes."

"Why have you come back?" I whisper. "Your birthday's over. My little crisis is over. I'm fine. You're fine. Goodbye."

"You're fine, *Madame*! Well, we're all contented! As for me, I hardly slept last night for working my way through your books. It was good lifting practice, but such a disappointment!

Not a single edition of Locke or Newton! On the other hand, no Descartes or that rubbishy Pascal. Some books of philosophy, literature, and history. And most wonderfully, anthologies and biographies pertaining to your modern theater."

"Those were my mother's books," I whisper through my teeth. "Those theater anthologies are fifty years old."

"The theater is *éternel*, *Madame*. A passion that knows no bounds. I recall a certain Mr. Bond in London – a very wealthy man. He loved my play *Zaïre* so much he produced it only so that he could star in the leading role. Well, on opening night, Mr. Bond was so enthusiastic about his death scene, he actually dropped dead on stage!"

"In front of the audience?"

"Now there's someone who appreciated drama! I tell you, the audience went wild."

"What did you do?"

He shrugs. "I was only sad that the performance couldn't be repeated. Ticket sales flew heavenward." One elegant digit points at my low ceiling beams.

"My mother never took her love of theater that seriously," I reflect.

The ghost is practicing moving Corn Puffs into the shape of a fleur-de-lis. "In one of your boxes I found nothing but factual books on Asiatic subjects and slim little novels about murder and death – a morbid obsession!"

"So they did send some of my books. I've given up journalism. I'm trying a new career as a mystery writer."

"Your husband's *bibliothèque* was more rewarding – Goethe, Schiller, and an encyclopaedia, unreadable of course, as it's in German. Frederick the Great and I corresponded in French for forty-two years. You and I can manage in English very well until you learn French. My dear friend Madame du Châtelet learned English in about six months. You'll just do the same, but in reverse."

"You can't stay here for six months — !"

He scrutinizes his surroundings. "Now, I look forward to hearing the boy's lessons."

"He can't see you – I hope?"

"I said I'll *listen*. Who's his tutor?"

Where to begin? Peter and I had looked forward to an escape from patronizing New York private school "educators" dripping phrases like "the gift of time," "age-appropriate," and "reading readiness." Now we find that Swiss youngsters learn by filling in worksheets as if they are all training to be clerks. Given Switzerland's fame for banking secrecy and hotel management, perhaps that's not far off.

Worse, in Switzerland, the sixth-grade teachers decide who will go to college. Is this some kind of scholastic homage to Genevan Calvinist theories of predestination? Alexander is already terrified by next year's "cut." You'd think his lack of French was the first concern, but no. His new teacher warned us he might not make college-track because his backpack is too messy.

Alexander, transformed into a huge wad of Goretex, shuffles through the kitchen into the laundry room. He never gives Monsieur Arouet a glance, although he stuffs the Corn Puff fleur-de-lis into his mouth. In a second, we hear him rummaging around for his snow boots.

"He goes to public school by train."

M. Arouet is astonished. "No tutor? By train? Alone? It's black as a Jesuit's cassock out there. Well, it was five minutes ago."

Dawn's pink rays are just cresting the Alps across the lake, waking a pack of huskies caged next door. Their howling fills the neighborhood and wakes up the second team down the road.

My skittish companion jumps in alarm. "A royal hunting pack?"

"Sled-dogs. Big winter sport around here."

M. Arouet recovers, but is still astonished at my callous maternal behavior. He wags one of his skinny fingers in my face.

"And you're sending your son to the dogs! I know this part of the world. A boy who reads such books deserves better! *Madame*, as the son of a mere Parisian notary, I was tutored at home by the Abbé de Châteauneuf, a man of wide culture and blessedly broad views."

The phantom turns reflective, "Ah, the Abbé! He was the last love of the great courtesan, Ninon de Lenclos, who seduced even Cardinal Richelieu in her time. In 1704 the Abbé took me to her house in Paris and there she was at eighty-four, still swathed in fine satins and lace." He leans over the table and giggles, "*She was dry as a mummy*."

"You don't say!" I too, leaning forward, repress a smile.

"Yes, but she bequeathed me 2,000 francs for book money – by the way, don't you drink coffee?"

This morbid picture of a dessicated courtesan makes me think Alexander might be just as well off with Swiss worksheets and neat backpacks.

"Did the Abbé introduce you to anything besides prostitutes?"

He straightens in indignation. "*Mais oui*! He taught me that religion was a device used by rulers to keep the ruled in order and awe. For saying that, *Madame*, he could be hung from the gallows! And he prepared me well for seven more years with the Jesuits in Paris, men who trained the mind of Descartes, and all the great dissenters of France."

He adds, "Although those damned Jesuits buggered me to such a degree that I shall never get over it as long as I live."

He gazes longingly at the coffee machine. "Perhaps some coffee flavored with cloves, the way they serve it in Versailles?"

Alexander returns from the laundry room and dons gloves and scarf. I have no wish to see him raped by priests, but I do wish he were going off to sharpen his wits on Aristotle, Epicurus, and Descartes. I kiss my first-born and pull his balaclava down over his forehead in a maternal gesture bravely borne.

Monsieur Arouet appears beside us in the doorway, struggling with a heavy woolen coat that covers his dressing gown and changing into hand-cobbled shoes. It seems he's come equipped with his own wardrobe.

"Where do you think you're going?"

"To the train, Mama. Bye." Alexander kisses my cheek and opens the kitchen door, shooting a blast of frozen air straight up my Japanese *yukata*.

"To the train! You are a careless woman, I vow. When nine-year-old 'Zozo' Arouet left for the Jesuit College of Louis-le-Grand, he did not walk alone. I was accompanied by a man-servant as well as my tutor."

"Well, as you may have noticed, *Zozo*," I retort, "we don't have any servants at all. The station's just down the hill. This isn't Paris, or for that matter, New York. He's perfectly safe."

But I can see it is more than concern for Alexander's physical welfare that is drawing this will-o'-the-wisp's attention.

"Which train, *Madame*?" Out of his pocket, M. Arouet takes an enormous jewel-encrusted watch on a gold chain.

"7:12. Why bother if he can't see you?"

"I'll be back *tout de suite* for coffee. Maybe mixed with champagne, or mustard, the way Frederick the Great served it? Or with a touch of ginger, Dutch-style?"

"How can you drink — ?" I protest, but the Phantom of the Overcoat's already scurrying after Alexander.

Amazed, I watch my son's slender form, bent over with the weight of his backpack, trudging through the pines at the end of our property and down the shoveled path between the snow banks. He never glances at the reedy figure dancing lightly at his side.

The winter sun rises behind them in a blood-red sky to the east of Europe's tallest mountain, Mont Blanc.

As the two of them turn at our gate, I hear the ghost's breathy voice in the morning air like an actor declaiming to an unseeing audience.

"I may have fought the Jesuits' doctrines all my life, but I never forgot what they taught me. The most industrious, frugal, regulated life possible . . . Nothing will ever erase in my heart the memory of Father Porée. Never did a man make study and virtue so pleasant . . ."

Alexander is oblivious to this flow of advice, but *something* has communicated itself to the child. A more positive breeze in the air? The rousing sight of a blazing sky? He straightens his shoulders as he disappears from my view.

My bones have felt chilled since I got off that plane, but now, thinking of M. Arouet at my son's side, my heart feels a welcome warmth. So what if Alexander can't see his talkative escort? I guess this lunacy is all mine to enjoy. Maybe I'll hold off the appointment with a shrink. This eighteenth-century blabbermouth has brought an unexpected perspective to all the newness of our life here by talking of things even stranger. His withered whores and buggering Jesuits pour balm on my panicked soul.

I'm shivering in my cotton wrap. I'll have to order one of those ugly duvet bathrobes from a catalogue, the kind that makes you look like a rolled-up mattress. Any pretense at being fashionably dressed is going down the tubes in this rustic setting. Since we left New York, I've piled on clothing without regard for cut or color, skipped my make-up, and scraped my hair into a careless ponytail.

Wait. This house ghost's got more style than me – and he's dead. I better slap on some blusher. I just hope he won't want to borrow my face powder.

I relinquish the bathroom to Peter, in a hurry to ferry our daughter in his arms to the clinic. Upstairs, I hear Theo starting up his asthma machine. It's at least comforting to know that when I packed up all our worldly and spiritual goods to come to Switzerland, my imagination came with me.

Call Me V.

While I was finishing the unpacking, I did some sneaky research among my mother's books and I've nailed down the Velvet One. Why me? I'm unworthy, to say the least. He's so cocky, I'm not ready to address him by his title just yet. I don't want to give him the satisfaction. I'll wait for him to announce himself.

"By the way, Monsieur Arouet is a bit formal. You may call me 'V' if you like. That's how I signed many of my letters," he says, breezing in. "I was in a hurry. I wrote some fifty thousand in all. They fill ninety volumes. You must get a set."

So he's taking the modest tack for a change. I could have done worse in the poltergeist department. He's quite the polite young gentleman. Not only does he not penetrate walls, but he's always exquisitely mannered and discreet, not to mention freshly attired, shaved, and ready to please. He even smells good.

His presence also helps in more concrete ways. With V. as company, I don't feel so besieged by workers who regard the restoration of our house as a communal T.V.A. project padding their wallets in time for Christmas shopping. When the carpenter announces after a three-hour lunch, "This is not America! I work to live, I don't live to work!" I swear I see V. push a winch off a shelf on to the carpenter's toes.

I also appreciate that the sprightly Monsieur Arouet is a dirty

"Entertainment Tonight!" broadcast in wigs and shoe buckles, a walking 1720s edition of *Vanity Fair*, a cavorting illustration of the joke, "I never repeat gossip, so listen well the first time."

Put another way, he never shuts up. We've moved on from his early childhood to his start in *salon* society. What a flake! How this rhyming flibbertigibbet in lace cuffs ever became the Great You-Know-Who mystifies me. He's obsessed with social tittle-tattle.

When he told me of the four Nesle sisters who served as mistresses to King Louis XV, each in her backstabbing turn more venal than her sibling, I stopped worrying so much about rivalry between Theo and Eva-Marie. When he described yesterday how Madame d'Étioles caught Louis' eye by hanging around the Sénart hunting grounds in a baroque carriage while the queen was looking the other way, I was relieved to learn that Peter's new secretary is a spinster who wears twinsets and pearls.

Nor do I dismiss the sympathy of sharing the house with someone who like me, is constantly cold. He's always wrapping his fleshless form in shawls and finely-fitted housecoats and vests.

But we all know how this plays out. I watched "Topper" on our black-and-white T.V. when I was a kid. The ghosts George and Marian always got the old fuddy-duddy Cosmo Topper into trouble by arguing with him in front of his dingbat wife. In every episode, Henrietta fussed, "What did you say, dear? Who were you talking to? Really, Cosmo! Pull yourself together!"

Or worse. I could slip into the *Mrs. Muir* scenario. That's where your uninvited haunter is so smooth and witty – in short, so superior to the mere mortals you're normally stuck with – that you decide to cross that final line of sanity and start turning see-through yourself.

I've resolved to remove Mr. Wig politely from the house, but I'm having trouble working the conversation around to eviction.

Oblivious to my decision, M. Arouet spends a full three days unpacking his personal necessities – books, globes, maps, telescopes and his own Sèvres porcelain coffee set. My office reeks of lavender, carnation, vetiver, and cloves. He insists he'll unpack himself, working non-stop on his powers of lifting, so as to resume material life, especially coffee-drinking, as he says, "*tout de suite.*"

"Ah, good morning, *Madame*! I've moved your collection of dismal volumes about people murdering other people to the shelf behind that pile of old newspaper clippings. I'll keep the oriental histories and maps. I always like to write about characters who travel long distances to exotic places. Have you read my story, *Micromégas* yet? I'm sure you noticed the influence of Swift's *Gulliver's Travels*, but mine was better, I think — ?"

"— those are my clips," I shout, reaching to stop him from dumping my own collected works behind the printer.

"Your ceilings are a bit low, but it's nicer than that sinkhole they gave me as official historian to the Court in Versailles," he says, untying cumbersome quarto editions of Milton.

"Is all this necessary? I mean, it's all part of the . . . the ghost-package, isn't it? You're sure no one else can see all this stuff, or trip over it?"

"I find it easier to work with things of no substance. Less heavy —"

My resolve is slipping again. Why am I feeling relieved nobody will notice all his *accoutrements?*

"— and you never know what you'll need in the country-side. Now Madame du Châtelet, my mistress —

"I think you've already mentioned her a few times —"

"She brought two hundred parcels when we fled Paris for the countryside of Cirey. I've left quite a lot behind —"

He's unrolling a larger-than-life oil painting of Catherine the Great at the foot of the guest bed.

"It's so pleasant to wake up with an Empress at my feet," he giggles, nailing the canvas Catherine to the wall.

"Really, I think you better stop right there," I say, as he empties his brass-bound trunk full of ruffled shirts and silk hose. "You won't need a wardrobe like that in St-Cergue. The men around here look like they sleep in their snow boots. Come to think of it, so do the women . . ."

"Ah, *Madame*," the Frenchman trills, "How sad they don't appreciate *the superfluous*, that element so *essential* to life!"

Okay, he's funny, at least funnier than the young painter downstairs who is crying midway through the morning into his cellphone to his therapist. Apparently his middle-aged partner (and gay lover, the tiling man discreetly explains to me in hushed voice), got hit by the ski train after a breakfast of coffee and white wine. St-Cergue's single train platform is now spattered like vintage Pollock with two cans of our bedroom's off-white latex acrylic, not to mention the various colors of the poor painter himself.

My kitchen has become an impromptu grief-counselling headquarters as the bereaved receives well-wishing electricians, wood-flooring teams, and plasterers for consolatory reminiscences and a drink. They're using my mother's crystal, goddamit. We've had two major snow storms, and it's the first time the snow-plow man has cleared away the slush blocking our gateway. Death as a one-time maintenance bonus.

A horrible scraping shakes the front of the house.

"*Mon Dieu*, what was that?" V. throws open my office window to the freezing air. The firewood man, Monsieur Berner, has just arrived in his delivery truck to offer condolences. We hear his engine go into reverse, followed by more horrible grating sounds. We feel the house suddenly wrenched and then released.

"What happened? *Qu'est-ce qu'est arrivé?*" I yell downstairs.

"It's all right, *Madame*," the carpenter yells back in thick dialect. "Monsieur Berner just had a *petit accident. Tranquillisez-vous. Le camion* attached itself into the rain gutter."

"I didn't understand the last bit," I complain.

"I translate, *Madame*. The gutter is no more. He says it'll be repaired soon. I say, don't expect anything before summer."

I clear away a foot of snow to peer over the window sill. Five feet of new copper tubing dangle from the roof edge below. The assembled mourners politely call up to me for permission to unpack another Hong Kong dining chair to seat Monsieur Berner. His unscratched truck sits smack on top of my snow-covered flower beds.

"What a fuss they're making! To the living we owe respect, but to the dead we owe only the truth – which I must now speak. The deceased was a lousy painter, *minable*." V. comments.

"I gather he was the younger painter's first great love."

"Ah, young love! One of my favorite subjects!"

Before he launches into yet another of his stories, I make my move.

"Monsieur Arouet. I've come to a decision. Please stop unpacking."

That refined profile swivels in my direction.

"I'm going to have to ask you to leave, or to return to, um, wherever you came from . . . uh, if there is a place . . . uh, you know . . . ?"

No response.

"I'm really sorry. Please don't take it personally. It was kind of you to come, but things are so busy and unsettled, I'm sure you understand."

Those brown eyes plead.

"How can I put this? You're a writer. Suppose we were both in a book together, or rather, a play? Well, I mean, it wouldn't fit, would it? We're the wrong mix, you and me. You belong in a literary masterpiece on a stage in Versailles, while my life is – well – kind of a T.V. sitcom."

"Tee vee sit come," he struggles.

"I knew you wouldn't get it. Excuse me."

The dancing brown eyes narrow to a slit. I hope firmness is

written all over my face as I leave him stunned in the middle of his linen pile.

"*Mais, Madame!*"

"Let's just say I'm an unworthy hostess, Monsieur Arouet. You won't find any Society here, no members of the Académie Française, and absolutely no Royals, not a single Louis I through XX in sight."

"Have I complained?"

"No. Please, stop following me. You're just going to cause confusion. I can't talk to ghosts all day. I've got my hands full. And in my free time, ha, ha, I have to learn French."

"But I can translate, assist you, guide you — " He clutches his antique book and stumbles downstairs after me.

I block him short, with both hands outstretched. "I'm just not ready for a – for a – a *Lumière*."

We circle the house down the bedroom stairs, past the mourners in the dining room, through the kitchen, across the living room and back up to my office.

He slumps down on the guest bed and crosses his spindly legs. He wags his head in bewilderment.

"I spent most of my life as a guest and was never made to feel unwelcome!"

"Well, maybe you can come next year. How's that?" I suggest. "By then I will have read your entire – what is this? – *Dictionnaire Philosophique*, and we can talk. This is covered with corrections. Haven't you already published this?"

"I never stop revising." He grabs the book back. "*Madame*, I resent this. I stayed with Madame de Bernières in Paris – but always paid my way – or the *adorable* Duc de Sully in the country. After my second stay in the Bastille, my great friends in England, the Ambassador Everard Falkener and Lord Bolingbroke were thrilled to receive me."

"Thrilled?"

"Ecstatic. And then I lived very happily for ten years with my mistress Madame du Châtelet and her husband in — "

"You spent your whole life crashing in other people's houses? Did you never own your own home?"

"Not 'til my sixties, but that is beside the point! I was never, *never* made to feel unwelcome!"

"House guests are like fish. They smell after three days. My mother taught me that."

"A witty saying proves nothing," he sniffs. "Well, maybe once or twice I chose to leave early," he adds, "but I never went anywhere I wasn't invited. I carried letters of introduction from Horatio Walpole, British ambassador to France, to the Duke of Newcastle, the Duchess of Marlborough, the Prince and Princess of Wales. That's it! Letters of introduction are lacking to us!"

"That's NOT it!"

He turns sarcastic. "A royal recommendation will not suffice? Madame de Pompadour gave me a room in Versailles. I was a guest at the Polish court-in-exile for years, and, oh, yes, I was invited to live with Frederick the Great in Potsdam to discuss affairs of state for three years."

His face clouds momentarily, "I did leave Potsdam under a *petit* cloud, but it was a case of mutual disillusionment, I assure you."

"You know, I don't know whether you're the King of Light, or the King of Name-Dropping, but as you're invisible, Peter can hardly talk Red Cross diplomacy with you."

"You don't have a lover?"

"Certainly not!"

"Perfect. Then it's just the three of us."

"I don't think Peter'll appreciate this *ménage à trois* at all, especially if he doesn't even know."

V. positively bristles.

"I don't see why Monsieur shouldn't be pleased! Madame du Châtelet and I lived with her husband in the Champagne country quite happily! I turned their home from a tenth-century ruin surrounded by iron forges and forest beasts into the intellectual headquarters of France! Who knows what I could do with this — !"

"Didn't he mind sharing his wife with her lover on his own estate?"

"*Poof*! Why? He was always off fighting Germans. Anyway, he ate with the children. He preferred regular meals to our little midnight snacks."

Our tiff is cut off by the church bells ringing noon. I hear the workers heading out of the kitchen, the mourner leading his entourage to Les Cytises Pizzas.

"They're sitting *shiva* on my dime, day after day," I grumble.

"His first love, you say . . . Oh, Pimpette!" V. sighs.

"A poodle?"

He shoots me a withering glance. "*Bien*, her real name was Olympe Dunoyer. My father hustled me off to work for the French ambassador to the Hague. I was wretched. I wrote Pimpette, 'Never love equaled mine, for never was there a person better worthy of love than you.' She married a count instead."

"I guess that happens — "

"No matter. Then I fell in love with Suzanne, just as my satires were making me the toast of all Paris. That was cut short by a *lettre de cachet*. 'Sieur Arouet must be arrested and taken to the Bastille.'"

"What's a *lettre* of *cachet?*"

His expression darkens and he whispers, "An instrument of terror, *Madame*, nothing less. Orders, signed by the King, for the imprisonment without trial of anyone who had incurred official displeasure."

"What had you done?"

V. shrugs his shoulders. "Boasted to a stranger in a café."

"A *stranger* sent you to jail?"

Monsieur Arouet glances behind both shoulders and spits out, "A police informer! Next thing I know, I'm dragged off with nothing but the clothes on my back! And irony of ironies, for verses that were not even mine! As soon as I was gone, my Suzanne fell into the waiting arms of my best friend, Lefèvre."

"She married him?"

"No. She married a wealthy *marquis*. Who cares? I had lost a woman, but I had gained new fame and a new name. I emerged from prison no longer François-Marie Arouet, but – surely you have now guessed?"

"You reinvented yourself, like Madonna?"

He frowns, "Well, even I could not compare to the Virgin, *mais oui*. Come, come, haven't you guessed yet?"

"Yes," I say playfully, "you're Racine."

He scowls.

"Molière? No? Corneille!"

I take pity on him. "Okay, okay, you re-named yourself *Voltaire* – Monsieur François Arouet de *Voltaire*."

He bows slightly, blushing with pleasure.

I looked up. "Did you ever see her again, Monsieur Voltaire?"

"Suzanne? Yes," he nods, thoughtfully, "after her husband died. Our reunion – such laughter! Such tears! I thought she would trip on her silks as she hurried down the stairs to fall into my waiting arms."

At this, he alights on my laser printer, his right hand precariously clutching a low ceiling beam. Stretching one graceful hand towards an invisible audience below, he declaims, "Young, gay, content, without care, without a thought for the future, limiting all our desires to our present delights – what need had we of youthful abundance? We had something far better; we had *happiness*."

He glances down at me, "For Suzanne. To make her feel bad about dumping me. Sounds better in French. Want to hear it again?" The hand shoots out in rhetorical readiness, as trained on the schoolboy boards of Louis-le-Grand.

"Wasn't there any hope of getting together with Suzanne again?"

"Yes, but by the time we got together again, I was eighty-four and she was eighty-three."

I turn away, hand on mouth, suppressing a giggle.

He's offended. "No less delightful all the same."

V. thrusts a couple of my old diaries aside to make room for his collection of ink bottles. A small photo flutters out of one. He scoops it off the carpet.

"Why this is a representation of Versailles!" he exclaims.

"Give me that." My spirit softens with recognition of this tiny black and white snap of my own first love, a French boy named François. The lens caught him sitting at a café table outside the Palace of Versailles during our brief reunion in Paris.

"A handsome youth."

"Named François — "

"Like me!"

"Like you. We met in Santa Cruz, California the summer I was nineteen."

A crazy summer with hardly any responsibility, the only summer of my life when I was truly free of obligations of family, studies, or job – just free, the only time in my life I made love five times a day, hitchhiked to Mexico with no-body's permission, tanned myself to the verge of Affirmative Action status, wore off-the-shoulder Romanian blouses. I have since then felt elegant, well-groomed, chic or sexy. But it was the only time in my life I felt beautiful.

And oh, he was so glamorous! His father was the political cartoonist for the French weekly, *L'Express*, and his mother a Russian-American expatriate painter. He was an Apollo, the bearer of all things European and civilized to my redwoody corner of the world infested with water beds, lava lamps, roach clips and lazy minds.

V. interrupts, "A town of the Holy Cross?"

"Santa Cruz? A faded resort in the mountains. Not unlike St-Cergue in its way."

"You accompanied this François to France?"

"No, he returned to New York to finish his architecture degree. I finished my Chinese studies in California. His love was that of any other normal nineteen-year-old – totally physical. But I don't think I ever fell in love that way again."

"And Versailles?"

"Five years later I went to Paris and looked him up. He rescued me from a flea-pit hotel and we went to Versailles for the weekend. I remember I joked, 'I'm not sure I'm ready for Versailles!' and he answered, 'The question is, is Versailles ready for you?'"

"And this, *Madame*?" V. rescues a faded slip of paper from the floor, from which he reads in the most perfect French:

> "*Voici pour Claire,*
> *L'oiseau solaire*
> *La grand tournesol*
> *Qui pleure et rigole*
> *Pour Claire*"*

It has been thirty years since I have seen this tiny verse dedicated to me using my middle name. I turn away from Monsieur Arouet to hide my sudden emotion. How was I to know at nineteen that this was the only poem anyone would ever write for me? I had forgotten this scrap casually slipped into my hand under the sun-dappled Californian redwoods. The smell of pine needles, Johnson's Baby Oil, and sandalwood soap floods my memory.

"All physical, *Madame*?" V. chastises me gently.

The pain of loss floods my heart. Until this second, the only gift I had remembered this golden youth giving me was the burning ambition to return to his arms one day a dazzlingly accomplished foreign correspondent, equal to his cosmopolitan

* This is for Claire, a sun bird, a tall sunflower, who laughs and jokes, for Claire

charms and sexual experience. Is there not something ironic
that after those thirty years of searching for success and adven-
ture in Asia, I ended up in a French-speaking village married to
a man also trained as an architect?

"Who knows? You might once again lay eyes on your
golden Apollo, *sportif et fort*."

"I doubt it. He moved from Manhattan to Manhattan
Beach."

"Not adjacent?"

"Not at all."

He shrugs, disgusted by my obstinacy. "I find this pessimism
depressing. You're discouraged, listless and sarcastic. Cut off
from your habitual circles and your professional rewards, you
can only complain your life is over."

He seizes an abandoned toy – Theo's plastic Hercules blade –
and hand held high, leads himself back and forth across the
room. At the click of a button, the toy clanks like iron and steel
clashing with enemy weaponry. Punctuating his pep talk with
Energizer acoustics, V. thrusts it, backing me into the corner of
the office.

"Did I sulk, sitting in the Bastille? Did I whine, fleeing
Versailles in disgrace? Did I moan, driven from the gaieties of
the Richelieu wedding in Montjeu to flee for my life from
château to château, retreating to exile in Champagne? Did I
groan leaving my post in the great Frederick's entourage in
Potsdam? Did I sit on my hands when finally exiled from
France at the age of sixty-five?"

I have a plastic blade pressed against my heart. "Uh, lemme
guess."

"*Madame*, NOTHING could be better for you than this
exile! I drafted my *Letters Concerning the English Nation* while in
exile! I wrote *Micromégas* and *Zadig* in exile! You were at grave
risk of wasting time —"

"Watching the Cooking Channel, only I can't get it over
here," I sigh.

"— thinking you were living just because events rolled you along!" He bursts out, "*Finalement*, I understand why I am here!"

"You do?" I whimper.

"*Mais, oui! L'art de vivre* has escaped you! I have come to teach you the fine art of being happy! There is nothing I haven't seen or done. Nothing can surprise me! Now," he tucks the Hercules sword in his belt, "finish decorating this house! Invite your wittiest friends! Write your next novel!"

"In other words, get to work."

"Use your time well! The world is full of lies, superstition, dishonesty, cruelty, prejudice, bureaucracy," he declaims. "*Écrasez l'infâme!*"

He has to have the last word. "And as for meeting old Apollos, judging from my experience with Suzanne, let's see, I was eighty-four, you're almost fifty, yes! You have thirty-four more years to go. Let's not waste them."

"Howbout I make dinner?" I escape the plastic sword and slink out of the office.

"I've almost finished unpacking," he says, satisfied. "I routinely employ all my daylight hours for research and correspondence," he adds, and flipping his coat-tails free of my desk chair, resumes scribbling in his leather book.

He's won another round. Where has the day fled? Already the workers are packing up. When I reach the kitchen, I stumble on proof that V. is right. The loss of young love can be endured. I surprised the bereaved painter standing in the middle of the kitchen in the comforting embrace of none other than the Ticinese tiling man.

The Bastille

A few days later, Alexander appears, panting, at the kitchen door. His back hunches over under its load of textbooks and his face is streaked with dust.

"Mama, I've gotta tell you something."

His face suddenly crumples into wrenching sobs, through which he croaks out, "I'm sorry. I didn't mean to."

"What's happened? Are you all right?"

"Please don't get mad at me."

I hate it when they do that. I'll have every reason to get mad, while information I need is held ransom for a guarantee of superhuman maternal restraint. I hold him by both thin shoulders and look him straight in the eyes.

"What happened?"

He heaves out the words, "I got . . . into . . . tr-tr-trouble."

"Why? What did you do?"

"I . . . I . . . was waiting for the train home and some guys were leaning against the train car on the siding and I went over and I started leaning on it too, and it – it just moved."

"I don't understand. You pushed a train?"

"No, NO, I didn't mean to push! It just moved! Then they arrested me."

He wails and falls into my arms as the backpack crashes to the floor. A ten-year-old jailbird. He's terrified. I cannot but help return the embrace.

"They ARRESTED you?"

He weeps, stammering through my sweater, "The ticket seller and the bus driver stopped the wagon from ro – roll – rolling away. The other boys ran away. So they grabbed me. They made me hand over my pass."

"Alexander! You lost your pass? How're you going to get to school now? And we just moved here. This is a small town. You want to be known all over the village as a juvenile delinquent?"

He can't know the real reason for my panic. The school director will be notified about Alexander's suspended train pass. Local mothers talk about the ruthless factors that eliminate children of his age from the university track. Fifth and sixth grade children are eliminated from college track not only because of poor academic performance, but also because of "lack of maturity." Troublemakers need not apply.

I hear myself shouting, "You realize that Monsieur Villar will get a letter about this?"

"Yes, Mama, I'm sorry." He's weeping uncontrollably. "Please don't yell at me."

"Go to your room immediately. I'm calling the train station."

Monsieur Voltaire rolls his eyes and resumes work at the dining table. It's the only surface long enough to accommodate some epic verse he's revising. The thick paper unscrolls off the table and snakes across the carpet. He whistles, amused, under his breath.

"My friend, the Duc de Richelieu, was thrown into the Bastille at fifteen for some boyish prank. He took his tutor with him, of course. I told you to engage a tutor. See what you get for not taking my advice?"

"Not now, thank you, *Monsieur*. Where's the phone directory?"

"Madame du Châtelet hired a certain Abbé Michel Linant as tutor to her boy. Although there was the problem of the tutor's sister . . . " he sighs.

"What should I look under? *Gare? Train?"*

"I haven't the slightest idea. Just send a messenger. We had to take in the tutor's sister and mother, too."

"Quite a crowd just so the boy could conjugate verbs," I joke, flipping through the directory.

"And then came Keyserlingk," V.'s expression sinks lower.

"Kaiser Anything doesn't sound too good. Okay, here's the number. Can you take this down for me? Three, six, six . . ."

"*De Keyserlingk*, to be exact," says V., his plumed pen scratching numbers furiously. "Prince Frederick of Prussia had compared me to Homer. Well, how could I resist the Prince's envoy to Cirey? Madame du Châtelet and I threw on little plays, music, fireworks spelling out Frederick's name as 'The Hope of the Human Race,' the usual red carpet stuff, and meanwhile the tutor, Linant, was just making a nuisance of himself. You see, the *Keyserlingk* was homosexual. Of course, coming from Potsdam, he had to be — "

I cut off V.'s flow, my finger poised on the directory. "Wait, you mean, the Prussian court was gay?"

"Oh, very jolly," V. tosses off, "and full of homosexuals, as well. As it turns out, so was our tutor, the Abbé Linant. The little ecclesiastical rodent was plotting with that nosy Keyserlingk to run off to illuminate Frederick's court in Potsdam! And that, *Madame*, is why our tutor had to go!"

"The sister?"

He growls, "Her, too."

"The mother?"

He peers at me through his magnifying glass with an eye now magnified four inches wide, "*Especially* the mother."

"And you still say hire a tutor for Alexander?"

V. looks at me fixedly, his memories of the rodent Linant refreshed.

"Maybe not."

The story from the train stationmaster is only slightly less garbled than my son's account. Glancing out of his window at the gaggle of pre-teens crushing the platform, he lifted his gaze to the sidings beyond just in time to see one of the spare wagons inching down the rails. By the time he and the bus driver had secured the wayward wagon, there was only one skinny American boy left standing at the scene of the crime – my freckled felon.

"It's a serious matter, *Madame*," the master insists.

"Yes, I know. He doesn't deny it. I only ask myself how my son could have managed to move a train car. He weighs less than eighty pounds, I mean, oh, what's that in kilos?"

The stationmaster is too busy to entertain this discussion with a foreigner who keeps muddling pounds with kilograms. The *Commune* will be in touch with us to set a date for the tribunal.

"A tribunal? Not just a reprimand?"

"*Oui, Madame, un tribunal. Heureusement, personne n'était blessé. C'est une affaire d'état.*"

I replace the phone. "Oh, great. They're calling it an affair of state."

V. looks up impatiently, "A train car, a poem, a little insult . . . *Lèse-majesté*. Nothing's changed. In my day, you were thrown into prison on a whim. I can't get any work done here! I'll go and watch the boy pack."

He starts to roll up his endless verse.

"Pack? Alexander isn't going anywhere!"

"He may be seized in the middle of the night. I was."

"Don't be absurd. Peter'll call the *Commune* and straighten all this out. I'll call his office now."

"Humph! Such a fuss! Be reassured, *Madame*. The Bastille was not so bad. They let me order in the essentials, you know, books, silver, family portraits, backgammon, mirrors, lamps, furniture, linen, perfume, and of course, a nightcap. Women took their maids. There was excellent food and wine. And the heating and laundry were provided by the King."

"No nail file?"

He laughs, "Why bother? All the best people, or at least the talented ones, passed through those stony chambers as 'special guests of the King.' The State could never afford a little pension here or there for a struggling poet, but it never minded how much it spent on them in prison!"

"No way my son is going to jail. I'm just worried about his school record."

"*Tranquillisez-vous, Madame!* The Bastille was like having the measles to someone well-born." V. turns confidential. "He'll meet the nicest people! I dined with the governor, played billiards and bowled with the guards. And *Madame*, I wrote *La Henriade*, my first real masterpiece, an epic that rivaled the *Iliad*, about Henri IV – bold, generous, *lecherous* – the usual bestseller stuff. I'm modernizing it right now for reissue."

He brandishes his yellowing scroll.

"They let you order in office supplies, with your take-out food?"

"Well, no," he sighs deeply, "that would have been expecting too much. After all, a pen in my hand is a deadly weapon."

"Of course," I nod, keeping a straight face.

"So I wrote it between the lines of a printed book."

"Well, that's better than the toilet paper the Chinese dissidents use these days. Will you excuse me, *Monsieur?*"

I hear Alexander sobbing with remorse behind his closed door up on the attic floor. Before I can comfort him, an annoying little tinkling bell summons me. One of the workers brought Eva-Marie a goat bell to ring for company or food. Sibling competition spurs Theodor during his ten days of recovery from the asthma attack to insist on an even bigger bell, as he's recuperating up on the third floor, farther from the action.

The afternoon speeds by answering bells. Finally Peter comes home from work, face drawn, to confront his tear-streaked son over the dinner table.

"Now, Alexander, tell us exactly what happened."

"Pierre-Edouard, Ludo, and some other guy were playing next to a wagon."

"Do you know these boys' last names so I can talk to their parents?"

"Only Pierre-Edouard Gruyère."

"Did they come forward when you were stopped by the stationmaster?"

"No, they ran away."

"Did you push the car?"

"I sort of joined in. I didn't think it would really move." Alexander eludes his father's angry gaze and studies his congealing mashed potatoes.

Once Alexander has been excused from the table and the dinner trays collected from the invalids, Peter briefs me on his conversation with a very stern *Commune* official who works by day for an insurance company.

"He must appear before a hearing Friday evening at six."

"Alone?"

"Apparently. If they're not satisfied by his answers, they may revoke his train privileges."

"How will he get to school without his pass?" I dread the answer.

"You'd have to drive him back and forth to Genolier for the rest of the year. Don't worry, we'll go with him. I'm not having him made a scapegoat."

"He's a human toothpick. He can hardly push our wheelbarrow."

"Well, obviously they haven't seen him yet. If they're picturing a fifth-grade Schwarzenegger, they're in for a shock."

It occurs to me that our bookworm Alexander, who never got into trouble in New York, has suffered from being the "new boy," with his faulty French and awkward, polite behavior. He's trying to be accepted by the other boys to the point of getting into trouble. Now he awaits his Friday summons to the Salle Communale with a blend of contrition and martial stoicism, as if he half wanted some kind of public censure.

Peter can avoid the tension of the coming trial by spending

his days on the usual distracting I.C.R.C. trivia – lost children in Afghanistan, security for aid workers in Burundi, prisoner exchanges in Colombia, disappearing office disbursements in Moscow, and funding flows from Washington and Tokyo.

For me, there's no easy escape. Left in the village to carry the family's coat-of-arms, I become more nervous than Alexander, unable to write or concentrate on the house repairs. Every bang of a worker's hammer, every electric saw whining away in a far corner of the house grates on my rattled nerves.

The tale of the runaway train car has circulated St-Cergue's main street already. Suddenly my most mundane transactions appear to me through a Hitchcockian lens of public guilt as that American Mother of the Train Pusher. Is it my imagination or does the bakery lady sell me my loaf of "*balois*" with a rather upbraiding *bonne journée?* The *tabac* proprietress, Madame Weber, has surely learned of Alexander's "state crime" as she dispenses papers, candies, cigarettes, and gossip – she hears absolutely everything. She hands me the French newspapers with an air of judgmental scrutiny.

"I didn't like the look she gave me," mutters V., clutching his fur-trimmed collar. We're walking uphill in a fluttering snowfall, my arms full of small purchases. "And I can't figure it out. Even in my day, carriages were secured with hand-brakes."

"She can't see *you*. She was scowling at me. Like we're a whole family of train saboteurs bent on mowing down little kids."

I'm not even safe in my own home. The laughter lacing our work team's mid-morning coffee break grows louder as Friday nears. The approaching tribunal looms over my shortening days. Having bought and restored one of the oldest buildings in the village, complete with its hefty tax bill, this is not the way Peter and I had envisaged our first official encounter with the village pooh-bahs. While waiting for the reckoning, I glare with accusatory fury at the mothers of the boys who escaped arrest.

"The family honor is at stake," Monsieur Voltaire announces

Friday morning, playing with a butter knife. "*Monsieur* must fight a duel."

"I don't think that's going to solve anything. What bothers me is this *omertà* among the other parents shielding their own sons."

"Exactly. *Monsieur* cannot let Alexander accept total responsibility. He must insist that this was an accident of childish miscalculation. In fact, he must go further, and demand an official apology from the *Commune*."

"An apology? Or — ?"

V. presses the butter knife on the nose of our new kitten, Frisbee.

" — or he must fight a duel with the chosen representative of the accusers."

"Yeah, right. Like you fought a duel. You're even more a featherweight than Alexander."

"Has history not recorded the insults I received at the hands of the Chevalier de Chabot Rohan? That lily-livered nobleman who kept taunting me, 'Monsieur Arouet, Monsieur de Voltaire, what really is your name?' The scoundrel kept it up for days, at the Opéra, and at the Comédie-Française, and this after I had been received at court and given a retainer of fifteen hundred livres by the Queen!"

"You didn't let him get away with it, I hope?"

Voltaire hoots with laugher. "*Non, non.* He was a nobody, just a worn-out old soldier and man-about-town who fancied my lover, the actress Adrienne Lecouvreur."

I shake my head. "Pimpette, Suzanne, now Adrienne. I can't keep track of your old girlfriends."

He laughs, "I tell you frankly, in the days before Madame du Châtelet, neither could I. Anyway, he wasn't even a *real* Rohan. His grandmother had lost that ancient Brittany name when she married. That was my offense. I reminded him of that. 'The difference, *Monsieur*,' I said, 'is that my name begins with me, yours *ends* with you.'"

"How did he take that?"

V. drops his lofty manner and glances at me slyly. This is a man who goes too far, relishes the delight of his victories small and large against the stupidities of the world and willingly pays the price.

"Um, not too well. While I was dining with the Duc de Sully at his *Hôtel*, I got a message to come to the gate. Six hired thugs leapt upon me. The Chevalier shouted at them from the safety of his carriage, 'Don't hit his head! Something good may come out of that!'"

"Well, if you really were the versifier of your age, it's like those attacks on Gangsta Rap stars by jealous rivals."

"Yes, by the way, I must ask you about these rap verses. They fascinate me as a commentary on the times. But I digress."

"I spent weeks hidden away in the Rue Saint-Martin, training with the fencer Leynault. I practiced pistol shooting as well as fencing. Finally, I summoned one of my relatives from the provinces to be my second."

"You actually fought a duel? Wow."

V. stands to attention, proudly determined. "It was my intention, but *non*. I tracked the rogue down at the theater, slobbering over Adrienne. I challenged him: 'If your latest money-squeezing affair has not made you forget your insult to me, I hope that you will meet me, man to man.'"

"Who won?" I ask, breathlessly.

"Nobody. On the night of April 18th, 1726, I was apprehended with two pistols in my pocket and taken to the Bastille for the second time. His so-called aristocratic family arranged it. It's all in the police records."

I'm unable to hide my disappointment at being cheated of a real live duel. Well, dead duel, but still.

"After all that build-up, all that training. What a bummer," I say.

"As you say, *quel bummé*."

Friday evening arrives. Father, Mother, Son and Unholy

Ghost drive the few village streets to the Salle Communale, a gloomy paneled chamber lined with hunting guns one floor above the police offices. V. is wearing a frighteningly formal outfit of black taffeta collar, screaming white tights, and a red hair ribbon at the nape of his powdered white wig. Peter has come straight from Geneva and is still in a dark suit.

The accused is wearing his St. Boniface blazer, suddenly too short in the sleeves.

Alexander enters the room first, and before I even clear the entrance, I hear a gasp of suppressed amusement from the six waiting elders. Clearly they expected a suspect of more heft.

A chinless woman in a hair band smiles slightly. I also see the chain-smoking fourth-grade teacher poised to serve as secretary. I recognize the father of a schoolmate of Alexander's. The designated spokesman at the head of the table is a very fat man, with rosy fondue-fed jowls enveloping the collar of a nylon anorak puffing out in all directions. I've seen him putting his trained hunting dogs into the back of his Terrano II lined with caging. One of these sinister black beasts now lies at his feet under the table.

The fat man orders Alexander to the foot of the table.

Alexander starts his plea, voice cracking when he gets to the part where the train moves out from under him. His French is hesitant and the words mischosen, but respectful. Then the questions fly.

"Is this the first time you played around the rails?"

"Were you pushing or leaning?"

"Were you aware of the danger?"

Alexander is shaking. No sooner have they pummeled him with one question, than another comes at him in colloquial French he struggles to understand. Things are not going well when the crucial question shoots from the teacher, tapping her pencil impatiently on the table.

"Don't you know the rules that were issued with your pass?" she rasps.

I shiver at the mention of the all-necessary train pass. V.'s eyes are burning with indignation.

Peter has followed the discussion calmly. At this last question, he suddenly raises his hand.

"May I put a question to my son?"

The inquisitors peer down the table to our little group sitting under the cantonal flag at the end of the room.

"Alexander, did you release the wagon's brakes?" he asks in French.

Monsieur Voltaire slaps his knee and explodes, "*Exactement!*"

Alexander has not understood his own father's French. "*Le frein?*"

"The brake, Alexander," Peter translates into English. "Did you or anyone else release the brake?"

"Nobody touched anything that looked like a brake."

"So the wagon wasn't secured when you started playing near it?"

The *Commune* officials glance at each other sideways, shifting slightly in their seats. I suspect none of them speaks English.

"I guess not. It just started to move."

Peter looks up at the village officials. "I see," he says simply, then switching into French, "my son has just clarified what was worrying me *a little;* that neither he nor the other boys touched the wagon's brake."

The council of six stares at us stonily. Voltaire makes a glaring face right back.

Peter continues, "My American wife and I have recently moved here, as you might know. We aren't familiar with local procedures, we admit, but are we to understand that the wagon was left unsecured on the platform during the hours of heaviest use by hundreds of schoolchildren?"

There is a painful pause. The hunting dog stirs and then drops his chin on his paws. The council members glance at each other and then from under lowered brows, scrutinize *me*.

"*Touché,*" murmurs Voltaire.

"You say you were not alone, *mon cher?*" the little woman in the hair band asks Alexander.

"No, *Madame*. I joined the other boys who were already there."

"Could you tell us the names of the other boys who started pushing the wagon?"

Alexander watched too many movies on the American Movie Channel back in New York for this turn in the questioning. He straightens his back and announces, "No, *Madame*. I will name no names."

"*Bravo!*" V. shouts. "To the Bastille with our heads high!"

Peter and I try not to smile and even the counsellors are squirming with embarrassment.

"Well," says the slight woman, "we take playing around the trains very seriously in this village. Three years ago, a child was pushed off the platform by a careless schoolmate into the path of a train. That child is dead. A house painter was killed recently by the train. I hope you understand our concern." She looks long and hard at Alexander.

The jowly hunter barks from the end of the table. "We won't revoke your train pass on one condition."

"*Oui, Monsieur?*"

"You warn those boys – when you see them – that if anything like this happens again you will all be severely punished. And they are to tell their parents about this meeting we've had with you today."

Alexander senses that torch will not be laid to stake tonight. He wags his head with frantic compliance; "*Oui, oui, Monsieur,* but don't blame me if Pierre-Edouard Gruyère doesn't tell his parents."

Peter sinks his head in his hands as the officials adjourn in giggles. We all shake hands and file out into the cold night.

"Peter, why was everybody staring at me when it was you who mentioned the brake?"

"Because, my dear wife, it reminded them that you are

American. I realized that although a Swiss would never dare contemplate charging the Swiss train authorities with negligence, everybody in that room would see you as a native of the Land of Crazy Lawsuits. Like most small-town bullies, the last thing that bunch wants us to do is to involve higher authorities."

He smiles and puts his arm around me, The Secret Weapon. "Oh, there was one other thing. This morning I found the hand brake of my car down. Strange, especially for me, to forget it. But it got me thinking . . ."

That night, I find Monsieur Voltaire dressed for bed in a flouncy nightshirt and nightcap. He is completely entwined in his revision of his "hit," *La Henriade*.

"Thanks for coming to the tribunal. At least Alexander didn't lose his pass. Or go to the Bastille."

"Your husband's interjection about the brakes was a deadly thrust. Admirable."

"But not as good as a duel?"

He sighs, "I would have made a wonderful second, but once again, all my training goes to waste."

"Maybe not. Was it just an inspired coincidence that Peter's car had been fiddled with?"

"Yes, that was very opportune," V. murmurs.

"Next time the family honor is threatened, I promise you'll be the second."

He smiles. "Any time, *Madame*, any time. In the end, there was no need to worry."

"No?"

"*Non*. Had the boy been condemned to the Bastille, I would have gone, too – to guarantee treatment worthy of your standing, of course."

He licks two fingers and pinches out the flame of his ghostly tallow.

Of course.

This Young House

In our cramped Manhattan apartment, I devoured "shelter porn" like *Elle Decor* and *Architectural Digest*. The glossies whet my appetite for home ownership; now I've got restoration indigestion, the life of *House and Nightmare*. This behemoth of bat-poop is unlike any of my rented apartments from Hong Kong to London to New York.

The *Commune* of St-Cergue archives date it from 1789, a two-story stone farmhouse with a wooden balcony running along the face of the second floor outside the main bedroom. We rip out a rickety outdoor stairway to discover a stone plaque dated 1894 thanking one Émile V. I. Berger for donating the house to the *Commune*.

A stable and granary were attached at one side. The granary door still bears someone's penciled notes: "*1898 décembre 31, neige,*" "*novembre 23, 1900, première neige . . .*" A farmer shellacked yellowed pages of his almanac to its planks. The water level in the reservoir next to the house is tabulated in a crooked column of figures. Voltaire instructs me on how to get Peter to get a local roofer to repair the gutters. Soon fresh-melted snow is filling the stone tank back up to eighteenth-century levels.

"Now you can shut off your water supply from town," V. crows.

The *Commune* passes us a yellowed photograph circa 1920

showing a self-satisfied gentleman-farmer and family in front of the house. An enormous tree is pictured in front of the kitchen door. The tree is now gone, but one day we realize that our terrace table was sliced out of this giant.

The house lured others, not all of them so contented. The records include a bitter correspondence between the *Commune* and its tenant over the appropriateness of installing indoor plumbing.

"*Heureusement*, the tenant won. I can't tolerate the smell of chamber pots," V. comments.

With the passing decades, the goat-house became a loft. The two-foot-wide stone walls were plastered over. The hay loft converted to bedrooms. In the late 1960s, the last farmer's son turned hippie and opened the house to the public as an East–West art gallery.

One morning I'm sweeping up toys. The marbles keep escaping the broom toward the south-eastern corner. Playmobil cannons, pingpong balls – everything rolls away. I giggle, despite my frustration; the playroom floor hugs the contours of the slope underneath. I'm suspended in childlike delight at a house so organic that it lies on the hill like a heavy cat fitting the contours of an old sofa. This house was born during the reign of the Emperor Ch'ien Lung over China, Louis XVI over France, Catherine the Great over Russia, and the presidency of George Washington over the infant U.S.A. This wayward floor was measured out the same year the *Bounty* was trolling the Tahitian islands for breadfruit. In 1789 builders rolled stones for these walls while French royalty rolled over cobbled Parisian streets to the guillotine.

"We were crazy to take this on," Peter mutters, standing on his toes in the dank basement, a pocket mirror in hand, to peer over our new red heater. The contractor positioned the digital read-out scarcely an inch from the ceiling and cheerily left us with a manual in seven languages – none of them English.

"Well, I'm glad we did, despite everything. Can you read it?"

"Upside down."

I realize I am going to love this house almost as much as I love the man who gave it to me.

Monsieur Voltaire despises it, starting with the heating.

"Your husband was cheated. I'm never warm. This climate is horrible. It's so difficult to work. Right now I would care for nothing but the sun." He wears half a dozen layers of clothes at all times, though all our Swiss neighbors comment that our expensive system overheats, implying immoral wastage.

"I'm sorry, *Monsieur*. Peter got up at four this morning to see why the heating stopped. Now's he trying a new program setting."

"Well," he rolls his eyes impatiently, "*Évidemment*, it doesn't work. In Cirey, I had up to forty fires burning at one time. My guests were always comfortable."

Second, he doesn't like the landscaping. Apparently he's an expert on that, too.

"You have no *allées*, no corridors, no front wings, no arches, *Madame*. You must allow me to assist you in the redesign of your estate. When we arrived at the Châtelet château, it was a derelict tenth-century ruin with no comforts, no refinements. Now, a little fountain or birdbath over there — "

" — would freeze up at these heights." I give him a chilly look.

V. pouts off to the office to rework some failure entitled *Artémire*. Apparently, the audience booed it off the stage the first time round, but nothing can discourage his appetite for rewriting.

A shutter suddenly slams against the window; the old bronze latch shaped like an angel has slipped a wing sideways. A snow storm is moving towards us in flurries of cotton batting lumps. This will be the third storm of the season, possibly the biggest yet. Snow starts tumbling down on the paving stones.

"Are you up to shoveling?" I shout at V. through a scarf wrapped tightly around my hat. My fashionable fur toque looked wonderful entering the Waldorf-Astoria Hotel for a United Nations General Assembly reception. Worn with a borrowed red ski suit at 1,100 meters, it looks ridiculous.

V. peers at me from the kitchen door through the whirling snow, sheltering his aquiline features with a pale hand.

"*Madame*, I do not shovel. This unhappy machine doesn't allow heavy labor of that sort. I am a playwright and versifier. Not to mention dead. All the concentration of energy in the world couldn't lift that."

"You know, you're not the only intellectual around here!" I shout over howling winds. "I'd rather be writing than doing this, don't kid yourself! If you don't 'do shovel,' what can you do?"

"Hunt venison?" he whimpers through swirling ice confetti. I'm not convinced that this is even something he did very often back in Champagne.

"Never fear, *Madame*! I know how to make myself useful." He dives back into the house, probably to read the coffee-machine instructions. After an hour of arctic misery, I shuffle back into the kitchen to shed my soggy boots.

"You should drink something to warm you," he scolds me.

"Thanks loads. Good God!" In my surprise, I trip over my half-discarded leggings.

"What is it?" He jumps too.

"Your hair!"

I can't help but gawk. His abundant curls are gone. Instead, lank brown hair lies flat against his skull, ending in fine tendrils at the nape of the neck. He reaches instinctively to the back of his head.

"My *hairs*? What is wrong with my *hairs*?"

"Oh, I guess that's it. It's your own hair. It's not a wig."

He sighs. "*Mais oui, Madame.* But it's hardly in good taste to comment on such things. I never mention your *tooths*."

"My *tooths*? What about my teeth?"

"Well, just as my wigs are false, obviously your teeth are,

shall we say a little too white, too straight? Hmm? I promise I won't jump to the ceiling on the day I see you take them out."

"How dare you! These are my own teeth!"

"You take me for a fool? A woman of nearly fifty with all her own teeth? Unheard of!" He laughs.

"I insist, Monsieur. These are all MY teeth."

He shakes his head. "Impossible."

I bare my gums at him. He leans forward, peering at the upper and lower sets of molars, shaking his head and muttering slowly, "*Ex-tra-ord-i-naire*. I have grasped the principles of the telephone and the flushing pierced chair, but this I cannot believe."

"Now that we've got the question of my teeth straightened out, please tell me how you've made yourself useful."

He leads me upstairs to my office, where I find my novel-in-progress scatterered over the desk.

"I hope you don't mind. I've been reviewing your papers. I might be able to help."

I've only published one small novel so far, so maybe he can be useful. After all, he's offering to let me pick the brains of the most successful French author of the eighteenth century.

"I gather it was one bestseller after another for you. What do you advise?"

"First, I think the subject of your novel is beneath you."

"Beneath me? It's a murder mystery set in Himalayan Tibet. I'd say that's pretty elevated."

"Very humorous, *Madame*. *Le Thibet* may be an interesting place for all I know. What I meant was, your writing is too vulgar, too commonplace, too literal. You should never, never, never write about real people or everyday things."

"Never? You just eliminated half the canon of twentieth-century literature."

"*Mais non!* A literary work must be lofty, relying on classical references, allegory, metaphor, and structure. You're writing about mountains? Then of course, *situez* your story on Mount Olympus. And all these silly chapters. Try to divide the action into five acts."

"Five acts."

"And of course, it must rhyme."

I smell trouble. Maybe hit literary formats don't endure over centuries as well as farmhouse foundations. But I don't want to offend Voltaire, of all people.

"Well, times have changed. Styles change. And remember, this is a novel, not a play."

"*Oui, bien sûr*, but surely the rules of literature – of good taste, of structure remain strict. Five acts is the rule."

"Structure and pace are important, of course. I'm just not so sure anybody wants to read a rhyming five-act mystery about Mount Olympus."

"It worked for me," he insists. "Now, to improve the dialogue, you should read your stories out loud. Better yet, ask your neighbors to read the parts."

"I'll read out loud. My neighbors? Forget it."

"When I ran out of neighbors, I used marionettes."

I look him square in the face. "You're sure this'll help get me published again?"

"What does your printer say?"

"Printer? You're sitting on it. Nowadays we go through agents and editors. My ex-agent sold my first mystery, divorced his second wife, and disappeared to Prague with his third."

"Editors! Reviewers! Insects that can only get themselves noticed by stinging! And literary agents? Even worse! I could show you all society poisoned by this class of person who can't find any honest occupation, be it manual labor or service. Unluckily knowing how to read and write, they become the brokers of literature, live on our works, steal our manuscripts, falsify them, and sell them."

"You must've spent time in New York."

He brushes off this dubious compliment and sits down in my

rocking chair, his fingers toying with an ornate silver letter opener.

"No, no, I'm just an old hand at publishing. My best childhood friend Thieriot acted as my agent. The rascal drove me mad! He spent all my earnings from *La Henriade* and told me that they were stolen from his house while he was attending Mass! We both know the man never prayed in his life!"

"Never!" I concur.

"And that so-called friend Maupertuis put out a pirate edition of one of my works. To prevent any more piracy, I split my story *Zadig* into two separate releases. Oh, then there were censors, lawsuits – nothing changes in the literary world! And one last thing . . . "

"Yes?"

"Could you write a bit lighter? A bit wittier?"

"Well, that's easy for you to say. Where's the Wit? I mean, like, 'Be Funny.' You can't do it on command, can you?"

He looks surprised. "Why not? It's easy. Of course, good writers are only witty in the right place, they never strive after smartness, they think sensibly, and express themselves clearly."

"Just like that, huh?"

He leans back and smiles from the sheer memory of his craft. "You just think of a startling comparison, or a delicate allusion, or a play on words. You might use a word one way when your listener will first hear it the other way. Or a sly way of juxtaposing ideas not usually associated with each other — "

Voltaire rises from the rocking chair and rests his chin on one laced cuff, gazing over the window sill at the distant lake, lost in memory of wittier days. "It is the art of finding a link between two dissimilars – or a difference between two similars, the art, *Madame*, of saying half of what you mean and leaving the rest to the imagination — "

V. breaks off his reverie and turns back to me, laughing at himself, " . . . and I would tell you much more about wit, if I had more of it myself."

"Aren't we modest? You never had any problems with writing, did you?"

"*Mais non*, I had failures all the time. I never stopped working long enough to worry. I was always revising, juggling my works in progress. I always had a new scene waiting in the wings, a book at the printers, a pamphlet in the bonfires."

"Keeping your name in play, so to speak."

"*Oui*. I read some of my chapters or verses at salons, just to get people gossiping and tittering, 'Oh! That will put him in the Bastille for sure!' People were always copying out what they heard, publishing it without my permission and leaving me to take the blame for some foul writing in the extreme. It is far better to be silent than to increase the number of bad books, you know."

"Maybe . . ." I say, trying to imagine reading my mystery to the electrician and carpenter over lunch at the pizza house down the road, " . . . any other suggestions?"

"Hmm, let's see. A literary feud? I got into an endless series of barbs with Jean-Jacques Rousseau – to set tongues wagging. Can't you pick a public argument with someone?"

I wonder with whom I could pick a literary fight, and more to the point, why they should care.

V. sees my downcast face and tries again. The poor guy is really trying to help.

"I've got it. Get yourself banned! Anytime the Keeper of the Royal Seal burned one of my works in the public square, it kept the printers up all night!"

"They don't burn books anymore," I inform him.

"That's bad news . . . from the publicity aspect."

The end of Royal Tyranny dampens his enthusiasm for a moment.

"Well," he says, slapping all the papers back into their file, "I wrote more than ninety-three volumes of verse, plays, fables and letters, and," he flicks a finger at my poor little mystery sitting on the shelf, "you've only started. If you're not up to a feud — ?" he looks hopefully in my direction.

"With whom?"

"And you can't leak your stories to a salon — ?"

"Unlikely."

"Nobody wants to burn your books?"

"'Fraid not."

"Well, you just have to get a new agent, and revise, revise, revise! I rewrote my satire of Joan of Arc, *La Pucelle*, for fifteen years before publication."

I explain yet again how difficult it is to work in two-hour intervals broken by the children's lunch hour, homework sessions, and music practices. Not to mention hours of staining wooden shelves, sewing curtains, and shoveling snow every day. I hint that I could use some practical help.

"Anyone can shovel, *Madame*. Anyone can sew. Not everyone can benefit from *les conseils* of the King of the Enlightenment." V. corrects me sternly.

"Sorry, I forgot. Mere mortals do the shoveling. Ghosts set the intellectual pace."

"You can't expect to accomplish anything in two-hour intervals, *Madame*. We will start at five — "

"Five in the *morning?*" I sputter.

"*Oui*, these days are too short and writers ought to be given a double ration of them, so we shall do exactly as Madame du Châtelet and I did in Cirey. We'll work from dawn through to the midday meal. I meant to talk to you about that, by the way, please change the main meal from evening to noon. It's much healthier. You'll excuse me, now, I must change for dinner."

I protest vehemently. "That's just the point! Dinner is the family meal. It's very important for – for – for family bonding."

"Oouf!" Voltaire waves family bonding aside with the swish of lace sleeve. "I realize you modern mothers have a bizarre, obsessive interest in your offspring, *Madame*, but they should eat in their rooms. Tomorrow morning we start at five, *as usual*, giving us seven hours before noon without fail every day."

"Very well for you not even to mention the cooking because you don't eat —"

"If you have house guests, slip away at midday while the coffee is being served —"

"Served by whom, exactly?"

He rubs his brow. "Exactly so. Refuse to receive them before tea. Madame du Châtelet and I often held poetry readings at dawn, and gave little theatricals around midnight for our house guests."

I groan to think of the exhaustion he is proposing. "Don't you – sorry, *didn't* you ever sleep?"

V.'s brown eyes scrutinize me. "Let's not lose a minute. The greatest expense is that of time. By the way, please move the coffee machine to the office, so much more convenient. I don't care about food, but the flow of coffee around here leaves even a phantom dissatisfied."

The next morning, V. and I tiptoe to my office in pitch darkness. A jolt of icy air hits my face. The hissing coffee machine is the only warm thing in the room. V. has opened the dormer window to the frozen skies; an impressive antique telescope points up at the black heavens.

He gestures upward and I gasp. The neon life of Manhattan always blotted out this glorious sight. Thousands of stars fill the nightscape, so many I can't find Orion or the Dipper.

"You see, the Earth which looks so noble and grand, is only an imperceptible point in the scheme of things," he says.

And two human souls, Voltaire and I, are dwarved together by the immensity of the universe spreading across the sky. The two centuries that separate our births are reduced to a meaningless nano-second. Suddenly my old house seems very young.

V. fixes his telescope on a distant target. "She is moved," he mutters to himself, noting the position in his little leather-bound notebook. Thoughtfully, he has shoved all of his astronomical charts out of my way. My poor manuscript waits on the desk. I turn to a passage describing a night in a Lhasa hotel and see that what I've drafted is totally inadequate in conveying the vast sense of place under the Himalayan skies.

I start to rewrite, "The wide Tibetan sky was punctured by more stars than she had ever seen in her lifetime of city living . . . " The words start to flow.

"Better than shoveling, *non*?" V. says, smiling back at me over his shoulder, framed by the glistening carpet of lights.

L'Académie Vaudoise

The following Saturday night finds me inching my car through a snowstorm down an unlit country road.

"I think we took a wrong turn in Duilliers," I say.

Wrapped in her Zurich furs, my sister-in-law Bea is re-reading by flashlight a ten-year-old's scrawled instructions to pick up his "*boum*" guests at the Givrins communal hall. The required party costume is "*rock et roll*." Alexander departed before dinner in palpable excitement wearing his old St. Boniface's school blazer, disguised as a Beatle.

"We should turn left at the well. Look, there's a well."

I turn the steering wheel too quickly and the car starts sliding. It sideswipes someone's parked snowblower. I hit the brake. All is still. The snow-covered stone houses look very picturesque, unless you're sitting in a scraped Subaru with your sister-in-law, lost as hell.

"Wrong well?" Bea suggests.

An elegant woman with a nearly royal profile and exquisite taste, she's deeply proud of her family's origins around the Alpine lakes near Lucerne and the founding canton of Switzerland, Schwyz. Now she's visiting her brother so far south of the "Rösti Belt," the border between Swiss-German and French speakers, she feels as much of a foreigner as I.

"It's almost eleven. We're late. I hope the party hasn't ended already." I wrench the steering wheel around.

"I see some lights over there."

With a daring manoeuvre of the car around a stone wall, we arrive in Givrins. Sure enough, here is Pierre-Edouard's mother Noelle Gruyère, greeting the parents in a foyer off the darkened dance room full of bopping pre-teens. Armed with a pack of Marlboros, she is wearing cobra-patterned leggings and a fishnet tank top over some kind of snake-skin bra.

"Mrs. Küng? You're Mrs. Küng?" she asks. "Alexander is such a gentleman, yah, yah, and he's having a real good time. They're all such sweet kids. I'm so glad that in the end, Alexander came."

"Oh, there was never any doubt," I say gratefully, "he's looked forward to this for days."

Noelle confides, "Well, you know, Pierre-Edouard didn't want to invite Alexander at first, because he was born in Hong Kong, you know, but I insisted. I reminded Pierre-Edouard that one year we invited a little refugee from Kosovo. And last year, we had an Afghan orphan. I teach him you have to make room for everybody, for all kinds. You have to be generous."

Bea hasn't quite caught Noelle's cheerful implications. There's something touching about my sister-in-law, the ex-wife of a director of the media giant EMI, charming the tobacco-wreathed Cobra Creature. Catching only that someone was born in Hong Kong, Bea asks, "Was Pierre-Edouard born in Hong Kong, too?"

The eyes of Pierre-Edouard's mother widen. She abandons us to greet parents who are less of "all kinds."

It's not as if being an immigrant into Swiss society is some kind of rare disease. Switzerland has welcomed foreigners since Voltaire's day. Last week, someone put up an election poster in our village picturing Nazi skin heads on the rampage. The slogan read, "Xenophobia isn't Swiss."

We're lucky to be in the "liberal" south-western tip of Switzerland that sticks into the ribs of France. Yet, there is an urgent air to our assimilation. It's not so much a racial issue as part of a larger French-language panic. The whole of Swiss-Romande society seems on red-alert when it comes to globalization, which equals Americanization, which equals English. Forget that the Swiss cereal box reads on the back, "*Let's chat sur Internet!*"

One lunchtime, I'm chatting to Eva-Marie as I carry her across the icy schoolyard to our car. Suddenly a teacher with up-turned nose and wiry hair darts like an attacking marmot across the yard to grab my arm, nearly landing us all on the treacherous ice.

She yells, "You mustn't speak English! You're in Switzerland!"

Well, I would gladly embrace the language of Molière, Proust, and – yes, Voltaire – if that was what I was hearing around me. Even V. has trouble with the local accent – thick Vaudois evolved from Julius Caesar's cavalry men once posted here – that renders even simple words like "*oui*" into an Appalachian "waah."

And the accent isn't the only problem. Eva-Marie's teacher has sent a brusque demand that I kindly return a *fiche*, which I don't understand. Happily, I have the Great French Playwright in residence.

"Ah . . . of course!" Voltaire responds. "The Paris police kept a *fiche* on me for decades. They just want her police file."

"Police file? She's six years old."

"That's what *fiche* means."

I come home from school that afternoon with egg on my face.

"A *fiche* can also mean a loose worksheet," I inform the master of eighteenth-century French.

"Pardon, *Madame*. I hope I caused no embarrassment."

"Only a little. I'll give you another chance. Shed some of your *lumière* on this — " I let him tackle Theo's latest school circular. "It's about a *Course d'École* — "

"A course of study?"

"No, it must be an outing. It lists hats, gloves and . . . a helmet. He has to bring something called a *K-Way*. What's a *K-Way*?"

V. starts flipping the Larousse. "There are no *K-Ways* in the *dictionnaire*," he says. "What's that? *Combis?* Let's see . . ."

"Wait, I heard it the other day at school! What was that kid putting on? It might mean a one–piece ski suit, you know, combined pants and top?" My pride in this linguistic victory is pathetic.

Voltaire sniffs. "*Combi* . . . an ugly word. *Les baskets?* That is English. To hold the picnic."

"No, *baskets* means sneakers, not baskets. Like in basketball shoes."

"But, *Madame*, this is not – what has happened to French?" V. shoves the sheet back at me.

"Don't shout. It's not English either! I've been trying to decipher these hieroglyphics for weeks! *A.C.T. de C.F.* means art, not acting, *CYT-2* stands for second grade. Look at this notebook, here! A multiplication tables assignment sounds like secret N.A.T.O. coordinates – *Fiche 27, Math 1: OP, livret 4!*"

Voltaire is in despair. "You'd think they'd never heard of the Académie Française. The French language is a very poor but proud woman. We have to give her alms against her will, but I dare say even she'd turn up her nose at *K-Way* or *combi*."

The school hours are harder for us to track than the jargon. Two days a week Eva-Marie and Theo start school at 8:05 (but not the same days), while three days a week they should arrive at 8:50, provided they don't have to come early for tutorials (noted in their *carnets* the night before). Eva-Marie has no school on Wednesday, Monday, and Thursday afternoons until after Christmas. Friday afternoon sessions start after Easter. Alexander is off Thursday afternoons as well as Wednesdays. On Tuesdays and Thursdays he comes home an hour earlier than on Mondays and Fridays.

Any Swiss mother with a full-time job outside the home is

fighting the entire school establishment of the canton of Vaud.

About a week after Noelle Gruyère's patronizing treatment of me as an immigrant, I experience the Swiss system's dismissive treatment of me as a mother.

Voltaire and I pay a visit to Theo's slow-moving *maîtresse*, Madame Vacher. I explain that her proposed class outing to the circus will conflict with Theo's after-school violin lesson. Our family is going to the circus that night, anyway, so Theo can spend Friday afternoon at home with me practicing his music.

"No," Madame Vacher says flatly. "Theo can't go home. He must spend the afternoon in the classroom." She resumes cleaning the backboard.

V. and I pursue the flying eraser in protest.

"Alone? Alone in the classroom while the others go to the circus? His violin lesson will seem like some kind of punishment."

"It's the law, *Madame*. The other teacher Gregory will look in on him from time to time."

V. tries blowing chalk dust in her face.

I protest, "Obviously, Theo would be better off practicing at home than sitting here alone."

"You'll have to make a request."

"Of whom?"

"Me."

"I just did."

"No, *Madame*," she turns to me with a superior smile on her face. "You attempted to *inform* me. The law requires an application making your request of me a week in advance, with an *attestation*."

"An attestation? Of what?"

She thrusts an application form into my astonished face.

V. and I storm out of the classroom. When we reach the house, my first thought is to call Peter with a resentful tirade. But that only doubles my indignation. Ever since I've arrived in Switzerland, I've felt like a child who needs constant introduction, translation and explanation, and now attestation from a real "grown-up."

"Don't worry. I'll sign that attestation," V. says with determination. "She is nothing but *une petite fonctionnaire*, a petty bureaucrat. She wouldn't dare challenge the name of Voltaire."

"Oh, right, good. Monsieur François Arouet de Voltaire, promises to babysit Theo. That's not the point. I'm an adult. I'm his mother. Why should I need an attestation, from you, or my husband, or anybody? Aren't mothers full citizens?"

"I assure you *Madame*, you are an adult." He bows in respect.

"Thank you."

"Moreover, that woman's French diction was so very poor! No rhetorical presence! No enunciation! Such slovenly posture! Graceless gestures! The attire of a peasant! Clearly she was never properly finished."

His eighteenth-century priorities make me smile, despite my fury.

"Well, I guess standards at the École Jean-Jacques Rousseau are not up to your buggering Jesuits at Louis-le-Grand."

Voltaire drops his silk scarf.

"École WHAT?"

"Jean-Jacques Rousseau. You said you knew him — ?"

V. spits out the question in a squeal of horror. "Know him? They named a school after that *coquin* traipsing around in an Armenian costume? That clock-maker's boy? That Judas to philosophy? That monster who sent his own children to a foundling home rather than care for them himself? That romantic idiot who wrote his Social Contract against the human species? No wonder they can't speak French!"

I watch Voltaire reach for Peter's armchair for support.

"I hate to break it to you, but they absolutely revere Rousseau around these parts. He is – as a god."

V. turns even whiter than usual. "Impossible! No man did more to undermine education and reason in arguing for Nature!

Bah! Why, I told him that reading his book made me want to run around on all fours but it was sixty years since I had done so, and it was impossible that I resume the practice."

V. circles the coffee table, dragging his knuckles on the carpet, in imitation of Rousseau's Natural Man, sending me into peals of laughter.

"You're wicked."

"Oh, *Madame*, never was anyone so witty as Rousseau when trying to turn us all into brutes again. I really wonder what they teach at that school. Surely it's obvious that Man is not corrupted by social institutions, man is civilized by them! Is this a school where they make sure the savage in Theodor is safely preserved? Come to think of it, Rousseau's novel *Julie* was full of grammatical errors, too."

I have never seen V. so caustic.

"There's a parent-teacher meeting tomorrow night. Why don't you come with me? It's about time you met the locals."

The taut lips curl at one end.

"You know, that's a felicitous idea."

V. appears in the kitchen after dinner with a self-conscious flourish. I haven't seen these green velvet breeches before, nor the knee-high polished boots and mauve silk stockings. His arrival is preceded by a whiff of lavender soap and he sports an Olympian wig of lush curls.

"Wow! This isn't opening night, Monsieur Voltaire," I've seen him working in his tufted green dressing gown for days on end, so I know this is a big gesture.

"Just a little something from the 'good old days'," he says, slightly abashed. "A debonair approach is always the mark of someone in control." He deftly tightens one of his stockings. "I hope the local dress has improved. When I took up residence near here, I found nothing but forty savages without even shoes to their names. One of the first things I did was start a stocking factory."

Crossing the school grounds, Peter and I greet Marius Metzler's parents, the Swiss-Germans who herd cows on the plateau above our house. They park their jeep embellished along its side with licking flames of red paint. Monsieur Metzler is wearing an embroidered peasant's work shirt under his leather jacket and a strange little skullcap. The cap is so picturesque, it might even qualify as what my fashionista friend Ruth back at the *Times* might christen a "fashion moment." Suddenly, I miss her.

Meanwhile, Voltaire is staring at Madame Metzler in her black anorak with the embroidered Chinese Dragon, skin-tight black jeans, red cowboy boots and a cigarette holder at the ready.

"*Madame*," he says, bowing as she struts right past him.

The classroom audience quickly divides into two: educated professionals assume places behind tiny desks along the front of the classroom, village blue-collar stiffs line up defensively along the back. The commuting women are still in their Geneva suits and expensive boots. The women at the back wear Madame Metzler's border chic – a fringed-leather cowboy look popular among the chalet dwellers.

I find my seat, indicated by a silhouette of Theo's head pasted on construction paper. He's left me a drawing of the Statue of Liberty in New York's harbor. The cartoon's expression is grim.

Voltaire sniffs a character next to him who is about thirty years old, undershaven, with two earrings in one ear lobe and a long quiff of blue-dyed hair at the nape of his neck. He ruffles through a crumpled packet of cigarettes for an unbroken candidate. V. settles on a tiny stool next to my chair.

"No doubt that is one of my friend Rousseau's Natural Men, a 'friendly and flowing savage who would return us to nature'."

The school director has arrived from "*en bas*," that is to say, the gentrified dormitory communities that lie closer to the lakeshore. Clearing his throat portentously, Monsieur Villar adjusts his bifocals, sets up his PowerMac on a table, and connects it to a projector. He will display his talk in outline form on the wall.

"Kind of like projected opera lyrics," I mutter to Peter.

" — for those of us who are literate!" V. whispers. "How thoughtful! I always found the Vaudois accent simply impenetrable."

In perfectly acceptable French, Villar announces that he is bringing the Canton of Vaud's educational system into line with more advanced parts of Switzerland. Every change appears on the wall, in outline form, with ponderous predictability. Each point is announced with a balletic flourish as Villar's index finger descends towards the PowerMac keyboard to announce Another New Idea.

His big message of the night is that no longer will the future of each child be engraved in stone by sixth grade. One can enter the university track a bit later than seventh grade with a sizable effort to jump from the "general track" to the "*baccalauréat* track," provided the student repeats years wasted on the general track. This is good news?

Villar now projects something resembling the map of the London Underground. Track lines move up and across, over and down, up, over and up again. These innovations were all tested and proven in – Quebec.

"The Land of the Huron Tribes, a model of educational reform?" V. grins. "That's why the school is named Rousseau!"

Despite Quebec's high unemployment, Villar seems to think the French-Canadian example will lead us out of the darkness of Vaud.

I am distracted from Villar's remarks by V.'s eyes which are circling hypnotically in time to the director's finger pointing to the white board, then diving towards the PowerMac, the tool of the Educated Man visiting the Peasants. Indeed, there is something of the courtier in Villar's minuet as he explains the "formation" of the masses.

"Excuse me, but is this man from Versailles, by any chance?" V. asks into my ear. "Those hand gestures remind me of my old friend, the Duc de Choiseul, demonstrating the latest dance at Versailles."

"Shush," I whisper, trying hard to translate Villar's windy replies.

"Oh, don't bother trying to understand everything he says. I've already concluded that this man must be very ignorant, for he answers every question that is asked of him," V. quips.

Next Madame Vacher shuffles forward to announce her big innovation: the kids will no longer just copy out vocabulary lists. They will try using new words in sentences, on themes they choose themselves!

I'm starting to wonder what century this school got stuck in.

Voltaire whispers dolefully, "Vocabulary lists? No great verses to inspire their hungry young minds? No Corneille? No Molière? No *Voltaire*? *Les pauvres enfants* . . . What a bleak century for education . . . '

One of the younger teachers – a tall, sporty blonde – follows the mumblings of Madame Vacher. V.'s expression brightens considerably. After all, this was a man who enjoyed very close relationships with many of the actresses in his plays. It's her unhappy task to explain the new grading system, discarding numerical grades for none other than American smiley faces.

The audience shifts in their under-sized seats as Villar draws the goofy circles on the blackboard. Parents of budding scholars manage to discuss *Les smileys*, without feeling too silly; the dignity of the evening erodes as less fortunate parents question the impact of *les demi-smileys*, *les straighties*, and *les frownies*, on the self-esteem of their dunces.

Madame Metzler suddenly launches at Villar in a ferocious attack, "*Les smileys* are infantile. Worse, they're American! They've got nothing to do with Swiss culture."

V. is delighted. Out of the corner of my eye, I see him smirking ludicrously at the parents in an imitation of *le smiley* drawn on the board – a Smiley clowning in an eighteenth-century wig. You can bury the man, but not the ham.

Other parents goad Madame Metzler on. Villar intervenes and says that instead of *les smileys*, some schools in the same district indicate the four levels of performance with the initials, L.A., A., M.A., and P.A., standing for largely acquired, acquired, less, or *moins*, acquired and poorly acquired.

But V. has wandered on to more mischief, poking blue-quiffed Natural Man into complaint that his older son in sixth grade is receiving marks in yet a third code, A.A., A-plus, A, N.A., standing for Achieved with Ease, Achieved with some Ease, Achieved and Not Achieved.

"Is the school system drowning in alphabet soup, or what?" Natural Man shouts to general applause. He takes a bow. Villar is retreating, his back against the chalk board. Traces of a Smiley grin at us from the back of his dark suit. At the back of the room a separate argument breaks out over *les frownies* versus not acquired, versus poorly acquired.

The meeting's gone haywire. Everyone is firing away at each other like machine guns in local dialect, waving cigarettes at Villar, who's packing up his PowerMac in retreat.

I drift off from the linguistic mayhem into memories of New York. St. Boniface parents never argued during a parents' evening. No one smoked Everyone smiled politely in their beige pant-suits while surreptitiously running their eyes down class lists to see who lived on East End, Fifth, or Park. Their Manolos tucked awkwardly under the little desks, the New York parents nodded at the classical allusions dropping from the headmaster's mouth. For $14,000 a year, this man would guarantee the boys Renaissance art and Etonian values, the keys to the Kingdom of Harvard, and the vice-president's corner office. Plus a field trip to Florence in the spring to soak up European culture.

But this is the reality of Europe; a roomful of over-taxed and angry parents drowning in an onslaught of mind-numbing vocabulary lists, educational software sales campaigns, distant bureaucracies, Disney movie posters, and textbooks from Quebec.

Peter and I leave the school meeting and walk home through the sleeping village. V. trails behind us, softly reciting some Homerian verses learnt by heart at Louis-le-Grand. We pass the abandoned youth hostel with shredded flyers stuck to the lobby floor and the tattooed locals sitting in the darkened rear of the café.

I smile to myself, realizing how different St-Cergue probably looks to a tourist here for a few hours of cross-country skiing. Each Saturday morning, the crafts boutiques spring to life, the *laiterie* lays out its runny cheeses, the social worker moonlights at his second-hand junk shop and M. Metzler drives tourists in a horse-drawn sleigh.

The town's latest stab at a renaissance is the restoration of the former home for unwed mothers into a chic art gallery. At the official opening I sipped my white wine and overheard another guest, none other than Dr Claude, disparage some of his patients as, "drop-outs, *marginals*, socially *unfrequentable*."

I start picking up threads of what Dr. Claude means. I'm told in a murmured aside, by a teacher no less, that one father "mistreats" his sullen older daughter of fifteen, but the details are only hinted at. What I see is that the girl rollerblades aimlessly outside the *tabac* until the new snowfall forces her indoors.

I can hear the Rochats fight with each other over his long hours in a backroom operation set up in the village by a British bank to take advantage of the lower wages here in the mountains.

Alexander gets off the train one day, his face swollen, his cheek bruised deep purple, beaten up for refusing to relinquish his seat. Having failed to budge Alexander with judo pinches to the nape of neck, the local bully Christophe finished up with full-fledged punches to his face.

"Why didn't anyone stop him? Where were the adults?"

"Two old ladies were watching."

Peter calls the perp's mother who invites my husband over for "a glass of white." Peter says the wine can wait; he'd prefer a written apology from the child. The next morning, I tackle the doyen of teachers to complain, and she only chuckles when I name the culprit.

"Christophe. He's already set fire to a car. That kid's a real case," she says, sauntering away.

Of course no written apology is forthcoming. Peter persists and drafts a letter giving Alexander's account of the incident. No answer. He follows up with a second call to the little thug's home and the father answers this time, and says his lawyer is preparing a case against us for "*menacement.*"

That night, Peter and I sit on the bedroom balcony, wrapped in blankets to wallow in the moonlight reflecting off the snow-covered lawn. We are no longer arrivals, spectators, or outsiders. We're being sued for harassment. Noelle Gruyère got it wrong. Events have fast made us locals ourselves.

There'll Always be an England

Normal people aren't regularly caught talking to themselves in empty rooms. Peter suggests I take a break.

I have finally waved off the last worker. Theo's back at school, his throat scarved against brisk winds. His gym class entails an inordinate number of chilly afternoons sledding or skiing on the village *piste*, but despite these exercises in group congelation, there's no more wheezing. The stoic, invalid's disposition that was settling over him in Manhattan has lifted to reveal an elfin optimism.

As serious as ever, Alexander devotes long hours on the attic floor memorizing French verbs, measuring triangles, and diagraming the laws of electricity to prove that a member of our family can make the cut for the university track despite an American accent.

These days even Eva-Marie seems almost whole again, winning snowball fights with the agility of someone born to plaster.

I've stuck to V.'s demonic pre-dawn timetable, although not his daily ingestion of twenty-five cups of coffee. The revision of the Tibet novel starts to trundle along despite my grumpiness. The only distraction is V.'s conversation, full of scandalous tidbits. Despite efforts to concentrate on work, I find myself muttering incredulously, "The Regent slept with his own daughter?"

I agree to Peter's get-away offer. Facing down fears of air-borne antibiotic-resistant T.B. germs, terrorist attacks, and lost luggage, I buy a cheap ticket to England to visit my god-daughter, Rebecca.

With a look of deepening consternation, V. watches me disconnect my computer and clear my desk. "It's all yours for three days. That'll give you time to write a new play. Well, knowing you, maybe two new plays."

He raises himself up to his full, if not imposing, height. He is too proud to ask me my plans, which in the end, I can't conceal.

"I'm going to England for a long weekend."

"A marvelous idea!" he leaps up with relief. "To return at last! It's been so long. My old haunts, my old friends — "

Which is how I find myself standing in a "ticketless" airline queue with a man who has tossed aside his green bathrobe for discount travel in his best polished boots, long brown velvet travelling coat with deep cuffs over a red brocade waistcoat, a high collar of wrapped linen frothing out in hand-worked lace, and on top of his elegant brow, an impossible wig of tumbling brown curls.

For what it's worth, I'm wearing a five-year-old black Anne Klein pant-suit that's gone shiny in the rear.

V. beams at me with unfettered delight as his enormous leather-bound trunk swings away with my red Samsonite between the rubber flaps and into the dubious mysteries of charter-flight baggage control.

He is flushed with excitement as we wander the duty-free counters. I have to stop him repeatedly from spritzing his lace cravat with Eau Sauvage – "Rousseau would have loved this one" – but my disapproval does nothing to dampen his anticipation.

"How I love the English! How I love people who say what they think! How I admire the English respect for facts, reality, utility, simplicity of manners, habits and dress!"

"I'm glad you're looking forward to it," I grunt, lugging an overloaded handbag. I would rather have left him at home, and he is no fool.

"What a relief from that Bastille of an office of yours! Now, do you have your letters of introduction? With whom are we staying first?"

"Don't worry. You haven't done too badly by my accommodations so far."

There are no reserved seats. V. insists I dump all my stuff on the seat next to me, so that he is sure of a place once everyone is settled.

"*Oui, Madame*, I have kept silent about your low ceilings, your inadequate heating, and the complete lack of intelligent Society because I am the soul of courtesy," he says, finally squeezing his velveted bottom into a seat that looks narrow even for his eighteenth-century pelvis.

"Even in the Bastille, I had the company of Madame de Tencin, the queen of the salons, but then, you must have heard all that in history class. Do you think they'll give us a coffee?"

"At these prices, I doubt it. What was Madame de Tencin in for?"

"Another Royal intrigue. In the Bastille, she and I were like Pyramis and Thisbe, a whispering wall between us and . . ."

"All right, all right. Anyway, you're sprung now from the doldrums of my office, so I hope you have a good time. We're staying with my friends, the Worthys, in Suffolk. Who did you stay with last time?"

"Henry John, Lord Bolingbroke."

He doesn't need to tell me that Bolingbroke was the Kissinger of his day, but before I can scour my memory for a few scraps about this familiar name, Monsieur Blabbermouth starts the usual boasting . . .

" . . . the Tory foreign minister who negotiated the Treaty of Utrecht, a political figure who strode both sides of the

Channel like a diplomatic Colossus, author of *Idea of a Patriot King* . . ."

"Oh, yeah, that Bolingbroke." I feel pathetic.

The Worthys and their two daughters are a delightful upper-middle-class English family, comfortably off thanks to Allen's endless toil in far-flung postings as an oil trader, but this will hardly be a weekend hobnobbing with regulars from Buckingham Palace. I try to warn V. that his hosts won't be titled aristocrats.

"No problem at all," he chides me. "In the three years I spent in England, I realized that the English classes divide up – much like their beer – with the froth at the top and the dregs at the bottom, but the middle is excellent!"

Will Katherine, a former women's page editor, chatelaine of a yellow Georgian rectory in Stowmarket, Suffolk – with her twice-weekly tennis doubles, needlepoint projects, and bread machine – appreciate comparison to a common brewski?

In ninety minutes, we've landed at Stansted, so sane and spacious it makes my memories of Heathrow in the late seventies compare with a Breughel painting of Hell. Gone are the clumsy diesel buses trundling across the tarmac. We whoosh our way from the landing gate via a sleek underground shuttle to the main terminal, pressed up against people with roughened faces, pale eyes, and the tired smiles of the freshly-vacationed.

"I landed on May 10th, 1726 at Greenwich, the week of the Fair," V. chatters on. "The Thames was covered with boats, the King was coming down in a barge, preceded by a band," he sighs, then adds, "this fat person is standing on my foot. Not that it pains me, but it is so very rude."

I gently edge aside the fat man wearing a T-shirt that advertises, "Bigger is better."

"No doubt you thought the revelers were coming to greet you," I comment dryly.

He looks at me out of the corner of his eye. "I admit at

thirty-two, I was stirred by the pretty girls, dressed in their finest, set off by their demure modesty, their rosy cheeks, but I quickly realized my elation was a little premature. When I reached London I found my banker had just declared bankruptcy. I was unexpectedly penniless . . ."

What day was it I finally landed in England, sometime in early spring, 1977? I'd already warmed up to the British experience by spending three years in the Crown Colony of Hong Kong, writing for the *South China Morning Post*. I'd done my time in the field, covering Vietnamese refugee camps, working eleven- and twelve-hour days for $200 a month, clothed myself in cut-price Chinese sandals and rejects from the factory outlets, eating local, living local.

The colony was also the "Fragrant Harbor" – like any successful port, an open culture; it drew all nationalities, particularly Commonwealth citizens. The raging war in Vietnam and a communist walled giant to the north fueled Hong Kong's teeming economy.

The *Post*'s newsroom wasn't England, but a microcosm of the British Empire, a crossfire of personalities: the boisterous self-parody of the Australian reporters, the dry irony of the New Delhi subs, the suave aloofness of the Sunday features editor from Sri Lanka, the slinky innuendo of the Cantonese, Harold, who covered the drugs beat by night, and the wild-man sentimentality of the New Zealand news editor who hired me virtually unseen.

An Australian sub on the *China Mail* propositioned me in the crudest possible three-worded question my second night at the Hong Kong Journalists' Club. I declined. He shouted down the length of the bar, "How I hate American women!"

The Scottish sportswriter returned from a drunken lunch at the Royal Hong Kong Jockey Club, knelt beside my desk in full view of our colleagues, and burred in an opera whisper that an illness had left him only one testicle, "but ah ashurrre ya, it wurrrks."

The newsroom was chaos even at its calmest. One night an Irish political writer tossed his typewriter across the newsroom and screamed, "I'm going home to Belfast for some peace and quiet!"

Not all of my encounters were with the wordsmiths of the *Post*. Since I came from a family in the entertainment business, I pulled the celebrity beat, as well as the drug rehabilitation beat, hotel and tourism, and relations with the American community. My U.C. Berkeley M.A. in Chinese Studies went ignored.

Robert Mitchum drunkenly scrawled obscenities on my notepad through a lunch on the Repulse Bay Hotel veranda while traveling pal Richard Egan looked on. Francis Ford Coppola pondered out loud to his production designer Dean Tavoularis and me about how well *Heart of Darkness* served as a starting point for his Vietnam war movie in progress. George Plimpton came looking for "Sex in Asia," for *Esquire* magazine. He pronounced my tour of live nude strip shows too mundane. Barry Humphries nervously aired his Edna Everage evening dresses in a banal Hilton suite, quizzing me for local gossip and peccadilloes that would spice up his dinner cabaret. President Omar Bongo suggested we do the interview in an aide's bedroom at the Mandarin Oriental, and thought the best place to do it was sitting on the end of the bed. When he started to finger my underwear, it took me a few seconds to register that, although I had never worked in Africa, this was unlikely normal interview behavior anywhere in the world. My editor protested to the Governor's Chief of Protocol – who, I recall, indicated that this was not the first phone call he'd received that week regarding His Excellency's visit.

Far from home and family, I was cutting my teeth as a journalist on "Daily Diary" pieces, Vietnam refugee news, and women's features. I was spending nights with the Royal Hong

Kong Police rounding up under-age whores from the brothels. I dined by day with a truculent Paul Bocuse or a nervous Sylvia Kristel promoting *Emanuelle*.

Finally, tiring of seeing the British in this crazy-mirror colonial version, I decided to visit the real thing. I boarded a plane for London, invited by Charles, a B.B.C. producer who had passed through Hong Kong a year before on assignment. I used my last paycheck to get to Heathrow . . .

V. waits for me behind the crowd around the luggage carousel. He's thumbing his tiny leather-bound English dictionary, full of spellings like "musick," and "rouze."

His enormous trunk tumbles and crashes off the conveyor belt.

"At least when I arrived in London, I spoke English. How did you ever manage?" I ask.

"Bolingbroke was married to a French woman, the widowed Marquise de Villette, whom he adored. She was older than he, but her charm endured past youthful beauty. Their marriage was an inspiration. But once I moved beyond their French-speaking circle, I was in trouble."

"I can imagine."

He rolls his eyes slightly. "*Désastre*. I was invited to sit by Alexander Pope's mother at dinner in Twickenham. I told her about the buggering Jesuits and she nearly fainted." He reflects, "It must have been my choice of words. Happily, I saw Pope himself many times after that."

"He was a hunchback, wasn't he?"

"*Oui*. I was shocked by the deformity, that grotesque torso laced into a harness all day. The suffering was obvious, but I was amazed by his sharpness of mind. At first we could hardly communicate. I fled back to the countryside and devoted myself to study for three months until I could converse and write in English."

I feel embarrassed that my progress in French after three months has been so slow.

"I told you before," V. scolds me, "go to the theater every night, and always learn the dirty words first. *Ah, voici la belle Katherine, non . . . ?*"

Katherine and my beanpole goddaughter Rebecca are waiting for us at Arrivals. Chattering in a flood of sunshine, Katherine drives us into the countryside. Their mutt, Sushi, is sitting on V., who's too busy reading *Time Out* to protest, checking out his old haunts – the Drury Lane and the Haymarket Theatres.

"Has the Lincoln's Inn Field Theatre closed?" he asks of no one in particular.

In the front seat, Katherine is catching me up on Allen's schedule. He'll arrive on his normal "commute" from Bahrain tomorrow morning. I am being sent to shop in London all day tomorrow and here is my train ticket. There will be a dinner party on Saturday night.

"I see that *Othello* is still playing," is the next comment from the back seat. "Unbelievable," V. bitches to himself, "how a woman can make an entire speech after she has been thoroughly strangled never made sense to me. Well, Shakespeare never had a spark of good taste or knew one rule of drama."

The Worthys' rectory is a Jane Austen vision, a large, square, two-story house, its foyer painted a bright and historically correct egg-yolk color, with Allen and Katherine's Japanese and Chinese statuary standing guard on the landings.

"So very modern," V. whispers with approval. He is even happier with the enormous guest room, lined with books and a *chaise longue* for his bed.

"Very elegant. The Bolingbrokes couldn't have done better. Is the toilet indoors or is that hoping for too much?"

That was not my worry when I first saw Charles' London apartment overlooking Chalcot Square that spring afternoon in

1977. The sunshine streaming into the living room through tall narrow windows hurt my eyes reddened by the all-night flight from Hong Kong. Within a week, it was obvious to me that Charles was absolutely too happy to see me, like a puppy with a new toy mail-ordered from America. He took me everywhere with him on his filming shoots. Within days, I had been introduced to two Members of Parliament, a future Foreign Secretary, the Prime Minister's son-in-law, and numerous television producers. The week ended on Friday at a B.B.C. cocktail party.

I felt very raw, very gauche, and very lost, until suddenly crossing the room, I saw a familiar face. I made out the soulful brown eyes and rotund figure of *The Times*' Hong Kong correspondent crossing the room, rescuing me from my oblivion. A sensitive and brilliant soul, David drank too much for his own good, but held a double first from Cambridge in Chinese and modern languages. By taking difficult and isolating postings in Cold War Moscow and Cultural Revolution Beijing, David ensured his professional reputation but by the time he reached his assignment in Hong Kong, he'd sealed the fate of his genius in a liquor bottle.

He and his Australian wife Judy hosted me along with young "journos" in their antique-filled living room in Hong Kong's leafy Pokfulam district. Judy's pretty face was framed by chin-length brown hair and windshield-wiper eyeglasses. Her delicious food and rippling laugher sustained a gaggle of David's admirers through obvious and hidden stresses.

In the presence of this couple, I was an awe-struck twenty-seven year old admiring a pair of well-matched intellectual and social talents, perhaps not unlike V.'s first glimpse of his Bolingbroke friends. It seems a small miracle to find David amid all these unfamiliar faces.

"Do you plan to stay in England?" this thoughtful man inquires as we survey the gathering from the margins.

"Yes, I'd like to stay on for a while," I reply.

David makes a call to the editor of the *Far Eastern Economic Review* in Hong Kong and within a few days, I become the *Review*'s London-based stringer, making editorial trips to Italy and Holland to review their relations with Asia. For his part, Charles urges me to write a letter to an executive producer at the B.B.C.'s Kensington House and within a few months, I'm also the "Beeb's" television coordinator for filming in China. Over the coming year and a half, I'm invited to become a member of the International Institute for Strategic Studies. I'm lunching at Chatham House listening to famous China scholars haggle the future of the Communist Party. I'm filing "voicers" to Toronto for the Canadian Broadcasting Company. I write a piece for the *Guardian* on Chinese family life.

How has all this happened to a foreigner? Like Voltaire, I discover new opportunities in England.

I loved England. Unfortunately, I did not love Charles as much as he perhaps deserved. Of medium height and finely built, his features were handsome enough, but I found his wit and generosity offset by an over-anxious gait and ingratiating style.

He liked to insert Cockney phrases into his speech – much as King Louis XIV's royal courtiers affected peasant accents for a joke, V. tells me – but with Charles there was a catch. Other B.B.C. producers affecting East End accents were products of Oxford or Cambridge. Their pose as "lads" was a gesture of equality cutting across class lines. Charles came from a warm family of East Enders but his background complicated the ambitions of the working-class achiever with a "redbrick" degree mixing with members of the Oxbridge elite affecting East End speech. These English class tensions confused and distanced me from the prospect of a life together. Although I wore Charles' ring, I was increasingly aware of my emotional fraud.

My reputation as a correspondent, thanks to David's introduction to the *Far Eastern Economic Review*, was growing and my trips to China for the B.B.C. became more frequent, extending my contacts in the China-watching world ever more distant from Charles.

One afternoon in Beijing, I discover David drinking alone in the cavernous dining room of his residence, The Beijing Minorities Hotel. At the table next to ours sits a well-known British trader who prides himself on having broken the 1950s' trade embargo with the Chinese Communists. We overhear him describe me to his companions in a whisper, "She *claims* she's a reporter."

This riles David, not so much for its aspersions on my modest talents, but as a slur aimed at a lady in his presence.

The English gentleman in David rears his head.

"Oh, what would you know about reporting, Edwin?" David retorts across the parquet. "You're hardly an authority. First you ran with the Poles, then you ran with the Russians, now you're running with the Chinese. You've never been anything but a running dog!"

Then to the astonishment of everyone in the dining room, this senior correspondent of *The Times* starts barking, yelping, and growling in the direction of Edwin's party. It gives new meaning to the phrase, "Mad dogs and Englishmen." Edwin and his guests flee their table in disarray. I don't know whether to laugh or sink under the table in embarrassment. Lao or "Old" Wang, the senior waiter, serves David a free brandy as the hubbub subsides. David downs the tiny glassful, but his fury isn't spent yet.

The dining room closes, so we continue the conversation in his shabby two-room suite on the sixth floor. Suddenly, David hoists himself up to stand tiptoe on an overstuffed chair and starts howling like a wolf into the heating-vent in the wall.

"Why are you doing that, David?" I ask wide-eyed.

"Oh, Edwin lives in the room next door," he replies.

*   *   *

Katherine breaks into my reveries of Englishmen I Have Known.

"Have you thought of looking up Charles?" She leans across the wooden kitchen table, offering a towering loaf of hot bread and a monumental Stilton.

"We lost touch," I answer.

I finally fled to Singapore from England with credentials to string for the *Economist* and the *Washington Post*. I offered to return Charles' diamond, but it now hangs on my goddaughter Rebecca's virginal neck, an English gem adorning an English jewel.

"Who in God's name is Charles?" Voltaire pipes up. He has descended from the guest room and joined us wearing his English country outfit, predictably tweedy and only slightly less fussy than his usual brocades. He's gone for the Scottish look in plaid scarves.

"None of your business," I reply.

"No harm intended, I'm sure," Katherine responds. Happily my rude retort doesn't dampen her good spirits. She serves up the hot, soft slices of bread and the blue veins of the cheese melt into the grainy clouds.

Rebecca and I set off for a walk through the broad, regular rows of beet poking through the frosty fields surrounding the house and its new tennis court. It is a relief to escape the snow, Switzerland, school commutes and French.

Sushi fetches the sticks we throw into tranquil ponds, their surface ice tinkling into glistening shards. Guinea hens strut down country lanes. Squawking pheasants streak out of bush-tops at our approach. The farms are prosperous; the landlords' children attend private schools.

Rebecca has just appeared in *Macbeth* at school, in the opening witches' scene.

> "When shall we three meet again,
> In thunder, lightning or in rain,

When the hurly-burly's done,
When the battle's lost or won."

We chant in happy unison.

"Still reciting lines by that drunken savage?" V. asks acidly, professional jealousy in evidence. "That Shakespeare's talent for fantasy is like plum pudding. It could only please the English."

I gape at his harsh estimation of the Bard, so he adds, "Well, and maybe Canadians."

Rebecca and I talk of her class's exploration of life in Ancient Rome. And this is the child described by her own mother as a hopeless television addict! What do mothers know? Maybe my cerebral Alexander sings Bow Wow rap lyrics on the train to school.

This is all very refreshing. I utterly failed my first godparent assignment in my twenties to a charming toddler in west L.A. – now a yoga instructor in Dublin. I'm tackling the godparent challenge for a second time in middle age. What does a godparent do? I'm still not sure. Free from the responsibility of raising a child with measured discipline and the yeast of sober example, one is merely asked to frost the cake with presents, contrarian ideas, and private confidences. The gamut of possible role models runs from Don Corleone to Auntie Mame.

Rebecca's little sister, the ebullient Molly, comes home from school, all refinement in a blue uniform, white blouse and regulation hat. For a minute, I feel sorry for my little Eva-Marie in St-Cergue, wrapped in jeans and snow leggings, surrounded by the coarse-mouthed kids of her class. Katherine's lasagne is delicious, even though one rarely goes to England for the food. I retire well-fed and exhausted to "our" grand room.

"Looking forward to tomorrow? We're taking the 9 a.m. London train from Stowmarket. I think Katherine wants to unload us for the day so that she can prepare for the dinner party in peace."

"I think we should lunch in the City," V. suggests. "I'd like to look into some investment opportunities there."

"Don't be ridiculous. We're going to buy Christmas presents in Oxford Street, and stop at John Lewis for wool gabardine."

"I want to go to the City."

He stamps his foot like a spoiled child. "I loathe Christmas and all organized religion. On the London Stock Exchange, Jews, Mohammedans and Christians meet as if they had a common religion and the only ungodliness we recognize there is the filing of a bankruptcy claim."

"Well, apart from worshiping at the altars of filthy lucre, exactly what can you do there?" I press him.

"I intend to invest in Euro exchange-rate futures contracts," he says with an absolute straight face. "They're at an all-time low."

This is a new and worrying facet of his personality.

I burst out laughing nervously. "You can't invest, Monsieur Voltaire. You're dead. And I won't lend you any money, so don't bother asking."

"Well, there's 'dead' and then there's *dead*," V. says, laying his wig on the top of a desk lamp and finger-fluffing it to look even more unruly. "I'll never be too dead to see a good opportunity when it exists. You're a fool if you think writing pays. I never made that mistake, and I was a millionaire by the age of forty. I always cultivated bankers who used me as a middle man. I made a tidy sum selling provisions and munitions to the army."

"A war profiteer?"

He glares at me, "A patriot, *je vous prie*. You don't think I lived on those puny family annuities and royal pensions, do you?"

I ponder this while brushing my teeth in the girls' bathroom – a huge room scattered with rugs, a standing tub, and an enormous basket of hotel soaps gathered by Allen on his oil-buying missions. When I return to our room, V. is in his nightshirt, picking his teeth decorously with a little ivory stick.

"You know, I've never imagined you as a financial type."

"Oh, I always lent at a healthy interest rate and was usually paid back on time. I once traveled from Paris to Nancy – that's one hundred and fifty miles – in two nights and a day to buy shares in a public fund issued by the Duc de Lorraine. I once made a killing of 500,000 francs on a lottery by using the mathematician Condamine's calculations to borrow from the bank and buy up the required number of tickets. The Comptroller sued me, but the courts backed me up."

I relent only a jot. "O.K., I'll buy you one lottery ticket for old times' sake – wait, don't look so pleased – you can forget futures, stocks, warrants, commodities — "

His brightening expression slumps. "Not even *un petit* thirty-day certificate of deposit?"

"No. N.O. . . . *N. O. N.*"

He heaves a discouraged sigh. "Well, then I'll just have to do my trading on margin. I don't see why I should stop being an investor now. Just because things went slightly awry the last time I came to England — "

He turns away, cutting off his sentence and reddening in the cheeks. I stare at him as he turns his face quickly towards the wall and stretches himself out for the night under the window. My black cashmere coat from New York serves as his blanket. Within seconds his head has disappeared under the collar.

I raise myself up from the pillows on one elbow, my eyes narrowing suspiciously at his prostrate form. A loud theatrical snore fools me not at all.

"What do you mean, things went awry that last time you were here?"

The snores subside and become more convincing. I give him a reprieve until morning.

The Froth at the Top

We scurry through beating rain from Katherine's car towards the Stowmarket platform. The train is delayed by a recent history of deadly crashes due to unseasonal inundations and antiquated equipment.

A few feet from where V. and I cower from the storm, a burly-bellied man in a shirt of loud pinstripes, red regimental tie, and gray flannels is braying into a cellphone.

Voltaire is riveted by every trading order this boor is barking down the line.

"He could be the son of a butcher, or the brother of a Lord," V. marvels. "That's what I love about England. A blue-blooded Frenchman of my day could never appreciate the merits of the market or the worthiness of trade."

I'm less impressed. "He's just a bad-mannered loud-mouth who works in the City," I retort.

V. is indignant at my under-appreciation. "Which is the more valuable citizen? A powdered and polite French lord who knows to a minute when the king gets up, goes to bed or even to the toilet, and who gives himself airs of grandeur while slaving in the antechamber of some minister —"

"Or this?" I glance with distaste at our neighbor.

" — Or this English merchant who enriches his country, and from his counting-house sends orders to Surat or Cairo, thereby contributing to the felicity of the world?"

"At least a well-mannered Frenchman wouldn't be waving his phone in everyone's face. Furthermore, our host Allen is an oil merchant in Bahrain, your absolutely ideal Englishman. He would never, ever, blather quotations of prices per barrel in public like that."

V. cuts me off, hovering over the conversation. "Shhh. He shouldn't sell Hewlett Packard just because the merger with Price Waterhouse is off," he whispers. "Tell him!"

"Stop shushing me. Since when did you become such a market maven?"

"I told you last night, I've been catching up. I signed my first promissory note at the age of thirteen. I read the financial pages you toss away."

"Is that where my *Economist* disappeared this week?"

He shrugs.

It is hard to believe now that I have to fight with a phantom for my *Economist*s, hard to believe that I even pay for them, since the last time I visited England in 1986, it was as that reputable journal's Hong Kong correspondent. I had come full circle; fleeing California for Hong Kong, Hong Kong for England, England for Singapore and then transferred in 1983 back to Hong Kong.

I suppose I should read it as a gesture of faith that an English institution entrusted its coverage of Hong Kong's handover to China to the hands of an American. I would be foolish, however, to credit them with over-generosity. The *Economist* never paid much and my talents, such as they were, came rather inexpensively. There was also the unspoken understanding that anything unacceptable I wrote would be changed by the self-assured and witty editors in St. James' Street.

Nevertheless, the years 1983 and 1984 in Hong Kong gave me a rare opportunity to witness the brilliant footwork executed by advisors loyal to the Hong Kong Governor Sir Edward Youde, a man of integrity so loyally devoted to the interests of the Hong Kong people that he died while on the job of fighting both Beijing and colleagues in the Foreign Office. I also observed the efforts of the Beijing-oriented Foreign Office mandarins to sell Hong Kong more cheaply than it deserved in the interests of Sino–British trade.

Two versions of the English character.

V. and I hustle ourselves into the train. I'm the last to join a foursome which includes a woman in a knitted cap and tweed skirt. She's on her cellphone, complaining to a friend about a book she's reading.

". . . I've got 'bout half-way through. That's the one . . . right . . . but it's still all about this girl and boy who fall in love, marry the wrong people, and after that, they all go mad. I don't know what you saw in it! Why did you tell me to read it? It's *dire*."

The cover of her paperback announces *Wuthering Heights*.

V. must stand for a good part of the journey, as I couldn't very well defend a seat for The Invisible Man. From time to time, I see him consulting his small leather notebook. He has steadfastly refused my offer to take him shopping. His itinerary includes checking out some French refugee haunt called the Rainbow Café in Marylebone that I am sure closed its shutters by the time Napoleon took office. He wants to attend a Quaker service to ensure that those plain folk are still a thriving antidote to the Vatican. Then he will haunt a session of Parliament to check out the state of free speech.

His passion for British free speech recalls a press conference in Hong Kong in early 1984 when the outlines of Hong Kong's diminished future under Beijing's thumb were starting to surface. Respectfully if timidly, the Hong Kong Cantonese reporters put their polite questions. I watched as they were fobbed off with carefully phrased half-answers concealing half-truths.

At the back of the press pack, I spot a familiar figure, emboldened by a largely liquid lunch. With those sad, dark-ringed eyes, David glares at the podium of visiting ponces from

London. The drink is starting to tell on David since that afternoon at the B.B.C. in London six years before. Diabetes and a damaged liver have bloated his good looks.

"One country, two systems." "Elections but not necessarily direct elections." On and on it goes, the Foreign Office jargon obfuscating the raw political capitulation. The language is too finely crafted for Cantonese reporters to publicly challenge, but David was trained by the same tutors as these pin-striped apologists.

"Shame," he suddenly intones in a low voice, seemingly at no one and at everyone at the same time. Heads swivel briefly to look with some embarrassment at David whose eyes are glistening with anger.

"SHAME," David repeats, "SHAME, SHAME," again and again, like the bell-wether ringing the knell of a true Englishman's conscience, while the red-faced spokesman behind the mike stammers on through his prepared statement.

I finish my story as V. and I make our way through Liverpool Street station.

"I must say that was light treatment for such *lèse majesté*. He would have suffered for a fraction of that insolence in the France of my day. I'm surprised he wasn't drawn and quartered, or at least whipped. In fact, were he French, I would not have been surprised to see your friend David's head impaled on a spike. But, there, you see! The French imitated the English in everything except liberty."

V. is momentarily distracted by a very pretty redhead, carrying two big Monsoon shopping bags, who ricochets unknowingly into him.

"It just proves my point that the English are free men. In comparison, everything French is rotten with frivolity and reaction. The English are true and orderly. The French are enslaved by superstition, tyranny, and unreasonable laws —

"But surely — "

"Compare the French, locked by their assumptions of Descartes' principles into a ridiculous definition of the universe swirling around in an invisible mass. Meanwhile Isaac Newton started out from his practical observations of the real world and developed his ideas of gravitational force only from what he could see and measure."

"I gather you're very keen on Newton."

"*Madame!* I introduced Newton to France! My own Madame du Châtelet was the genius who translated his work, no less. I stood here in London, awestruck at thirty-three years of age as I watched dukes and earls follow the coffin of that great thinker as he was borne away to an honored burial site. The French had forgotten how to think and almost as bad, how to honor their thinkers and artists. The English are greater philosophers and possessed of more courage than we."

"You actually saw Newton's funeral?"

"I watched in awe, then hurried to meet his disciple, Samuel Clarke, and his niece, Mrs. Conduit. Newton was the star of one of my *Letters Concerning the English Nation*, that made my fame as an essayist! Surely you've read those at least?"

"I'm sorry, no."

Voltaire stops short in his tracks. "Exactly who do you think reported the story of the falling apples that gave Newton the idea for gravity?"

"I should have guessed," I mutter.

"But you miss my point," V. says, resuming his steps. "Compare the homage paid here to Newton with our attitude in France, where Molière's body was interred under cover of night. Madame Molière had to scatter money to a howling mob to distract them from impeding his burial even then. The English buried their greatest actress Anne Oldfield in Westminster Abbey, while we tossed Adrienne Lecouvreur in a lime pit without a single blessing."

We bustle with hundreds of commuters through the tunnels

that lead toward the Central Line.

"You aren't coming toy shopping?"

"Oh, I think not. I've heard of an interesting establishment of ladies with a talent for, well, just say a specialty in — "

"You're going WHORING?" I explode.

"Doing research, like any writer visiting a foreign land," he protests.

"Do you intend to make a habit of prostitutes while we're visiting my friends?"

"*Mais, non, non, Madame.* Once, out of curiosity, is understandable. Twice would make me a pervert. *Adieu.*"

He dives into the crowd. I don't wish to keep him from his reunion with eighteenth-century phantom French refugees in their Huguenot hide-out, or rouged English tarts, if he can possibly find them. Years of working with male journalists in Hong Kong taught me just to avoid those avenues of experience.

As V. rounds the last curve of the tunnel, I see him pulling from under his greatcoat a marvelous hat with plumes that brush the low ceilings of the Underground. Even with those hand-cobbled shoes, his gait is steady and firm. Despite his constant petty ailments, he's in his prime this morning. He's lost that hounded expression. It must be the cassia purges he takes twice a week.

I'm surrounded by strangers, yet curiously free for the first time in weeks, with time on my hands to splurge at Hamleys. After two hours of weighing the merits of baby dolls that really piss versus those that really burp, I emerge with two enormous bags of Christmas gifts and an empty purse. At a bank only a few feet away, a Bureau de Change is ready to relieve me of more Swiss francs. Ahead of me in the queue an African father juggles his Playstation 2 purchases, trying to count out his wad of Zimbabwean dollars. I'm transported back to that week in Hong Kong when London friends asked me to introduce a Rhodesian-born journalist around Hong Kong on a whistle-stop tour of Asia. I lined up the usual contacts – brokers, China-hands and bankers – who briefed him willingly, but the interviews didn't go smoothly. We lurched uncomfortably from one appointment to the next, me silently wondering why he bothered if he knew everything already. On the final day of his visit, we arrive for an interview with the deputy chief of the New China News Agency, but our taxi driver refuses to wait for us outside the sinister new office tower that houses the Communists' headquarters.

"No parking, no parking," the wizened Cantonese insists, pointing at various traffic signs and barriers that protect the Party enclave from protesters and suicide car bombs.

"Just tell the man to wait here," the reporter barks.

"No stop. Lose licence." The driver shakes his head.

Being a product of British colonial Africa, my boss doesn't like insolence from natives. He clearly thinks me inept for not being able to handle one.

"You tell him I'll pay his fine." He pulls out a HK$100 note and tosses it at the man behind the wheel.

"There," he shouts at the old man, and points at his watch. "One hour. You be here."

The Cantonese shifts calmly on his bamboo-beaded seat cover and delicately picks up the money covered in Imperialist cooties. He places it in front of our noses. He speaks to me with a serene smile in deliberate Chinese, meant for careful translation.

"Lady, tell your white devil big boss Englishman to go jerk off on his mother's dirty underpants."

There is no point in trying to explain in this steamy diesel cab in the middle of Queen's Road East that my guest has possibly less claim as a "Zimbabwean" to English status than the Colony-residing Chinese himself.

It's a pity (I reflect in the tube heading back to Liverpool Street laden with Christmas presents), that Voltaire didn't have a chance to enjoy the full influences of the English whom he so idolized – the Antipodean editors, the Indian sub-editors, the Zimbabwean ex-colonials, the "British" Cantonese.

I returned nauseous with depression that day to my Hong Kong apartment to find Allen and Katherine Worthy visiting from Tokyo. They were expecting a baby who would become my goddaughter. Katherine spent a lot of her time as my guest making me, the hostess, cups of tea.

Some things don't change.

"I've made you tea. I'm putting you to work," Katherine warns me cheerily as Voltaire and I descend to the kitchen in Suffolk on Saturday morning. Katherine has laid out squid, tofu, beef, and vegetables to be sliced for tonight's Mongolian Hot Pot dinner. Molly and I slice frozen bits until our numb fingers turn blue – while Katherine studies a cookbook on the other side of the table.

V. is reading cookbooks too.

"I'm relieved to see people have abandoned their overuse of ham essence and morels."

"Disgusting."

"The cooks at Versailles could never use enough essence of ham, pepper, nutmeg and morels. But for the life of me, I can't imagine eating this stuff *tou-fue*."

"Oh? I always thought you liked squid," Katherine answers me innocently.

Voltaire's dressed this morning for "hunting," probably to do nothing more than shoo pheasants out of hedges with Sushi barking alongside, but old habits die hard. This way, he escapes kitchen duty.

"'Must make being dead a comfort," I mutter, nursing smelly, frozen fingers.

"Considering the *tou-fue*, I'll stick with hot chocolate tonight." V. slides out the back door with Sushi.

Our elusive host Allen lies in state upstairs on the excuse he is recovering from his overnight flight. He's still asleep when V. returns from his jaunts and entertains himself riffling through Allen's library. A gasp of appreciation greets the discovery of a yellowed paperback in the lower corner of the shelves.

"My *Age of Louis XIV*!"

"I told you Allen was your ideal Englishman."

V. reads his own opening lines, "It is not merely the life of Louis XIV that we propose to write; we have a wider aim in view." He sighs with satisfaction.

"Good lead, as they say in the newsroom."

"Well, I had practice. In England I started my first history, that of Charles XII. As he had been dead for only thirteen years, I could consult living acquaintances of Charles for a new kind of history, one that recorded the history and thinking of the age, not merely dates and events in a man's life."

"I think what you're saying is that while you were in England, you invented modern historiography."

"Oh, I have no doubt." V. agrees, with typical immodesty. "But I really don't know where there is an argument between your modern micro- and macro-historians. I don't see how anecdote can replace history, nor can a vast panorama of history be insensible to anecdote."

I'm scanning the shelves myself. "Look! there's Allen's *Leibniz*, over there on the upper shelf."

"Leibniz! Here IS a man I can talk to! Where is this *Alain*? Why is he still napping? I held with Leibniz for some time, arguing that a God without flaws cannot make a world with flaws, therefore we must be living in the best possible of worlds. By that reasoning, even the most distressing or con-fusing events must have occurred for a reason."

"I'll make sure we discuss it with him."

"Of course, Leibniz was wrong. He also thought the whole world was composed of monads, little entities with their own souls. I had my doubts but now when I hear about the map-ping of the human genome, I'm thinking maybe monads weren't so far off after all . . ."

If I thought V. was going to make himself the social center of tonight's dinner party, I'm mistaken. He wasn't joking about staying in bed.

"I always avoided small talk and endless evenings," he announces. "Say I'm not feeling well."

"I'm sure you dazzled the diners at Versailles while you were in favor. And you were fit enough yesterday to walk the entire City in the rain collecting mutual fund brochures," I add. "I saw them spread all over your trunk."

"Well, I'm genuinely unwell now." He coughs up some rather convincing phlegm. I worry he's caught something serious until he adds, "Illness has great advantages; it spares one society."

Over my protests, he changes into his green dressing gown, and settles down to revise his history of King Louis. "There are always some little improvements one can make."

"Your passion for revision, especially two hundred years after the printers' ink has dried, never ceases to amaze me, but I'm not accepting any excuses tonight."

"It is simply too cold down there. I'm catching pneumonia."

Indeed, I've noticed that the Rectory is a tad polar. Always chilled to his fleshless bones, V. has taken to wearing his overcoat, even when standing next to Katherine's heavy Aga.

As Katherine and I lay out the Extra-Hot Crunchy Bombay Mix, the guests arrive – two couples – the men swathed in woolens and cashmeres, one woman in a long skirt, the other in tight velvet pants, braced for Inuit hospitality. However, Katherine has heeded a small comment I made as to frozen toes in the night.

"Gosh, it's warm in here. Katherine, what have you done? Have you actually turned on the heat?" cries the lively Deenie, an immediately likable women in her early forties with an English countrywoman's heartiness.

"Good Lord, has anyone called the fire engines?" jokes her husband Ralph.

The shy Welsh beauty Gwyneth has relinquished her coat, but is hanging on to her shawl, thank you, in case someone puts out the blaze.

"I warned Miles that he better remember a jumper for the Worthys."

Katherine takes this teasing in her stride and the evening is full of good spirits and getting-to-know you conversation. We are among friends, who take me and my foreignness on board without the usual tiresome joking aimed at Americans. They accept me so easily, in fact, that it is with a shock that I realize that I am the oldest person in the room. When did that happen? Katherine brings out a birthday cake for Miles and there are only thirty-eight candles on it. This dark-lashed charmer on my right is a mere youth.

Miles' excessive courtesy to me, I realize with horror, is deference to an older woman. This is a ghastly development, but on the crest of my fiftieth year, I should have seen it coming. All my lively charm and banter, mildly flirtatious comments – should I tone these down from now on for fear of looking a bit pathetic?

The dinner is otherwise very enjoyable, the conversation light, apolitical, unphilosophical, consisting of jolly stories and funny references to mutual friends and their foibles as well as endless frustrations with the Hot Pot experiment. The height of the evening is a story about an eccentrically stuffed squirrel that Katherine passed up at a school auction only to find it staring at her from Deenie's mantel a week later. The guests seem fairly contented with their lives and with each other.

Well after midnight, I leave Allen and Katherine cuddling by the fire to find V. furiously scribbling all over his fund brochures calculating interest rates.

"Did they discuss Newton or Locke?" he asks.

I shake my head, no.

"Quakerism? The theater? Smallpox inoculation? Monads?"

"They talked yard sales, the disappointment of skiing in Wengen, and the irresistibility of a stuffed squirred. We had a wonderful evening."

"Not exactly the sort of thing I overheard in London dining rooms," he clucks. "What's happened to the English?"

For his benefit, I recall a very different dinner in fashionable Mayfair in 1981, at the home of Charles' friends, Vanessa and Richard. It is an evening full of floating tension running the length of the great oak table stretched between the host, the son of a peer, and his wife, a working-class Manchester girl. The guests include a couple in advertising, a talk-show pundit and a female banker who is allegedly tussling with an invest-ment report Richard has submitted. A rather feckless au pair also makes an appearance from time to time to report on the antics of the two children in the upstairs nursery.

The conversation is pointed, dry, cynical, competitive and sardonic. Would their M.P. still be standing in the next election? Who will get that elusive interview with the Princess of Wales? Who has rented the best holiday villa in Tuscany?

The question that should have been asked (although I didn't know it at the time), was "Who has yet to sleep with our host?"

To be honest, the hostess was in the dark as well.

"I only learned the truth about Richard years later, after they were divorced," I tell V. in the half-light of the guest room.

"And how did the lady discover her aristocratic husband was catting around?"

"That woman banker who brought a huge bouquet of flowers for Vanessa the night I was there gave the game away. She and Richard had already had two children. She wanted to change their name to Richard's, especially as it was such a well-known family 'of rank.' Her petition had to be posted in *The Times*. Poor Vanessa went into shock. Through all those years of dinner parties in Mayfair, Richard was raising a second family right around the corner."

"Did you dally with this Richard?" V. asks me pointedly.

I shake my head ruefully. "Apparently I was the only woman in London who didn't. Even the au pair who served dinner that night had a go. Come to think of it, it's rather insulting he didn't even try."

V. bursts out laughing at my brush with the titled.

"Didn't I tell you the English upper classes are froth?"

Allen rises early the next morning to get us back to Stansted. We've got his copies of *Louis XIV* and *Leibniz* in V.'s trunk.

"Didn't you know my university thesis was on Leibniz?" Allen asks. But like V., Allen has long ago moved beyond Leibniz. Thanks to my English friend's eclectic tastes in authors, I've read Simon Ley's novel about Napoleon, Mikhail Bulgakov's political satire, *The Master and Margarita*, and *The Bridge On the Drina*, by Ivo Andrić.

"But the guy who is really fascinating me these days is John Gribbin," Allen says excitedly as we pull out of the driveway. "You have to read *In Search of Schrodinger's Cat*." Allen explains quantum mechanics in layman's terms. He claims it is possible – although he admits, not very likely – that all the molecules of the car, the baggage and ourselves will shift to one corner of the front seat.

"I'd rather make my plane on time," I say, laughing.

From the back seat, V. butts in. "This is too interesting. For what it's worth, I say forget the flight and shift the molecules."

In twenty years, my polymath friend Allen has never bored me. Isn't he the very kind of Englishman who opened V.'s eyes to a world of science and philosophy untrammeled by the Church and superstition and "first principles?" When I'm around Allen, I realize how little I've been paying attention to the world at large, from the latest rock bands half my age to the most rewarding Eastern European writers banned from print fifty years ago. His mind is open, voracious, and quixotic. He seems unprejudiced against anything except what V. would call "flummery."

V. is scribbling notes on the back of our "ticketless" airline print-out. "This is better than Newton."

As we scurry to the check-in counter. V. starts a heated argument when I hand the print-out to the airline staff.

"Those are my notes!" he protests.

"Oh, shut-up, or you ride in cargo."

He retreats, pouting, to the display of new authors at the book stall.

"I don't see any Richard Dawkins or Stephen Hawking," he groans. "*The Life of Britney Spears*, hmm. She reminds me of an actress in my *Zaïre*."

"They're calling our flight. I'll teach you how to order books online when we get home."

I instantly realize that this might be the riskiest gesture yet since making V.'s dangerous acquaintance.

"I'm glad you enjoyed the visit, even though we didn't visit the Court and you didn't get a chance to look in on Boling-broke's descendants. But you did like Allen and Katherine?"

"She makes a formidable quince and apple tart, that *Katherine*," he nods. "As for *Alain*, he would have made a wonderful eighteenth-century man. I see that mine were simpler days, when one man could still realize the height of scientific thought, the apex of literary achievement, and poli-tical influence within a single lifetime by simply being ready to apply himself with an open mind."

"Yes, well, you should know. Allen is hardly likely to master the intricacies of space-age physics and become a rock star while holding down his day job as an oil trader, but I respect him for not giving up."

Then I quote V. back to his face, "How I love these English who say what they think, their respect for facts, reality, utility, simplicity of manners, habits and dress!"

He nods. "I said it before: If ever I smelled a Resurrection or had a chance to return after death to Earth, I prayed God would make me be born in England, the Land of Liberty!"

"Well, half your prayers were answered. At least you returned, if not as an Englishman."

"*Oui*. I thank you for bringing me." He tips his wide-brimmed hat.

"Don't mention it."

He exclaims as he sees the coast of England recede below our window, "Just imagine how Newton, Locke, Clarke, and Leibniz would have been persecuted in my France or imprisoned in Rome or burned in Lisbon. What is one to think of human reason? That it was born in my century in that England, right down there!"

I'll refrain from arguing the case for Plato or Aquinas, but I'm glad to finally close the door on so many contradictory experiences with the British Empire. In the end, I was no more English than was Voltaire.

"You know what? I'm glad to be going home."

V. looks at me in surprise. "Switzerland! Your home? That's the first time I've heard you say it."

"That's the first time I've felt it," I smile. "It's the first time I return to St-Cergue from abroad."

"Perhaps my influence on you is not so negative, despite your constant efforts to dislodge me," he says, smiling rather wickedly.

"You can stay a bit longer if you tell me one thing. Why did you have to leave London so quickly last time?"

"Well, as it was so many years ago – let's see, very early in '29, – I can admit now there was rather a *petite* question of some counterfeit banknotes. It was really a technicality, only it would have been difficult, not to say time-consuming, to clear my name and avoid a hanging. Far easier just to return to France under a royal pardon. I didn't get back my pension from the King, but the English sales of my *Henri* saga set me up nicely. And I always had a scheme or two in the market."

Considering he's stuffed his trunk with brochures on security technology and pharmaceutical funds, I'm lucky to get V. back to Switzerland without the Securities and Exchange Commissioner of England on our tail.

"Shall I bother to fasten my seat belt?" he asks winsomely.

His innocent act doesn't deflect me. "Exactly what did you do in the City while I was shopping?" I ask, my heart sinking at the thought he might have discovered how to trade on margin.

He ignores my question. He's circling exchange rates in the *F.T.*

Elementary, My Dear Voltaire

The Mystery Writers of America bulletin arrives in the mail. I'll miss the Edgar Awards in New York next April. I'll miss everything in New York next spring.

I start addressing Christmas cards, but they only remind me of the distance between family and friends, and me. What I'm really avoiding is a third rewrite of the Tibet mystery.

It's easier to gaze out of the kitchen window. Peter has sawn a hole in the six-foot-high wall of snow lining our front walkway. Through this glistening window, I can just make out Mont Blanc. The killer peak's razor edges gleam a deceptively innocent pink.

Voltaire saunters into the kitchen.

"And how is *Mischief in the Land of the Snow Lion* this morning?"

I've noticed that for a mere illusion, he does look after himself remarkably well. I've lost count of his linen shirts, lace cuffs and kerchiefs, damask coats, and neatly rolled stockings. His teeth aren't holding up too well, but that's a twenty-first-century quibble. I can see why the starlets of his day fell across his casting couch with enthusiasm.

"I've renamed it, *Shadows of Shigatse*."

He shrugged. "That's as far as you've got? When I returned to France from England, I plunged into work. I gathered together the actors needed for my new play *Brutus*, but their reaction to it was very negative," he laughs ruefully. "Or should I say, brutal? I revised like the devil. The first night's performance was glorious, yes, glorious, but only because the audience was completely made up of my friends and admirers. *Brutus* closed after fifteen days."

"I am so heartened by your failures, Monsieur Voltaire."

"At your service," he favors me with a slight bow, adding, "The list is long – *Ériphyle*, *Artémire* – but it never bothers me, as long as I have successes, too. I always have five or six irons in the fire at one time . . . speaking of fire," he lights the gas under the coffee pot, "have you run out of sugar again? Have your suppliers send it in bulk."

I've lost track of his daily coffee intake, but one evening he was up to forty cups. Is it caffeine nerves or do I detect a growing irritation at our family's happy preoccupation with the coming of Christmas – what he keeps disparaging as "that Jesuit myth?" Then he gets more jittery reading newspaper headlines about "infamy" unleashed and has to calm himself down with hot chocolate. He's constantly complaining of digestion problems.

He picks up a Christmas card that shows three cartoon reindeer logging on to the Internet to view a lady reindeer in a bikini.

"*Mon Dieu*, how vulgar! I once wrote *The Temple of Taste*, but now I'd rename it the *The Temple of Bad Taste* . . . You know, your endeavors make me think I might write a mystery myself."

"You! Write a mystery?"

"Why not?" He adopts a sinister expression. "*The Poisoned Priest, Venom at Versailles, The Cardinal's Cutlass* — "

He has me holding my stomach at his antics, creeping around the kitchen like a vaudeville villain.

"Great titles, but it's the plotting that's hard."

"I've already got my plot – the murder of my friend, Adrienne."

Intrigued, I follow him out of the kitchen to the terrace, to settle at the table in the sun. A horrible scrambling wail hits our ears from the icy lane beyond our gate. A wire fence meant to restrain the sled dogs next door is caving over under the weight of accumulated snow. Two young huskies have mounted a drift and leap to freedom. In a moment's scramble, the dogs spot one of the wild cats that hunt our hillside basking on a hot, dry rock. The panicked feline dashes towards a parked van, but her hind legs are captured in the merciless jaws of a dog. The victim is yanked from the van's underbelly, and with the ferocious help of the other dog, she's ripped into two pieces like a piece of toffee.

V. is the first to recover from shock. After all, unlike me, he's already seen murder first hand.

"Do you think anybody's going to clean that mess up off the snow?" I ask feebly, collapsing into a chair next to him.

"Here, drink some coffee. At least death came swiftly. Now take the lingering demise of Adrienne. Paris's most famous actress, my ex-lover and good friend died in my arms after four days of painful dysentery and inflammation. She was only thirty-eight years old."

"She was really murdered?" I drag my horrified attention away from the shreds of cat scattered outside our gate.

Voltaire gazes absent-mindedly at Mont Blanc through the icy hole. "Well, everyone said she was murdered by the Duchesse de Bouillon. I did not join fashionable Society in pointing the finger."

"You thought it was a natural death, huh?"

"I didn't say that," he turns, his sharp cheekbones catching the morning rays. "I said I didn't point my finger. Naming another culprit might be as good as signing my own death warrant. But I reckon as we're ALL dead now, it's safe to tell the truth."

"A real murder?"

"It's a long story," he warns me, discarding his tufted jacket of white *matelasse* and unbuttoning his brocade vest. "Ah, I can finally warm my frozen bones."

The walls of crystalline snow transform the terrace into a sheltered courtyard. Eye-splitting sunshine bathes the wooden table. Voltaire pulls a pair of sunglasses out of his vest pocket and sets out his Berlin coffee service featuring a crown of laurels surrounding the lyre of Apollo, according to a design by Frederick the Great.

I lean towards him. "Monsieur Voltaire, excuse me, but those sunglasses look just like my husband's."

"They are your husband's . . . so ingenious . . . look, the frames regain their shape no matter which way they're twisted." He contorts Peter's $300 wire frames into an S shape. "Italians are such wonderful artisans, *non?* These are signed by a craftsman named Armani. "

"Peter might miss them," I say through gritted teeth. Having the greatest mind of the eighteenth century as your imaginary friend makes for delightful conversation, but when he appropriates Peter's few real luxuries, he gets on my nerves.

"Not while the poor man slaves down in all that fog," Voltaire waves one dismissive hand in the direction of the Red Cross headquarters. "Now, here's my mystery. You'll help me modernize it later for publication. Much of what I'm going to tell you leaked out from the Paris police reports of the day . . . "

"You must first understand that Adrienne was the most honest and talented of Frenchwomen. Her father, a humble hatter, moved his family to Paris from Reims when she was only ten. She grew up a few streets from the Théâtre-Français and dreamed of stardom. At fourteen, she organized a little group of players to perform around Paris in the most exclusive salons."

"What did she look like?"

"Oh, striking in every way. Not slim, according to your

modern fashion, but her voice was like music – natural, not singsong. Her figure was graceful, her expressions so mobile! When she was on the stage, she didn't prance from one corner of the rectangle to the other, she didn't *recite*."

"She really acted. She became her characters," I prompt him.

He sips his brew. "*Précisément*. And that alone was a theatrical revolution for which any playwright of my time was grateful. It was all real to her.

"Now, enter, stage right, another character, the one true love of Adrienne's life, Maurice of Saxony. Picture the illegitimate son, one of three hundred bastards of Augustus the Strong who had deposed the Polish King Stanislaus, father-in-law to none other than our King Louis — "

"— XV. I know. What did Maurice look like?"

"A brute," Voltaire sniffs, glancing at me over the rim of Peter's shades. "It's true that Maurice took my place in Adrienne's bed, but I am not one to brood. No, Maurice was an ambitious cad. All right, he was tall, his face slightly too wide to be called classically handsome, curling hair parted in the middle, robust build, sensual, courageous, ambitious, and brave — "

"Mmm . . . " I wonder if Maurice wasn't a bit too manly for V. to swallow.

"Yes, and penniless. Of course, as talented as he was in the battlefield, it was in the boudoir that he intended to conquer. He aimed high, and used all of Adrienne's pawned jewels, some 40,000 livres' worth, to woo the hand of the widowed Duchess of Courland, one Anna Ivanovna, later Empress of Russia."

"Poor Adrienne. Did she know?"

"Yes, she lent Maurice her jewels open-heartedly, ready to be a friend as well as his adoring conquest. But Maurice's father, Augustus, feared the marriage for political reasons. So although Maurice bedded Anna, as well as her sister – he could never leave a bedcover unturned – he failed to win his duchy and came back to Paris. For over three years, Adrienne had kept herself for him alone, but one hardly expected his kind of man to return the favor."

"Adrienne's starting to sound more like a doormat than a celebrity actress."

"I warned her. She was four years older than Maurice. She welcomed him back without a single reproach about the little opera singer Marie Carton who followed him from military camp all the way back to Paris. Marie was now enjoying most of his lusty attentions backstage, you might say."

"Was he a great military hero?"

"*Madame!*" V. groans at my ignorance. "Surely you know he became the Maréchal de France and one of the greatest military strategists of all time!"

"I'm with you so far. Adrienne the actress loved Maurice the Cad, and he came home to her after his attempt on the Duchess of Courland fell through, with the singing Marie in tow. But I thought you said that somebody named Bouillon murdered Adrienne? Where does she fit in, this Duchess of Broth?"

V. lets one of his typically brittle laughs escape.

"She wasn't chicken stock, *Madame*, far from it. *Non*, our suspect, the Duchesse de Bouillon was of very royal blood. Louise Henriette Françoise de Guise de Lorraine, the sister-in-law of the Duc de Richelieu, married off at eighteen to an old toad, Emanuel Théodore de La Tour d'Aubergne, Duc de Bouillon. Oh, by the way, our Duchesse, too, had granted Maurice her favors — "

"He really got around!"

"Oh, he was the subject of much gossip. But his liaison with the Duchesse, was, as you would say, cold coffee." He pours himself a fresh cup.

"Didn't all this bother the Duke of Bouillon?"

"*Mais non!* He was forty years older than the Duchesse! The Duc was far wiser than his wife. The Duchesse was incapable of accepting Maurice's indifference. In the torment of jealousy, she hatched a plan against Adrienne."

"I thought you said the Duchess wasn't guilty."

"*Madame*, I implore you to listen, for here is where my story leaves the territory of the banal *ménage à trois*."

I interrupt, "Four, if you count Marie."

V. waves a limp hand. "Nobody ever counted Marie."

He leans forward. "Now, listen. Enter, stage left, the most unusual character in my little mystery, Siméon Bouret. He was a hunchbacked abbé of only eighteen, seeking a career in Paris as a miniature portraitist. Hah! Sorry, I meant no pun. These little pictures on rings, brooches, trinkets, it's the fashion, *non*? He escapes his nasty rooming house every evening by going to the Théâtre-Français. One day he meets a young man dressed in livery who turns out to be the page of the Duchesse —"

"Bullion!?"

"Hardly a heart of gold," Voltaire sneers. "They chat and the page invites the abbé to the Hôtel de Bouillon to paint the Duchesse. Why not? She's a well-connected beauty of twenty-two, tall, black-eyed, with dark hair and a large beauty mark near the right eye, if I remember correctly . . ."

"It all sounds slightly too easy."

"Well, there was indeed, a strange catch . . ."

Voltaire takes a deep breath and leans his bony face back in the bright sunlight, his eyes closed. He seems far away from our farmhouse. I imagine he is once again in the Paris salons, drinking up every detail of the great sex-and-murder scandal of 1729.

"Want more coffee?" I heat up some more water and in a few minutes, rejoin him, still basking like a sly, thin cat in the streaming rays. Outside our gate, the lady dog-sled owner has come bouncing out of her chalet with a pail of scraps only to discover that two of her dogs are missing. I watch her boot plunge into a glistening pool of blood. Her startled cries rouse her husband.

V. smiles to himself at this tableau and goes on with the intrigue.

" . . . During the third sitting for the abbé, the Duchesse works the conversation around to the theater. She asks rather pointedly, 'Do you know the actress Lecouvreur?' Well, of course he doesn't know Adrienne personally, but the Duchesse urges him to get to know her, and even then dictates a letter to the abbé to deliver, a silly piece of business purportedly signed by a prince of the blood asking Adrienne to break off her affair with Maurice."

"How do you know all this?"

"Read it yourself. It's in the police report."

"Did he deliver the letter?"

"No. That doesn't stop our jealous Duchesse. The next day, she asks for the letter back, but tells the abbé to be at the gate of the Tuileries that same night."

"I hope he didn't go."

"Well, he does go, and there he's met by two masked men."

"Oh, c'mon! Too fishy. I warn you, no mystery reader is going to buy two masked men!"

"I vow to you, *Madame*, there they are, two powdered rascals, fresh from the Palais Royal ball. They ask the abbé if he wants to make some money in exchange for gaining access to Adrienne and giving her a few pills filled with a potion to make her fall out of love with Maurice and in love with someone else."

"Beyond fishy. Your story just moved from *poisson* to poison."

"*Oui*," V. laughs. "They lead the abbé over to the Duchesse herself, crying and repeating Maurice's name over and over again."

At this Voltaire starts playfully weeping into a handkerchief. "Mademoiselle Lecouvreur is an unworthy woman. It would be doing a service to the state to put her out of the way. You can be sure of a reward."

This is a man who loved to act in any of his fifty plays.

"Oh, stop it, I get the idea. The Duchess sounds like a case."

Voltaire instantly stops sobbing. "Ah, yes, but a murderess?"

"Finally our hunchback hero finishes the portrait, but still hasn't met Adrienne. The thugs of the Duchesse hound him. He writes a desperate note to Adrienne asking for a meeting on the terrace of the Luxembourg."

"Would an actress of her fame answer such a note?"

"Oh, you can be sure my wise friend was there. The abbé warns her she is in danger of being poisoned. Adrienne asks, 'Is it from the Opéra that the danger is threatening me?' referring to the singer Marie. 'No,' says the abbé. 'Then it must be from the Hôtel de Bouillon!' Adrienne guesses. She tells the abbé she wants to ask the advice of a competent man — "

"Maurice of Saxony."

Voltaire looks miffed. "I am the author here! Yes, Maurice. Maurice and Adrienne meet the abbé. Maurice accuses him of making up stories, but Adrienne is convinced, 'This threat comes from the Duchesse de Bouillon,' she says."

"Good instincts," I comment.

"Better than those of the Duchesse herself," Voltaire points out, "who never guessed her real rival was Marie. The following day, the poor abbé is dragged to a meeting on the Quai de l'École with the two masked men and now a third man in disguise. They order him to go the next day from Pont Tournant in the direction of the marble statue through a little alley of trees. In the second tree on the right he will find a package of pills, most of which are harmless; but three wrapped in a separate paper are meant for the actress."

"Masked men, poison pills, marble statues. Your story has historical color." I keep my opinon of the plot to myself. He can be so touchy.

Voltaire leans back, sweeping his lace cuffs free. "It is what you call the True Crime. You will help me put in the red salmons later — "

"Red herrings."

"As you say. Abbé Bouret brings the pills to Adrienne and Maurice. Just sniffing them makes all three nauseous. They alert the police commissioner Hérault."

"Haven't I heard his name before?"

Voltaire nods with a knowing smile. "*Oui*, the snob Hérault who threw me into the Bastille. Of course, he favors the Bouillon tribe over a bumpkin cleric and a mere actress. He sends the poor abbé to Saint-Lazare — "

"Prison?"

"*Oui*, for three months. And he sends the pills to L'Académie des Sciences for testing, but they say they need more pills to form a reliable opinion."

Something here troubles me.

Voltaire cocks an eyebrow and continues, "The police accuse the abbé of inventing the entire story because he's in love with Adrienne. They charge him with using poison and giving false information!"

"Can I ask you something?"

His long-fingered hand sweeps up gracefully and the long cuffs flop back on his large-buttoned sleeve.

"Not yet. Poor Bouret remained in jail. Adrienne, trouper that she was, played in *Horace* in January and in *Electra* and *Le Florentin* in February and then a month passed before she returned to the stage in March in *Le Malade Imaginaire*."

"A rather prophetic title."

"Indeed. If only what happened next had been an imaginary malady," Voltaire says. "On March 15th, Adrienne collapsed on stage with a violent case of dysentery. The doctors couldn't stop the internal bleeding that followed. On the morning of the 20th, she died. I was at her side."

Loud voices erupt beyond our gate. One of our other neighbors, the mother of a new-born girl has emerged from her chalet to collect the mail. She has stumbled upon our sled-dog neighbor clearing the snow of cat guts.

V. and I can catch snatches of hysterical exchanges in colloquial French, to the effect, "Why aren't these dogs under better control?" "What if that had been my baby?" "What makes you think they were my dogs?" and so on.

V. and I overhear defensive retorts about the supervision of the second dog-team at the end of the road. An element of doubt has been introduced as to the guilty canine culprits. There's no doubt in my mind whose fence gave way to the vicious pair, but the tracks are too jumbled now to wrest a conviction.

I pose the obvious theory. "So after all, the Duchess poisoned Adrienne."

Voltaire purses his mouth as if warning me not to be so hasty. "Note that on her own deathbed, although she confessed to a Herculean stable of mortal transgressions, the Duchesse de Bouillon did NOT confess to the murder of Adrienne Lecouvreur."

"Well . . ."

"Ah, ah, ah, be careful, *Madame*. My generation took their deathbed absolutions very seriously."

"Well, absence of a deathbed confession certainly wouldn't clear her name today. I'm more struck by other things. Take the police report. If a mere whiff of these noxious pills knocked over three healthy people, why couldn't the Academy form an opinion? Maybe they never saw the real poison pills?"

"A very good point," V. encourages me.

I venture further, "And even if nobody wants to believe an actress or a starstruck abbé, why don't we hear a loud protest from Maurice of Saxony, future Maréchal of France? After all, he's spent all of Adrienne's 40,000 livres. He owes her at least some support."

Voltaire's eyebrows lift suggestively, so I go on.

"And didn't you say the thugs were accompanied by a mysterious third man? Who was he?"

"Go on."

"Well," I play Watson to his Holmes, "it seems to me that once her plot was blown, even that hysterical Duchess would want to lie low. She could only hope that nobody would interview those funny friends who stuff poison pills into trees. Would she make another attempt so soon after the first? She'd be blamed."

V. interjects, "Oh, she was vilified in whispers. Only her titled position protected her while Adrienne's humble birth and vulgar profession condemned her to a shameful burial in a hole filled with quicklime like a dog with no Church rites! I wrote some very passionate verses about the hypocrisy of that, I can tell you!"

It's futile to stop him from leaping to his feet and with one hand dramatically pointing at our snow-clogged roof gutters, bursting into verse:

Ah, verrai-je toujours ma faible nation,
Incertaine en ses voeux, flétrir ce qui'il admire
Nos moeurs avec nos lois toujours se contredire
Et le Français volage endormi sous l'empire
De la superstition –

He throws me a glance, "You're not listening. Do you need a translation?"

"No, sit down, sit down. I've got the idea, Empire of Superstition, a weak nation that doesn't know its own mind, yadda, yadda, yadda . . ."

Voltaire is indignant. "Some say it was my finest poem. It was set to music by Frederick the Great — "

"Oh, no . . ." A frisson of fear runs down my spine.

"Cold? There's more sun over here."

"It's not that, Monsieur Voltaire. I just thought of another possibility. But it's so cynical. If . . . naw . . . !"

"If what?"

"Well, Adrienne knew someone was trying to poison her.

119

She wouldn't put anything strange into her mouth. If I were her, I'd have my food tasted."

"Yes, she knew she was in danger, but she wasn't sure from whom. She suspected Marie, and then the Duchesse de Bouillon."

I'm swept by an urge to protect an honest and talented woman dead for more than two centuries.

"In fact, she wouldn't trust anybody except Maurice, who had seen the poison pills himself. After all, she loved him enough to re-establish him in Paris with her life savings, even when he was sleeping with an opera singer down the street."

"*Exactement*. Maurice handled the poisoned pills. As you say, perhaps the police authorities never tested the real pills at all. Because in the end, the poison was used, *n'est-ce pas*?" Voltaire rises from the table and carefully lifts his *matelasse* coat off the back of the chair.

"Maurice?" I gasp.

The argument beyond the gate has finished. The ghastly remains of the dead cat are buried in a snow drift. Our sledding neighbor works in waist-deep snow, repairing the damaged fence and cursing under her breath.

"Well, at least our two neighborhood murderers have been caught," V. says, heading indoors. He concludes, "As for Adrienne, as we might have said in France, *cherchez l'homme.*"

"It's not a bad story."

"*Merci, Madame*. And as you know my secretary Longchamp is nowhere to be found, would you be so kind as to put it all down on paper?"

"I don't have time."

He stops inside the kitchen doorway and a strange expression crosses his face. Little did I know this was going to be the seed of so much trouble to come.

"I have a better idea," he says. "Why don't you teach me?"

"Teach you? To write?"

He rolls his eyes. "*Mon Dieu. Non, Madame*, teach me to *type*."

The Eternal Contest

The nights are at their longest now. Dusk falls around five, lingering only lightly on Mont Blanc's violet ridges before dying altogether. I'm listening in a desultory way to "Europe Today" on the B.B.C. World Service, but European Union events hover permanently below the watermark of "interesting." I realize I couldn't care less what a Dutch parliamentarian from the Green Party thinks of U.S. foreign policy towards Iraq.

V.'s warming himself by the fire, scanning the cartoons in a six-week-old *New Yorker*, sighing with frustration, "I don't get that one . . . nor that one . . . why is that funny . . . ?"

He tosses the magazine aside. "*Madame*, you should switch on the terrace light. We wouldn't want *Monsieur* to slip on the ice."

"You're right." I heave myself out of my favorite armchair.

On her doubled winter rations, Frisbee is starting to waddle, not run, to the door when we put her out for the night. Surviving the cold by sleeping under the heating tank, she's lucky compared to the wild cats clinging to the stony cliffs that shelter us from the storms sweeping the plateau above.

This is the "high" season in St-Cergue when the funky, smoky restaurants along the main street fill up with visiting Genevan families reddened by hours of skiing and sledding. The shops are full and no longer close exactly on time, the doors merrily jangling their bells with the entry and exit of customers. There's a cheerful, money-making expression on everyone's face, giving a new meaning to "Jingle Bells."

The ski slope opposite École Jean-Jacques Rousseau is busy until ten each night. Passing in my car, I can make out tiny, darting figures flying downhill, moving in and out of the floodlights that compete with the full moon. I cherish these glimpses of hidden beauty, fleeting and unplanned. There's no *après-ski* glamor to speak of. There are no private airstrips, Versace wardrobes, or Fergie photo ops. We are not in Gstaad or Klosters or Chamonix. St-Cergue's last royal visit was in the 1920s when posters in London advertised "Fly this morning and ski in St-Cergue by tea-time."

Tea-time these days means bottles of local white wine sloshing down gelatinous cheese fondues. Old art-deco post-cards of St-Cergue illustrating fashionable flappers in tweedy ski pants and leather ski bindings sell out quickly at the grocery store of Monsieur Reymond. His late father was the mayor of St-Cergue for decades. Our Monsieur Reymond is a stooped, kind-eyed man, ranging bottles of "*sirop*" and instant-soup packets along the shelves while his wife briskly handles the cash register.

One day, to help my Alexander in a history assignment, this Monsieur Reymond describes the old St-Cergue of his youth. The town was only one third its present size, but teeming with wealthy English tourists in high season come to frolic, dance and flirt, ice-skate, curl heavy irons across the ice, or ski pulled along through town by horse-drawn sleighs.

Talking to my ten-year-old, this seventy-year-old is momentarily again a child himself. His eyes grow wistful, leaving my young interviewer sitting through an uncomfort-able silence, his little worksheet half-filled. No one wants to forget the golden years, even as the town slips deeper into the cracks between semi-alcoholic decline and commuter gentrifi-cation.

In this deep winter quiet, my life is more meditative than ever before. V. and I burrow like hibernating animals sheltered by thick stone walls and low-beamed ceilings. When Theo and I play our daily duets, we turn on all the lamps to read the music.

I have never known till now the dead silence of a mountain town completely swathed in snow. Sometimes I walk with Alexander past the dog-sled cages to his early morning train. With all the street lamps illuminating the snow banks high on each side of the street, it looks like a moonwalk. The footfalls of youngsters trudging out of the night into the glare of the train station parking lot are muffled down to a gentle crunch. The cars of dawn commuters crawl and slide in and out of the village on a whisper. Occasionally, we hear a gunning engine grinding itself deeper into a muddy rut.

"I miss New York. I miss my Council meetings," I complain to Peter. Few of my first Christmas cards from St-Cergue back to the States have been reciprocated. The New Yorkers are the last to keep in contact and I realize why.

I Left New York, *ergo*, I Am Not.

"I don't miss the hissing brakes of the bus outside our bedroom window every dawn," Peter answers firmly, stretching full-length to enjoy a leisurely bath. "And I don't miss that straight-backed bathtub, that forced my knees up to my chin."

This winter offers time to think, to digest. The days of obliterating magazine deadlines are over. Some hopes, or memories, or regrets rise to the surface, others settle once and for all to the murky bottom of my subconscious. Scenes of the past reorder themselves, other events – so weighty at the time! – float downwards into irrelevance. Certain passages in my life telescope into oblivion, others zoom forward like slides under a microscope. My life feels whitewashed in ice, dormant, await-ing rebirth. Like Allen's shifting molecules, the elements of my new existence reorder themselves, randomly floating around in this vacuum, making experience, knowledge, friendship, disappointment – all the things that used to press in on me – seem only particles that interact by some as yet, undiscovered set of physical principles.

This impression of time collapsing and expanding is almost tangible to me these days, Einsteinian in its obviousness. I try to explain it to V. He enjoys this interplay between time and physics, distance and experience. He spent years working out scientific problems in his laboratory at Cirey.

And after all, what is his visit to my house, but an exercise in time travel?

"When I wrote *Micromégas*," he explains, stoking the dying fire with a poker and brushing the ashes off his velvet trousers, "I imagined two visitors to Earth arriving by means of a convenient comet. One visitor is six thousand feet tall from Saturn and the other a full eight leagues high, from the star Sirius. They watch as tiny figures on Earth, some dressed in turbans, some in tall hats, slaughter each other. Their enormous size makes all of our terrestrial wars and follies seem no more than the toing and froing of insects."

"You ridiculed war between Christians and Muslims by reducing it to an anthill?"

"Precisely. Now that I visit you, *Madame*, Time refracts my memories, like . . . like a prism breaks light into color. I see so many things much more clearly from a distance, as it were."

"And what strikes you most?"

"That my greatest energies were spent on my least lasting endeavors. Take, for example, *La Pucelle*, my naughty epic about Joan of Arc."

"Never heard of it until you mentioned it the other day."

"Precisely. It started as a salon game, a challenge to write some clever verse about a tap maid burnt at the stake. It was a useless burlesque that I spent twenty-five years writing in secret. In order to evade the censors and elude the Bastille, I filled it with lots of vulgar stuff that no one could possibly imagine I would lower myself to write. Madame du Châtelet was so worried about it, she kept it hidden behind multiple locks."

He shrugs his shoulders, "Rubbish. I can hardly read it now."

"Anything else a waste of time? I mean, relatively speaking."

"Hmm. Well, I spent years working in the pursuit of scientific progress . . . Oh yes," he smiles to himself, a bit abashed. "Oh, *mon Dieu*," he starts chuckling, "what fun that was . . . Oh, by the way, you wouldn't by any chance have a Réamur thermometer around the house?"

For weeks, V. has carried around his list of science books without saying anything. Then one day, he insists that I place an order on the Internet for all of them. He wants anything on "negative gravity," "string theory," and – well, the rest of it I can hardly follow. He jabbers at length about two detectors in Antarctica that have picked up minute patterns in a glow from primordial gases – possible traces of the cosmic match that ignited the Big Bang and led to the creation of the universe fourteen billion years ago – he explains with a great waving of his arms, "traces of colossal waves, like sound waves, that the fluctuations probably set in motion, roiling the young universe."

Voltaire's immersion into the world of modern science seems contagious, or is it merely coincidence that during that same week, Alexander's class starts studying magnetic forces, and Eva-Marie is seized with a passion for division?

"Give me a *calcul*," she orders, bundling herself into her ski jacket.

"Say 'division' in English. Forty-two divided by seven. No fingers."

"Good, we haven't done the seven *livrets* yet," she says, satisfied by the challenge. "I'll get the fastest score. Faster than Levy."

"Tell me your answers at lunch." I watch my littlest one

limp off to battle her clever pal, Levy, over the multiplication computer game. The orthopaedist promised that the dragging of the leg, still in a walking cast, will correct itself. The beauty of her lovely, straight nose is forever marred. Although the crater dug by a tree branch has healed over, her best feature now bears a shiny dent. I massage the nose faithfully each night with cream, hoping to diminish the damage.

I still can't adjust to Eva-Marie's rapid adaptation to Switzerland, every move she makes to fit in with local life taking her farther away from that Manhattan princess I dressed for the United Nations Christmas party in red velvet and ribbons. As she chatters in local dialect to a playmate in the schoolyard, my once-graceful girl looks a stranger to me. When she learns a French word before she's heard the English equivalent, I feel a trifle betrayed. All my life I wanted a daughter. I did not foresee the irony that the only one of my three children born in the U.S. would turn out the least American.

Other aspects of her acculturation bother me. She's quickly assimilated from some of the village children the Vaudois defiant slyness in the face of authority, an opaque manner. I start to notice that the first explanation of anything from Eva-Marie will always differ from the last. She's tailoring truth to suit my reaction. She's leading a double life.

When I challenge her, I see she has already tagged me as different. "You don't understand my new lifestyle," is her flippant reply. We argue about brushing her tangled hair, the choice of grubby pants. At the same time, she's increasingly vain, testing my perfume without permission. One morning, after yet another argument, I despair of her willfulness, her calculated coquetry, her sharp bilingual tongue, her *foreignness*. She exhausts my reserves of patience without feeling my profound love and sympathy for her.

Distracted by this female wrangling, V. puts down some perusal of *The Satellite Atlas of the World* to watch her with affection written all over his face.

"That performance amused you?" I ask, once Eva-Marie is safely off to school.

He shrugs with a chuckle. "She's determined. She learns the rules, but only so she can successfully flaunt them. She will have physical passion, you can see that in her daring athletics. Look at how bravely she works to strengthen that leg. She'd already be sailing downhill again on those infernal sticks, if you hadn't locked them up. Of course, she's calculating. Your daughter will be one of life's gamblers."

"She worries me."

He smiles fondly to himself. "She reminds me of an ambitious Marquise, an incorrigible cardplayer, a flagrantly adulterous mother of three, and a domineering housekeeper. A woman who wore her best diamonds twenty-four hours a day, but who was too busy refuting Descartes' theory of the vortices to brush her hair."

"Sounds a real harpy. Someone at Versailles?"

"No, she came one night with friends to a simple supper after I returned from England. She stayed with me for thirteen years."

I blush. "Your mistress, Madame du Châtelet!"

"*Oui*, my beloved Émilie, or to introduce her properly, Gabrielle Émilie Le Tonnelier de Breteuil, La Marquise du Châtelet-Lomont. The official French translator of Newton's *Principia*."

"Does Eva-Marie look like Émilie?"

"Oh, *non, non, pas du tout*. Émilie had dark, curly hair tied up like a child's, and sea-green eyes, while your daughter has brown eyes and hair like streams of honey. But Émilie was taller than average, like *Mademoiselle*, and the energy! Émilie could work all night on a mathematical problem, study English all morning, and still preside over a houseful of guests at Cirey for a lively dinner."

"She sounds rather tempestuous," I comment, "and not so easy to live with," looking in the direction my own termagant has taken to school.

He shrugs, "I had my own wing in Cirey, with my library, my scientific instruments, my bedroom. She had her wing, decorated in light blue and yellow with a boudoir lined with panels by Watteau and filled with bowls of rings, snuff boxes and other baubles."

"She liked jewelry?" I ask, smiling.

"Oh, yes. I gave her a ring with a tiny portrait of myself engraved by Monsieur Barier, with this little verse:

> *Barier grave ces traits déslinés pour vos veux;*
> *Avec quelque plaisir daignez les reconnaître!*
> *Les vôtres dans mon coeur furent gravés bien mieux,*
> *Mais ce fut par un plus grand maître.**

I sigh. "That's lovely."

He bows slightly, flushing with pleasure. "Aha, the sweet intoxication of praise untainted by flattery! Such a little bagatelle! Émilie liked it. I was really smitten, although I was thirty-nine, and she was already twenty-seven, hardly young."

I let that last bit pass. There is something about this passionate partnership that reminds me of my six-year affair with a fellow journalist, a New Yorker named Sean. It began as I turned thirty, "hardly young." Introduced by colleagues in Hong Kong, here at last was my soul mate! Here was another journalist who could understand the pressure of deadlines, the thrill of pinning down a scoop, the late-night torture of crafting the elusively perfect "lead," the challenge of the telling "nut" graph, the hashing out of political theories over drinks with other correspondents.

Soft-spoken, courteous, tall, with curly-brown hair, large

---

* *Barier engraved these features, as you asked:*
  With whatever pleasure you may deign to recognize them!
  Your features were engraved much better on my heart,
  But then, done by a much greater Master.

green eyes, and a muscular build, Sean made our first date a tropical fantasy of dining on the veranda of a romantic colonial hotel, followed by a midnight swim in his borrowed shirt.

Like V. and Madame du Châtelet buried in the wilds of Champagne, we hid ourselves away in the palmy suburbs of Singapore, where it was never winter, cold or dark. We reveled in the equatorial strangeness of the island that combined high-rise banking centers and teak-poled *kampung* shanty-towns.

However, our working idyll was overshadowed by the Singaporean government, as ever-present an authority as an eighteenth-century Keeper of the Seal. Our telex traffic moved the old-fashioned way out of the Reuters' external service punching room: certainly nothing we filed to faraway desks was private. The stories we were assigned by our editors inevitably concerned some of the city-state's touchier spots: trade union politics, weapons exports, treatment of the island's single Indian parliamentarian who stood in opposition to the ruling People's Action Party, social engineering policies, and political detentions.

We persisted in our jobs despite the whispered warnings of a British diplomat over private lunches and hints from American Embassy staffers that we were dealing with sensitive issues. The jungle that surrounded our apartment building turned more ominous than romantic. Promised interviews with Singaporeans were cancelled without explanation. U.S. Embassy officials would only meet us outside their offices. Little slurs began to circulate and grow, and finally reached our ears. Sean was described to me at a cocktail party as a "communist trouble-maker," when in truth, the only thing markedly leftist about Sean was his handwriting. These imagined political affiliations were repeated by Singaporeans to other foreigners. Nor did I escape the innuendo. Although I was writing for the *Washington Post*, the *I.H.T.* and others with an accreditation from the government press office as a reporter, I was dismissed as Sean's "camp follower."

Our apartment, its large veranda opened to the equatorial breezes, began to seem as private as a fish bowl. There was no way we could lock away our writing in a drawer as did Voltaire. We had professional reputations already established outside Singapore and we had to ride it out, but the mounting tension made an already competitive relationship now paranoid and fractious.

After eighteen months, Sean's application to renew his work visa was refused. De facto expulsion from Singapore came as a relief, trailed as it was by questions in a public session of the Singapore Parliament and coverage by the B.B.C. World Service.

"She could not bear it," V. interjects.

"Couldn't bear what?" I look up to see Voltaire nodding.

"Émilie couldn't bear the stress, her fear of the state taking revenge for my writing. I had to run for my life to Holland because a copy of *Le Mondain* was found in the drawer of a dead bishop."

"What was so incriminating about *Le Mondain*?"

He shrugs, "I dared to say that I preferred an age with fine clothing, civilized books, and Gobelin tapestries on the walls to running around the Garden of Eden stark naked. Adam and Eve had long dirty nails, unkempt hair, no knives or forks, and no decent bedding. Let's face it, they knew no sanitation and, without cleanliness, even the happiest love is nothing more than a shameful base instinct."

"Seems pretty obvious to me."

"The Church took offense. I fled in secret for months, disguised as Monsieur Revol, travelling from Brussels to Antwerp, to Amsterdam, to Leyden. Émilie interceded for me by letter and in person with as many influential people as she could contact. I confess, I was so pre-occupied with proof-reading my book on Newton's theories in Holland, I neglected my poor friend back in Cirey. She grew quite frantic."

Frantic – ah, yes. After his deportation to Hong Kong, Sean

neglected me, too. There were long weeks of silence, then a brief, unsuccessful reunion in Malaysia. After six months I joined him in Hong Kong, but the romance was over. We lasted a few more years together, but he didn't want a partner so much as a handmaiden to his talent. Lost items needed to be retrieved, dry cleaning had to be dropped off, forgotten secretarial chores became "little favors," that would prove my love.

I came to resent his assumption that I would edit his copy at any time of day or night. He called me, "unsupportive, disloyal." Our volatile relationship became a subject of barfly gossip. After one final and very public break, I found myself giggling at the delicious relief of solitude.

"How did you, with all your talents, live with Émilie without immolating your relationship in competition?" I ask V. as he fiddles with an antique Bunsen burner. Every day, my office looks more like Dr. Frankenstein's lab. Émilie and her scientific passions have become an unseen presence.

"Ah, *ma belle Uranie*, she was so much better at mathematics and calculations than I, I had no chance there. But I had a different type of talent. Newton's theories had been buried for twenty-seven years in a warehouse and only the most academic scholars in England, Germany, Holland and Russia had probed his depths or understood his reasoning. Émilie could translate, but even she couldn't *explain*. If I understood Newton's proof of a general gravitational force, then I knew how to explain it, and then – well, all Paris understood, too."

"You two were always able to work side by side without any jealousy or rivalry? What was this story about her locking herself up with Clairaut to study mathematics until you kicked the door down?"

"Clairaut was annoying, yes," he nods, still unable to take his eyes off a curious prism shining a rainbow of streaming light on my desktop.

"And this Maupertuis whom she was always begging to give her extra lessons?"

"A very handsome, hard, disagreeable man. But looking back on all that now, one must make allowances for a woman so different from all the others of her time."

"Was she able to suffer being second to the great Voltaire?"

I think of Eva-Marie's constant resentment of her brothers, my resentment of Sean's successes.

He sits back from his work at last and considers, then beams fondly, "Of course. I had forgotten. The Contest."

He takes off the heavy linen apron covering a fine shirt of cotton lawn. He carefully rebuttons the exquisite lace cuffs. I've noticed the appearance of deep expression lines around his eyes and mouth. Are they due to his spending the long nights peering up at the stars through a lens?

Or is my handsome friend ageing before my eyes?

"Oh, the Contest!" he laughs to himself again. "You see, in 1738, l'Académie des Sciences in Paris offered a prize for the best essay on the 'Nature and Diffusion of Fire'."

He smiles wickedly, "I had wheedled the theme of the contest out of Maupertuis the year before. Well, you know me. I ordered the best chemical equipment available and set up my dark-room and physical apparatus. First, I carried out an experiment suggested by Newton, to prove that the reflection in a prism does not come to an end when the glass is surrounded by a vacuum instead of air. I tried then to deter-mine the nature of heat, using every resource known at the time; a balance, a Réamur thermometer, and a Musschenbroek pyrometer by which I could observe how heated bodies expand."

"I wondered what that thing was." I point to a contraption of glass, wires and pipes warping the wood of my Ming side table.

"I even carried out some experiments measuring the weight of iron before and after burning at a nearby foundry, and by setting fire to the back forest of the estate — "

"Which you will not repeat in our back yard — " I say firmly.

"*Tranquillisez-vous, Madame.* My forest fires were too expensive to clean up, but what I discovered was very interesting — "

"Smokey-the-Bear taking snuff?"

He ignores that. " — I observed that the same amounts of different fluids, such as oil, water, vinegar, of different temperatures, do not take an average temperature when mixed."

"And that means?"

His disdainful glance conveys I am a complete ignoramus. "That I was on the brink of discovering the specific warmth of the physical body, of course."

"Of course."

"Had I developed a little further my *idées* of the calcination of metals and of the compound nature of air, it is I, François Arouet de Voltaire, who would have been the first to discover oxygen!"

"Is that what this is?" I ask, pointing to the total, happily ephemeral, mess he's made of my office. It would be nice to think it was in the furtherance of science, even retroactive science.

"Yes, I'm repeating the experiments of Scheele, carried out forty years after mine, using superior instruments and finer measurements which were not available to me then."

"Well, clean up when you finish. What did Émilie do for the contest?"

"As far as I knew, nothing. My essay was nearly finished and she betrayed no interest at all. I only learned later that she was obsessed with the idea of winning, and can you imagine – opposing all my ideas!"

"How dare she?" I mocked him.

"Indeed," he commented, with a completely straight face. "Keeping her little secret, she worked without practical experiments of any kind through the nights for a week, sleeping only an hour before dawn. Her entry argued that fire has no weight, that it is possibly neither spirit nor matter, but a substance of an unknown nature, like the empty space whose existence can also be taken as proven but whose composition defies us."

"Did she win?" I'm secretly hoping Émilie blew them away.

"No, we both got honorable mentions," he says with obvious chagrin. "Of course, there was one thing I liked. Émilie supposed that the colors of a spectrum contain heat in varying degrees, red being the warmest and violet the coldest. Forty years later, Rochon proved she was right."

"Well, who did win?"

"The mathematician Euler."

"I've actually heard of him."

"I'm not surprised. Second and third prize went to a Cartesian, one Count Créquy – the Académie was riddled with Cartesians – and a Jesuit named de Fiesc who believed in those silly vortices of Descartes."

I imagine Émilie, sleepless in her diamonds and silks, exiled far from Paris in the forests of Champagne, learning of her honor.

"Émilie was happy she got a mention?"

"*Mon Dieu, non!* She wrote to the Académie begging she remain anonymous. 'I have a thousand reasons for asking it,' she pleaded, but — " he turns to me confidingly, "she had only one."

"The scandal of living with you in sin," I nod in sympathy.

"*Mais non*, sinning with me was a feather in her cap! No, obviously it was ridiculous in Society for a woman to be so learned."

I raise one eyebrow. "Obviously."

"She didn't want to seem a fool! Now you must excuse me, I'm going to finish this before the apparatus cools."

That evening, Alexander is upstairs studying geography. Theo practices a Bach bourrée in the living room. Eva-Marie sits on the playroom floor, painting fake blood on her discarded hip-length plaster cast which we've preserved for future games of "The Mummy."

"Levy beat me at the math game today," she reports. "So I

putzed him at basketball.''

''With a walking cast on your leg?''

''No problem. I just stand there and toss the ball over his head. He's got a computer at home to practice division, but there's no software that can make him as tall as me.''

Maybe Émilie was right to hide her entry in the contest from Voltaire, maybe not. It came out all right in the end, and it's interesting to think that V. might have won but for the Cartesian obsession with vortices stuck in the antediluvian brains of the Academicians of Paris in 1738.

Still, one question lingers in my mind as I set the table for dinner. What if Émilie had won? I won't ask Voltaire, that's for sure. He has the hindsight of the dead, but he's still just a man.

May the Force be Damned

It's almost Christmas. I adjust a pair of expensive corduroy pants to fit over Eva-Marie's cast underneath a midnight blue velvet dress. The plaster leg has its upside. Even her teacher admits Eva-Marie will be unable to hop around the stage in a herd of twenty youngsters sporting donkey's ears made of construction paper.

Spared making a literal ass of herself, Eva-Marie will hobble downstage to a standing microphone to recite a poem about a Tibetan yak coming from the far Himalayas to worship at the manger. Her costume will consist of one of my fur-trimmed hats from Lhasa.

She is only one of two children in her class who will directly address the audience. It marks a little watershed for our family; the first theatrical occasion in which a Küng child speaks French, but I say nothing. Being so small, she takes it in her stride. And there is something about her recitation that pains me. Like the yak in the poem, my children have come so far in so short a time. I drag behind their determined little caravan, my heart in a cast, reluctant to leave New York for good and follow them.

At least, we've found music is an international language to ease the children's integration. We've located a Chinese piano teacher for Alexander who can understand the newly-arrived American mother speaking Mandarin, and a Swiss-German violin teacher who can happily confer with Theo's father. Already Theo has been assigned to his music school's orchestra in time for the Christmas concert. We head nervously to his first rehearsal.

The Music Conservatory of West Vaud, freshly painted in deep Renaissance tones, sits in a lakeside villa in Nyon. The rehearsal hall, once the ballroom, is a silvery gray with maroon trim and burgundy velvet drapes. The only person who seems to be correctly dressed for the décor is Voltaire, who nonchalantly props his elaborate hat on top of a bust of Handel with an affectionate pat, "*Bon soir, mon cher Georges.*"

Amidst the zip and clatter of violin cases and stands, Theo looks tiny. The Conservatory has a philosophy of starting children on string instruments around the age of seven, when Suzuki-trained Japanese prodigies are already haggling recording fees with Sony. Like a lot of New York music students, Theo took up the violin at four. Thus he's the youngest tonight, eclipsed behind a buxom blonde teen in a pierced navel ring and platform sneakers.

Hans-Walter Hirzel, the genial Swiss-German conductor, taps for "attention" with his baton and addresses his team. He's arrived in good humor, his hair still wet from riding a bicycle through a light snow along Nyon's ancient lanes laid out by a Roman city-planner two thousand years ago.

"I'm sorry the sheet music wasn't ready until tonight, but that is the fault of the printers in Lausanne," Hirzel explains. "So we'll read it through."

Even I can discern the hint of Lucerne in his French.

"We're going to play a concerto by Arcangelo Corelli, who was born in 1653 and died in 1713. Corelli tells us it was *fatto per la notte di natale*, that is, written for the night of Christ's birth. It's a typically baroque piece. The violin soloists will be answered by the first violin section, then the second, etc. Right. Let's start."

A forest of poised cat gut obscures Theo's expression as he

encounters a nineteen-page thicket of black notes in the company of twenty-five strangers. I can only imagine his panic. He's no sight-reading prodigy.

With a downward gesture of Hirzel's baton, off they go. Corelli has ordered up a majestic first chord, aching and prolonged. Then a long pause follows, broken suddenly by a low instrumental groan from Hirzel's right. The graceful cellist with a rope of hair reaching the back of her waist and glasses like Coca-Cola bottle bottoms has lingered too long.

"*Non, non,*" Hirzel gently scolds her. "Like a sword thrust, like this," he slashes the air.

V. nods with enthusiasm, illustrating a fencer's slice, for no one's benefit but mine.

"Again." Hirzel orders. V. slices through the air again.

The chord comes again, plaintive, but brief. The cellist, eyes wide with attention, this time holds her fire. Then the second, mounting harmonic plea. Another strategic pause. Then ten firm, lilting chords close the phrase.

Hirzel lowers his arms. "Good," he says. "An excellent start, even if that's all we accomplish tonight."

Everyone breaks into laughter. They repeat the chords from the beginning and then plunge after the elfin Hirzel into the cold waters of unknown notes, like faithful lemmings jumping off a cliff. As juvenile Christmas performances go, this first run-through is rough, but I have to admit, already a big improvement on "*I Saw Mommy Kissing Santa Claus,*" back at St. Boniface.

V. settles himself down amidst the discarded coats behind the second violin section. He seems perfectly comfortable admiring Hirzel's management of his troupe. After all, the theater is more home to Voltaire than the many houses in which he lodged. He spent years like this, perched on the end of a stage. He's enthralled to be back at a rehearsal, but to my astonishment, his slender fingers are dancing to the music *off the beat.*

I find this very distracting, as well as slightly unbelievable.

My eyes glance from time to time at his drumming fingers, lightly brushing the rounds of his brocade-covered knees. But something is wrong.

Voltaire has no, repeat no, sense of rhythm whatsoever. How can this be?

I hear Corelli's music shift from movement to movement, from $\frac{4}{4}$ to $\frac{3}{4}$, from $\frac{12}{8}$ back to $\frac{4}{4}$, but to any sentient human being who can multiply by two or three, musical *binaires* or *ternaires* are hardly a challenge. And yet, even a sea of violin bows cannot drag my enlightened buddy on the downbeat in time.

"Did you ever study music?" I ask in a whisper, affecting disinterest.

He looks at me, innocently surprised, his fingers dancing their own crazy polka, "*Mais, non.* Since I turned twelve, I guessed the enormous quantity of things for which I have no talent. I know that my organs are not arranged to go very far in music. Why do you ask?"

This is the first time it has occurred to me that V. might actually be bad at something! I am exhilarated, liberated, elated. Is every friendship, even an imaginary one, fraught with this kind of secret jealousy? Of course. No friendship could long survive such inequality in talent, and it's pretty obvious I'm never going to be called the Mind of My Century, or for that matter, the Woman of Any Given Day. After weeks of hearing about his hit plays, his royal dinners, his love affairs with celebrity actresses and marquises, his endless print runs, his scientific discoveries, and political notoriety, I have discovered that God is Just. Oh joy! V. isn't tone deaf – one wouldn't want that – but obviously the guy ain't got much rhythm.

Meanwhile, Theo is stretching his talents to the limits. From where I sit, I can only see the point of his half-sized bow, rising and falling behind the others. Is he faking it? If he is, so what? I am so proud of him, this "Theo Dor," this "gift of God," whom I almost miscarried in my third month of pregnancy. His good humor in the face of his chronic asthma, and his natural generosity towards a well-meaning, but pedantic brother and temperamental little sister are essential pieces of ballast stabilizing our family ship. He has earned his family nickname, borrowed from the Peanuts strip, "Sweet Baboo," this plucky little soul sawing away in $\frac{12}{8}$ time punctuated by Hirzel's shouts.

And I reflect on the sheer guts of children – what they'll take in their stride, what they'll do on trust. After less than six months out of Manhattan, one tackling Corelli cold under a stranger's baton, another delivering a Christmas poem to three hundred locals in their own dialect, a third standing up to a tribunal to confess a local "crime" in his newly-learnt French. How dare I take them for granted?

On and on go the musicians, movement by movement. Pimply complexions break into beads of sweat. Grimaced mouths press against orthodontic appliances.

Two hours after that first, brisk chord Theo finally surfaces, flushed and relieved, from a welter of slamming cases and clanging music stands.

"How did you feel back there?" I ask.

"Well," he grins, "I got behind the wheel and stayed in my seat, but it was like I forgot to fasten my seat belt."

I haven't seen him glow like this since we left New York, since I saw him hang over the uppermost balcony of Carnegie Hall, peering down at Yuri Bashmet playing the viola. Something tells me that tonight, our wandering Sweet Baboo has found his tribe.

We have all been so lonely in our different ways. In October Theo asked, "If I don't learn French, can we go home to New York?" I think of the Statue of Liberty drawing on his desk and Alexander's sketch of a boy, tears flowing down his cheek, sitting in an airplane watching his beloved cityscape – the Empire State Building, the Chrysler Building, the World Trade Center – recede below.

Eva-Marie doesn't cry or draw, but she wakes up at night

from a nightmare in which she shouts in French one minute and in English another.

Peter is reluctant to admit we've lost anything by moving to Switzerland. He hated the hypocrisy and bureaucracy of the U.N., the bumper-to-bumper commute in Third Avenue traffic, the lack of fresh air and heights. He cites Theo's sufferings in Manhattan's pollution, or the struggle to keep St. Boniface from putting Alexander on ritalin, or our worries whenever Eva-Marie was so much as ten minutes late returning from Carl Schurz Park at nightfall.

"Don't you miss anything?" I ask, hungering for sympathy.

My husband thinks for a moment, then smiles and answers, "Eartha Kitt at the Carlyle."

The more we share our reminiscences, the more I realize that Peter lived the U.N., while I lived New York. When Ruth, my style guru, took me to fashion shows, Peter was meeting the Bulgarian ambassador to resolve his country's customs officials' theft of Red Cross fuel for trucks delivering assistance to Bosnian and Serb civilians. While I sat at the Council on Foreign Relations listening to discussions of China policy, Peter had to meet the Chinese ambassador to be refused, yet again, the right to carry out prison inspections. While I caught up with *Business Week* friends over lunch, P. was subjected to a harangue about humanitarian imperialism from an African general whose army had just murdered three Red Cross colleagues.

The New York Christmas was the hardest for Peter, who could no more relate to the schmaltz of *We Need a Little Christmas*, or the joyless brutality of *Home Alone*, than I could to the austerity of Christmas spent in Switzerland; a handful of wooden toys, and days spent almost entirely outdoors celebrating the Return of the Great Snow Being.

Peter spent five years longing for the traditional (real!) candles burning on the tree (a sure fire hazard, I quipped), the choir in the breathtaking baroque Abbey of Einsiedeln, the charade of departing sleigh bells his parents played on the four Küng siblings in post-war central Switzerland.

Now I struggle with the elusive Christmas spirit, facing Christmas without the assistance of the giant tree at the Metropolitan Museum of Art, Looney Rooney the Magician at the U.N. Christmas party, Rudolph Giuliani leading son Andrew Giuliani down the main aisle of St. Monica's Church at Christmas morning Mass.

I've conveniently forgotten the ridiculousness of Christmas in New York – the inability to find a single *crèche* for sale in the Bloomingdales' Christmas Boutique, the nullifying political correctness at the nursery schools when Kwanzaa songs were sung around the Christmas tree, or tiny Marys and Josephs hopped to "Hava Nageela," as if these festivals had no separate historical or theological integrity. I've forgotten the $8,000 toy cars at F.A.O. Schwartz, the frozen sleet underfoot on a taxi-less morning, the crazy urge to forget the whole thing and fly to Punta Cana on a last-minute Club Med deal.

I launch myself into wrapping paper with Rosemary Clooney warbling on the C.D. player. V. has seized the morning to watch T.V. Our video library fascinates him, but his choices are usually drowned out by the kids' arguments over *Groundhog Day* versus *The Pink Panther*.

An hour later, I hear his light step mounting the stairs to my office.

"Lord, let this cup pass from me, yet not as I will, but as thou wilt, sayeth E.T."

"Excuse me?" I stop ripping scotch tape and look up at him, leaning in the doorway, tapping his small leather notebook with a quill.

"I refer, *Madame*, to the Agony in the Garden, St. Matthew 26. It has been revised by one Monsieur Spielberg. He cast a monk-like alien as Christ who goes in agony into the garden on the eve of his death in a plastic tunnel overseen by Philistines in microbe-proof space-suits who don't recognize him as the Messiah."

V. takes a huge breath, before continuing, "*Le E.T.* then dies and miraculously rises from the dead, ascends into heaven, and no doubt is now seated at the right hand of the Father, a Greater Alien than Ourselves, forever and ever, Amen."

"E.T.? Jesus?"

"*Madame*," he sneers, "Is that light bulb of a little red heart beating away in his reptilian breast not an illusion to the pierced Sacred Heart of Jesus? *Non?*"

"Possibly. What are you up to?"

He refers to his notes. "Well, there is *The Lion, The Witch and The Wardrobe*. Of course, the lion Aslan is another Jesus, crucified on the stone table. His disciples Lucy and Susan – two soppy Magdalenes if ever I saw – weep as the noble Beast offers up his life in atonement for that nasty Edmund's sins. Then, whoosh!" V.'s quill flies through the air tickling my nose, "The Lion rises from the dead and vanquishes the White Witch." He adds dryly, "*Quelle surprise.*"

"Well that's easy. The Narnia books were written by C.S. Lewis, a Christian theologian — "

V. silences me with impatience, "And now, *Star Wars* — "

"*Star Wars?*"

"Clearly penned by Jesuits. There is the virgin birth of Arkadan, and then the Trinity of the Father and the Son who is named Luke Somebody – where is it?" he checks his notes, "A nice reference to the Book of Luke. Anyway, there is the lost son, in whom godlike powers are dormant until manhood, when he discovers that The Force is With Him – *excusez-moi* – with us. Everybody goes around saying, 'It is the will of the Force,' just like 'the will of God' dribbled off the lips of priests. Actually, I think The Force is much better than the Holy Ghost, *n'est-ce pas*? After all, we wouldn't want to insult ghosts, would we? Hmm?"

"Well, what do you think?" I ask guardedly, leaning back from the rolls of green and red paper scattered around me.

"Think?" V. shouts, waving his hands in frustration. "I'm HORRIFIED, *Madame*! It was bad enough when the Jesuits thrust these impossible fables down the throats of children in my time. Now it's an *infamy*. They're indoctrinating your children with stories coded as astronomical animal adventures!"

"And you've broken the code?"

"*Madame*, I know Christian theology when I see it! I had two hundred volumes on Christianity in my library and what's worse, I read them all."

He mutters to himself at the memory, "It was like doing the rounds of a lunatic asylum."

"Now wait. You believe in God. You refer to him often."

He waves an elegant hand in protest. "That's not the issue. *Madame*. These works are ill-disguised reiterations of the Christ myth. A disgusting insinuation of organized religion into innocent minds. I find no Enlightenment in your playroom!"

"*Miracle on 34th Street?* One of my favorites, I should warn you."

"Abominable! That poor little Sharon, battling unassisted for the powers of Deductive Reasoning, is defeated by a tidal wave of superstition and sentiment in the name of a mythical figure called Santa Claus – of whom I've never heard. Frankly, I prefer even Christ to that idiotic fat man."

"What else have you been watching?"

"Um, *Heidi!* Yes!" He flips eagerly through his notes. "Another disgusting Jesus allegory, the way Heidi cures Clara in a wheelchair with nothing more than a wave of her hand. '*Rise up and walk.*' Surely you recognize Jesus curing the Paralytic at Capernaum, St. Luke, chapter five!"

"Now how did I miss that? *Thomas the Tank Engine?*"

He breathes a sigh of relief. "Ah, now, I like Thomas. A faithful representation of the natural social order. Sir Topham Hat is the nobility, the engines are the bourgeoisie, and the disruptive wagon cars the illiterate laborers in the field. It would be hopeless to try to educate the *canaille* – it only spoils them for the plow – and the engines do a good job of managing them. No argument there."

"It was written by a clergyman."

His eyebrows fly upwards in alarm. "A Catholic?"

"No, an English Protestant."

I hate that smug smile.

"Well, do you believe in God?"

"But certainly, *Madame*. Can you examine the workings of a clock and not believe that there was a watchmaker responsible? The existence of the universe proves there is a God. But everything that goes beyond the adoration of a Supreme Being and submitting one's heart to his eternal order is sheer superstition. Still this Christmas!" He waves a disgusted arm over my glittery mess. "By now, I would have expected to find a worthy successor to Christianity, a secular faith, if you will."

"You're visiting the post-Christian era. We've replaced Mass with crystals, astrology, numerology, and aromatherapy. We use candles and incense to worship in our bubble bath, instead of at the altar."

He looks confused, but hopeful. "Astronomy has become the new religion? The study of the stars?"

"You misheard me. I said astrology. Tea leaves for airheads."

"Ah, you mean superstition. That must be attacked. Madame du Châtelet wrote six volumes exposing the contradictions, improbabilities and injustices described in the Bible – surely you've heard of her *Examination of Genesis?*"

"'Fraid not."

"Tssk, tssk. How delinquent your modern printing houses are! Religion is something for one's housemaid. Mass is for the masses. I insisted that d'Alembert and Condorcet wait until my servants left the dining room before we conversed openly about the proofs of God's existence or otherwise."

"Very wise, I'm sure." I'm trying hard to keep a straight face.

"But Faith, now you might ask what is Faith?" V. muses to himself.

"I'll bite. What's Faith?"

"Is it to believe that which is evident? No. It is perfectly evident to my mind that there exists a necessary, eternal, supreme and intelligent Being. I need no Faith for that."

I rest back on my haunches, Dentist Barbie in one hand. "Monsieur Voltaire, does all this mean you're coming to Christmas Mass with us, or not?"

He heaves a weary sigh.

"In Paris, Midnight Mass was just one big social event. While I was burying myself in Cirey, restoring Madame du Châtelet's derelict dump of a house, she was gallivanting all over Paris entreating that mathematician Maupertuis to go to Mass with her."

He sounds as green as his emerald ring.

"How do you know?"

"I have evidence! Listen to what I found hidden amongst all the jewelry I gave her — "

He unfolds a faded pastel sheet of paper from his vest pocket. A beautiful scent of heliotrope, musk, and roses hits my nostrils. He assumes what must have been the typical posture of a Versailles coquette. With one hand, he fans himself with his little notebook, as if it were a lacy delicacy rimmed with feathers.

His voice jumps an octave and he reads the note, simpering, "'Paris, Friday, Christmas night, 1734, I would rather still be in Cirey and know that you were still in Basle, than to see as little of you as I do. I want to celebrate Elohim's birthday with you' and by Elohim she means Jesus, of course. 'See that you come tonight and drink his health with me and Clairaut. I shall expect you between eight and nine and then we shall go together to Midnight Mass and listen to the Christmas psalms — '"

"Hardly incriminating — "

"Wait, wait, listen . . . 'accompanied by organ music; from there I shall take you home. I am counting on this.'" Voltaire's brown eyes glint red. "*Take you home?*"

"Well, maybe now I know why you really dislike Christmas," I say under my breath watching him flounce down the office stairs in a huff.

Peter and I have decided the children are still too young for Midnight Mass, which is a shame because our priest is a Congolese missionary. Facing a dearth of home-grown priests in millennial Switzerland, Holy Mother the Church has assigned this blackest of shepherds to minister to us lost white sheep of St-Cergue. This is somewhat like the village's namesake, the Irish monk St. Cyr who crossed the Jura range a thousand years ago carrying the written word back to illiterate Europe. He reached our crossroads, and as the legend goes, stopped at a hut where Les Cytises now stands, for a drink. The bar service was no doubt even slower in those days, so the good saint moved on.

It's time to start some new traditions. I've settled on reading *A Christmas Carol* out loud every night, although Dickens's vocabulary is a little difficult for Eva-Marie. The children are wide-eyed under Eva-Marie's lumpy duvet as they await the arrival of the third and most frightening of Dickens's ghosts, the withering child-spectre of Christmas Future.

What strikes me rereading Dickens's passages is not the cheery Victorian Christmas "future" of plum pudding and jigs, but the Christmas "past," – the industrial bleakness of polluted fog seeping through frozen keyholes, rapacious rag dealers, whisky-sodden revelers, thin scarves, and second-hand ribbons. And after hearing V.'s relentless attacks on the domination of the Church, I've noticed for the first time that Dickens's characters are celebrating a Christmas almost as secular as any in twenty-first-century New York.

Finally, Scrooge falls on his knees, screeching, "Spirit, hear me! I am not the man I was," and ends up spraying his money and good cheer all over town. Tiny Tim did NOT die after all.

"God bless us, everyone," I cheer in my best crippled-little-

English-boy voice. I close the book. Not a sound. I look up and see that both Theo and Eva-Marie are sound asleep.

"That was pretty good, Mama," Alexander says.

"Get upstairs before Santa Claus finds you here in the hallway," I whisper.

He looks at me with those huge eyes for a long minute. I realize he is about to tell me something I'm not ready to hear. Somewhere between last Christmas and this, between 80th Street and our farmhouse, my eldest son who half-believes in Voldemort has stopped believing altogether in Santa Claus. Reading my dismayed expression, he checks his impulse.

"Okay," he says. As he drags his sluggish brother up to the third floor, I hear Theo mumbling, "Did I miss the fourth ghost?"

"You must love Dickens," I say to V. "I don't think Jesus was mentioned even once."

"Oh, I appreciate religion, *Madame*, a noble lie, damned stuff for the mob, but a consoling myth. Imagine the risks of atheism to social peace. One needs a mythology to keep the majority in check. In short, if God did not exist, it would be necessary to invent him."

"Merry Christmas, Monsieur Scrooge."

With obvious affection, he wishes me, "*Joyeux Noel, ma très chère Madame*," and with an elegant bow and the slightest of kisses blown from his fingers, he retires.

Mission Implausible

Hong Kong's fascination included meeting all varieties of people and learning how they'd ended up in the Colony. Usually something had driven them from home – say, the dreariness of a farmhouse in Topeka, the poverty of a paddy field in Guangdong, the banality of a sunbleached, Sydney suburb, or the depression of a grim industrial town in northern England.

Sharing these origins around the Foreign Correspondents' Club bar, or better yet, watching someone hide them, was intriguing. Story-telling. This was how I grew up in L. A., a teenager in braces and a scoliosis body cast, listening to my parent's friends tell stories over a Sunday meal.

The guests were often actors or movie production people who had come from all over the country to take their chance on "the industry." These brunches might break up as late as six in the evening, leaving my impressionable ears full of wonderful anecdotes or sadder tales of broken dreams. One Italian-American actor, Michael had just finished a film where he played an Apache next to cowboys Fonda, Stewart, Widmark and other stars. Gulping his Bloody Mary, Michael told my parents ruefully, "When the cast met on set for the first day's shooting, I was the only guy there I didn't know . . ."

In St-Cergue, everyone knows everyone. Two days after Christmas, I see our lanky, erstwhile carpenter and spouse –

like Jack Sprat and his heavyset wife – clearing snow around
the stone cottage behind Eva-Marie's two-room schoolhouse.
They themselves live in a wooden chalet not far from our
farmhouse. A couple of explanations occur to me: that bereft of
carpentry work, they're shoveling to meet the bills, or else (and
more charitably), that a disabled neighbor needs assistance.

The truth does not occur to me, not even once, and that just
shows how little I've grasped the social underpinnings of this
hamlet.

The house belongs to his own mother.

It never crossed my mind: that this village is peopled with
many generations of the same family, that it's normal for a
European village to be full of the people that we emigrant
Americans left behind. For hundreds of years, my neighbors
have been distilled by farewell party after farewell party down
to the people who want absolutely *no change*.

Any day now, DNA experts may map the "we never
moved" gene. They should name it after St-Cergue.

Peter jokes he will run for mayor and, no doubt, win on the
success of his campaign slogan, *PAS DE CHANGEMENT!*
NO CHANGES!

I try to organize the local mothers into a roster for a "Lunch
Club," so that we could take turns babysitting the kids at the
school gym. The system is based on a patrol calender that St.
Boniface parents devised to rid the streets around East Side
private schools of drug-pushers. I propose as follows: one lunch
hour of surveillance per month is required of each mother, and
in exchange, she can send her kid with a brown-bag lunch as
often as she likes the rest of the month.

Three dozen mothers sign up, thrilled at help with lunchtime
babysitting. All but two are outsiders like me.

"It's obvious why you can think up something like that,"
says the plumber admiringly as he replaces the toilet seat he
himself broke four months ago during the first installation job.
"You're a foreigner."

"You'll never get the locals up there to change their ways. Those women *like* preparing a hot lunch every day, it's their *raison d'être*," smugly warns school director M. Villar when we solicit his written support.

Sadly, M. Villar is right. The "Lunch Club" gets off the ground, but never flies higher than the treetops. A hostile curiosity pervades the schoolyard at École Jean-Jacques Rousseau as the local women watch the kids of "outsiders" troop off to "Lunch Club." They lean against their gas-guzzling jeeps and murmur through their anorak collars. If we foreign mothers don't cook a decent hot lunch for our kids, and we're not doing the nine-to-five down in Geneva, *what are we doing with our stolen time? Who the hell do we think we are?*

Peter is short-tempered these days with my inability to see the positive side of village life. When I complain that life is boring here, his curt response is, "Of course there is intrigue in a village. Lots of it. Nothing but intrigue." He sips his morning coffee quickly.

"Yeah, right, the raging passions of the lady who runs the tourist kiosk. I'm talking about big-time intrigue – diplomatic secrets, arms dealing — "

"Arms dealing? Everyday life as a foreign correspondent, I suppose . . ."

"Well, not every single day, but people, events, were un-predictable. They told great stories. They lived great stories. It wasn't such a bad life."

"The life I dragged you away from to give you a six-bedroom house in a ski resort, three children, and the freedom to write your mysteries." Peter frowns, discouraged. "I thought you wanted a different life." He's getting that testy sound in his voice.

"I never said that. I liked my life as a foreign correspondent. It just wasn't compatible with raising three kids without leaving them in the care of some hired person, which I don't want to do. But that doesn't mean I signed up for life in purdah. At least in New York, I could have lunch with old colleagues from *Business Week . . . "*

V. raises an eyebrow with disapproval as he eavesdrops on our marital tiff. He hisses urgently, "*Madame,* curb your discontent! When a man has left his youth behind he needs a woman of easy temper. The burden of affairs makes such consolation all the more necessary. "

He then indulges in one of his least appealing habits – sticking small bundles of snuff up his nose.

Peter looks at the coffee machine. "Is that machine hissing?"

"You're going to be late," I answer glumly.

Angered that he's made to feel guilty for going to the office during Christmas week, Peter reacts defensively. With just enough of a displeased clink of his C-SPAN mug on the counter, he exits for work.

My husband has a point. I was hardly addicted to the adrenaline of the battlefront, but he's figured that out anyway. My beat was business and politics – China's boom and bust economic cycles, the Taiwan issue, the Hong Kong property market, the end of the Colony itself . . .

V. clears his throat and blows half the snuff back out of his nose into a square of fine linen. He's disgusting.

"Arms dealing? Exactly what do you know of arms dealing? Wasn't it you who accused me of profiting from the war trade? Hmm?"

"I've had my moments of intrigue," I protest weakly.

He looks skeptical. "I tried intrigue myself. I wanted to be a diplomat, a go-between, an *intriguant.* I actually offered to spy on my friend, Frederick the Great."

"You?" No one as indiscreet, as vain, as *out there*, as Voltaire could pull off diplomatic spying.

"It's true," V. insists. "On October 20th, 1740, the ruler of the Austro-Hungarian empire died, leaving the throne to the young Maria Theresa. All eyes turned to Prussia where my friend and admirer, the young Frederick not-yet-so Great, was visibly aching to use his army of 100,000. Was my philosophy pupil going to turn out to be a warmonger like all the other kings?"

This grand introduction has not deterred me from clearing the breakfast dishes. Irritated by the indifferent bustle around him, V. stands to attention, "I wrote to the French minister, Cardinal Fleury, and offered my services as Secret Agent for France."

I stop, cups and saucers balanced mid-air, and shake my head. "A spy for Versailles? They'd just run you out of town."

"Yes, well, I was determined to raise my standing a little around court by winning Prussia's friendship for France."

"Wasn't Fred already a friend of France?"

"*Eh bien*, he was under-impressed, you might say, by King Louis' military record. As Frederick said to me, an army that runs away for three years in succession and is defeated every-where it shows its face, is not exactly a troop worthy of Caesar or Alexander."

Always the perfect gentleman, V. carries a single dirty cup to the sink. "None the less, I left Paris with secret instructions from the Foreign Minister Amelot to make clear to King Frederick the danger that threatened him from Austria, which had just attacked us in France. I would induce Frederick to ally with the French."

"You just turned up in Prussia for a chat?"

"Ah, *non*, you're right, I needed a pretext. So I contrived a very public quarrel with that ass of a Bishop of Mirepoix, and I wrote to Frederick that I wished to find refuge with him at the Court of Prussia. The Bishop was, of course, informed that I had insulted him."

"He didn't mind his new international reputation as an ass?"

"Oh, yes, the old bishop complained to King Louis who assured him that his ordained asshood was agreed upon for state reasons."

Something tells me that insulting Church leaders is a typically misguided Voltairean start to his new espionage career.

"Of course, I got Frederick to pay all my expenses for my journey."

"You were spying for King Louis. Why didn't he pay?"

"Oh, I had a separate deal with Louis that my cousin became the French army's supplier of food and uniforms, with a percentage for me. Then I negotiated a cut from the Brothers Pâris for the food supplies I had already procured."

"So to recap, you were a spy for peace paid with war profits?"

Ignoring my insinuations, he continues, "*Meanwhile*, I set about my mission. For three months, I waged my secret diplomacy, first from Frederick's palace in the Hague. Through the aid of the Prussian Ambassador's mistress, wife of an influential Dutch official, I obtained copies of secret agreements between states hostile to France. I passed to Versailles exact information about military expenses and strengths of the Dutch troops."

"That's not bad," I concede.

"Then I proceeded to Berlin where I used all my flattery and wit to persuade Frederick to ally himself with Louis."

"So far so good. Now," I slam the dishwasher door shut and start up the machine, "exactly where did you go wrong?"

He stiffens with surprise. "Why do you ask that?"

"I start to know you."

He sheepishly mutters, "The French ambassador to Berlin felt upstaged by my scheme. He informed Frederick he was nurturing a spy in his bosom. Frederick started opening my letters — "

"You were probably opening his — "

" — whenever I got a chance. But I think what he really didn't like was paying me back the three thousand thalers he owed me for publishing his critique of Machiavelli in France; that and my travelling costs."

"In short, Fred didn't like paying for the pleasure of being spied on?"

V. straightens his sleeves and brushes croissant crumbs off his lacy cuff. "Well, that hardly justifies starting the First Silesian War over the Austrian succession. Eight years of bloodshed because I wanted my outlays repaid! Really!"

I laugh, agreeing wholeheartedly that this is an instance of expense account bickering gone horribly wrong.

I look at him directly. "That wasn't the real reason."

"No," V. admits, "Frederick allied himself with France on and off when it suited him, but no thanks to my efforts. You see, *Madame*, intrigue does not always live up to its reputation."

"Well, you blew it with your Berliner. Now listen to my story about a German arms smuggler. Your mistake was assuming there was intrigue waiting for you. I assumed there was no intrigue at all, but boy, was I wrong."

"Is this a true story or one of your thriller efforts?"

"It's true. In fact, I'm so afraid that the villain might turn up at my door for revenge, I'm going to change the names."

"The weather that January morning of 1989 is cold and humid. The office windows leak wet gusts and our secretary, Dorothy, empties the plastic bin of the dehumidifier twice before lunch.

"Dori Jones Yang had hired me away from the *Economist* to *Business Week* only a few months before. It's early days for me with a new publication. I have to prove myself.

"Our two workspaces are divided by a sliding cardboard partition somewhat warped by steamy summers. Our swivel chairs are upholstered in plastic leather so cracked the stuffing pokes through. McGraw Hill's steel-and-glass tower on the Avenue of the Americas in Manhattan is a far cry from these low-rent accommodations.

"Dori thrusts a telex from New York at me and asks off-handedly, 'Can you look into this? I don't think it'll come to much, but we have to answer it anyway.'

"I can see Dori's working flat out to finish a cover story. The pressure is obvious from two telltale signs; she's forgotten to remove a metal hair clip before leaving home this morning, and she has immediately scattered the top of her desk with M&M candies, her deadline fuel.

"A little discouraged, I scan this tag end of a job. New York asks us to follow up a curious news item coming out of Germany. A chemical weapons plant capable of producing both mustard and Sarin gas is close to completion in Rabta, Libya. A Hong Kong company, the innocuous-sounding Wing-wing Trading, appears to have sold equipment made in Germany by Von Stall Chemie to Colonel Gaddafi. Yesterday, Dr. Von Stall appeared at a press conference in Bonn denying all knowledge of the deal.

"'Oh, God,' I sigh. 'Lemme read this again. Von Stall equipment sold by a Hong Kong company was photographed in Libya . . .'

"Dori laughs a little apologetically. 'Yeah, it sounds like a wild goose chase.'

"'I'll make some calls,' I say. Rousing myself, I stalk stoically a couple of blocks through the clanging streets. All umbrellas seemed perfectly aimed at my eyeline, garbage clogs up the gutters, and anything that makes Hong Kong a glamorous tourist destination seems to have taken refuge on the far side of the island.

"I ride the soulless elevator up to Hong Kong's very un-picturesque Office of Business Registrations to set off on a paper trail. I call for Wing-wing Trading's file number and wait twenty minutes in a crowd of teenage Cantonese office boys. I wish I had remembered to buy a sandwich on the way.

"A harried clerk slams a tower of tape-bound government files on the main counter. A rugby scrum breaks out while the files, grubby cotton tapes flying, are handed out. I flip through the thin Wing-wing file. It seems that Wing-wing Trading is owned by a textile firm, Wing Trading Corp. That means another quarter of an hour's wait to open another anorexic file revealing that Wing Trading Corp. is run by a certain Martin W.W. Chong and Cecilia P.K. Tso, directors of something called Q&K Secretaries.

"Back to request Q&K Secretaries, to surface from the basement archives. The file contains only a couple of sheets of paper and enjoys a cross-holding arrangement with yet another company bearing the curious name, Kwok Medical Center.

"The lunch hour is crawling past me, while I wait for Queen Elizabeth's loyal clerks to wipe the curry chicken noodles off their chins and rummage through their basement of battered folders yet again.

"I feel desolate. I let myself be lured from a decent beat analyzing Chinese Communist politics at the *Economist* for a career at *Business Week* plugging up little holes in other people's stories. Pile after pile of bound files slam down on the front desk. My number for Kwok Medical Center is finally shouted out over the running hubbub — "

Voltaire looks worriedly at his empty mug. "Is this a long story?" he asks.

"Longer than your spy episode, but not as long as your actress murder," I say pointedly, annoyed at his impatience.

"If there are more of these files to wait for, I'd better boil more water," he says.

"No, now it gets more interesting . . .

"Kwok Medical Center's file is much fatter, and I wend back through quarter after quarter of unimpressive earnings, to come across an inexplicable shift in the company's fortunes. Kwok was founded by a couple of Germans back in the seventies to trade in Chinese herbal medicines. Hippie healing had fallen on moribund times, but they struggled along on tiny profits. Then in 1984 control of the limping Kwok Medical Center shifted to the mysterious Cantonese cotton-trading duo in Mongkok, the directors of Wing-wing."

"So there was a German connection!" V. lights up.

"Exactly. I jot down the addresses, noting that Wing-wing's Chong and Tso live in the same Kowloon apartment, possibly as man and wife. The Wing-wing operation sits in Mongkok, Hong Kong's most crowded industrial district — "

" — and as far from the desert wastelands of Libya as one could imagine," V. comments perceptively.

"Indeed. When I emerge from the Mongkok metro station, it's pissing with rain. The neighborhood is a wilderness of rackety trams and double-parked trucks. The sidewalks are impassable, blocked up with hawkers selling hot chestnuts or tacky baby clothes. I get to Wing-wing's office block – you have to imagine – cement corridors stinking of dog shit – this is the secret hideout of a global poison-gas fiend?

"Inside the nondescript offices of Wing-wing Trading Corp. and Kwok Medical Center there are these two secretaries slurping curry noodles and tea. They just gape open-mouthed at this *guay-po* arriving out of nowhere."

"What's a *guay-po*?" V. interrupts.

"Cantonese for foreign devil woman. I start to introduce myself, and trip over bales of cotton samples. They start giggling behind their hands. Bundles of fabric are blocking the entry, piled on the shelves, everywhere. I glance inside Chong's inner office door and – surprise, surprise – the International Sarin Smuggler is out to lunch. All over his office I see these Rotary club plaques and jokey desk toys – I mean, obviously this guy is just one of thousands of little nobodies running textile businesses across the Chinese border. A medical center? There isn't a pharmaceutical degree in sight!"

"Much less a signed portrait of Gaddafi," V. adds.

"Precisely. I stop near the front door, you know, just to think. I've lost an hour. And I'm standing there by the fax machine, and I notice the usual list of auto-dialling codes on the wall. I expect to see area codes for China or Britain. But no – the first six area codes are for Germany, Liechtenstein, and Austria."

"Another German connection!"

"Well, it's something unusual. I write the numbers down, although I still feel a bit of a jerk.

"Back in the office, Dori's spirits are flying high, working with inserts from our colleagues in Tokyo, Seoul and Paris. I tell her all I've got are six note pages of shareholdings and addresses of these dummy companies that trade cotton shirts."

Voltaire interrupts, "You didn't abandon the hunt?"

"I was tempted. It was typical Hong Kong. You're a businessman, *Monsieur*, but you don't know the Chinese mania for sequestering wealth behind a string of nominee companies."

"Well, I bought and sold a lot of properties in my time," shrugs V. "But I didn't trust shareholdings after the collapse of Law's banking scheme bankrupted the French Crown. Do go on."

"Well, just when I'm about to give up, I notice something in my notes. Before it became a meaningless plaque on Mr. Chong's mildewed wall, Kwok's offices were in the Central district. And there's a time gap between the German herbal hippies and the cotton-trading Rotarian. So instead of listening to Dori munch M&Ms, I take a taxi to the address – a spooky, old colonial low-rise in the oldest part of Hong Kong. Next to a heavy mahogany door upstairs, there's this elegant teak signboard painted with the names of about two hundred companies. I've stumbled into an office devoted to managing 'shelf companies.'"

"Shells? Seafood vendors?" Voltaire looks startled, trying to follow.

I laugh. "No, companies that just sit on shelves and hold other companies."

"Fascinating . . ." My friend Voltaire takes a note, I fear for his own future financial shenanigans.

"A beautiful secretary ushers me into the office of Mr. Woo, a whip-thin Chinese in pin-stripes. We drink jasmine tea while the willowy Iris looks up Kwok.

"'Oh, yes, I remember the Kwok sale, about five years ago,' says Woo. 'A European stranger came here in person. I believe he left his card. It should be here in the file.'

"Iris deposits the Kwok ringbinder into my lap. An oversize piece of pasteboard, an almost royal calling card, has been punched and ringed, along with the company papers. It reads: 'Dr. Gerhard Von Stall, Managing Director, Von Stall Companies.'"

"*Extraordinaire!*"

"Yes! Just like that! Sitting in my lap! Photocopies of letters, bank records and shareholdings, showing how the 'innocent' son-in-law of the patriarch of the German chemical giant Von Stall Chemie walked Hong Kong's streets like, like, well, a spider weaving a web to avoid international sanctions selling chemical weapons to Libya.

"He purchased Kwok off the shelf and then opened a new Swiss bank account in Hong Kong for it, giving Kwok a 23% shareholding in the venerable Von Stall Chemie GMBH, which would have been worth millions to the hapless 'director,' the Rotarian Chong, had he ever known. His account application has telefax numbers identical to Von Stall's Liechtenstein branch – the same numbers I copied off Chong's wall back in Mongkok. Then Kwok opens a Hamburg subsidiary in 1987, allowing the deadly Von Stall equipment to be sold to a German entity with a Hong Kong headquarters, thereby evading export control laws.

"Like a good German schoolboy, Von Stall entered Kwok's business purpose as, 'trading chemicals outside Hong Kong.'"

I lean back and beam at Voltaire. His third pot of coffee sits untouched. His mouth is hanging open.

"Did you get him?"

I blush only a little.

"Not alone of course, but I supplied the missing proof. U.S. Defense Intelligence Agency officers photocopied the documents the day after *Business Week* published its eight-column story. Dr. Gerhard von Stall was convicted and sentenced to five years in prison. *Stern* ran a two-page photo spread of him in a nifty pair of handcuffs. It made a handsome wall decoration for our office."

V. is shaking his head in wonder. "Quite intriguing."

"You might have made a good spy if Frederick hadn't been so quick-witted."

"To be sure," V. admits. "To be sure. Your own German was a monumentally clumsy *intriguant*, if I may say so."

"Don't be jealous. They say every criminal has a tell-tale *modus operandi*, a sort of operational calling card that can be read by the well-trained eye. In my case, the culprit left his actual calling card!"

V. sniffs. "Never underestimate the arrogance of the Germans, or for that matter, the aristocracy in any century. And you realize, when you set out that ordinary rainy morning, you could not have imagined the day would end in international triumph. You didn't think you would find anything so fascinating, hmm?"

I don't like where this is heading.

"You're hinting that I shouldn't dismiss the possibilities of village life in Switzerland?"

"Perhaps?"

"All right, I'll stop saying it's dull. For example, there's something weird about the local ceramist — "

He nods, " — making teapots with the spouts that look like — "

"Uncircumcised penises!" I burst out laughing, "Have you seen them in the window next to the *tabac?*"

"Tasteless kitsch! Madame de Pompadour put France's state budget back on track by setting up her porcelain factory. You could use a Madame de Pompadour here, if only to improve the quality of the handicrafts."

"Tell me about Pompadour," I urge him. I'm afraid that he's going to make his excuses to run off and leave me alone making lunch. He's always busy with something.

"Once I've finished my new entries in the *Dictionnaire Philo-sophique*." V. strolls away, murmuring, "Hmm, shelf company."

Like I said, things are getting predictable around here, even the ghosts. However, I was determined to hear more about Pompadour later.

A Morsel for a King

During my years in England and China, a fellow Californian was following a different path.

A lanky screenwriter whom no one could call a classic beauty, she was blessed with humor, a broad smile, and a self-protective *sangfroid*. When we became friends in Hong Kong, she hadn't yet written the first of many award-winning movies. She dropped a dead-end affair with a married film director to marry a rising leading-man. To read later that this "action" star was worth over three billion dollars to the film industry made me feel momentarily dizzy as I recalled my girlfriend's insouciance during their on-set courtship.

The tabloids reported that the husband preferred carpentry and car-collecting, home and kids to carousing or clubbing. Theirs was a marriage that defied the Hollywood odds, a "happy ever after" ending.

Until this Christmas. After more than twenty years of well-documented togetherness, Mr. Perfect goes off the connubial rails no less publicly. A formal separation is announced by both sides. My girlfriend disappears from the pages of the glossy mags, to be replaced by a doll-sized, doe-eyed television actress hanging on the Star's arm up and down red carpets from Hollywood to Deauville.

So much for fairy tales.

"Leszczynska, that's her only option," V. comments, crumbling a doughnut and reading the paper over my shoulder. The sun is rising a bit earlier now that Christmas has passed, but is still low enough to streak almost horizontally across the kitchen and bounce off my late mother-in-law's pewter coffee service.

"Did you just sneeze into my Bran Flakes?"

He groans. "No, I said, *Leszczynska*. Marie Leszczynska, Louis XV's Polish-born queen. That's the only role your friend will play from now on. Don't tell me royalty is dead in the twenty-first century. In my day, kings, not actors, dispensed fortunes like that. This man earns millions of dollars just for appearing on stage — "

"On film — "

"Appearing *professionally*. Let's pass over the pittance I paid my own actors, even though I always gave them all my ticket earnings. What this man is paid an hour is more than King Louis XV got for a lifetime of going to the toilet in public, even if I calculate the exchange rate conservatively. That makes your friend the Queen, just like Marie Leszczynska. Sweet, religious — "

"Come to think of it, she's very keen on the Dalai Lama — "

He nods as he applies a dab of marmalade to his doughnut. "Yes, I know the type. Queens typically go all pious as they mature. Tolerant, patient, religious – and dumped. Your friend is the Official Wife and has no choice in the face of the King's infidelity, but exile or acceptance."

"There's a third option nowadays. She's hired Tom Cruise's lawyer."

"Very practical, I'm sure. Now, our Polish Marie was a practical girl. Her father was sitting in Lorraine, deposed from his throne. Where could she go? She chose acceptance. Mistresses quaked as she passed. The little Madame d'Étioles did everything she could do to please the Queen, and as Madame de Pompadour, she lasted twenty years in the King's bed."

"I don't think my Californian friend wants to put up with a Pompadour."

"Billions are at stake. Influence, contacts. Will she risk exile? I don't think so. These newspapers will lie to the vulgar public, but of course, within the walls of royal society, The Courts of New York and Hollywood know all. I predict an accommodation."

V. fans his napkin like a feathered plume. "Society women don't change. I can hear them gossiping from here. 'The King's taste for his Consort has faded, *c'est évident.* Just look at this photo! She has reached *un certain âge,*' they twitter."

"Times are different." At forty-nine, I'm squirming.

"After forty, women are old," V. says.

"Are not!"

"*Mais oui!* She's an old woman. But she can still rule Society, like Marie Leszczynska. And should she not be grateful? Louis was faithful to Marie for far longer than anyone expected. They had many children together. But then his duty was done. Nothing endures forever."

"What makes you so sure?" I ask. "You never lived in New York."

"Oh, *Madame,* I know the salons of New York without stepping foot on Park Avenue. Gradually, my old friend Madame d'Étioles, now elevated to Madame de Pompadour, worked her magic on the King. Don't forget, I was invited back into royal society. I was appointed Official Historian. I dined at their table."

"That must have been a relief after all those lonely years in Cirey."

"Actually, it was stifling."

I refuse to abandon my rosy optimism, even if it rests uneasily on the gossip columns. "It says here that my friend and her husband may be getting back together."

V. sighs, bored with my naiveté. "*Madame,* after working his way through the Nesle sisters and who knows how many other mistresses, King Louis suffered a sudden illness in Metz. He panicked and rediscovered religion. He ran back to his Queen

Marie on bended knee. All of Paris rejoiced, the streets were filled with hysterical crowds who called him 'Louis the Well-Loved'. It lasted until the beautiful Pompadour crossed his path in the hunting grounds of Versailles."

"What was she like, Pompadour? Hot stuff, huh?"

V. rolls his eyes with appreciation. "Raised to be a 'morsel for the King,' that's what we called her. White skin, soft cow eyes, wonderful sense of style, beautifully dressed. But what I recall best was her wit, her delightful singing voice, her virtuosity at the keyboard – an excellent musician, a brilliant actress! Trained to seduce the great seducer himself."

Should I confess to V. my own seduction of my husband?

My mother always said, "Either an old man's darling or a young man's slave." At least this was more practical than her other adage, "Never drink more than two martinis with a man you're not engaged to."

The buddy role with Sean hadn't suited me. Was I ready for the "old man's darling" bit? And did the man have to be so very old? I was only thirty-six and deep down inside, I knew that when I reached forty, some would think me old, just as V. said.

I redecorated the dilapidated harbor-view apartment on Victoria Peak in Hong Kong. I changed Sean's museum-white, glass, and chrome New York modernity to a pastel mélange of Easter almond yellows and pinks set against white wicker furniture. I tossed mohair and lace around the living room, bought silken underwear and new sheets. More hard-nosed than ever in my work, I softened at home, let my practical haircut grow long, sewed an ankle-length red coat, splurged on a pair of absurd party earrings from which dangled tiny filigree bottles that could hold perfume.

Though I desperately needed to replace my rusting Honda Civic, I even plumped down an impetuous $2,000 for an ageing German grand piano. My Versailles was ready.

Miraculously, the man appeared. I knew he was the Louis of

my life, with his noble profile and courtly, gracious European manners. He presided over a diplomatic reception as the new International Red Cross delegate to Asia like a visiting prince. We were introduced by a fellow reporter, the correspondent for the German daily, *Handelsblatt*, who smiled on with the calculations of a Richelieu.

Like Pompadour driving her carriage between the King's horses and hounds in the hunting ground of Versailles, I bided my time, content to be viewed. I resolved that any new courtship in my life would consist of more than comparing notes on personnel changes in the Chinese politburo over a bottle of cheap wine at the Foreign Correspondents' Club.

Unlike Louis XV, Peter had neither Queen nor illegitimate bastards, but at the age of forty-seven, there was the faint whiff of jaded dissipation creeping up on his chiseled features and generous mouth. After years of overseas missions for the Red Cross – negotiating cease-fires and assisting war victims – his string of girlfriends was mythic back at Geneva headquarters. I heard "court" gossip during lazy junk outings on a hot Sunday afternoon on the China Sea. At dinner parties where diplomats and journalists mixed, there was curious speculation. Would this eligible bachelor seek a consort in Hong Kong?

"Pompadour and the King finally met in 1745 at the Masked Ball of the Yew Trees," V. says, as we climb home from the village. We're wrapped in coats, shawls and mittens, but V. still insists on his morning constitutional. Madame Weber has been disappointingly short on gossip this morning and V. has resorted to buying the French weeklies for the latest on actresses and the corrupt doings at the Monaco Court and the Quai d'Orsay.

"What a night that was! Avenue de Paris was a river of light, illuminating a double line of coaches and carriages coming from the capital!"

"Were you invited?"

"Of course! All of Paris came! The Ball was open to anyone

in costume and the concierge rented out swords to those not equipped. What a sight!"

"And Pompadour?"

"Ah, don't rush me! Rumors were flying that Madame d'Étioles, as she was then known, had caught Louis' eye. That didn't stop every pretty girl in Paris from coming to the ball to try her luck, but where was the King? Queen Marie had made her appearance, covered in pearls. The Dauphin and his new wife had arrived as the guests of honor, disguised as a gardener and flower girl. But the King, ah, the King, he was very late."

"Then the door to the King's antechamber flies open, the guests press forward and – a parade of trees walks into the room! You see, determined to be anonymous, Louis disguised himself as one of eight yew trees, just like the ones lit up by bonfires and torches along the walkway to Versailles. One of the trees promptly carried off Mademoiselle Portail to a dark corner of the castle."

"To play a new version of 'I love yew'?" I can't resist.

"*Oui*," V. chuckles, "but having made her contribution to ardor in the arbor, the poor Portail made her disheveled way back to the ballroom only to find the real King was deep in conversation with the girl he would soon rename, 'Madame de Pompadour'!"

All very amusing, but I feel I'm becoming more a Marie than a Pompadour these days. Is my marriage slipping into Royal Torpor? We would all prefer to be Pompadour. After the usual morning hours spent at my laptop, I hunt down V. I find him in the guest bathroom, powdering his wig for the day. His vest is embroidered with gold threads and his white stockings fresh and smooth, but he's sending wig powder in little clouds all over the clean sink.

"What were her tricks? How did she keep Louis interested?"

"Pompadour?"

"Yeah. I need some love tips. Everything is so, well — "

"*Sombre*." Voltaire grimaces.

"You feel it too, huh? I'm worn down car-pooling to catechism classes, music classes, dance classes, getting the kids to do their homework. Jesus, just *translating* their assignments takes hours. When I'm not trying to write, I'm taking Eva-Marie to the orthopaedist, Theo to the paediatrician, or Alexander to the optometrist."

I think fleetingly of long weekends spent uninterrupted in bed with Peter, voluptuous, carefree Sundays doing nothing but making —

"Amusements. Entertainments."

"Sorry?"

V. sounds impatient. "Pompadour, of course. She understood the King's profound melancholia." He wipes his engraved ivory comb on a clean bath towel.

"Louis was a dissipated man, fawned over, indulged from birth. Pompadour's trick was to constantly surprise him, amuse him, spirit him off to hideaways, groves, châteaux. Produce plays, operas, picnics, *n'importe quoi*. Remove him from his court, hide him from his diplomatic visitors, do anything to fend off boredom."

I hesitate. "This approach sounds . . . expensive."

V. waves this aside. "She charged it to the state – thirty-six million francs in twenty years."

"My credit card limit is a bit lower."

He shrugs, sending a flurry of fresh powder up my nose. "Your friend bought her movie star a vintage car, *un Austin Healey*. An old car can't be that expensive."

"Fat lot of good that did her. I must do something. After so many years, I must resuscitate my inner Pompadour."

V. looks up, his eyes bright. "An entertainment? A party? Real people at last?"

"You should talk! Yes, real people. A New Year's Eve party. As long as I have to live here I might as well meet some people. It'll be a sort of house-warming for Peter to get some of his friends to drag their unwilling carcasses up from Geneva. Will you help?"

V. skips with excitement. "Yes, yes, but only four days to go. I have no time to erect a theater," he mutters. "There is so little time to rehearse the parts. But Alexander will make a marvelous *Brutus*."

I clear my throat. "Moral support will do. No revealing yourself to my kids. And no yew tree costumes."

"The food must be really good," he mutters to himself. "Nothing would be more tiresome than eating and drinking had God not made them a pleasure as well as a necessity. The pleasure comes from God."

"As long as the menu comes from you."

By noon, V. has scribbled down food suggestions – in his best English for my benefit.

"This is one meal?" I protest. "Remember who's doing the cooking. What's this? Truffled turkey?"

"*La d'Inde*, you know? The large bird from the West Indies? Find some Jesuits who breed them – one of the few things they produce in which I have faith. The rest, I've kept very modest. No *foie gras*, given your budget. Order the best *café moka* from the islands – Genevan coffee is terrible – and chocolate with double vanilla for sweetening. Make sure the olive oil smells of olives. Do you trust your suppliers?"

"These days we have supermarkets."

"Do you think that's wise? There's still time to order the best from Paris or Lyon. I thought up the cranberries myself as a little *touche Américaine*. Come to think of it, my American play *Alzire* would be perfect. It was a big success in 1736 – all about the cruelty and fanaticism, Spanish barbarity and intolerance in the Americas, and you're an American, so we could —"

"Conquistadors for New Year's Eve?"

"A shortened version of *La Princesse de Navarre*, perhaps? Just a little fantasy I threw together for the Court. My friend Richelieu got the job of King's Chamberlain and commissioned it for the wedding of the Dauphin to the Infanta of

Spain. It was a big success."

At my skeptic glance from under lowered lids, he insists, "*Énorme!* It won me that title of Royal Historian and two thousand livres a year in salary."

He gives my unmade-up face some razor-sharp scrutiny. "You're too old to play the princess," he says, "We'll do it with marionettes — "

"NO puppets!"

"The Genevans *still* prohibit all theatre? Tsk, tsk, pathetic, aren't they? I said they were a cold and complicated people, but I would have thought things had loosened up a little by now. *Bon*, then it's just the music and magic tricks. Eva-Marie must learn not to show the front of her cards by Saturday night. And no matter how well Alexander plays his jazz, he must learn to take a bow properly. You must make him execute it like this."

V. bends his head to buckled knee breeches while his hand makes a supersonic arc through the air.

The next day, he explodes.

"You've taught your children nothing, *Madame, rien!* I can't work with talent like this! Especially when they can neither see nor hear me. Better to use marionettes as we did in Cirey."

"I'm sure it'll be fine on the night. A bad dress rehearsal, they say, means a great show."

V. casts me a warning scowl. "Remember, nothing is punished so viciously as the desire to please – if that desire has failed."

I haven't seen V. this animated in days. He insists that we need ten at the table, minimum. He's crawling up the cookbook shelf like a frustrated gekko in velveteen breeches.

"Where's your Massialot? You know, *Cuisinier royal et bourgeois?*"

"Probably out of print," I suggest.

"Humph! It was good enough for the cooks at Court. What's this, the *Joie* of Cooking? Well, that'll have to do. Damn, if only Bonnesauce were here!"

"You had a cook named Good Sauce?"

"For 180 livres a year. Worth every coin."

I know he's thinking less of my cuisine than his audience for this little entertainment he's cooking up. That sturdy canvas work apron he's donned is all for show; it's me pulling out the pots and pans. Even as Peter is finding last-minute guests, I'm having second thoughts just looking at Voltaire's menu.

I invite one fellow U.C. Santa Cruz buddy, a rather mercurial television producer of "Believe It or Not" segments, to drive down from Paris. He will help me face our Swiss guests with their elegant culinary expectations for *Le Réveillon*, as the French term New Year's Eve. If the middle-class Pompadour faced down the taunts and whispers of Versailles as she braved their rude verses and mockery, I can do this, I will do this for my Louis, but I need at least one trusty friend at court.

I re-examine V.'s menu. He's a Versailles vet.

Red and black caviar on star-shaped puff pastry
Oysters on ice
Sherried parsnip soup with hazelnut and basil garnish
Lac Léman trout
Partridge pie
Truffled turkey
Épinards in sauce Béchamel
Gruyère, rampon, bean gratin à l'Italienne
Salade mélangé, assorted cheeses and biscuits
Compote of Seville orange in honeyed white wine dressing
Caramelized flans with candied zest and Grand Marnier praliné
Cranberry nut tarte with sauce caramel and vanille glacé

"But the *pièce de résistance*! Aha!" he crows with excitement. "We will serve them an exotic treat at the end of the meal. Something they will never, ever, forget!"

"What? What? What?"

"BANANAS! In winter! You will be the talk of Geneva!"

Poor V. means well, but disaster looms. Since I've arrived in St-Cergue, I've avoided contact with Geneva, the strange Calvinist, exclusive manners of Genevans, and their insular social judgments. It's going to take more than out-of-season fruit to make the evening a success.

"How the hell am I going to serve all this, much less cook it?"

No answer from my co-host. V. is busy preparing the "grounds." He's inspired Eva-Marie to gild empty peanut butter jars for hanging on the branches of all the pine trees near the garage, and place votive candles inside. A trail of more little candles will sit on mounds the boys fashion by overturning my salad bowl filled with snow along the walkway in front of the house.

I gaze out of the kitchen window as he points proudly to the mounds.

"A corridor of fairy lights to mark the entrance of the Court," he explains. "Once Pompadour, dressed as 'Night,' led us through the dark forest to a clearing where she had a troupe of players waiting to play for the King. The guests, even Louis himself, picnicked on logs and stones. It was a great success. What do you think? *Mon Dieu*, it'd better not rain."

I glance down during this distraction at a caramel sauce that has suddenly granulated into something like maple sugar. My furious expression is all the answer V. needs. He backs off before I can caramelize his wig.

"*Bien. Une idée, simplement.*"

I can't keep track of V. after that, although I hear laughter and wild violin bowing coming from the playroom. The cooking proceeds, less by inspiration than by putting one pan in front of another, hour after hour. I'll break it to V. later that I'm skipping the truffled turkey, but at least I found pigeons at the supermarket to fill in for partridges. The fresh trout will give Peter a last-minute errand to keep him out of my hair. I'm investing a paint-by-numbers faith in cookbooks, clearing out the freezer for sauces and gratins that seem to multiply upwards like stones of the Egyptian pyramids. You don't know how the Egyptians got to the pinnacle, but they did.

Ed, my familiar face at "court," arrives from Paris with his own wild card in tow – an opera singer, a cuddly Russian beauty half his age with the improbable name of Khatuna. They have known each other all of three weeks, he explains with the delight of a boy who has found a new toy. She speaks Georgian, Russian and Italian and clearly adores my old friend, hugging and snuggling and cooing to him, "*Ours, ours.*" Bear, bear.

Peter gives me an amused glance. "I have a feeling I know where she does her best singing," he whispers.

"Do you think she's one of those illegal passport hunters? Where will we put her at the table?" I ask Peter on the night. "Compared to everyone else, she's another generation. Which one of your guests can babysit in Italian?"

"Maybe Jean. He's got a summer house in Tuscany."

I try to imagine the aristocratic Jean spending his New Year's Eve next to the lusty Russian. Ed good-naturedly volunteers to prepare the pile of seventy-five oysters. An hour later my oven mitts are stinking, frayed memories of their former selves, but sixty-nine glistening oysters are on ice-filled, foil-wrapped cookie trays laid outside in the snow under the rising moon. Six bad oysters have been tossed aside in the bushes. I think of the smell luring wild cats that haunt our back cliffs, but what can we do?

"There wasn't any room in the fridge," Ed explains, and heads upstairs to change.

"*MADAME!*" Voltaire shrieks, rushing in from the dining room. "Who laid the table? Where is the gold and silver plate?"

"I don't own any gold or silver plate. That's my best china."

Voltaire throws up his hands. "*Mon Dieu!*"

The rest of the guests arrive in a sudden downfall, like an avalanche of snow poured from the inside of a tourist van.

That's how I'll survive this evening. I'll be a tourist attraction, I think, with my faulty French, Americanized food, and missing footmen. Flowers and bottles fly around the kitchen. Everybody is kissing everybody. Jean and Christine's tiny daughter, Charlotte, is swept off by my kids to the playroom. Estelle, the new baby of Peter's former Hong Kong assistant, Catherine, is settled upstairs in my office in a carrycot, right next to V.'s invisible oxygen experiment.

The Court of Geneva has descended on our little Versailles. Nobody notices Voltaire, standing at the door bowing to each guest, a preposterously happy grin on his face. The women from Geneva are dressed like Calvinist priests in sober black pant-suits devoid of adornment, their men in sober dark suits – hardly festive gear.

Voltaire is dressed entirely in crimson velvet. It hasn't occurred to me, preoccupied with my own new isolation, that V. has spent far longer than me waiting for the good times to roll. Something over two hundred years.

A Cat Can Look at an Oyster

Already I can see that one guest has come to have a bad time. While the arrivals are tossing off their heavy coats, offering champagne bottles, and distributing presents to my over-eager children, a woman slightly older than myself is muttering, "I'll keep my coat on this evening, thank you. It's so cold in these mountains! And all those curves! I'm completely carsick! How can you stand the commute, Peter?"

I feel like sinking through the kitchen floor. Or kicking this prematurely gray spirit, Ghislaine. Pompadour had beauty and charm to spare when dealing with the powerful women of Versailles, the royals who mocked her. I lack those advantages, but there is no time to brood. V. flies across the kitchen behind the cluster of guests, snow fluttering off his wig.

"The fairy lights were a grand success. Where did that infant go?"

"To the office."

He's horrified. "To my suite? You've already put that Irish-American and his Russian *coquette* in my bed!"

Just then Ed and Khatuna descend from Voltaire's rooms into the living room. It's hard to know where to look. They are resplendently overdressed, he in a tuxedo with green satin cummerbund and she in sequins and a very tight skirt.

I catch sight of the unhappy Ghislaine smiling to herself meanly at the over-the-top foreigners from Paris. I'm already christening her the Duchess of Geneva, a Calvinist bastion of restraint and rigidity.

"The caviar stars by the fireside!" V. prompts.

The guests settle themselves strategically, the elegant Jean inquiring of Catherine, "Where do I remember you from?" Catherine's doting and obedient husband, until very recently her imperious, dashing boss, is singing the baby to sleep upstairs while she sips her aperitif downstairs.

V. whispers to me, "Jean reminds me of the Duc de Richelieu – when he finally became first Chamberlain to King Louis – like Richelieu, he immediately tries his hand with the prettiest girl in the room."

"I was a guest in your own house at your own table less than two years ago," Catherine pertly replies to Jean. Beneath his handsome features, Jean blushes with embarrassment at betraying the forgetfulness of age. Jean's wife, Christine, hides an indulgent smile.

"That is just like Richelieu," V. nods. "And his wife, Christine, just like the Duchesse de Richelieu, full of *sagesse*, with smiling blue eyes."

"Enough about Richelieu. I'm worried about the oysters and the wild cats," I mutter to V. "I thought I heard some wailing outside."

The party is under way, and V. and I can safely sneak out of the kitchen door as Peter pours out drinks and stokes the fire with the help of Roger, Ghislaine's husband. Ghislaine has made such a point of her chilblains that she has been accorded a prime chair near the hearth.

Christine is trying unsuccessfully to make conversation with Ghislaine, quite unconcerned at Jean's flirtatious efforts in Catherine's direction. Ed and his songbird are cuddling at the end of the sofa.

I'm stunned by the frigid air that slaps my cheeks. Foggy day has turned to polar evening.

And the oysters have turned to – ice.

"They're frozen to the front lawn!" I gasp.

"*Oui.*" V. says lamely, staring down at Ed's improvised platters of oysters frozen solid in their juice to the snow. The plume on his party hat blows low over his brow.

"Quick! Do something! You know the French. They've got to have their oysters or the whole evening doesn't count as a New Year's Eve."

"Worse, *Madame*. The French have a sense of humor. You have a roomful of Genevans. They have no sense of humor whatsoever —Wait!"

He suggests we fetch Theo's "Little Carpenter" IKEA tool-kit. I try to saw the ice away from the trays while V. wields the pliers. The oysters won't give and the saw breaks instantly. V. runs into the house again to look for more tools just as I see two ominous feline silhouettes slink through the pines. They rest on their haunches just outside the margins of the flickering candles.

Four green eyes calmly survey my panic.

"Scat! Shoo!" I start throwing pine cones to scare them off.

The eyes don't move. These are warriors of the cliffs, hardy, sharp-clawed hunters. I've seen them attack each other, put out eyes, fend off huskies, polish off hedgehogs. I've no doubt there were moments when Pompadour's entertainments in the woods hit obstacles. I wonder what Old Pomp would do with these circumstances.

"*Voilà!*" V. is back brandishing fireplace tongs. He makes a fulcrum from a log and together we fix the iron rods under one of the trays and shove, stomp, and kick. Despite his unathletic build, V.'s concentration is only too successful. One of the cookie sheets flies loose, thirty oysters fly skyward, then disappear into the deep snow. There is a satisfied growling sound from the starving onlookers. We scramble to excavate our oysters with our bare fingers. The nasty, savage cats lower their heads and move slowly forward.

"*Allez-y!*" V. roars, flinging the tongs at the cats. They back off angrily, knocking over a fairy light, but retreat no farther than the circle of light coming from the house.

Through the living room window I spy our guests chatting amiably.

"*Huîtres!*" I announce brightly, only a few minutes later, floating graciously into the living room with trays of oysters.

I watch the grimaces of pain as the guests realize that what I have served is not so much oysters as "oystercicles." Jean gallantly shows how a little warm breath and a dollop of lemon juice will loosen them from their shells, and following his example, they finish them off. Ed takes a bow for his manly shucking. We move to the next course in the dining room.

"What's in this soup?" demands Ghislaine, the Duchess of Disdain.

"Celery, onion, leeks, shallots and — " I hesitate. In English, parsnips might sound acceptable, but the French for parsnips is "country turnips," and I realize how rustic and ill-chosen this will seem for New Year's Eve customers expecting lobster bisque.

I play for time, "Um, I can't remember . . ."

"There is *quelque chose*,"the Duchess presses me.

"Hazelnuts," I smile.

"*Non, non, non,*" she smiles back, and I feel her teeth as if they were in my ankle. "Something a little — "

I put down my soup spoon and surrender, "Something a little *WEIRD*?"

"*Oui . . . Étrange . . .*"

Suddenly four guests rise to their feet and leave through the kitchen door. To throw up? I look up at V. in total dismay. He's enjoying Khatuna's *décolletage*. He shrugs in confusion. Peter addresses me from his throne at the other end of the long table.

"Smokers," he explains. "I just told them about Theo's asthma."

Ed is laughing at Khatuna. She has found no common language at the party and so is making kissy faces at her lover across the table. As I clear the empty soup plates, I find all but three of our guests standing blue-faced, wrapped in blankets, sucking on cigarettes, stamping their feet and no doubt, comparing notes on turnip soup, the Duchess among them. Six feral silhouettes watch them from the shadows of the pines, licking their paws.

"Never have I been forced to leave a New Year's Eve just to smoke!" Ghislaine protests.

The trout and pigeon courses are survived, eaten even, as a sort of accompaniment to constant cigarette breaks. Catherine's husband is so addicted to tobacco that I realize he's hosting a smokers' New Year's Eve party outside.

Towards the end of the main course, Ed insists I open his "hostess gift." He's just finished shooting a documentary about miracles and has brought us a plastic bottle in the form of the Virgin Mary containing genuine water from the Shrine of Lourdes.

V. shakes his head with amazement to see such a thing in the twenty-first century.

The Duchess of Darkness hasn't given up. She challenges Ed from the other end of the table. "Surely you don't believe in miracles and all the rest of that Catholic, well, myth."

It's obvious she was about to say the French equivalent of "drivel." As a free-lance producer, Ed's favorite miracle is probably a paycheck sent on time, but since he doesn't like the Duchess, his face betrays an urge to make mischief.

"Well, more than sixty miracles have been attributed to Lourdes and tested by independent science," he says, straight-faced.

"But in this day and age, surely . . ." Catherine equivocates with slightly more charm than the Duchess.

"Absolutely proven, documented by outsiders, including atheist medical experts," the joker Ed persists. His twinkling Irish-American-Catholic humor shines forth, leaving the

Genevans unsure. Is he pulling her leg? Have they fallen into a den of Papist fanatics?

I scramble to serve the salads and cheeses. Jean sneaks into the kitchen to find me struggling with plastic bags of pre-cut lettuce.

"You're not supposed to be in here," I protest, as he empties the leaves on to the waiting plates. "You'll have to pretend you saw me wash this stuff."

"Why do you think we all buy it in bags?" he says with courtly forgiveness.

I realize with complete shock that with six courses down, punctuated by frequent sessions of glacial smoking, it's already 11:35.

"Where the hell is the entertainment?" I quiz my co-host. I suspect V. of breaking his usual rule of coffee only, as an opened champagne bottle left in the kitchen is looking in-explicably empty.

"Here they come," V. signals with a flourish of his hand, and I see my three costumed children descend the stairs over-looking the dining table. Alexander is carrying a box of magic tricks, Eva-Marie has sparkles in her hair. Theo is carrying a wand. Little Charlotte is watching my older kids, fascinated.

They circle the table of overfed guests, each child addressing one person, and then another in rotation. I hear their sur-prisingly professional magic spiels with delighted surprise as they tackle these strangers with their, "Can you believe it?" "Please tell me when to stop," "Now take a card," "Please choose the middle card," "Tell me what you see," and so on. There is laughter, and good-natured, "Oh, I know this one," "I'll take this one instead," "No, no, I want to take that one!" V. is darting around the table, unobtrusively adjusting a card here, smoothing down a handkerchief there.

At last, I start to enjoy the party. As the show nears its conclusion, Theo slips off to the living room, and we hear the first strains of a half-sized violin playing by the fireside, heralding the fast-approaching turn of the New Year with a "Russian Fantasy," by Portnoff. The guests move through the kitchen back to the fireside. Encouraged by his audience, Theo puts impressive energy into his bowing. The music quickens and crescendos, climaxes and finally, Theo takes his bow. I see V. in the corner nodding with an impresario's approval – off the beat, but who's to know?

The Duchess suddenly speaks. "He has touched my heart," she announces to everyone. "Come, Theo. Let me kiss you."

Who needs Lourdes for miracles?

The stroke of midnight sounds with the recorded cry of a mullah calling the prayers of an Islamic dawn. From Peter's bedside table, V. has stolen the Bahraini clock-radio Allen gave me in England, and has set the alarm for twelve! There is laughter from all of Peter's old friends who remember their shared missions in Beirut, Aden, Kabul and Kandahar. Missions in the Middle East and other war zones on this of all nights are remembered, and toasted.

Amid much kissing all around, I take a picture of Ed happily crushing his starched shirt in a passionate embrace with Khatuna.

Alexander takes his turn at the piano with a piece of jazz and everyone sips more champagne. Somehow I find Peter in time for a kiss, as I listen to the mellow riffs that without warning bring a painful yearning for New York. But this wave of nostalgia is broken when Eva-Marie replaces her brother at the keyboard with a rousing "Indian War Dance."

"Why is she playing with all five fingers rounded, even using her thumbs?" V. asks. "I never noticed that before. She looks like a monkey clutching at the instrument."

I am bewildered. "Well, how would you play?"

"With only three middle fingers, and flat, not curved," he says. "Everybody plays the clavichord like that." He shakes his head, muttering as he wanders off, "I've never seen anyone play so strangely . . . imagine, the whole hand!"

"And now Khatuna'll sing for us," Ed announces proudly.

And now I'm worried. I have no evidence that we have an opera singer in our midst and I wonder how much proof even the besotted Ed has.

"Did you have a chance to rehearse this?" I ask V. He shakes his head, no.

All eyes and ears rest on Khatuna. To my surprise, she stays seated. What opera singer sings sitting down? Social panic closes in on me. There is a terrible silence of judgment about to fall from the Duchess of Sour Notes.

Ed sits erectly in a chair next to Khatuna, his lips pressed together in a tense smile.

Nothing comes for seconds. She looks at Ed, her hands clenched tight.

Slowly, a low note rises up out of her high bosom. My first impression is that at least she's singing, and it takes a few seconds to be sure that what we are hearing is a pure alto-soprano voice. She has chosen to start with a Georgian folk song, and the low notes reverberate around the hushed audience. I watch Ed's lips smiling more easily now as he beams proudly through two folk songs.

I think of my college girlfriend who married Ed long ago. B. committed suicide so young, almost as young as the girl who is sitting in front of this room of strangers twice her age.

"I talk to B. every day," Ed confessed to me once. How many years since she left us? I've forgotten and feel guilty. I watch Khatuna and wonder whether this rosy-cheeked, button-eyed girl is a harbinger of happiness. Ed and I are fifty now, I think. His hair is white and thinning, his belly straining at the cummerbund. I am no longer François' long-legged, sun-kissed California girl. Ed is no longer B.'s maverick love, the water-balloon king of U.C. Santa Cruz.

I hear my guests burst into applause and Khatuna smiles, relieved. Then she stands up and belts out a Donizetti aria like a pro.

The evening draws to a close. It was not a complete disaster, although the verdict of my King has yet to be heard.

"Have you had enough?" the Duchess asks Roger. We can't tell whether she's referring with *ennui* to the festivities or his liquor intake. She turns to Peter and confesses as they depart, "Thank you for the invitation. I should explain. I didn't want to come this evening for one simple reason. I grew up in this village and hated every minute of it."

My boys have disappeared to the third floor and collapsed, still dressed, in their thick duvets. Charlotte, still robed like a Richelieu princess in layers of festive purple taffeta, is snoring on the playroom floor. The unwatched *Pocahontas* video dribbles softly in French.

The indefatigable Eva-Marie is playing caroms expertly against Jean by the fireside. As the little wooden disks ricochet into the corner pockets, V. watches nervously. "I hope she's not playing for money. Émilie was always calculating the odds, but one night in Versailles, she lost heavily."

"What was heavy in your day?"

"Eighty-four thousand livres. I warned her, in English of course, that she was playing with cheats." He clears his throat, recalling his ill-timed *lèse-majesté*. "Unfortunately, one or two onlookers understood English. We had to evacuate the court the same night."

"Party was over, huh?"

"*Totalement.*" He nods his head with regret at the abrupt loss of his day job as Court Historiographer.

Slowly, coats are gathered, the baby bed collapsed, Estelle carried away in Catherine's arms, the heavy-lidded Charlotte wrapped up in a heavy blanket, farewells and good wishes exchanged once more.

Outside, a few of V.'s candles still flicker bravely from the pines, although some of the glasses on the mounds of snow have cracked open from the cold. V. and I spot a tell-tale oyster shell pushed into the snow and surrounded by cat prints. We exchange smiles with conspiratorial relief.

Peter waves off the last of the guests. My husband, who claims he needs no social life, who has no "real friends," who first seemed indifferent to the suggestion of a party, is flushed and happy, loving and young. Despite the early morning hours, that persistent look of harassed fatigue has disappeared from his face.

We sleep late the next morning. In the afternoon, life resumes some normalcy. Our first holiday season in our new Swiss home draws to a close.

V. finds me throwing a dozen white napkins in the washing machine and emptying the third load of plates from the dishwasher. We discover a flower pot on the terrace table filled to the brim with cigarette butts.

He is looking slightly less perky than usual. He winks at me over the high collar of his best white *matelasse* dressing gown, with its oversized buttons lining the wide cuffs and the six gold-tasseled bows on either side of the lapels.

He clears his throat, politely raising his eyebrows. "How was the King this morning?" he ventures.

I blush a little, thinking of my exhausted husband left sleeping off his happy dissipation and connubial pleasures in our chambers.

"I don't think Pompadour would have complained at the royal reaction."

"*Bien.*"

Birth and Death in Exile

My offspring have fallen in love with the movie *Casablanca*. Theo seems especially impressed when the raffish Vichy officer, Captain Reynaud, switches allegiances to join Rick and the Resistance. So I am not too startled one day by the following scene: our Polish-American friend, Joanna, arrives from New York on a working visit from her office with Human Rights Watch to observe the Geneva session of the U.N. Commission for Human Rights. Theo knows that Joanna is fighting for the "underdog," and he greets her formally at our front door in a home-made Vichy uniform. He gives her a snappy salute and announces, "Unoccupied Switzerland Welcomes you to St-Cergue!"

Certainly, St-Cergue does seem removed from the world, the least likely place to find reflections of a post-Cold War Switzerland seeking a new identity. It's hard to believe that Switzerland holds more foreigners per capita than any other Western European country, even Germany; foreign-born residents comprise 18% of the Swiss population, compared to 9% in the U.S.

And four of those foreign-born are us.

Moving here requires rotating my psychological compass. It takes more than a few months for the body and mind to shift its deepest bearings, to automatically reckon the new time zones between my aunt in Detroit, or e-mail buddies – in Beijing,

New York, Buenos Aires and Harare – and me. I slowly shift my sense, not only of this place, but of my new coordinates on the broader map.

"You're not the first," says V. Despite the cold weather, he suggests a walk into the hills overlooking the village. Alexander, worried his mother will lose her way, offers to come along.

"I'm only going to see the Vieux Château," I tell Alexander, repeating Voltaire's proposal.

"You won't find it," Alexander warns me.

"Sure I will." I've completely misread the skepticism on my junior historian's face.

Huge clumps of snow thump off the overhanging pines as we set off. Voltaire hobbles along in those hand-made boots, leaning on his walking stick.

"To defend their property around here, the good, ahem, monks of the Abbey of Saint-Oyens nearby decided in 1279 to build a château that could overlook the entire lake all the way to Geneva and beyond. And because they were monks, they inveigled the wealthiest neighbor, the Seigneur de Thoiry, to build it for them. It was constructed on the ruins of a look-out left by the ancient Romans."

"You won't find it," Alexander sings to me, shivering hands thrust deep into his anorak.

Sure enough, after twenty minutes of hard climbing, we arrive at a breathtaking summit with a clear view of the Alps, Lac Léman, and Geneva shimmering in the distant haze.

"Where's the château?" I demand. V. is futilely thrashing at the bushes with his stick for traces of a thirteenth-century castle.

Alexander stands facing me, hands outstretched in frustration. "Mama, I've been trying to get your attention all the way here. The château was destroyed in 1476 when Charles-the-Bold took refuge after his defeat at Morat. The Bernese promised to rebuild it, and sent an engineer, but . . ."

"Well, I'm pissed off. I was promised a thirteenth-century fortress."

"By whom?"

Should we break the news to V. over there, scrambling around on his hands and knees, scraping at underbrush, and muttering to himself, "Damnable monks!"

"Come here, Mama," says Alexander. I follow him to the edge of the precipice. "This was the highest lookout of the Roman cavalrymen sent to Nyon by Julius Caesar. In 1958, two archaeologists excavated this site. They found nine skeletons right here, all buried facing that way," his thin arm stretches south-eastwards, towards Rome. Proof we are hardly the first and surely not the last to adjust our bearings in exile.

Europe, too, is shifting its bearings and its center, broadening out to embrace tentatively the east. Meanwhile, is my version of Switzerland – which extends roughly from Peter's first floor office in Geneva up the lakeshore coast of suburbs and mounting the fifty-five curves from Nyon to St-Cergue – is my little corner of this country in a state of social flux?

As far as I can see, no.

One of St-Cergue's old "ruling families," the Jaquet clan, still holds primacy, thanks to their ownership of a fleet of mammoth snow plows. They've held sway in an unbroken line from their eighteenth-century dominance of the cowherd chalet rentals in summer to the management of the hockey team at the turn of the last century. Some things don't change.

Occasionally the outside world intrudes. One morning the mothers in the schoolyard gossip that a bearded man wearing a Kosovo Liberation Army insignia had been seen waiting for a train. The Albanians buy some of their arms down in Geneva. What was he doing up here?

Likewise, rumors fly when a Russian mafioso's wife tips a maternity nurse at the Genolier clinic a thousand francs, fresh from the laundry of some Genevan bank.

Such are the ripples of contact with the darker world that lies east of us. Supposedly there are some 40,000 Chinese immigrants poised on the border of the former Yugoslavia just waiting for "snakeheads" to smuggle them westward. Please, I pray, drop off a couple of decent Sichuanese cooks at the base of our hill. I wait in vain.

There is a Bosnian refugee family living in an apartment at the top of the little ski run behind our road, but this is small beer compared to the immigrant influx down in Geneva. The father cleans chimneys and the mother cleans houses. Both look exhausted as they climb the steep slope to their *quartier* every evening. One day in the parking lot, I'm asked to sign a petition to allow the immigrant mother and father to work legally. As a Swiss-passport holder, I sign, thanking God that the entire village is not exercising a similar door-to-door referendum on me.

During World War II, St-Cergue filled to bursting with Polish, Russian and Dutch refugees, the grocer M. Reymond told Alexander. "They built and repaired half our roads."

Most of the foreigners renting the chalets sprinkled across our mountainside are indeed refugees, not from war, but from recent layoffs at Digital Corp. They're hardly the type of person who would linger in Rick's Café offering to trade a night of illicit passion with Captain Reynaud for an exit visa.

There are other echoes of Switzerland's situation squat in the middle of Europe.

The Swiss daily, *Neue Zürcher Zeitung*, recently published the Zurich city map issued by Moscow to K.G.B. spies during the Cold War. The best dead-letter drop-off points and anonymous meeting places are carefully transcribed from Swiss-German into Russian Cyrillic letters. Peter finds this hysterically funny, deciphering over dinner the names of his favorite streets and hangouts from the clumsy Russian transliteration back into Zurich dialect. A quick glance shows that the Zurich Zoo Cafeteria was an espionage hotbed.

The faint echoes of that Switzerland, a neutral zone peopled by trench-coated Le Carré wannabes lurking in the Cold between East and West Europe – the memory of that Switzerland – resonates around this map as a quaint joke.

Even St-Cergue was the center of intrigue only fifty years ago, as the only outing allowed the Eastern bloc communists assigned to diplomatic missions in Geneva. Every weekend, our little village became a Swiss version of the old Bullwinkle cartoon – alive with duplicitous Natashas and their panting Borises swapping secrets and having illicit love affairs.

All in all, one has to admit that at least it was a useful Switzerland. To what purpose now is this Switzerland in the very heart of Europe, yet holding itself aloof, from a European Union about to admit Poland, among others, to its ranks? Time and again, the Swiss vote against union. This conservative sentiment has leaped a generation from the ageing mountain-fast Alpine villagers to the internet-surfing eco-protesters in their twenties fighting the anonymities of corporate globalism. I'm surprised to feel a sneaky admiration for this resistance. After all, what is so appealing up close about the black economy of Berlusconi's Italy, the corruption of the Chiracs and Dumas in Paris, the racist neo-Nazis in Germany and Austria?

This is not to say Switzerland isn't still Europe's *mittel*-ground, a half-way house for the merging worlds of post-Yalta, post-Berlin Wall Europe.

I confide to Joanna that I've yet to meet anyone in St-Cergue with whom I've got any common interests besides raising children. She's quick to sympathize.

"It's odd you've never run into Dzidka Kierkowska," she says. "I haven't met her, but we have mutual friends in Geneva. She's an actress from Krakow who supposedly lives just up the street from here in the apartment complex at the top of the ski slope. She's exactly your age."

"An actress?" V. speaks up from his revisions of *Mérope*, a play he claims earned him the first calls for "author!" in the history of the theater. "A professional actress? Here in this backwater?"

I'm happy to see my Ghost-in-Residence perk up. Since New Year's Eve, he's been ailing with one complaint after another. He announced one morning that one of his teeth had fallen out. I was horrified, but he's taken this dental disaster in his stride.

"Just another consequence of a malady with which I was born, Life." He shrugs. He tosses his tooth in the wastebasket, where it vanishes from sight.

"No wonder you don't eat. That's the third molar you've lost since I met you."

He looks surprised at my distress. "*Madame*, everyone has within him, from the first moment of his life, the cause of his death. We must live with the foe until he kills us."

He's looking older every day, complains that he is "an old man," that anybody over forty has no right to feel as old as he does. Or did he say fifty? Happily, the news of an actress in the neighborhood brings a smile to his face for the next day or two.

"Aren't you a little old for actresses?" I tease. "Just this week you were saying that you'd given up women, even your dear Émilie, at the age of forty-six out of sheer physical exhaustion."

"Poor Émilie found my amorous retirement hard to accept," he acknowledges. "I don't suppose it was much of a comfort to her that I delivered the bad news as poetically as I could." He waves an ink blotter in the air, marking the rhythm of his lines:

> *Si vous voulez que j'aime encore,*
> *Rendez-moi l'âge des amours,*
> *Au crépuscule de mes jours*
> *Rejoignez, s'il se peut, l'aurore.*
> *On meurt deux fois, je le vois bien,*
> *Cesser d'aimer et d'être aimable*
> *C'est une mort insupportable,*
> *Cesser de vivre ce n'est rien.*

A Visit from Voltaire

Du ciel alors daignant descendre,
l'amitié vint à mon secours,
Elle est plus égale, aussi tendre
Et moins vive que les amours.
Touché de sa beauté nouvelle,
Et de sa lumière éclairée,
Je la suivis mais je pleurais
*De ne plus pouvoir suivre qu'elle.**

"You gave up sex at forty-six because you were too old? Peter didn't even marry me 'til he was forty-eight!"

He shakes his head, which makes his wig shift slightly back from his balding forehead.

"She'd worn me out. Well, you know Émilie. She didn't take it well. I suppose my suggestion we be no more than friends was a sad surprise for her. She had a very ardent nature and had to take hot baths every morning to subdue her needs."

"That's okay, I don't need to hear the details." I'm blushing.

"I agree. Let's change the subject. When does the Polish beauty visit?" he asks, brightening up.

"This Saturday, for a buffet lunch. The Polish actress, her

---

* If you wish me still to love,
  Bring me back the age of loving,
  In the twilight of my days,
  Revive if possible, the dawn.
  We die twice, I see it well,
  To cease to love and be lovable
  Is an unbearable death
  To cease living, that's nothing.
  Then deigning to fall from heaven
  Friendship came to my rescue
  Steadier and more tender
  Less lively than affairs.
  Touched by her new beauty
  And by her illuminated light
  I followed her, but would weep
  To be able to follow only her.

professor husband Henryk, Joanna's two Polish friends Dzidek and Beta, who are international human rights experts, and a Polish explorer who at sixty-five is about to launch a solo crossing to the North Pole. His name is Jurek."

"Just like Lunéville!" he exclaims. "Just like Maupertuis' expedition to Lapland! Oh, how well I remember it! He came back with two Lap sisters, both his lovers. Exotic trifles, but hard to discard later."

"Looneyville? I know my New Year's Party was shambolic, but —"

"Tsk, tsk, Lunéville, *Madame*, the Polish court-in-exile in Lorraine, where Madame du Châtelet and I were forced to take refuge after the gambling incident in Versailles."

"Oh, that."

"Yes, that. Well, I couldn't stay shuttered up in the Château de Scéaux forever, could I? I hid out there for months, writing one little novel after another to amuse my hostess, the old Duchesse du Maine. Let's see, I wrote five short novels —

" — only five, think of that — " Here I am still struggling with that damned Tibet mystery. I hate him.

He ticks them off on his bony fingers, "*Babouc, Memnon, Scarmentado, Micromégas, Zadig* — "

"Where was Émilie?"

"Oh, busy paying off the 84,000 livres she lost at the gaming tables, and apologizing to those scoundrels. Everybody promised to forgive and forget, especially the biggest cheats, but still — " his voice trails off. Émilie, it seems, was left to fend for herself.

"Who was in this Polish court — ?"

" — in-exile. You recall Maurice's father, Augustus the Strong had kicked out — "

"Why King Stanislaus Leszczynski, of course! Wait a minute. That means you fled Versailles and the wrath of Queen Marie by taking refuge with — "

He flashes a wicked smile. "Her father! Why not? Émilie

finally joined me from Paris, and after we'd sorted out a Châtelet family lawsuit in Brussels, we headed for Lorraine. Oh, Émilie could be so charming, she quickly became the bosom friend of the King's mistress, Madame Boufflers, and her two other lovers, the King's Chamberlain and Jean-François, the Marquis de Saint-Lambert, and all would have been well, until — " his face clouds over. He clams up.

"Until what? What happened?"

To my astonishment, after mentioning this Saint-Lambert person, V. turns and exits the room without explanation, his dark expression racked by some awful memory.

For the next few days, he barricades himself in the office.

"Do you need anything?"

He groans. "Usually asses' milk helps. Or maybe a small grilled ortolan with a glass of Alcante wine on the side? And if there's any mail, or the chemistry books arrive from Amazon, give them to Longchamp."

Ortolans? Imported wines?

"Need I remind you that your secretary isn't here?" I retort a bit tartly. I hear a discouraged whimper. "Are you all right in there? Open the door!"

"I'm weak," he moans. "I have lived to be fifty-eight years old, with a very feeble body, and have seen the most robust die in the flower of their age: care has saved me until now. So let me die in peace."

"Hellooo? You're already dead! Get up and help me put together this lunch. This is my chance to meet the few sentient life forms who live in the village. What do you have against Poles all of a sudden?"

The door opens and his unshaven, grouchy face appears momentarily to say, "I have nothing against Poles! I am merely dying, *Madame*, dying. But for God's sake, don't call a priest!" Then the door shuts, not too gently, in my face.

He has struggled with ill health for some weeks now, that's true. I was so used to him being sick with one complaint or another, I stopped taking any special notice.

"Shall I call a doctor?" It sounds absurd to suggest medical treatment two hundred years after death.

I hear his voice, muffled by a thick scarf, "Each man must be his own doctor, must live by rules, now and again assist nature without forcing her; and above all, he must know how to suffer, grow old and die."

"Well, suit yourself," I say, clearing away his tray from the floor outside his door, "get well by Saturday."

He descends the stairs on Saturday, just as the bells of the two churches in the village finish their daily chime-out for God. He's wearing a spotless coat of dark rose brocade and white stockings under blue-black breeches. He's masked his sallow complexion with some powdery paste, but at least he smells wonderfully of lilac water.

The seating at the table is a puzzler, but at this V. is an expert.

"I assume French is our lingua franca," he asks.

"That's your wishful thinking. Joanna speaks Polish and English. Jurek is bringing a girlfriend who speaks only Polish. Peter and I speak English and French, of course, but no Polish. Jurek, Dzidka and Beta speak Polish and French. Luckily, Henryk and Dzidek speak all three.

This social conundrum reminds me of those children's riddles: "Mr. Green has a dog and lives in a white house. Mrs. Smith drives a Ford and lives next door to Mr. Black. Mr. Baker has a cat and lives in blue house. The owner of the brown house drives a Studebaker . . . who drives a Fiat?"

Jurek arrives first with a nearly-mute girl half his age in tow. He's an attractively gnarled Antarctic trekker. Were his remains to be found frozen in some iceberg, no doubt the defrosting team would nickname him, "Sinew Man." His teeth, the result of decades in Eastern Europe's socialist dental chairs, are no setback to his glamor.

This seasoned adventurer has brought us a present, a large

poster of himself standing at the South Pole. He is butt-naked save for Arctic climbing boots. I blush to notice that Jurek is a very fit sixty-five, and that makes him nearly twenty years older than V., yet Jurek seems in no mood for sexual retirement. He holds a small Polish flag positioned modestly in front of his groin. The poster's slogan reads, "Oldest to the Coldest." The unfortunate axiom that men can become more attractive as they age and women less so, was never better illustrated.

I dart into the kitchen for dishes of nuts and olives and find V. supervising Peter's uncorking of the wine.

"I think that's a pretty jazzy introduction, handing out nudes of yourself. I must try it before it's too late!" I exclaim.

"I think he's sucking in his stomach a bit obviously," Peter comments.

"The verse is acceptable, but the flag is very *small*," adds V. Both men seem a little snappish these days on the question of virility, and Jurek is a walking advertisement for hormonal endurance.

Joanna, beautifully dressed, descends the stairs, leaving me momentarily wistful for Bloomingdales fashion ads in the Sunday *New York Times*. Despite our repeated protests, she's weighed down with presents for the children. Amidst the flurry of unwrapping Beanie Babies and Star Wars Playing Cards, introductions get temporarily muddled.

In her immediate wake come the thick-set Dzidek and his blonde cherub-faced Beta. Then lanky, professorial Henryk, as courteous as a count, with his lately-gained bride, the willowy star of the Krakow State Theatre, the actress, Dzidka. She is dressed like a modern Rosalind, in slim black pants, a long slim black leather jacket and a red shirt.

"My actress?" V. rubs his hands eagerly.

"She's all yours," I laugh. "Maybe Peter and you can show her his collection of Polish theater posters, and I'm sure she'll tell you all about her career." Peter and V. do just that, while I quickly cook the mussels in white wine and parsley and set out

the thick, crusty *pain de levain*. The freshly-plucked ducks from
the Divonne open market are turning crispy brown on the
oven spit. When everyone has been warmed with a drink, and
the mussels are popping open in their broth, we sit in the
winter sunshine wrapped in blankets and briney steam.

There is so much life and warmth among these people. I
realize that none of us is home; each of us, including my
husband from his Alpine roots to the north, is an immigrant to
this place, but is it more than that? I'm feeling a robust Slavic
lust for life that would shame the correct Anglo-Saxon, over-
whelm the Calvinist Genevan, horrify the overbred Parisian,
and challenge even the reputation of the "salty" Cantonese,
"hot-blooded Irish," and the earthy Koreans.

" . . . That was a drama for us already when there was the
vote over Poland and N.A.T.O.," Dzidek is saying, "because it
was really a reflection of whether, finally, we were going to be
accepted by the Western Europeans, as members of the European family. And for us this was very, very important. You
could hear everybody in Poland practically holding their
breath. It was going to reverse something that we felt had been
done to us at Yalta, saying we weren't really part of Europe."

It strikes me viscerally where I am, literally, sitting. I have
never lived so far "east" of the "West," so close to what I was
raised to think of as the Iron Curtain countries. This existential
shock hits me with renewed force.

"Some of my colleagues in Geneva have the same reaction as
you," Dzidek jokes, "especially when I make a short visit to
Warsaw for a long weekend. They are always shocked to think
that Warsaw is just an hour and a half away by plane. It's
nothing, nothing."

Indeed, Jurek has just driven from Poland this weekend. Yet
for me, Eastern Europe's invisible curtain lingers, psycho-
logically as impassable as the invisible wall that barricades
Buñuel's diners in *The Exterminating Angel*.

"I'd like to visit the Eastern bloc," I muse vaguely.

"Too late, you missed it," Peter jokes.

"What was it?" V. asks no one in particular.

Dzidek chuckles. "We joke now that for twenty years we were told to 'Think Party and Say Lenin,' then for the next twenty years, 'Think Lenin, Say Party,' and all we can do now is laugh and shrug our shoulders and admit that for the last forty years, we were saying one thing and thinking another!"

And what Dzidek and Peter are trying to convey to my American mind is that Eastern Europe as it sits on the compass of my imagination – that remote, gray, no-man's-land of barbed wire minds and German shepherd borders, of second-guessing the machinations of Karla, of Len Deighton's Berlin-buried moles – that territory is *gone*.

Voltaire has no inkling of my 1950s Cold War images. His century also saw the disintegration of eastern Europe from the Holy Roman Empire into dozens of state-lets. But the sinister totalitarianism, I realize with a shock, was not in the East for V., but at home in France, headquartered in Versailles and anywhere the Church and the whims of the nobility persecuted his freedom of speech.

For him, Russia of all places, was the home of his devoted correspondent and imperial German-born pupil, Catherine the Great, trying to smash feudal shackles, not forge them. Compared to France, the east of Europe was a fluid region of experimentation and change. The French King persecuted V. and all his *philosophe* friends, while in Moscow, Catherine the Great hosted Diderot to dinner and let him slap her thigh in his enthusiasm for debate. In France, warrant after warrant went out for Voltaire's arrest, while in Lunéville, he was free to speak his mind. And more and more, the safe haven of Frederick the Great's Potsdam (sixteen miles from Berlin!), beckoned V. from Émilie's embrace.

How can V. encompass, during his stay at my little farm-house, the extraordinary shifts of fascism, socialism and communism that took the East hostage, kept Spain sclerotic, and left the English, French and West Germans together, battered and embattled, but free to speak their minds?

My guests are busy studying an atlas spread across the remains of the lunch. Jurek is tracing his proposed route across Antarctica. No one has noticed V.'s distraction. Court life goes on.

Voltaire seems preoccupied with working off his strange, private melancholy. He collects himself just enough to ask me, "*Madame*, have you forgotten the coffee?" We all take our cups inside, abandoning the fading sun and escaping the inevitable chill for the comforts of the fireside.

All language barriers have been broken by good will and fine wine. It no longer matters where people sit. Using the excuse that, he of all people, can't find a place to settle himself, Voltaire discreetly slips up the stairs. I watch his sad figure retreat. What is wrong with the greatest literary courtier of the Polish Royal Court?

Double Delivery

"Why are you so troubled by memories of Lunéville?" I ask V. as we launch back into work on Monday. He's rewriting his play *Sémiramis*. After its first première, he listened in disguise to the exiting audience. Working from notes jotted down on that long-ago evening, his pen is flying this morning.

Watching him from the other end of the room, I'm swamped with the envy of a worker bee watching a talented butterfly. I'm thinking of dumping the Tibet book. I'm not Voltaire and there are only so many times I can revise something before rejection makes me collapse inside.

I try distracting him again. "So, why the big melancholy?"

"Please, *Madame*, if you will allow me to tighten this dialogue for Lekain, you know . . . brilliant actor . . ." he scribbles away. "There! With that, I'll outdo Pompadour's favorite playwright, Crébillon! In fact, I've set myself to do a new play based on each of his themes – *Sémiramis* will just be the first – that'll show him up, the tired-out has-been!"

"You seem in a better mood now."

He casts an irritated eye in my direction and at last the furious pen is laid aside.

"Oh, all right, I'll tell you. The morality of Lunéville was even more debased than in Versailles. King Stanislaus shared his Madame Boufflers with his Chamberlain. The King showered her with compliments, praised her skin, her eyes, the whiteness of her throat, but if she became bored with the old man, he just left the room, saying, "All right, I'll send my Chamberlain to finish the job."

I laugh at the decadence of Stanislaus. "Why would that upset you?"

V. clears his throat, hesitating over some difficulty. "*Alors*, well, here I was, in a beautiful palace, a free man, my host a king, with all my historical books and references, and with Madame du Châtelet. And I was one of the unhappiest creatures on earth."

"Why?" I insist.

He lowers his voice and leans towards me as if making a shameful confession. "Madame Boufflers had a third man in her bed, the *so-called* poet Saint-Lambert. Even in Lunéville, three lovers at a time was a little *de trop* — "

"Over the top?"

"Exactly. Saint-Lambert was forced to sneak in disguise into La Boufflers' rooms once the King and his Chamberlain had finished for the night. Such a charade became tiresome to Saint-Lambert, not a greatly energetic man despite his good looks."

"I still don't understand why — "

"This game of musical beds had a terrible consequence for my poor Émilie," he explains. "One day I finished work early. I went to Émilie's chambers to fetch her for dinner. The candles weren't lit. I proceeded without hesitation through the dark to the last of her rooms where I discovered Saint-Lambert and Émilie — "

"Oh. I see."

All of V.'s fame and riches, and all of Émilie's brilliance at algebraic formulae couldn't protect them from the passage of time and passion. How shallow and wasteful all of these flirtations and parties must have seemed to V., how foolish and disloyal Émilie's sudden infatuation with a mediocre courtier ten years her junior!

He goes on, "Do you remember when the Polish actress was chatting of her days on the boards in Krakow?"

"When Peter showed off his collection of Polish theater posters?"

"Yes. And Dzidka explained that the end of socialism meant the end of state subsidies for her theater group?" V. sighs. "I too, lost my royal pension when I was exiled from Versailles."

"That's when you whispered to me that it was too bad Dzidka didn't have kids," I say. I am realizing what a blessing the children have been in dragging me into this unfamiliar environment. When life's road bends suddenly and curves away in an unexpected direction, it is dangerous to have only two wheels.

"And I said – I said I supposed it was too late for Dzidka to have children," I fumble.

"I didn't tell you what I was thinking, yesterday, when you said that," he continued. "I was thinking, it was too late for Émilie," V. mutters.

"What do you mean? The Châtelets had three kids. By the time you got to Lunéville, the youngest must have been, let me see — "

He waves these offspring aside. "Oh, the youngest Châtelet was already seventeen. But with Saint-Lambert — "

"She had a child by Saint-Lambert?"

He nods gravely. "Pregnant at forty-three, a figure of ridicule!"

"C'mon, many women have babies now at that age. Madonna, Cherie Blair – having late babies hasn't made them figures of ridicule."

He looks at me, those penetrating eyes filling with sadness, but says nothing.

"I had Eva-Marie after forty!" I protest.

"No one had babies at that age!" He slams his walking stick across the face of my desk. *Sémiramis* goes flying in all directions.

Well, I didn't say it was easy.

Motherhood for me started when I went to my gynae-cologist because a reporting trip to India had left me with a persistent stomach ailment.

"Well, it's not exactly Delhi Belly," Dr. Siu said slowly, reading the test results. I feared cancer – she was sliding the Kleenex box across her desk nearer to my reach. When I heard the diagnosis, I did shed tears – of shock and excitement. Precautions had failed, leaving me feeling this child was some kind of unexpected gift.

Dr. Siu was a delicately-built southern Cantonese. She was sure that at thirty-nine, I would need a Caesarean. On the other hand, my new obstetrician, Dr. Liang, a tall, lumbering woman of China's hardy north, predicted a natural delivery. I thought this was a difference of medical opinion. I was forgetting the Chinese cultural factor. True to Hong Kong's passion for horse-racing and mah-jongg, the two Chinese doctors had laid bets on my endurance over a friendly dimsum lunch. The biggest event of my life was just another good-natured round of Chinese gambling.

As an embryo, Alexander went "on assignment" outside Hong Kong eleven times: at five months' gestation, he bounced along the ring road of Beijing with demonstrating students headed towards Tiananmen Square. He traveled to Taiwan, Shanghai, and points south.

Lying on my back in a Jakarta hotel swimming pool, my nine-month stomach ballooning up to the heavy equatorial sky, I let tropical rain wash my face and abandoned myself at last to physical fate. I could no longer deny his "otherness." This person inside me was going to acquire an independent existence soon.

After twelve hours of painful labor, assisted by laughing gas and Peter's exhortations to breathe, the baby came. Alexander's first seconds of life were celebrated by a Chinese doctor in a yellow plastic delivery apron shouting down a delivery room phone, "No Caesarean! I won! I won!"

Twenty months after Alexander's birth, the edges of my health and nerves were fraying. I was about to give birth a second time. Maybe Voltaire's right. Pregnancy at forty-one was not to be taken so lightly. After weeks of bleeding, Dr. Liang warned, "You may be losing this one. Let nature take its course." Happily, Theo did not want to be lost.

And so soon – the grueling last months of waiting for our Eva-Marie's arrival in Manhattan – slogging that February past shoulder-high snow drifts.

All the insouciance of that first pregnancy was gone. Now I was as fearful as Émilie of losing my strength, my work, my independence. Forget hopping on planes. I trudged no farther than the 79th St. Diner at First Avenue to buy a bran muffin. I was too wrung out to change diapers, to clean rooms or make beds. I collapsed with relief at the first sound of Peter's key in the latch. One evening I realized he'd been tending to the boys for more than an hour, and still had not had the chance to shed his raincoat.

Yes, Émilie, how frightened and how alone you must have felt, married to an old military bore, reduced to friendship by your greatest love, and knocked up by a second-rate dilettante. Listening to Voltaire, my heart fills with sympathy for mercurial Émilie, pregnant at forty-three – so brilliant, so passionate, so foolish, and so unlucky!

"What was worse, the social stigma or her health?" I ask V.

We're taking advantage of some early spring sunshine to collect the kids for lunch by foot. V. insists we exercise every day, though he still recoils at the suggestion of shoveling snow.

"Her health. She fought night and day to finish her translation of Newton's *Principia*. She worked from eight until three, then took coffee, then worked from four until ten, then dined and talked with me until midnight, after which she resumed her work through the night until dawn. This occupation helped her deal with the humiliation."

"The baby's illegitimacy was a problem, huh?"

He chuckles with indifference to that small matter. "Oh, that was easily managed. Saint-Lambert and I urged poor Châtelet to visit us. We wined and dined him while Émilie flirted shamelessly with her own husband and lo! a brief but effective second honeymoon with the homecoming soldier won the future child the name of Châtelet!"

"Didn't he guess?" I shout above the noise of screaming children flooding the playground. I find it impossible to believe the genial Marquis was that stupid.

"Never underestimate the vanity of men," V. wags a finger at me. "The old goat couldn't stop boasting. Behind his back, Saint-Lambert and I discreetly categorized the pregnancy as one of Émilie's 'Miscellaneous Works.' But that was our private joke."

"Ha. Ha."

"I assure you *Madame*, there was ridicule. Even Frederick the Great, who hated Émilie for keeping me all those years from joining his court in Potsdam, even a king as noble as Frederick could not resist composing a nasty little verse of victory over my poor friend:

> A question of a life lost
> In a double delivery
> Of a philosophical treatise
> And an unlucky newborn.
> Who knows precisely
> Which one stole her from us?
> Of this fatal event
> Whose opinion should be followed?
> Saint-Lambert chooses the book
> Voltaire blames the *child*."

Spitting out the last line. V. makes Frederick's disdain quite clear.

"Ah, ha, *les enfants!*" Our conversation is interrupted as we march uphill with Eva-Marie and Theo. I heat up frozen pizzas which the children detest. They are my culinary protest against the school dismissing them at 11:30 a.m. in the first place.

Against the background of a violinist sawing manfully on Dolfein's "Higher Positions" exercises next door, V. watches me clear away the half-eaten crusts.

"A life lost? Now I understand. Is that why you've been locked up for so many days?"

"*Oui*. It all came flooding back to me. The infant, a girl, came without difficulty after all. Émilie felt weak, but otherwise everything was *très bien*. Then, a few days after the birth, on September 10th, 1749, Émilie started choking." V. gazes across the lake at Mont Blanc, still catching the late sun. His voice falls to a whisper. "It was very hot that evening. We gave her a glass of ice-cooled almond milk and dined with Madame Boufflers. Only Longchamp and her chambermaid du Thil and — " he hesitates, covering his eyes with a shaking palm.

"Sorry, I'll tell Theo to stop that."

To everyone's relief, Theo switches to Vivaldi.

"Saint-Lambert offered to watch over Émilie. Ten minutes after we left them, there was a terrible sound between hiccuping and rattling. She fell unconscious. We made her smell vinegar to revive her, slapped her hands and limbs. It was no use."

I reach over to take his shaking hand in mine, but he brushes me off.

"She was gone." He stammers on, "I – I – I asked for the ring she wore, the one which had held my tiny portrait hidden inside. Boufflers had already removed it from her finger. You see, they knew Émilie had replaced my portrait with Saint-Lambert's. It was he who killed her! Whatever gave him the idea of getting her with child!"

V. sobs quietly to no one in particular assaulted by unbearable memories, locked up for so long. Where do everyone's strongest memories go, when they die? All that grief, that energy, that electrical passion left crackling around us? Do the emotions of the dead just drift away like lost radio signals?

"I want you to have this," he says, handing me a yellowed sheaf of papers. "It's Émilie's essay on Happiness," he says softly. "She knew she had lost my passion by then, but I did not realize I would lose her so soon . . ."

For a moment, it seems that he is too overwrought by the flood of memories even to go on. He appears fatigued beyond my limited human measure, worn out by the ordeal of relating it to me. Who could relive all their life's griefs a second time, knowing the pains and disappointments ahead?

Suddenly he takes off his worn wig. The stiff brown ringlets splay across the table. Now, V.'s just another person in middle-age with graying hair at the temples. The gap of centuries between us closes.

I read Émilie's essay out loud to her ageing mate, translating with effort.

"'The ideal would be two individuals who are so attracted, so attracted to each other, that their passions would never cool or —'"

"' — or become surfeited —'"

"' — or become surfeited. One cannot hope for such harmony of two persons. That would be too perfect. A heart which would be capable of such love —'"

He takes the papers from me, "'. . . a soul which would be so steadfast and so affectionate, is perhaps born once in a century . . .' You see, *Madame*, I had not lost just a mistress, but half of myself, a soul for whom mine was made. There would be none like her ever again in my life."

I can imagine that the laughter and gaiety and inflections of French-speaking Polish Lunéville were hardly interrupted by the loss of that difficult, demanding, brash, insecure, passionate French Marquise, her black curls and untidy aprons covered with chemicals, her ringed fingers stained with the ink of calculations, so faithless and loyal all in one. Here in the midst of my best efforts to make new friends, to find a place for myself in this willing exile with someone I love, so far from friends and family, V. reminds me that there will always be people who are irreplaceable.

It is painful to think Peter and I won't be together forever, that after all the years of wrong choices, finding the "harmony of two persons," is, even at best, only a temporary state.

That night, as I sip red wine next to Peter over the remains of dinner, I drink a silent farewell to the long-suffering, headstrong, lovable Émilie.

The Bodhisattva Babes

"You're really coming all this way just to see me? I feel like Sally Field waving her stupid Oscar and squealing, you like me, you really like me! You're coming all the way to Switzerland for only five days?"

"Yes, I can't believe I'm doing this. I haven't even told my bosses that I'm leaving the country. I haven't even told my mother. I took some of my vacation time and said I wouldn't be back until Friday. Natalya's coming down from Boston tomorrow and we leave from Kennedy on Saturday night."

Jane is a "China" friend who works at a New York daily editing overseas coverage. She is bringing her best friend of thirty years, Natalya, whose life intersects with mine in strange synchronicity, even though we've never been introduced. My parents rented Natalya's house for the year I attended sixth grade, just after our move to California. Natalya and I attended the same junior high and high school, separated by two years, and we tangentially shared acquaintances and teachers.

"It is time you two met," Jane says, "it's a karmic necessity, and I am going to make this happen."

I envisage them as timely Bodhisattvas, each representing half of my life – the one a pre-China youth in California, and the other, a young adulthood spent in the Far East. Maybe they've come to signal closure of some kind – come to bury my past, if not to praise it? Perhaps the disjointed chapters of my life will be reconciled somehow?

Moreover, I childishly await their judgment of my new life; if a foreign editor of a major daily and the programs director of a Boston museum deem my isolation on the top of a Swiss mountain as, hey, awesome, then will I feel better? Can I turn my wood and stone heap into a mountain sanctuary, a Tibetan monastery, a Zen retreat, a rustic spa? Will freshly-starched cotton *yukatas*, grapefruit bath mousse, and a long-handled back brush do the trick?

Peter just looks forward to having a houseful of lively women for a week.

"Bring on the babes," he jokes.

The morning of their arrival, the sky above Mont Blanc is an unmarred blue, leaving us awash in a celestial purity of snow and light. However, something is wrong with the frontyard.

"Do you see something poking out of the snow?"

Voltaire thrusts his nose towards the window and proclaims, "The leaves *poussent*." Then he disappears upstairs to bury himself in a rotting, leather-bound tome, *Description of the Chinese Empire*, by somebody named Du Halde. His moldy books flake all over my freshly-vacuumed rugs.

I try again with someone in my own century.

"Peter, what's that sticking out of the snow? Am I hallucinating? Someone planted the yard in a yin and yang pattern?"

My husband, redolent of some after-shave unearthed from the back of the closet in honor of the visitors, follows my gaze along swirls of inch-high spiky protuberances. "When I bought the house, I did see lines of tulips . . ."

"Like this?" I draw the distinctive in-and-out half circles.

"Um. That hippie son of Föllmi, the old farmer, probably planted them. He also brought the trees over there from the Himalayas."

"God has changed her dress," Eva-Marie interrupts.

"Is God a She?" I ask my woman-in-progress.

Eva-Marie nods and sweeping her arm in a graceful arc at the pink and blue horizon, "She changes her dress depending on Her mood. This is a good mood."

"Yeah, but when She takes a shower, it rains," Theo teases.

We must ready the guest room for Jane and Natalya. V. sweeps away the cobwebs from the low eaves. Various mementos of working in China hang around the room: replicas of *Business Week* covers, some photos of B.B.C. film shoots in the countryside. Next to an Overseas Press Club award from 1991 stands a tiny snapshot of me grinning into the sun with some Chinese college girls "sent down" to the countryside during the Cultural Revolution.

That photo dates from 1972 and the girl that was me wears two long braids, like the Chinese trio with their black tresses. These two pieces of cardboard – the photo of me on a Maoist commune and the award earned twenty years later – are the symbolic bookends of my China career.

"You know," V. sighs, "I once championed the Chinese above all the other nations of the world. I studied the Jesuit, Trigault, who explained the Chinese civil service. And there was that other Jesuit, Kircher, who praised the Chinese philosopher-kings. The problem with the Jesuits was that they compared Confucius to the school of that man Jesus. The cart before the horse, *non?*"

"China has changed. The system of civil service exams rotted away two centuries ago. Jiang Zemin ain't no philosopher-king."

"Well, how lucky you were to see the Celestial Kingdom!" Voltaire insists, "That country of virtue and rule of law!"

My first impression of China in 1972 was less of a country of virtue and rule of law than of a country suppressed by lawless Maoism into paralyzing fear. But whatever political dissension, economic illogicality and bloodshed the Chinese successfully hid from their prying American guests during that hot August, nothing could have put me off left-wing revolution more than the bickering of our own band of teachers and students –

hosted by the quixotic Prince Norodim Sihanouk – paying tribute to the Central Kingdom's Great Leader.

It was a rocky tour, and no doubt a traumatic exposure to the West for the Chinese.

From Tianjin, one of our party, a professor's wife, sent home a "Dear John" letter. Our patient hosts relayed the angry husband's pleas from Berkeley via one rural, hand-cranked telephone to another. The Latin American Leninist in our group decided the South Asian expert was a Trotskyist, so those two stopped speaking. Our youngest member broke down because she couldn't take crowds; an untimely discovery when our every appearance commanded an audience of thousands of gaping Chinese on foot or bicycle.

"Does it hurt?" a little Chinese boy in Henan asked me. His mother hastily explained that her son meant no insult. He'd never seen a foreigner before and assumed my blonde hair and blue eyes were the symptoms of a painful disfigurement.

Finally reaching Beijing, our Hispanic member thanked our flummoxed Chinese translators at the farewell banquet for giving him the courage to "come out of the closet." This was not in their Foreign Ministry phrase books.

Twenty years in China followed, but where did it go? Into dozens of notebooks – filled with hundreds of Chinese, interviewed and quoted – now dumped in the corner of my office.

V. dusts his wardrobe with a silver-handled brush. Something must be done with him. I can't stick him in a box with the discarded notebooks.

"The room looks great. I'm leaving now for the airport. Have you seen my car keys?"

"*Ici, Madame.*"

"Good. Thanks. Now what are you going to do while I'm with my guests? Natalya and I will be reminiscing about our Californian childhoods. And you'll be bored listening to me talk to Jane about China. I'm afraid you'll be kind of out of it for a week . . . what the hell are you wearing?"

V. isn't listening, as usual. He is following me out of the house, half striding, half stumbling along in a preposterous outfit of embroidered turquoise brocade that reaches all the way to black cotton slippers with pointed toes. His usual headgear has been replaced with something featuring upside-down Mickey-Mouse ears on either side, festooned by tassels and long ribbons hanging down the nape of his neck. His long, drooping sleeve catches on the car door handle.

"Out of it? *Madame*, I will be deeply in it!" he screeches, yanking at the dangling sleeve. "Did I not dedicate the first three chapters of my world history to the achievements of ancient Cathay? Did I not devote the last chapter of my history of Louis XIV to the bitter arguments between the Jesuits and Dominicans over the Confucian Rites? The Devil with this sleeve!"

I scrutinize him over the top of the Subaru. "You aren't coming to the airport in that get-up."

"We are greeting an accomplished Sinologist, *non?* Was I not the father of modern Sinology?"

His headdress hits the roof of the car as he gathers up the voluminous folds of his silk robe.

"Thank God nobody but me can see you."

"Ah, *La Chine!*" he sighs, as he settles himself next to me. "Do you know my play, *The Chinese Orphan?* I'm wearing the costume of Zamti, the Confucian mandarin! I did everything I could to represent the customs and morals of the Chinese, right down to the style of Manchu dress. Your friend Jane might appreciate it, seeing as she herself is married to a mandarin."

Jane's husband, Wu Ming, is a Chinese academic employed in New York. He researches in Beijing on a half-year basis.

"Give Jane my Chinese play. She must judge how accurately I showed that a truly virtuous monarch could be governed by justice and an absolute absence of religious prejudice!"

"Sounds like a roaring hit. Bring on the dancing priests for the Rites Controversy Revue!" I tease, navigating the curves down the mountain toward the highway.

"Oh, you must at least have heard of it. The loyal Zamti offers his only infant son to be killed by the invading Genghis Khan in place of the heir to the throne. But his beautiful wife Idame, beloved by Genghis Khan in his previous days as a wandering barbarian —"

"A convenient coincidence,"

"A theatrical device! The wife Idame woos the Tartar invader with her virtue until he spares both her infant and the baby prince."

"Doesn't sound like any Genghis Khan I've heard of."

V. bristles. "One hundred and ninety performances in Paris in 1775 say you're wrong, *Madame*. It was based on the play by one Ji Jun-xiang, *The Orphan of Tschao*. What could be more authentic than that?"

I've offended my friend again. This guy is so touchy. He pouts for at least fifteen minutes until I try to make peace.

"Sorry. I never took you for the China-hand type. I mean, what with all your other accomplishments."

"*Madame*, I studied things Chinese for over forty years! Not for me, the *petites chinoiseries* that captured all the ladies – the parasols, the porcelains, the little bibelots of the Chinese export trade."

"No? The Voltaire I know never yet turned down a luxury that money could buy."

"*Mais non!* To me, what was China but proof that the Scriptures did not contain all the truths of mankind!"

Of course. It's all about his battles with the Church again. I should have known.

"Why, Confucius was recording some thirty-six solar eclipses when, according to the theologians of my vulgar era, Noah was selling seats on his silly ark. China was printing books when we couldn't read or write. A nation that can prove its antiquity independent of the Holy Scriptures is a very useful country indeed. The Chinese were deists without the Church, without the Trinity, without a lot of superstitious transcend-entalism, in short, with nothing but tolerance for all."

"I start to understand the big draw."

"Oh, why couldn't France have been like that, with a virtuous monarch with only one priority – like a father concerned with the well-being of his children?"

"I think you idealized China a bit."

"Ah, China, the most beautiful, the most ancient, the most vast, the most populated and the most *policé* in the world. "

"I'll agree on the 'most populated and the most policed'."

He gives me a piercing glare. "*Policé* means well-regulated, civilized, not policed. So civilized that Emperor Qian Long wrote verses. An emperor who writes poetry can't possibly be cruel, don't you agree?"

"You've overlooked that famous painter, Hitler, not to mention Nero, master of the lyre . . . So that's your China? Everybody reciting Confucian sayings and competing to be the most virtuous? Sounds a pretty boring night at the theater to me."

He sniffs. "Well, maybe my Chinese was a little stilted, but that wasn't my fault!"

"Oh, no, of course not . . . "

"Well, if the French hadn't been so damned French, I could've made my Chinese more Chinese and my Genghis a real Tartar! I had to water down my ideas and costumes so as to avoid provoking the laughter of people who mocked anything that didn't match their fashions and customs."

"That's the watered-down costume you're wearing now?"

"Well, it fitted the actor Lekain, so it's a bit big for me – anyway, anything Chinese was all the rage in those days. It was a huge success."

"Goes without saying." China mania sweeping Versailles . . . the Beatles and the Maharishi . . . Richard Gere and the Dalai Lama . . . some things never change.

"Can you drive more slowly? I'm getting carsick." Green-tinged, he slumps into a heap of silk.

Twenty minutes later, I scan the arrivals screen at Geneva's Cointrin airport. Jane and Natalya finally emerge from customs, Jane in Donna Karan nylon sports clothes, Natalya in lycra separates and mules. I feel very "cotton" all of a sudden and count the months since I shopped for new clothes.

We stop off at the street market in Divonne – lanes of fresh fruits piled high in baskets and earthenware bowls, ducks and geese hanging from hooks, spices filling the air, and blue and yellow fabrics from Provençe. Can I pretend that I do all my shopping here in this cover photo for *Condé Nast Traveler*?

I buy our lunch, romantically wrapped in French newspapers and crisp white paper bags. Jane is tempted by the fabrics and Natalya considers hand-cut blocks of lavender soap. V. trips good-naturedly behind us, sniffing flowers, and pretending he doesn't mind being ignored.

"This reminds me of Xin Ping Lu," sighs Jane, referring to the famous Guangdong market filled with butchered pigs, pressed ducks, skinned dogs, gleaming rows of bright green cabbages and scallions, mountains of pomelos and dusty, bumpy red lichees. At last a friend has arrived who can help me connect the dots! This is going to be a great week.

Back at home, we unload the food and launch into five days of conversation.

The weather cooperates. The sun beats down and for a few days, I can watch the tulips tattoo their yin and yang message through the snow. Only Tibetan prayer wheels, flapping flags, and Buddhist gongs are lacking to make this a sanctuary of reflection.

If I had hoped that two women could be my Bodhisattvas, I am not too disappointed, but it's possible they're also taking this break in search of more than my own personal enlightenment.

Natalya goes for long walks every morning. Eva-Marie nicknames her, "The Lady Who's Out Walking," while Jane seems to be catching up on months of late-night calls to Wu Ming in Beijing, for she becomes "The Lady Who's Sleeping Upstairs."

When they're not walking or sleeping, there are the long conversations I long for, the companionship without explanation that anyone in exile misses more than food or weather or streets.

Natalya recalls many forgotten scenes of our West L.A. youth! Like the Latin teacher with the biggest dandruff flakes ever recorded who giggled with titillation when we staged the "Roman Games." Or, the celebrity parents sending their kids to recitals in thousand-dollar costumes borrowed "off the lot" with an indulgent wink from the "wardrobe lady." Whatever became of our fellow students, the offspring of Jerry Lewis, Burt Lancaster and Jayne Mansfield? We review Natalya's years studying drama, her divorce, and single-parenthood.

V. listens wide-eyed. "It certainly doesn't sound like my school days at Louis-le-Grand. The Jesuits may have been perverts, but they never made us act out orgies in bed sheets . . . A shame Natalya didn't continue acting. She would be marvelous as the New World princess in my *Alzire*."

V. manages little better with Jane, with whom he hoped to compare his notes on the Confucian virtues.

"Ask her about the legacy of Confucius. I always said he was the most perfect practitioner of natural religion — "

"Which is — ?"

" — Ethics founded on reason and independent of metaphysics except for belief in God. *Vas-y*, go ahead, ask her."

Instead Jane and I talk of her hopes to pull together Wu Ming's expanding career in China with the financial security of her New York salary. Jane says she hoped a solution to this dilemma would present itself while she stays with us, maybe even while she sleeps? Like those Buddhist visions appearing to meditating Tibetan monks: a lake, an unknown house, a rainstorm, a child in the distance . . . What clues would appear in

Jane's dreams? – a shimmering image of an apartment in smoggy Hong Kong or a rhyming allusion to an overseas posting?

The visions don't come, but at least Jane's looking rested.

One morning, I leave Walking Buddha and Sleeping Buddha chatting in the kitchen while I tow Theo and Eva-Marie to school.

Eva-Marie's teacher collars me with a big smile on her face.

"Bonjour, *Madame*, you are ready for tomorrow?" she chirps, her ski-freckled face, bright blue eyes, and shining blonde mane the kind of scrubbed beauty that all first-graders deserve.

Tomorrow? I'm drawing a blank.

"So many kids signed up for your Chinese class that we've limited it to the ten oldest. You've been assigned *Atelier Onze* starting at 8:45. *Bonne chance!*" And she takes off on legs so long they seem to have cross-country skis permanently attached.

My I-almost-understood-your-French smile stays frozen on my face just long enough to propel me home. Sure enough, amidst Eva-Marie's cereal-box dinosaur trading cards, a wad of hardened chewing gum, her scuffed *pantoufles* and an ear-warming headband she claimed to have lost – aha! – I fish up a dog-eared circular inviting parents to volunteer to teach foreign language and culture during a "*Jour multi-culturel.*"

Suspiciously, the sign-up coupon at the bottom is missing. MISSING! I count the hours until I can subject that little monkey to the third degree.

Noon finally rolls around, and my two Bodhisattvas are kitting up for a leisurely lunch at the village's best restaurant. They bid me farewell after we reach the village junction and sail off wafting an air of international glamor over the lunch-time hustle.

A village *patrouilleuse* mans her post nearby. She wields her stop-sign like a battle shield. Yellow poncho flapping, this protective harpie brings a careening Peugeot roaring down from the direction of the French border to an infuriated halt. With studied care, she shepherds my children across the road.

Eva-Marie's lingering limp slows her down. The driver, a young Frenchman with a cigarette hanging off his lower lip, impatiently glares at us, then revs off in a wave of slushy snow towards Nyon.

"Drives the French crazy when I stop them," the mother grins at me, then she nods in the direction of Natalya and Jane, "Your friends from New York?"

"Yes. How did you know?" I am embarrassed to admit I don't know this woman's name.

"Madame Delacroz overheard their accents last Monday."

Are we talking about Natalya and Jane here or the surveillance of two international cocaine smugglers? This is worse than those biddies the Chinese Communists installed in every commune to spy on their neighbors.

"Um, they arrived on Sunday."

She nods, satisfied. "*Bien.* Until tomorrow!"

"Well, yes, uh, so long," I say, pulling Eva-Marie and Theo safely away from Village Intelligence Services.

I round on my littlest child with machine-gun intensity, "Eva-Marie, did you promise I would teach Chinese tomorrow morning?"

"Oh, yeah, I forgot to tell you."

She ticks off the names of mothers who will teach Italian, Serbo-Croat, Dutch, Hebrew, Greek, Polish, Spanish, Swiss-German and German, "And you!"

"But they're teaching their native languages! Chinese isn't my native language. Why didn't you sign me up for English?"

Eva-Marie looks confused and distressed at losing face. "Luke's mother is teaching English, because she is English. You're not English. I promised you'd teach them how to write those funny letters. You know." Her little hand swooshes through the air. "Don't worry. You'll be the best. I promised."

This heartbreaking confusion in her mind between competing to win and at last winning herself some friends is in painful evidence.

And so it is that the next morning, I reluctantly leave my two house guests to face one of the toughest audiences in the world – ten kids whose idea of a good time is running their snow boards over the next guy's collarbone. Crossing the slushy playground, I give myself a pep talk to pump up my confidence with only partial success.

I can't do this. Yes, I can. But what if I've forgotten all my Chinese? A wicked thought springs to mind. So what if I can't speak a word of Chinese anymore, well, then, what the hell? Who's going to know? There isn't a genuine Chinese speaker within twenty miles! These brats won't know the difference.

On this tide of fragile bravado, I go for the kill. The band of roughnecks tries to storm the classroom, but I've brought a hand puppet who starts barking Chinese, not allowing a single kid to pass into the room until he or she has identified himself in Chinese. Saucer-eyed and giggling, they realize this puppet means business. The papier mâché "Monsieur Bang" is a take-no-prisoners kinda guy. There'll be no Italian pizza, no British game-stall, no kitschy German cartoons, no Serbo-Croat folk dances, and no Dutch butter cookies. They wanted Chinese, these little thugs, and they'll get it. It'll be over in sixty minutes, and I'll be the one left standing.

My fearless little puppet chants at them. Within ten minutes, they're reciting the numbers from one to ten in sing-song perfection. "*Yi, er, san, si, wu, liow, chi, ba, jeou, shi*," faster!, faster!

What's happened? I wanted to bring these little souls the serenity of classical Chinese, but the demonic hand puppet has taken over! *Yi, er, san, si*, his victims shout like a bunch of fanatic Red Guards waving Mao's little book.

After half an hour of games with big Chinese numbers hanging on their chests like political prisoners in some kind of mock struggle session, the kids have to beg Monsieur Bang in Chinese for their brushes and ink. I choose the roughest customer, Gerard, to read out all the characters hanging on the walls. He sweats tiny little-kid bullets as he struggles with Mandarin's third tone. Last September this kid tried to set fire to our back forest and stole my kids' new sleds one month after our arrival. Monsieur Bang takes revenge.

The puppet holds his mammoth brush upright and demonstrates the correct brush stroke order. To my astonishment, ten thick brushes move up and down, press and lift, making bold, black suns, men, sedan chairs, rivers, mountains, sheep. The children check each other's work with the furrowed concentration of T'ang dynasty scholars.

"Chinese has no plurals, no conjugations of the future, passé composé, or imperfect tense, no he or she, no feminine or masculine nouns," I comment.

The budding mafioso Gerard sighs, "I adore Chinese." Suddenly, the school bell rings and I am released.

"My, my, how things must've changed in six months for the locals to start trusting that strange *Américaine* with their children," says a sarcastic voice from the doorway. V. is wearing a quilted jacket, flowing pants of silk tucked into soft leather riding boots, and a curved saber made of cardboard.

"Ah, Genghis Khan, I presume. How long have you been standing there?"

Voltaire laughs. "Long enough to know you're lucky an eighteenth-century bachelor like me doesn't know the twenty-first century definition of child abuse."

"Well, I can't understand their Vaudois accent. I had no choice but to take the sink-or-swim approach."

"The Jesuits who whipped me at Louis-le-Grand would have hired you in a minute." He saunters around the desks, showing off the swish of his trousers.

"Listen to this. It's my Epistle to the Emperor of China, published in 1771." He starts to recite from a wad of hand-written verse, while I detach sheets of ideographs from the cork board. Most of his poem is about rival French poets and literary foes.

"Stop, please. It all rhymes, but I can't imagine what the Emperor Qian Lung, sitting in Beijing, made of all that."

I scan the stanzas, "Who is Linguet the lawyer? Who is Ribalier of the Collège Mazarin? Who is Marmontel of the Académie Française? This hasn't got anything to do with China."

Voltaire sighs and folds up his epistle. "That's often the case with China-watching, isn't it? Thanks to you, these kids discovered their own 'China'. For that little rascal Gerard, China's a world of no more irregular verbs, for the little girls, it's the swoosh of ink on paper. For me, China was Not France – a world without arguments between Jesuits and Dominicans, without petty literary rivalries, Church injustice, judicial persecution, censoring of thought and belief."

"No more *l'infâme*."

"Precisely. The Emperor expelled the Jesuits, but he didn't behead them. For me, China was tolerance. Now, tell me, what was it for you?"

I dry off the clutch of brushes with a paper towel.

"Let me think back that far. I was nineteen years old. My forty-five-year-old father had just died of oesophageal cancer. I was temping summers as a secretary at a film studio. I guess for me China was the pure dedication of the Revolution, the secret language of an exclusive world, the spartan aesthetic of the Un-Hollywood, the news assignment my father's illness kept him from keeping, the diplomatic career my mother cut off when she returned from the U.S. Embassy in Nicaragua to marry my father . . ."

Voltaire springs to his feet. "Yes! It represented everywhere you were not, an escape from everything that oppressed or saddened you, a chance at everything your parents couldn't finish."

V. watches me rinse out the ink saucers. We toss Mr. Bang in a shopping bag, and head home for lunch.

"Perhaps, *chère Madame*, you left your Chinese world because you had exhausted what it meant to you. My own interest in things Chinese faded when I realized that the Middle Kingdom was not quite so perfect as I had pictured it. I wouldn't worry about the occasional outbreak of nostalgia."

"Yes, but — " I laugh at myself a little helplessly, pushing microwave buttons, " — but all those years of China studies just so I could teach that brat Gerard how to write 'sedan chair'?"

V. distracts me by pouring some reheated coffee into an exquisite cup and saucer.

"Where did you get that cup?"

"A gift to me from the Emperor in 1768," he crows.

"Come on, if the Emperor of China had actually sent you a gift, you would have mentioned it before this. You showed off Frederick the Great's letter to anybody who even set foot in Cirey."

"Well, at least it came to me from China. I like to think it was the Emperor's acknowledgement of my efforts to expand appreciation of China throughout the French kingdom. Here, read the inscription on the saucer," he prompts, lifting the delicate cup.

Next to a swallow painted in blue and white, I read the ideographs:

> "Like snow, he scatters a divine, gold embroidery of
> Sunlight, mixed with scarlet more radiant,
> Alone, atop the great straight branches
> When the luxuriant garden is already deserted."

"Exactly." V. takes a big breath larded with self-love.

"Monsieur Voltaire, this is a poem about a bird."

"Sunlight, enlightenment? Alone at the top of a straight tree? Hmm?"

"Yeeesss." I'm groping . . .

"*C'est moi*, of course! The Emperor of China compares me,

Voltaire, to the bird *unique*, solitary at the pinnacle of achievement, surrounded by snow reflecting sunlight. You see, here, divinely-embroidered sunlight? Enlightenment?"

"It's kind of a stretch."

"Hmmph!"

The last night of their stay, Peter offers Jane and Natalya some of his grandfather's home-made 1946 kirsch. We listen to Jane's nightmare experience in Beijing on June 4th, as she lay on the stones at the edge of Tiananmen Square, her shoe grazed by a bullet, her clothing soaking up the blood of wounded students. All around her stood armed teenagers wearing the uniform of the People's Liberation Army, rural youths brought in to quell the "turmoil."

I think of Voltaire's romantic illusions about the distant Chinese, ruled by virtue and tolerance. He's come to realize that his ideal country now executes more people than any country on earth, that they torture suspects and detain political prisoners in psychiatric wards. And yet, as a teenage soldier told Jane that murderous night, staring down her petrified expression, "Don't fear us. We're good people."

By the firelight, the ageing French philosopher and playwright listens, his brow troubled. For all of us who imagined China as an alternative – more moderate, just, equal, exotic, peaceful, refined – the realization always returns; when you dig a hole through the center of the earth, you don't come upon a land of perfect opposites on the other side. Nor is China the worst of all possible worlds.

Jane and Natalya must finally pack up, and with them, their stories of two lifestreams I didn't navigate. Natalya stayed closer to our roots in the States. Jean married a Chinese. I chose to leave Hollywood, and then China, and follow Peter.

Straining under the weight of East Coast fashions, Alexander lugs their bags back out to the car and twenty minutes later, I've seen off their flight with regret.

"Did you enjoy the Babes?" I ask Peter as he sweeps up the

empty bottles of our final evening.

"Very much, except that I'm totally jet-lagged. They managed to move our sleep schedule on to New York time instead of the reverse."

"I had a great time listening to their stories," Voltaire chirps up. "Do you think we could visit Wu Ming in Beijing?"

I glance at his Genghis pants.

"Of course, I'll get myself a more up-to-date set of silks."

The Best of All Possible Worlds

I thrust my face through the car window at V. who is glued to the back seat, clutching a wool blanket around his shoulders. "Don't you want to wave him off?"

Theo's departure for a week of ski camp with his class is such a victory of spirit over corporal frailty that I can't help insisting that V. bear witness. For two weeks, our boy has determinedly fought off first a flu bug and then a runny nose, religiously inhaled his medications, and sat through two appointments with his paediatrician, all so that he could board the school bus headed to the resort area, Les Diablerets.

"I want to be normal," Theo said the night before his departure, his fist clenched on his pillow. "I want to go with my gang."

"I didn't know you had a gang."

So on this snow-tossed Monday morning in late winter, certain that Theo doesn't have bronchitis, pneumonia, or tuberculosis, nothing will stop me putting my towhead into that goddamned bus full of screaming kids.

"*Bougez* your butt," I bark at V. "You could take a lesson from that child!"

"*Madame*, it's a tempest out there! I prefer to remain warm here in the car."

"You prefer to listen to the radio," I say dryly.

"A discussion of French theater." Radio Suisse Romande

has launched another interminable discussion in cultivated voices about preserving the integrity of French drama against the onslaught of Tom Cruise and Spike Jonze.

"News to snooze by," I retort.

V. has hurt my feelings. This is a big day for our family. Alexander has already returned from a week of cross-country skiing with his class. I hardly recognized him the night he came back, his rake-thin form toned and looking two inches taller, his round cheeks reddened by the Alpine altitudes. Monsieur Martignier, the camp director, has taken my bookish, neurasthenic first-born and driven him thirty kilometres a day on skis. Now he looks like a poster boy for the Swiss Cheese Association.

We can't hope that Theo will be transformed that dramatically, but maybe he can have something approaching a good time. Peter finishes briefing Martignier on emergency measures in case Theo falls short of breath.

"This Martignier looks responsible enough, but would you believe I had to explain to him what an inhaler is," Peter warns me, his face creased with worry.

"Oh, oh, Toto, something tells me we're not in Kansas," I joke.

"Or Manhattan," Peter corrects me. Marriage to a Swiss brings its tiny trials.

Clusters of chatting parents, sucking on cigarettes, clutching umbrellas in the snow flurry, clog the asphalt around the luggage hold. I carry the skis and poles and Peter follows me, lugging Theo's heavy backpack, and a second bag containing his nebulizer.

The bus engine grinds into action and anxious parents are shooed out of the way. Theo gives me a thumbs-up sign out of the back window. I say a little prayer to his guardian angel as they pull out of the parking lot. I kiss Peter off to work and struggle back through pelting ice flakes to my own car.

"What did I miss?" I ask V.

"A revival of Molière next month in Paris," V. mutters. He sees I'm too distracted by Theo's drama to get his point. "Jean-Baptiste Poquelin Molière, born 1622, died 1673."

He turns his anguished face to me and repeats, "1673! One hundred and five years before *me*!"

His silence as we continue down the hill to do the weekly grocery shopping in Nyon worries me. Until today, no excursion has been complete without some fun story of dirty sheets at Versailles, theatrical performances at Cirey, or letters from Fred the Great in Potsdam.

"Nothing survives," he murmurs.

"I beg your pardon?" I'm concentrating on the curves in the road.

"Nothing of mine has survived. Not the *Dictionnaire Philosophique*, *Micromégas*, *Zadig*, *l'Orphelin de la Chine*, *Cataline*, *Oreste*, *rien*, *rien*, *rien*! After *La Henriade* was published, all of Paris called it better than the *Iliad*! I wrote to my best friend Thieriot, 'Epic poetry is my forté, or I am much deceived.'"

"Well," he concludes in despair, "I was much deceived!"

"Stop whining. They named a boutique in Paris, 'Voltaire and Zadig.' I just saw it advertised in *Elle*."

"A ladies' shop? Bah!"

"And there's a Voltaire County in North Dakota. Oh, did you know that Napoleon tried to get through exile in Elba by rewriting one of your tragedies?"

"Which one?"

"Sorry, I don't know."

He favors me with a curl of his thin upper lip.

"I'm just trying to cheer you up."

We continue driving in silence.

Suddenly, a torrent of resentment pours out of my friend.

"I checked Amazon.com without you. Entered my name in the little 'search' box. I know the facts, *Madame*. Now I know why you did not fall back in joy at my arrival. All my plays are out of print. A few anthologies are available on 'special order'."

"Why not try the French web sites? Anyway, a lot of respectable people are only read by special order. Even my murder mystery is available only by print-on-demand from some entity named Replica Books. Sounds like something out of *Blade Runner*, doesn't it?"

"I haven't the slightest idea of what you speak. Even if my *oeuvre* is for sale, it's not read, not debated." He bursts out, "Do you know what my Amazon ranking is? *5,457,000!* Do you know the sales figure of *Hamlet*?" Now he turns really bitchy. "Well, that depends on which edition you choose, doesn't it? The name of Voltaire lingers on no one's lips. I am not the gossip of the salons. My first drafts are not smuggled eagerly across borders. I am discussed nowhere except some moldy classrooms presided over by mediocre *professeurs de collège*!"

He sinks deep into an exhausted heap of hand-stitched velvet, out of my view.

"Oh, gimme a break. Okay, you're no longer a household name, but you've got a *quai* named after you in Paris, and a street in Geneva. As has-been legends go, you've got it made. Historians say the eighteenth-century practically belonged to you. You want the twenty-first too? Aren't you being a leetle beet greedy?"

He shakes his head, his voice dripping with disdain. "I am nothing more than required reading. I'm dead — deader than Aristotle or Euripides, deader than Molière, *mon Dieu*, I am deader even than that Shakespeare! I read of a movie about him, and I taste gall. Is anybody accepting Oscars for '*Voltaire in Love*'? And I was in love many, many times!"

"Stop pounding the window! You're not being fair to yourself. Was there anyone to compare with Shakespeare?"

His eyes are burning. This would have mortally wounded him, if he weren't already deceased.

"I wrote some fifty tragedies for the stage, *Madame*. Fifty, from *L'Œdipe* to *Irène*. It was I who introduced to the French nation a few pearls which I found in Shakespeare's enormous dung-heap of verse! I admit he was natural, but had not *le bon goût*, not so much as a single spark of good taste, or knew one rule of the drama."

I'm shocked by V.'s amazing egotism.

He backs off a little. "Well, all right, he had some good passages. '*Demeure, il faut choisir et passer à l'instant, De la vie à la mort ou de l'Être au néant. Dieux cruels.*'"

"Cruel Gods? Where did they come from? Was that your version? That's nothing like '*To be or not to be, that is the question*'. You've lost Hamlet's rhythm entirely!"

V. starts with indignation. "Certainly, you don't imagine that I translated Shakespeare in a slavish way? There was always room for improvement. '*Qui suis-je? Qui m'arrête! Et qu'est-ce que c'est la Mort?*'"

"No, no, listen, this is how it goes, '*To die, to sleep – no more – and by a sleep to say we end the heartache,*' and, let me see, '*For who would bear the whips and scorns of time —*'"

V. translates, "'*Qui pourrait sans Toi supporter cette vie de nos Prêtres menteurs bénir l'hypocrisie —*'"

"Hamlet never said anything about 'lying, hypocritical priests'!"

"Well, he does in my version. I hated priests then, I hate them now, and I shall hate them till Doomsday! It adds to the spirit."

This sounds almost apologetic. Luckily I'm driving and have to keep a straight face. He is inconsolable, determined to wallow in artistic self-pity.

"Name one of my plays that breathes on stage today."

I can think of no production of any Voltaire play ever advertised anywhere in my entire life. This is bad.

He derives masochistic delight from my silence. "You see! How Jean-Baptiste Rousseau must be laughing at me! It was he who wrote *Ode to Posterity*, it was I who quipped so cruelly, 'I fear, *Monsieur*, your work will never reach its address!'"

"That's quite a put-down."

"Now it is I who lies prostrate, down put by Posterity."

We trudge the aisles piled with tuna fish cans and instant fondue. I've never known someone who can sulk so aggressively. His vanity is ridiculous, yet I pity him with his powdered wig tied neatly at the nape of his neck, his stockings clean, his shoes polished, his shirt ruffles nicely ironed, his long coat brushed. All that for a four-story shopping mall. He deserves better.

Later that afternoon, I prepare the terrain. "Are you so sure you missed the twentieth century?"

He's brooding in my office, fiddling with the geometry compass he's filched from Alexander's backpack. He pretends to be matching his calculations to a solar system illustration in a kid's science book.

"I think this is incorrect, the distance between the sun and this Pluto, whoever that is," he says.

"Pluto's orbit interchanges position with Neptune's on a regular basis, so you're probably both right. Put that down and follow me. I want to show you something."

We go downstairs to the bookshelves by the piano. I reach up for the photo of Leonard Bernstein unpacked so many frantic months ago.

"Do you recognize this man?"

V. stands back, one foot posed behind the other, hands stretched out in a rectangle, as if he were Watteau composing a royal portrait sitting. He considers, he measures, he estimates. He moves closer and takes a single lens out of his breast pocket to examine Lenny's black and white pores.

"*Non.*" He shakes his head. "I would have remembered the pistol." He glances at the handwriting on the back of the picture, while I continue, "He was one of the greatest composers and theatrical geniuses of the twentieth century."

He refers to the signature on the back. "Monsieur Arthur Elgort?"

"No, Monsieur Bernstein. Elgort's the photographer. Read

what Bernstein is saying, here, written down near the edge of the frame."

V. reads to himself under his breath, "The critics will kill me."

He hands the photo back to me. "Well, if Monsieur Bernstein was an enemy of the critics, then I'm sure he was a genius. Critics are nothing more than gnats who lay their eggs up the backsides of racehorses. It's the only way they get to run the race."

I laugh. "They say, those who can, do, and those who can't, teach."

"Those who can't even teach are appointed to the Royal Court as critics."

Still despondent despite this sally, he heads back to the staircase, no doubt planning a whole afternoon of pondering his vacant eternity of unfame after a brilliant life of combating "*l'infâme*."

I don't give up that easily.

"Are you sure you didn't haunt Leonard Bernstein around 1955 or '56?" I call up the stairs.

"Why are you so insistent, *Madame*?" he retorts over the banister. "You cannot change what is. Or in my case, what isn't. My plays and histories are forgotten. I am *nul*."

"But one of your stories, your *contes*, survived as a play, a musical play. *Candide*!"

He shouts back in rebuke. "That silly fable about Westphalia and the Baron Thunder-ten-tronckh? You attribute to me that pack of nonsense? I have, thank God, better occupations."

"Nice try! You might've been able to deny authorship in your own day, but you can't deny it now. Everybody knows you wrote it. It's your most famous work. Set to music by this man, Leonard Bernstein."

The wigged head reappears over the top of the banister. A wave of relief passes through me. He descends the stairs with a little lilt in his step. He hesitates, then dances some kind of tuneless minuet back and forth, barely able to disguise his delight.

"*Candide?* Really? That little trifle? Who would've thought it?"

"A huge hit in New York."

"Five acts? Full orchestration?"

"Three acts. Don't pretend you're not thrilled. I can order the recording."

"If you like," he says, shrugging. "*S'il vous plaît,* I mean to say, if it pleases you, *Madame.*" He bows slightly and skips upstairs to resume his astronomical calculations. Worried his point hasn't sunk in, he yells down the staircase. "We can listen to it any time, *Madame.*"

I carry the telephone in my pocket, hoping it never rings with news of an asthma attack. It rings the very next morning.

"Hello, Mama?" says Theo's voice, so small.

"Are you all right?"

"I'm blowing my nose a lot. I forgot my goggles. Can you send them?"

"Is that all?" I'm ready to jump in the car to save him.

"Yeah. I skied yesterday afternoon. It's boring. My monitor is Hélène but everybody says Gregory is better."

"Are you feeling all right? No short breathing?"

"Yeah."

"Oh."

"I'll give you the address to send the goggles, okay?"

V. lingers in the mornings by the mailbox, pretending he is measuring the snow-patched front lawn for a vineyard. Maybe they can grow grapes in Lebanon or Sicily at 1,100 meters' altitude, but our latitude rules out any viniculture, no matter how many more centuries of global warming V. sits out. He watches the postwoman buzzing back and forth between the chalets in her black and yellow van, like a mail-crazed bee.

This goes on as the week progresses – the excitement before the van arrives, the little sigh once we've thrown out the junk mail, sorted the medical and tax bills, put aside the magazines, and tussled over the paper. He fills the time assembling a clipping pile of horrors – slavery in Sudan, prostitution in Thailand, debt bondage in South Asia – and filing it all in a ring binder labeled "*L'Infâme.*"

The morning before Theo returns, I find V. in the kitchen trying to open a large brown package with the food processor blade. He has discarded my Chinese chopper and my best paring knife.

"Nothing is sharp enough," he complains. "I use all my concentration and I can't cut through this — "

"Let me. These boxes weren't designed with the eighteenth-century ghost in mind."

I wonder how he'll handle his disappointment. This box is big enough for a dozen C.D.s. The packaging disgorges a thick edition of the latest *Writer's Market (8000 Editors Who Buy What You Write!).*

"*Quel horreur!*" V. mutters, shrinking back, pulling back his ruffled cuffs in self-defense. "What is that?"

"One thousand, one hundred and twelve pages of raised hopes and a mailbag of rejections. But I ordered it to motivate me. You've been nagging me for weeks to get back into the fray. I figure if I just keep sending out my manuscripts, one of these eight thousand people will buy another novel of mine."

"*Regardez, le* C.D.!" he exclaims with hope, spying into the discarded bubble-pack.

"Online access to the Writer's Digest Data Bank," I read.

His face falls. "Not my musical play."

"'Fraid not."

At last, *Candide* arrives. V. rips it open with Peter's Swiss Army knife.

"Book by Lillian Hellman, lyrics by John Latouche and Dorothy Parker." I open the notes. "'A rich blend of various elements'," I continue. "Sounds promising, doesn't it?"

V. strains to read ahead of me. "'An impending disaster,'" he intones.

"Wait, I'm not there yet. 'Bernstein's strong admiration for Voltaire' . . . see, here?"

"'An insurmountable task . . .'" he scans.

"C'mon. You're just reading the negative stuff."

"I can't help it," he protests. "That's the way I am. I've never taken criticism well."

"You sure know how to hand it out. Listen to this, 'A brilliant show!' Feel better now?"

"'Nonsensical plot?'" his voice cracks at that sentence.

"'One of Bernstein's strongest scores —'"

"'Only rarely strikes the right note —'"

"'THROWS LIGHT ON ALL THE DARK PLACES —'"

"'AN UNWORKABLE BOOK —'"

"Oh, I'm giving up on you!" I cry. "Listen! It says right here that this show was, 'A le-gen-dar-y and u-nique clas-sic!'"

He leans over, stabbing one of his long fingers at the C.D.'s flyer unwinding across my lap. "And it says here, 'Pretentious!' *Prétentieux!*"

"'Broadway craftsmanship at its most magical!'"

He snatches the little white booklet and practically screams at me, quoting, "A MESS!" and throws the paper tangle on the floor at my feet, running to the bathroom, mumbling over his shoulder, "I'm going to be sick."

"You're always sick," I yell at the slamming bathroom door. "Besides, it doesn't matter if you're sick. You're dead."

A dreadful sound emerges from behind the bathroom door.

"Monsieur Voltaire, are you – are you throwing up?"

He returns from the bathroom, his face a pale green. "No less unpleasant when you're dead."

"This was just the first production. We could order the revivals. You know, I don't think you're giving this a chance. It should cheer you up."

His complexion, always pale, is now bleached. One lethal eyebrow is aimed at me, unconvinced.

"Shall we give it a try?" I persist.

He is mopping his brow with a lacy handkerchief. Who will do this man's ironing when his linen supply runs out?

I look at his rococo finery, his proud stance, his expression rigid with pride, and it hits me, I am looking at the greatest playwright of the Enlightenment overcome with Opening Night nerves, a man who took so badly to the boos greeting the debut of his *Artémire* that he mounted the stage to argue and heckle right back at his audience. How is a dead playwright going to argue with an equally dead audience if this doesn't go down well?

In goes the C.D., and the overture strikes up.

We give Bernstein his head. Bold and a hundred percent American Broadway, the opening strains send homesickness for New York flooding over my being. How confident the young Bernstein was! Who else would put an operatic aria in the middle of a musical comedy? Who else but Dorothy Parker and Lillian Hellman could marry the satirical brittleness of Voltaire's age to the martini-dry cynicism of the Wall Street suits of the fifties? Take V.'s lovers star-crossed by eighteenth-century greed, lust, and war, and turn them into a twentieth-century couple arguing between a future on Park Avenue versus the Connecticut countryside?

Max Andersen's portrayal of Pangloss is acerbically bright. Barbara Cook's lilting Cunégonde has turned Voltaire's two-dimensional character into a canny, sexy, worldly Parisian *demi-mondaine*. And when New Yorkers, expecting something corn-fed like *Oklahoma*'s Curley the Cowboy or *South Pacific*'s Nellie Forbush, rubbed their eyes at Professor Pangloss singing a parody of Leibniz's philosophy, "The Best of All Possible Worlds," who else but Lenny would publish a defense of his opera in *The New York Times*? Come to think of it, Voltaire would.

I lean back and for the next hour, soak it in. This is the young Bernstein – brave and brilliant. The composer plays with form: tangos, waltzes, mazurkas, and gavottes sparkle, one after another. It's improbable, ambitious, and simply wonderful.

I'm heartsick for it all – the overflowing theater district sidewalks during intermission, yellow cabs with immigrant drivers, sunny winds sweeping up leaves in Central Park, the fall fashion line-up, umbrella hawkers in the rain, stretch limos gliding up Lexington, an empty August weekend rollerblading in the humidity-thick air down squishy-soft asphalt streets. I think of the first sign of autumn, the banners of the Met flapping in the quickening September breezes, Christmas windows at Saks.

Too soon, the swelling finale lifts me up and then suddenly, it's over.

I have been so moved, tears are running down my cheeks. Outside the front yard, the unwelcome whine of old Berner's power-saw breaks my reverie. This is the twenty-first century, the place St-Cergue, Switzerland. I'm sitting on the floor in my gardening jeans and old moccasins, but I've just been transported to a first night in 1956 in an overheated Manhattan theater, my nose full of cigarette smoke and Chanel No. 5, my ears filled with gorgeous harmonies and witty delivery.

V. clears his throat and surveys my tear-streaked face.

Finally he speaks. "The music was rather loud."

I look at him in a harmony-induced haze.

"But not bad. *Pas du tout*. Not bad. I liked Cunégonde's aria, yes, very much."

The rest of the day is anti-climactic. I hide my disappointment. What did I expect? How could a man of his time attuned to Handel, not even familiar with Beethoven, turn on to Leonard Bernstein? V. was used to kicking unwashed theatergoers out of his path from the wings in order to perform, accustomed to small-scale amateur theatricals in palaces and private villas. His fans preferred little recitations in a country garden or a whispering salon. How could Voltaire imagine the excitement generated by an original Broadway musical in those golden days of Bernstein, Rogers and Hammerstein, Lerner and Loewe?

What a stupid idea. The C.D. case lies open and abandoned in a corner of the living room. I splash cold water on my puffy eyelids and drive downhill to meet Theo's bus. I ask him too often whether he enjoyed himself. Is he glad he went? Was his breathing okay? Did he fall down a lot? Was the food good?

He says he had a "pretty" good time. The skiing went "okay." The food was "all right." At dinner, the family hears the details.

"Mick cried every night because his parents told him just before he got on the bus that they're getting a divorce," he announces. "I stayed home on Friday morning because I was a little breathless. The teacher told me to vacuum the chalet because she said I had nothing to do. Mathias offered to stay behind. He's one of my buddies. He wiped the tables."

"Where was your teacher?"

"Playing with her new baby."

It all sounds a little bleak. "I guess you're sorry you went?"

He looks at us startled. "Oh, no, we spent the evenings capturing girls and administering the Tickle Torture. I was the Chief Executioner."

I sleep deeply, relieved to have Theo safely under our roof again, until I'm awakened by the sound of shuffling feet. My bedside clock reads two in the morning. What's wrong now?

All the children are zonked out in their beds. I creep across the second floor. V.'s bed is empty. Peering down through the banister into the living room, I spy him, waltzing in circles. He's wearing the stereo earphones over his nightcap, and tangling his dancing slippers up in the cord. He is singing to himself, his thin lips barely moving, the billowing sleeves of his nightshirt waving as he moves with the score.

He looks so *alive!* The sadness that lingered after Émilie's death was relived has finally dispersed. He doesn't see me, so lost is he in the soaring flights of his singing characters. One showman captured the spirit of another across the centuries, and now that attention and appreciation are reciprocated. I feel quite left out by their genius. I slip back to bed.

The next morning I find V. hollow-eyed, but good-humored at breakfast, mixing the dregs of his first coffee-pot of the day with a fresh pot of chocolate. He is humming what sounds a lot like Bernstein's "Eldorado" number. He eyes me carefully, but says nothing. He's holding something back, but why? Never shy or fearful, what would silence that whiplash tongue? Again and again, he glances across the table over the top of the Bran Flakes box.

He stirs a little sugar into his Qian Lung cup with the only silver spoon he could find, a baptismal gift engraved with Alexander's "A." It may be my imagination, but the tinkling of silver on porcelain seems unusually energetic.

"Oh, what is it?" I give in.

He draws himself up and clears his throat. "Oh, nothing, really. I have been thinking, I admit. Perhaps it is a folly, nothing more, *Madame*, but I beg your counsel."

This is suspiciously coy.

Finally, he spits it out. "I simply ask myself whether this gentleman, this Monsieur Bernstein, would care to look at some of my other works for musical adaptation? *Alzire*, I think, since it's set in America? Or, *Zaïre*, perhaps? He'll find in it traces of *Othello*, and I admit that while in exile in England, certain themes used by English authors attracted me irresistibly, so that later, I borrowed them . . ."

It's going to be a long day.

Courts and Clubs

A brilliant morning signals the end of winter in the mountains. The sun's rays skate across the distant lake surface and bounce off the icicles clinging to our pines. Icy drips drill deep holes through the snowy crust of our yard.

In late autumn, the ground floor of the house was shadowy and cold under its wide, low eaves. Now the low-lying sun shoots its beams right into my office. V. has hung an orange Indonesian sarong as a make-shift curtain to shield his eyes. The thin cotton gives the room a lovely glow, and certainly perks up the complexion of any dead middle-aged house poet and well-known throne-licker who happens to be staying on *indefinitely*.

Although I feel V. is getting a bit underfoot, he's been careful never to get under Peter's feet, nor to move anything in his presence. In fact, V. spends as little time in my husband's company as he spent in poor Monsieur du Châtelet's. Today, however, my phantom friend is hopping this way and that to avoid my husband who criss-crosses the house with a measuring tape in his hand, counting out the square meters of our house and cursing under his breath.

Peter hired a local accountant to do our first Swiss tax return. This Einstein has just confessed to a costly mistake involving the "rental value" of our residence. This refers to the absurd tax due on the profit we would theoretically make if we rented out every square meter of livable space, even though we're occupying the house ourselves. Sometimes the Swiss seem determined to make their country unwelcoming. I now realize why so many Swiss rent rather than buy their home. This tax flies in the face of American experience that home ownership builds communities. In our case, paying it will wipe out the last of our savings, already savaged by the vague mathematics of our long-gone contractor.

In his willingness to push us over the final brink into bankruptcy, our accountant tossed off revised figures that include floor space under sharply slanting roofs – space that only Stuart Little could comfortably occupy. My Swiss husband is law-abiding within a centimeter of the regulations and he's measuring every centimeter himself. He marches back and forth across the house, crawling around corners, eliminating hundreds of francs worth of rental value, and bringing the taxes down, franc by desperate franc.

"Why don't we just hire a new accountant?" I ask.

He glowers. "Why would the next be any different? I think we can manage if they agree to take the payment in installments."

I beat a retreat, muttering, "Sorry, I still think in inches," to find V. in his frothy shirt sleeves of finest lawn, poking away at my laptop keyboard. The printer churns out fresh pages. We've argued politely for some weeks over the use of my computer. This guy is a fireball of words bursting to get out. Will he try to equal the ninety volumes he wrote during his lifetime before he vacates my office?

More worrying, will he ever vacate my office?

He charmed my Internet password out of me just last week and within twenty-four hours, had set up a day-trading account with Charles Schwab. I shut that down before he landed both of us in debt, and quickly changed my code. Now I catch him filling his leather notebook with calculations, trying to work out the likely variations on the spelling of my name. I've foiled him, with an all-numerical password.

Of course we are paragons of *politesse* at all times, never discussing this openly, but he leaks frustration.

Just last week he whined, "I always paid for the outgoing post of my house guests! You can check the correspondence of that tedious Madame Graffigny who lived with Émilie and me at Cirey. It's one of the few nice things she said about me in her letters. Now, I want to use the *é*-mail."

"E-mail. Eee, not *é*, and the answer to you, *Monsieur*, is snail mail. *La poste des limaces*. I'll be happy to pay your postage."

Lately, he's obsessed with his correspondence with Frederick the Great. Frederick's boys-only entourage seems to have made V. impatient with me, with all women who would delay his rise to Chief Groupie at yet another European throne. I would have thought his disenchantment with Versailles had cured him of seeking kingly approval.

Moreover, the repeated refusal of the Académie Française to admit V. to its ranks should have taught him the irrelevance of joining elite clubs. But, oh no. Now he's pining to return to the posturings of that motley court in Potsdam. Possibly because when Fred heard V. couldn't get into the Académie, he said, "If Voltaire can't get in, then who the devil is in it?"

Well, the next time he threatens to move to Fred's, I'll personally pack up all his scientific junk and rotting books myself. As they don't weigh a material ounce, the shipping should run cheap. He's only headed for another disappointment, but then, he lived before Groucho Marx.

Not that I don't understand the attraction of "courts." When we arrived in New York from Hong Kong, I was more than ready to tackle a fresh crowd. The excitement I felt for our new life at the United Nations lasted so briefly, it is hard to recall my initial enthusiasm for the diplomatic whirl. It was soon evident that under the then-Secretary-General Boutros Boutros-Ghali, the atmosphere was clubby and elitist enough to please Voltaire. The whiff of corruption lingered on from the days of Perez de Cuellar, with appointments within the Secretariat distributed like party favors, and scandals of sexual favoritism or harassment stinking up certain corridors.

Peter was appointed the first full-time Permanent Observer to the United Nations for the I.C.R.C. This status was shared along a bank of seats in the General Assembly with permanent observers of the Holy See, the European Union, the Palestinian Liberation Organization, and even Switzerland, not yet a member.

Formal protocol dictated that during the heady autumn days of the General Assembly meetings, we would dine out once or twice a week, always seated in the middle of the long banquet table while pride of place at the head and foot of the table was reserved for the ambassadors and wives of Security Council permanent member states. This meant that more often than not, I found myself next to the P.L.O.'s Observer, a dentist-turned-diplomat. Our conversation stuck to the safe stuff: real estate, local schools, vacation spots. Occasionally I got the Papal Nuncio instead. He liked to talk about Jean-Paul II's Popemobile.

Cocktail receptions filled the calendar. The point was to circulate, to meet, to represent, to discuss, to fix dates for more meetings to discuss. At times, racing past two or even three other harried U.N. couples to make an appearance at the same five receptions in one evening, the obligations seemed less onerous than comic. Night after night, the same people, the same discretion that prevented any substantial conversation for fear of diplomatic offense.

U.N. wives quickly arrived at their own pecking order. The wives of Security Council permanent members were the head chickens, these matrons reigning from their apartments on Sutton Place, the Waldorf Astoria or Park Avenue. The wives of alternative members of the Security Council exploited their husband's temporary rotation on to the pantheon with a social fury, knowing that a good performance in New York might mean the appointment of their spouse as Foreign Minister at home.

Those wives with intellectual ambitions presided over foreign policy tea-parties, while others blessed with more beauty than brains kept their mouths shut but dressed to the nines.

Some Middle-Eastern wives carried heavy political baggage in their little chain-link purses. During the Gulf War, some of the Arab ladies were awkward with my friend Christine, the charming French wife of the Palestinian dentist because she wasn't Arab. The Europeans treated her carefully because she was married to an Arab rather than a European. Of course, the Israelis and Americans labelled her clearly in the Palestinian camp . . . Well, Christine and I laughed together; all these relations ebbed and flowed one season or peace agreement later with no more court fanfare than a rise in hemlines.

The wife of one of the Balkan ambassadors was very insistent on Serbia's millennial claim to Kosovo. While she bent my ear over a minuscule but chic plate of fusion cuisine at the restaurant Vong, I was embarrassed by a flash of bare breast underneath her expensive leather vest, her nipples stiff with political excitement. She enlivened all our years at the U.N. with her argumentative passion and excruciating dress sense. Her most memorable entrance was at a reception attended by President Clinton, Nelson Mandela, Douglas Hurd and others at the opening of the General Assembly. It was easy to spot her in a crowd of hundreds. She wore a hat with a two-foot high antenna springing skywards, ending in a white ping pong ball – the Martian from Belgrade.

A place could be earned at "court" by good humor, discretion, and usefulness. A lack of interest in craft bazaars could be dangerous. An ironic aside could get you labelled. An inability to sit through a three-hour lunch culminating in an hour-long raffle of native products could prove lethal. To someone like myself, who had prodded, questioned and investigated to earn my keep, this life was a strange form of mental repression.

Some women tried innovation, like the Finnish lady who served reindeer hors d'œuvres or the cheerful New Zealander who decorated her sunny apartment with bold Kiwi paintings.

Other wives were clearly overwhelmed and miserable – birds in gilded cages. The statuesque young blonde Lebanese bride of the middle-aged German ambassador inexplicably fled halfway through her second year of duty. The wife of an under-Secretary General departed New York permanently when her husband took his secretary-cum-mistress to official functions in her place. Such spectres lingered like remembered casualties in Chanel haunting the forced gaiety of the social battleground.

Somewhere beyond all of this, there were real casualties, real tragedies and real U.N. operations, Red Cross delegations, struggling in often impossible, and even dangerous conditions in the field to help victims of poverty, hunger and war. All that was far, far away from U.N. headquarters.

One April evening, I recall, a shoulder-to-shoulder crush of party-goers attending an E.U. cocktail soirée parted like the Red Sea to avoid conversation with my husband: he had made himself deeply unpopular earlier that day by being one of the first to officially categorize the slaughter in Rwanda as "geno-cide." Terminology like that was a dangerous call to action and might force the U.N. community to, well, actually do some-thing.

So, in as much as I understand the political courts of my day, I grasp the *ennui* behind V.'s soulful comment:

"The French in Paris, I was tired of them. They played, supped, talked of scandal, wrote bad verses and slept like fools to recommence on the morrow the same round of careless frivolity."

"And Freder —"

"Oh," he says, clasping his hands, "Frederick was the anti-Louis, he was a Horace, a Catullus, a Maecenas, an Alexander,

a Socrates, a Trajan, an Augustus, he was Solomon of the
North, he was *God-Frederick!*"

I see disaster looming.

"Haven't we been here before? One, running away from
England over some forgery scandal? Two, a midnight escape
from Versailles to avoid a duel? Just because you liked Frederick — "

"Liked him? Someone who had flattered me for years with
his verses, his political thoughts, his invitations? I *loved*
Frederick." V. coos like a dove.

"I hear he called you a 'beautiful genius with the charming
ways and all the malice of a monkey'."

V. flashes back. "Where did you hear that?"

How can Monsieur Voltaire be so intellectually bright and so
socially dim at the same time?

For weeks I've been hearing this and that about Frederick.
One minute it's true love, the next minute it's bitter complaint.
V. talks so much about this German paragon, I feel I know the
guy myself – short, acidic, brilliant, unwashed, sleeping more
regularly with his dogs than with his boy attendants, desperate
to capture the jewel of French verse – His Truly – to adorn his
collection of celebrity brains.

V. is fussing with his papers as if the coach for Prussia were
about to leave without him.

"He offered me the post of Chamberlain, free lodgings and a
salary of 5,000 thalers. I made sure he advanced the cost of the
journey. With Émilie dead, how could I keep putting him off?"

"He sounds more like a suitor than king."

"Oh, kings! Pompadour did her best, but Louis had had
enough of me. All he said was, 'That will make one more
madman at the Prussian court and one less at Versailles!' While
Frederick promised that I would be received as the Virgil of my
age! Oh, you see *Madame*, I left for Berlin without any
regrets."

Back in New York, the stifling atmosphere of the U.N.

"court" prompted me to seek other outlets. I signed up to work on the Overseas Press Club's Committee for Freedom of Speech so at least I, for one, would be allowed freedom of speech, even if I couldn't obtain it for others by writing letters of protest and meeting with visiting foreign journalists and publishing accounts of oppression.

In the afternoons, while the housekeeper took our three diapered offspring to Carl Schurz Park, I bashed out letters to heads of state all over the world. I protested against the bodies of journalists washing up headless on alien shores, the corpses of newsreaders found incinerated in cars, investigative reporters shot off their motorcycles, and for variety, the living dead in chains, behind bars, under house arrest, or just, "disappeared." Co-chairman Norman Schorr and I waged battle by fax.

I also toiled on a novel, ostensibly a nanny-killer-thriller, but as with so much in fiction, the subconscious wormed its way into make-believe. The winter had turned cruel. My mother was dying of cancer on the West Coast.

Finally, on an early April evening, I sat sweltering in one of my wool U.N. suits beside a rented hospital bed installed in the tiny front room of her West L.A. bungalow. Outside the open screen door, the cicadas of my childhood hummed in tune with her rasping breaths. The fine, dry heat of a Southern California spring bathed me in memories. Why had I fled all this? Why had I left her to the resentful attendance of my brother? Why and where had I been for twenty years?

Back in New York following the funeral, dispirited by a dentist's failed attempt to anaesthetize a cracked molar, I strolled half-numbed around F.A.O. Schwartz. I looked like hell, grimacing with pain, and dressed too casually for uptown. So I was startled at bumping into an old American acquaintance from Beijing and even more surprised that Steve, natty in a three-piece business suit and looking not a day, much less a decade older, even recognized me. It had been fifteen years since we breezily exchanged hellos in the Beijing Hotel.

On this miserable day in New York, he took it into his head that I should join the Council on Foreign Relations. Another club beckoned.

"You know, you'll have to write, or research, or do something," Steve warned me. I was more than happy to sign up for round tables on Sino-U.S. trade, seminars on South-east Asian foreign policy, lunches on North Korean security threats, speakers on Japanese-U.S. defense policy. I dove into research on China's role at the U.N., wrote a booklet covering an Asian policy conference, anything, anything, thankful for a means of merging my reporting past with my current existence at the U.N. and the press freedom work at the O.P.C.

In short, I had found a court I liked and it wasn't the U.N. I was going to make the most of it for the time we remained in Manhattan. It was certainly more useful than cooking pies for ladies' luncheons.

I also knew the gratification of belonging does not necessarily last forever. Maybe for once, I have a piece of wisdom to share with the Enlightened One – not that he ever listens to me.

The morning after V. announces that Frederick is his ideal sovereign, I open the mail and with the blood draining out of my face, take no more than ten seconds to hunt him down. I storm into my office, where I find V. marking up a long page of verse.

"What's this?" I nearly shout, thrusting a print-out of figures into his face, but he shoos me off impatiently.

"*Tranquillisez-vous, Madame*, I'm going over some of Frederick's verses. Really, sometimes it is tiresome making all these corrections. The man even sends me his suicide notes to edit and then doesn't have the decency to act on them — "

"I will not tranquilize myself! Sixty-seven trades in one month! Are you out of your mind? The market is sinking, Amazon shares are down 88% from their high, and you're churning all these security-system stocks? What the hell are you trading with?"

He doesn't even look up at me, flicking that little *plume* back and forth, changing verb endings, and muttering, "Wrong tense, if I change the ending here . . ."

I am glazed with fury.

"Oh, what is it!" he looks up suddenly, and pounds a frustrated fist on the desk – my desk!

"What is it? This! These accounts. Trading online! On my computer! Using my password! My credit, no doubt! Look at this!"

His expression darkens, his eyes glower. "You've been opening my mail!"

My voice drips with sarcasm. "Oh, no, I haven't. It's mail addressed to — " I read the names on a fistful of envelopes, "'Monsieur Revol' and 'Madame D'Azilli.' Did you think such silly aliases would fool me?"

"Well, they fooled Louis XV's court censors," he mutters.

"Well, Monsieur Revol and Madame D'Azilli can sell out their accounts as soon as they break even."

V. is paying no attention to me, cursing under his breath at yards of handwritten poetry unraveling across the desk. "Does Frederick expect me to go on washing his dirty linen for ever?"

"Are you listening to me?"

"Every day, I go over his mediocre poetry, but it never gets any better than it was the first time I saw it. In fact, that whole Potsdam was second-rate, except that bastard Maupertuis who was always feeding Frederick lies."

"Who's second rate?"

"The whole of Frederick's court. Like that Algarotti who dabbles in Newton."

"Your house guest at Cirey who wrote 'Newton for Dummies'?"

"*Newtonism for Ladies*, meant for simple females at court, yes."

"So Potsdam didn't live up to its billing?"

"Truth is never to be found near a throne," he remarks.

I am secretly pleased.

"Besides, only that Maupertuis was worth anything, and I've never got on with him. I find him in Potsdam suggesting that doctors should be paid only for cures, that we should dig a hole to the center of the earth, or build a city where only Latin is spoken – *quel* lunatic!"

"Yes, an irritating fellow," I demur diplomatically, recalling Émilie's Christmas Eve love note to this lunatic. "Now, *Monsieur*, about this Charles Schwab business . . ."

"By the way, *Madame*, what in God's name is your husband doing? I have tripped over him more than once. Why is he underfoot, imitating Rousseau's savage ideal, crawling around on all fours?"

"He's recalculating the rental value of this house — "

"The what?"

"The money we would earn if we rented it and — "

"I said I'll pay you back just as I have always paid my — "

"This has nothing to do with you and as you have lived here rent-free for almost four months now, you had better think twice before you complain of my husband's presence. Anyway, you're so hot on Frederick and Potsdam? When are you going back?"

"Oh, you couldn't send me back there, *Madame*, I implore you. Prussian wine is like vinegar, no – donkey's piss – and the food at Frederick's court is only as passable as possible in a country without any decent game or butcher's meat."

"For example?"

"He ignores his French chef and tells the German to make pasta mixed with Russian beef marinated in eau-de-vie on top of polenta stuffed with crushed garlic and parmesan cheese. *Blah!*"

"Food is no longer the point. I'm sure your old friend still misses you, wherever he ended up."

"Hmm," V. looks abashed at this. "I'm not so sure."

"What did you do?" I press him.

"Well . . ." his face assumes an ingratiating expression. "You see," and then he stops to choose his words a little too carefully, as if phrasing a defense, "three months after I arrived in Frederick's court, I heard from a Jewish financier, one estimable Abraham Hirschel, that one could buy tax certificates issued in Saxony for half their face value. Part of Frederick's treaty with Saxony guaranteed any Prussian holding these notes a full refund."

"Oh, no! Don't tell me you tried to – you're not Prussian!"

"*Un petit détail, Madame.* Hirschel went to Dresden and bought 40,000 francs' worth for me, but — "

"You were caught, weren't you?"

He nods in sheepish admission.

I sit down next to him. "Frederick figured out that his genius of French literature was a little bent when it came to making a buck?"

"I gave the money to Hirschel to purchase jewels and furs for me."

"Rubbish. Just like you're weasling about this day-trading now. Frederick saw through you."

"I won the lawsuit."

"But not Frederick's respect."

Two hundred and fifty-three years later, it's obvious this incident caused Voltaire pointless humiliation.

"He told La Mettrie he was almost finished with me," V. whispers, then imitating Frederick's imperial whine, "*Bah! Vhen von has sucked za orange, von throws avay za peel.*"

"The King of Prussia called the Great Voltaire an orange peel?" After all, this mutual admiration society between V. and Frederick had sustained both men for years.

"He did. After that, what could I do?"

"You left?"

"For three months I played sick — "

"Well, you're sick all the time anyway — "

"I fled to Leipzig. Frederick panicked, thinking I was carrying away his letters mocking the French court. He put me under house arrest when I reached Frankfurt until I handed over his stupid poems. I took off in a hired coach, but Frederick dragged me back again. Madame Denis, Longchamp, and the servants joined me from Strasbourg – so Frederick arrested them, too!"

"Obviously you finally got away."

"Only after I had bribed the Frankfurt officials with a hefty sum to cover my 'board and lodging' while in captivity! And you complain of your 'rental value' tax!" he laughs dryly.

"What a bastard!"

"*Non, Madame.*" V. fights back. "Frederick was the only monarch of his time to declare in that dark age that he was a free-thinker, to brandish a philosophical spirit unleashed from the superstition of the Church, to let so-called 'religious crimes' go unpunished."

"You still defend a guy who called you an orange peel?"

"You don't understand my debt to Frederick. Until Potsdam, my work had been literary, scientific or a jab at the priests, nothing truly great. Thanks to him, from then on, well . . ."

V. stops, a steely look in his eyes. The amusing court jester, the sly wheeler-dealer, the foppish theater wizard, these make way for a Voltaire I've never seen before. It's not just that he's aged. I'm afraid of V. for the first time since he arrived.

"Frederick gave me courage that lasted the rest of my life."

"Where did you go?"

His voice drops back to a whisper. "I was a hunted man. In the public squares of Paris, they were making bonfires out of my satire of Maupertuis, *The Story of Dr. Akakia and the Native of St. Malo.* I stopped in Alsace, but the Jesuits evicted me from Colmar though I went to Mass, even took Holy Communion! Anyway, Colmar was a dump – half German, half French and so uncivilized it might as well have been totally Iroquois."

"Didn't anyone help you?"

"I wasn't the only one forced on the run. The French

Inquisition was bursting into flames everywhere I looked. People were burned, hung, branded, whipped, pilloried, sent to the galleys for owning books! My *Charles XII* was banned, the *Henriade* suppressed, the *Letters Concerning the English Nation* publicly burned by a hangman. Imagine my shock when I went to see my old friend Cardinal de Tencin in Lyon and he refused to be with me for longer than a minute. A minute!"

I can see the mounting flames of intolerance licking their reflection in V.'s terrified eyes. Deep creases of middle age line his cheeks. Is it the sunlight burning through my orange sarong that is washing his features this frightening color?

Seeing me standing alone, transfixed over my desk, Peter stops in the doorway of my office, still dangling a long measuring tape wrapped around his neck.

"We've been over-taxed by two thousand francs. I just faxed the proof to the accountant." He shines with triumph.

"Oh!" I take a deep breath. "What did he say? Did he apologize for leaving you to do it?"

"Of course not. He's so stunned, he can't speak. I had the feeling I was the first of his clients to ever challenge the tax officials in Lausanne."

Peter concludes that taxpayers in this historically colonized part of Switzerland have given up questioning anybody, and they've had a lot of practice, since they've scraped by under the bureaucratic yoke of Julius Caesar, the Duke of Burgundy, Napoleon Bonaparte, and the distant burghers of Berne with scarcely a breather. It's a miracle that anybody can even stand up straight around here. Peter, however, was not raised to bow to Rome, Paris, or Berne.

He hums to himself as he leaves my office. I'm sure he will prevail. Does this prove that sooner or later, we all get our day "in court?"

I turn back to a subdued Voltaire. "Where did you go?"

"I considered America, drawn by the spirit of Benjamin Franklin and William Penn, but I was forty years too old to try the New World. In the end, I sent a desperate letter to Geneva."

He sighs and wipes his brow with a handkerchief.

"The Calvinists' permission reached me in hiding just in time. There were no more courts for me to turn to, no more crowns to shield me. At the turn of 1755, I crossed the River Arve on the Lyon Road, leaving the hypocrisy of France on one side and the misery of Sardinia on the other, into Switzerland – and safety."

The Walls Can Talk

So that's what hounded him to Switzerland. I start to understand why V. feels so at home here, and why he is so damned
hard to dislodge. Maybe he's got nowhere else to go? That
doesn't stop him from complaining.

"Is this house haunted, *Madame*?" he says through his
shivers, pulling a shawl over his brocade dressing-gown even
tighter. His claw-like feet cling to soft kid slippers.

I laugh a little. "Have you looked in a mirror lately, Mr.
Apparition?"

"I tried," he rubs the deep circles under his eyes with dismay,
"but it's too early in the day. Unless I really concentrate, I don't
reflect much light . . ."

He pours himself a second coffee, more proof that the
caffeine habit can be tenacious, even beyond the grave. He
squanders all that psychic energy that could go into great
rewrites just to digest endless cups of java.

"Lay off that stuff."

"Just to open the eyes, *Madame*. I couldn't sleep all night
because of a woeful moaning in the walls that speaks of misery,
hunger and all the evils of this world."

That afternoon, I hear low groans coming from beneath the
floorboards under my feet. I check the living room below. No
one there.

That afternoon, Alexander comes to me, his worried moon-face pale under its spread of freckles. "Mama, I think Frisbee's trapped in the wood pile outside the living room."

We brave piercing ice flurries to remove layer after layer of logs. Then feeling like total dorks, we notice Frisbee observing our frantic search from a cozy indoor perch on the living room window sill.

The wailing travels through the bowels of the house. Peter hears it coming from the wall of his study. There are animal laments over the kitchen table during dinnertime and groans mid-morning in the laundry-room to the sound of the B.B.C. World Service. V. is right. It sounds like a desperate soul mourning the sadnesses of the whole world.

Peter is not the kind of man who tolerates this Muzak of Misery without an explanation. When a low growl starts up during dinner, Peter slams down his fork, and the kids giggle nervously.

"What the hell is it?" he asks.

"So you admit it's more than wooden floorboards warming up after a long winter. I told you yesterday, that is a *creature!*"

"Ooooooooh," Eva-Marie interjects.

"Ooooooooh," the Thing returns and we all jump out of our seats.

"It's a bird," Theo suggests.

"It's a plane!" Alexander sings.

Just then we hear a horrible squawk, a sudden fluttering of feathers, a scuffle breaking out directly over our heads, followed by the unmistakable sound of jaws crunching on bone.

"Omigod! It's eating something!" squeals Eva-Marie.

"Now *that's* a bird," Alexander says. "I mean, it *was* a bird."

"Walled up, like Edgar Allan Poe's *Cask of the Amontillado*," I say with a shudder.

"There's a hunter of some kind trapped inside the insulation of the house," Peter concludes.

We search for the entry point of this mystery beast and locate one possibility; a loose chunk of molding at the base of the house's exterior that seems to lead nowhere. Peter loosens the opening to release the captive, but the scuffling and crunching continues for another week. Worse, the Phantom of the Farmhouse has come to love us and regularly caterwauls through the ceiling boards along with our mealtime conversations.

This macabre atmosphere, more suited to Halloween than March, pervades our household. One day, V. has just graciously admitted me into my own office, when a small voice cries out, "BOO!"

I look down to see the face of Frankenstein rendered on green construction paper staring up at me. My little girl's hazel eyes twinkle through two jagged holes.

"D'I scare you?"

"Not me, but you might knock out someone more delicate who's not ready for the shock." I glance at V. staggering against my desk, clutching his fragile ribcage.

"What's it for, sweetheart? It's not Halloween."

"They don't have Halloween here. They have *Carnaval*. Is it really horrible?"

"Suits you perfectly."

"I made one, and then Levy and Nicholas copied me, so there were three Frankensteins in class today. Everybody else wanted to be a princess or Pikachu. So boring."

Eva-Marie got her idea, I assume, from Alexander's French edition of *Frankenstein*.

"This is one of the most horrible and moving stories I've ever read," he intones solemnly over his breakfast cereal.

I'm not entirely happy thinking my children will make their way through the English classics via French translations.

"It'd be better in the original language," I suggest.

"Why? This is already horrible enough. It's wonderful."

He cannot put the book down. Its ghoulish illustrations enliven every meal. He must be still very young, I reflect, to wallow safely in gore and mutilation with such innocent glee.

I can think of enough horrible things without Frankenstein's help. And sometimes, I think, things are getting worse as I get older. Or do I simply feel more helpless about the horror we thought we could change when we were so young, so ambitious, so busy?

The China-watcher Jonathan Mirsky e-mails a copy of his latest editorial for the *I.H.T.* He cites reports that mainland Chinese jailers are torturing followers of the religious movement, Falun Gong. An officer has castrated one convert with a clothes hanger, before bludgeoning him to death in front of his wife. Of course, there was no trial, neither for the Falun Gong adherent, nor for the state sadist.

I cannot do anything about the horrors in Afghanistan or Africa, the abuses in South America, the poverty in Eastern Europe. But China was once my stomping ground, my playing field. I feel somehow responsible that too little has changed, for all the talk of rising living standards and social freedoms. And far away in a sleepy Swiss village, I brood on these reports of modern horror.

"You look fatigued, *Madame*," V. says gently. He has found me sitting with a mug of green tea on the balcony off the bedroom. The Alps range across the horizon in the distance, rivaling in grandeur my memory of the Himalayas.

"Don't you think it's ironic that I'm sitting here obsessing about the persecution of the religious in China, when you spent your whole life fighting persecution of the irreligious? You've got to admit, were you Voltaire today, you'd be on the other side."

He growls, "I will always be Voltaire."

"You know what I mean."

" — and it's not true I fought for the irreligious, but I fought against the evils of the established Church, against the persecution of anyone who disagreed, including the religious. I argued for tolerance. I tell you that one should regard all human beings as one's brothers. A Turk my brother? A Chinaman my brother? A Jew? A Siamese? Yes, of course. Are we not all children of the same father and creatures of the same God?"

He takes off his knitted cap, scratching at his scalp, and turns his face to the sun. "Take Calas for instance. You must have heard of that affair."

"um . . ."

He's astonished at my ignorance. "But for Calas, I might be a forgotten scribe, a mere poet."

"Sounds unlikely."

"Ah, *Madame*, Calas was the turning point of my life. May I?"

He callously tosses Frisbee – a tiger-striped rug of snoring fur – off the seat and takes her place next to me. Indignant, Frisbee stares at the empty air.

"Jean Calas was a Huguenot, a Calvinist Protestant, among the few left in Toulouse after a century of rabid Church persecution. By then, Huguenots couldn't hold office, couldn't be lawyers, doctors, midwives or booksellers, goldsmiths or grocers. Their marriages were illegal, their wives considered concubines, their children bastards. Anyone found at a Huguenot service was arrested; the men sent to the galleys of the French navy for life, women put in prison, their clergymen put to death."

Not so far below us, the two little churches of St-Cergue – Protestant and Catholic – chime out noon bells. Voltaire smiles cynically while he waits for the clanging to stop.

"Depressed one night because his faith prevented him from pursuing a law career, one of Jean Calas's sons hung himself from the rafters of the family linen shop. The terrified members of the family knew Toulouse law ruled that a suicide must be drawn naked through the streets to be pelted with mud and stones, and then be hanged. Jean Calas lied to the police, saying his son had died a natural death. The police seized the father, accusing him of murdering his own son to prevent him from converting to Catholicism in order to practice law."

"Surely friends and neighbors knew better."

"Of course, but two trials and a parade of witnesses full of hearsay and gossip silenced those who knew Calas was innocent. The Calas family governess, a Catholic no less, was jailed for five years for defending her employer. A friend who had dined upstairs with the family the very night of the tragedy was sent to the galleys for telling the truth."

V. glances at me, "You do know what that means?"

"Well, I saw *Ben Hur* — "

"The Navy's powers in the Mediterranean had to be maintained. The rowing benches had to be filled! On thirty double benches sat three hundred rowers, shackled six to an oar. Naked to the waist they were never, never, unchained, winter or summer, day or night. They ate and slept on that bench. Think of it, *Madame*, a gentleman named Jean Pierre Espinas was sentenced to the galleys for life, chained to one spot for twenty-three years because he once gave a night's lodging to a Protestant clergyman. Many killed themselves and became corpses chained to an oar."

"What happened to Calas?"

"You talk of horror, *Madame*. Your society devours Monsieur King's books and watches these Hannibal-cannibal movies. You have never endured daily horror as we did in France. Is it not telling to you, a child of the twentieth-century's revulsion at Nazism, that it was to Germany that I first fled the tortures and killings of France, even though it was Germany who taught the French torturers the use of the stake and wheel? It was the French who turned torture into an exercise of such legal precision."

He spits contemptuously over the balcony.

"Please, tell me, what happened to Calas?"

"Imagine, after months of court testimony, you are condemned for killing your own beloved son. You deny it. You are subjected to the *question ordinaire*." He shudders, and sees from my bewildered expression that I have no idea of the *question ordinaire*.

"Your arms and legs are stretched, *Madame*, until they pop from their sockets. Your hands and feet are twisted until they disconnect from the limbs."

I gulp.

"After a short pause, you are revived, to be put to the *question extraordinaire*. Still curious? Fifteen pints of water are poured down your throat. Calas, of course, protested his innocence. Another fifteen pints, forced down him until his broken, useless body swelled to twice its normal size. Then he was dragged to a public square before the cathedral and laid upon a cross. An executioner, with exactly eleven blows of an iron bar, broke each of his limbs in two places. The old man, calling upon Jesus Christ, proclaimed his innocence still, but that was not enough to convince the screaming mob. He dangled there, his head still connected to a pulped, swelling mass of mangled guts, until mercifully, he was strangled, bound to a stake and burned."

"When did this happen?"

"March 10th, 1762."

"March 10 . . . Why that's today!"

He takes a deep breath, and sighs, "Yes, the same as today, a beautiful spring day." He gestures towards the scattered French villages nestling across the base of the powerful mountains in the distance. Off in Toulouse, the great-great-great-great grandchildren of that frenzied, shrieking mob are taking their lunchbreak.

The air is thin. Only the bright sun protects us from a chill. When V. discovered me on the balcony, I felt I was gazing far across the world, removed from ancient schedules, petty anxieties, old deadlines met, trivial obligations discarded. I will be fifty years old in a month and time is shrinking for me. Strange road signs mark the passage of years. This week the U.N. High Commissioner will visit Beijing to plead, among other things, for medical parole for the dissident Xu Wenli, locked up in a Chinese jail.

I met Xu before he served the entirety of his first, eleven-year sentence. We sat in his bare, tiny concrete hutch of an apartment. His small daughter helped her mother make us tea. It was the spring of 1980, in the flush of the Democracy Wall movement. Xu spoke to our visiting B.B.C. film team of his desire to reform the Communist Party, not to overthrow it. His friends turned their faces safely away from the camera. Although the fingers that held his cheap cigarette shook uncontrollably, this skinny fellow faced the lens. His was only a thin voice rising from a little cement box out of a city of faceless millions. He dared to become a face.

No sooner was he released from prison, than he joined the founders of a new democratic party for China. The hammer fell on his head again. Another sentence, this time thirteen years.

How this stubborn toothpick of a prematurely ageing man, struggling with hepatitis B two years into his second sentence in a fetid cell, seems to terrorize the communist gerontocracy cowering behind the high walls of Beijing's Jongnanhai! Just after leaving Hong Kong for good, I got a reporting award in New York. I can only think of the irony that Xu serves a quarter of his life behind bars while I'm feted with a free dinner at the New York Hilton for merely writing about the Chinese prison system.

From time to time, I e-mail or write encouragement to that little tea-making daughter, Jing, now a grown woman, a sculptress in Boston. And the years . . . the years . . . the years tick by, and I count them.

The older I get, the more important that soul chained-up from wife and daughter is to me, I tell V.

"I didn't urge the overthrow of the monarchy," says V.

"Let's face it. You idolized Frederick and Catherine."

"Only because of the potential for good that lay in their power. Yet they say I fathered the French Revolution just by calling for the truth."

"Yes, but I'm sitting in St-Cergue. There's nothing anybody could do for Xu Wenli from a Swiss border town."

He snaps at me, "*Madame*, I did everything from Switzerland's border! You think someone with your energy can sit on the things you've seen, and wrap them up like those little sandwiches your children devour? One speaks out, *Madame*, one makes trouble, one doesn't equivocate or compromise! There are enough people who will do the compromising for you.

"Where did the desperate Calas family seek my help? In Switzerland! I wrote to the Cardinal de Bernis, to d'Argental, to the Duchesse d'Enville, to the Marquise de Nicolaï, to the Duc de Villars, to the Duc de Richelieu. I begged the King's ministers – Choiseul, Saint-Florentin – to investigate the Calas trial. I engaged lawyers, I published a pamphlet, a treatise, then more pamphlets. I begged fellow authors, 'Cry out yourself and let others cry out; cry out for the Calas family. Cry out against fanaticism, stupidity, oppression. Shout everywhere, I beg you, for it is *l'infâme* that has caused their misery.'"

"The infamy again?"

He shakes his head. "*Non, non*, not *l'infamie*. *L'infâme*. That meant the murderous Church with its lies, tortures, hypocrisies, its terror so despicable and vile. The name Voltaire was quickly everywhere, linked to that of Jean Calas. *Écrasez l'infâme*, crush the monster! became my slogan. By the time I was sixty-eight, I suffered almost all the time from colic, but whenever I attacked *l'infâme*, the pains mysteriously disappeared. I had the energy of a youth and why not?"

"You were taking on the whole of Mother Church."

"*Madame*, I was taking on the most powerful institution in the history of mankind! A prominent lawyer in Paris prepared the case for the Council of State. I raised contributions from a hundred quarters, including the Queen of England, the Empress of Russia, the King of Poland."

He leans back, to catch his breath, then adds, "Finally, I appealed to God."

"And what did you say to Him?" It's no longer ridiculous that God would listen to Voltaire.

"I wrote, 'Thou hast not given us hearts to hate, nor hands to kill one another. May the trifling differences in the garments that cover our frail bodies, in the mode of expressing our thoughts, in our ridiculous customs and imperfect laws not be used by us as signal of mutual hatred and persecution.'"

"Pretty wordy. Did God answer?"

"Of course."

My eyes widen.

"Well, through Louis the King. The King's Council pronounced Jean Calas innocent in 1765. The King granted 30,000 livres to the widow and children for loss of property."

"And you did all that with your pen . . ."

"When I heard the decision, I wept for joy. Me at seventy-one, crying like *un enfant*! I did it all over again for the Sirven family, accused in Toulouse of killing their own daughter who had converted to Catholicism and committed suicide by throwing herself down a well. Sirven saw with horror what had happened to Jean Calas. His trial was to be heard in Toulouse before the same authorities who had pulled Calas limb from limb. The Sirven family fled to Geneva. It took two hours to condemn that man to death and nine years for me to prove him innocent."

"So the royal entertainer and science buff became a crusader?"

V. starts. "A Crusader? Hardly."

I explain, "I mean someone who campaigns doggedly against impossible odds."

"Not a seeker for the Holy Grail?"

"In your case, the Grail was Enlightenment."

He likes this comparison. "Yes and freedom from guilt. The sort of guilt you feel sitting on this balcony in the sun while the Messieurs Xus of our world sit in rancid cells."

Of our world. He's right, of course. When Xu's first trial

came up, his words were twisted against him, the verdict as rigged as that against Calas. His Beijing friends asked the B.B.C. for its recording of the entire interview. The tape would prove he hadn't argued for "revolution" but had called for reform within the Socialist system. No one in London could find the cassette which had been tossed away after the broadcast.

I feel sick recalling the disappointment in Beijing.

"Never feel guilty. If you were perfect, you would be God."

"That's good to remember."

He chuckles, "Oh, I felt guilt, but I had better reason than you. A general's son of nineteen years old named La Barre was charged with smearing a crucifix with *ordure*. La Barre confirmed he was a heretic, that he couldn't understand why anyone would celebrate the Host at Mass or what he dared to call The God of Dough. Among his books, they found my *Dictionnaire Philosophique*. The Parliament of Paris argued that I was the real criminal, but that as I was safe from their clutches, hiding in Rolle — "

"That's only a few villages away from here — !"

"My disciple should suffer in my stead. They ordered his tongue be torn out. He was beheaded and his body burnt while they were looking for mine. Hearing they had carried out the execution and were now hunting for me, I laid in a large supply of Holy Water."

He tosses me a wicked wink.

"How can you joke?"

"Oh, one jokes to cover fear. And there was so much to do! So many cases, so many letters to write! I petitioned Louis XV, then Louis XVI, attacking the extremists of the Church. A Protestant minister in Geneva said to me, 'You attack Christianity, yet do a Christian's work.'"

That night Peter takes his turn to do something Christian for a tortured soul. As an I.C.R.C veteran of prison visits in war-torn countries, he's used to shedding light into dark places.

"I've had it with the Thing buried alive in our walls."

He disappears, returning moments later with a saw and a step ladder.

"You're not going to saw a hole in the ceiling of my new kitchen!"

It's too late. My spouse has already pencilled a large circle on the white-painted trim. He saws around it and removes a neat plug of wood. Two huge, demonic green eyes blink out of the hole at us, totally blinded by the light.

Eva-Marie shrieks, "It's the Thing!"

I think of the animals that populate the forested plateau behind our house – foxes, marmosets, and bats.

"Why doesn't it move?" Theo whispers.

Peter looks into the blinking orbs. "It's blinded by the light. And it's used to our voices by now."

He fetches a strip of ham and very carefully places it at the edge of the hole. In a split-second, the meat has been whipped off his fingertips.

"Aiiihhh!" Peter grabs his bleeding fingers. "*Um Gottes'wille!*" he swears in Swiss-German. "At least its sense of smell is intact."

Suddenly a black, elongated wraith slithers and stumbles out of the hole, flipping and scrambling down the cookbook shelves. The kids are screaming as the pipe-like beast flings itself from room to room in a panicked search for an exit from the house.

"This way! It went this way," Eva-Marie yells. "Into the playroom."

The Thing cowers in a corner under the videotapes.

Peter shouts, "Block all the doorways." He throws open the kitchen door to the terrace. The Thing makes a desperate dash, here blocked by Alexander like a hockey goalie from the living room, there blocked by Theo like a line-back from the route up the stairs. The maddened beast ricochets off the walls, knocking down Lego set-ups, snow boots, and brooms, until at last it flies out of the kitchen and streaks away across the frozen yard.

"It was a cat," Eva-Marie says, a bit let down.

"Probably a wild kitten hidden for the winter by its mother inside our insulation piping. It got trapped and lived on bats from the attic — " Peter speculates.

"The crunching sound! Eewwwwww," says Alexander.

"I vant to drink your blooood," Theo says with a Dracula leer.

If only it were so easy to shed light on suffering.

Voltaire showed what could be done with a witty, persistent pen. He was Europe's first one-man N.G.O., the first modern humanitarian organization. Now women and men fight the powers-that-be for causes all over the world – against drug barons, Mafiosi, child prostitution, child soldiers, hunger, powdered milk, corruption, assault weapons, slavery, corporate greed, on and on.

It has been some years since I saw my byline in a newspaper. Something that once seemed so easy, so accessible, now gives me pause. I wrote beneath the standard of a magazine or sheltered behind the authority of a respected institution. The girl who put a chemical weapons smuggler behind German bars from her obscure Hong Kong two-room office, who won an award for prison labor coverage, who shot out letter after letter from New York demanding release and relief for imprisoned journalists – well? What has happened to that feisty female? Alone, without a calling card, she has been muffled by Swiss expectations of motherhood, by those deadly social anaesthetizers – laundry and lunch-boxes.

Xu Wenli sits in a barred cell, hidden away from the Potemkinesque China shown the visiting Olympic Committee from Lausanne. My friends in China e-mail me that China has changed beyond my ken, that I know nothing about the "new" China. They cannot erase this fact, however; the innocent Xu rots in jail. If V. can send a message from Switzerland, so can I. I e-mail the *I.H.T.*

Dear Editors,
Regarding Olympic Sleuths Need to See Through the Beijing
Whitewash *by Jonathan Mirsky and* China Quiets Critics for
Olympic Visit *by Elizabeth Rosenthal: Might I suggest a logo for*
Beijing's Olympics? How about a set of interlinked handcuffs
replacing the traditional Olympian hoops, and two circles of barbed
wire for the "zeros" in 2008?

"Bravo!" Three days later, V. returns grinning from our mailbox, brandishing the paper. "Your few lines reached beyond
the schoolyard! Beyond Arzier, Genolier, Givrins, Trelex,
down to Nyon, across to Geneva and Lausanne, up to Zurich,
Paris, London, New York, and hee! hee! Beijing! Ah, the
golden years! The years when the whole world knew what I
fought for! What I fought against!"

He narrows his eyes and adds pointedly, "Some of us even
did it without e-mail! You know, you give me an idea,
Madame . . ."

Why does he look like Frisbee when she's just caught a bird?

L'Infâme.org

I tackle my house ghost trying to sneak the coffee machine back up to his office. This Sisyphean feat of psychic lifting has been going on for weeks, although V. practically fades into half-transparency for hours after plugging it in. Peter yanks it back to the kitchen counter and mutters about my early morning habits, and V. smuggles it back up the next morning.

"Monsieur Voltaire!"

He futilely tries hiding the coffee machine behind his back. A soft white ink-stained cap gives his graying hair a sheepish air.

"Forget the machine," I scoff. "Who's this?" I point to this morning's "Letters to the Editor" column in the *I.H.T.* The very first letter is from a "Frank Arouet, Philosopher and Playwright."

"Oh, that. *C'est moi.*"

"*Frank* Arouet?"

"No one would believe François Voltaire, for obvious reasons."

"And what is Frank Arouet doing, exactly?"

"Oh, in print again at last! I was inspired by your little note to the newspaper. I sent in my thoughts on globalization and the inevitability of a single morality governing the behavior of civilized men of different cultures. This is delightful!"

Voltaire has overstayed his welcome. Despite our long hours,

I'm getting very little writing done because he insists on reading aloud to me everything he composes. He may be a playwright-turned-polemicist, but at heart, he'll always be a ham.

And an expensive ham . . .

"I'm sorry to bring up these costs, but I may have to give you up for Lent," I joke a little to ease the blow.

"Ah, it is the Lenten season, of course. Is there a higher tax on beef and pork? Are the profits being given to the hospitals? Do they still do that?"

"Not any more. The meat prices are rock bottom, more thanks to mad cow disease than Church laws and – stop changing the subject! This is the Mastercard bill. Last month you spent more than $500 on book orders from Amazon and Alibris. And now long distance calls to Pakistan! Would you care to explain those?"

"It's the comfortable people like you who have to suffer price rises." He wags a finger. "Don't complain. Remember, the poor fast all the year long."

"I'm sure. Now about these calls to Pakistan — ?"

"I should have known that the Lenten laws would change. It's just like I say here in the paper. All societies do not have the same laws. What is a crime in Europe might be a virtue in Asia, just as certain German stews will never please the French epicures. All societies will not have the same laws, but no society will be without any laws at all. Here, read this line, right here, it's quite good — "

I read out loud, "The good of society is established by all men from Beijing to Ireland as the immutable rule of virtue; what is *useful to society* will be therefore good in all countries."

"Exactly!" He straightens with pride. "Now, *Madame*, mail these, if you would be so kind!"

He balances the machine on one buckled knee breech, while he fishes in his canvas apron for a bundle of hand-addressed envelopes bound together with coarse string.

The top envelope is addressed to "Monsieur le Secretary-General, Kofi Annan," the next one to "Monsieur George Soros," the next to "Le President Vicente Fox," and so on.

Return addressee: Frank Arouet.

"There are more than two dozen letters here, *Frank*." I arch an eyebrow.

"Send them all by messenger to the Hotel Steigenberger Belvédère in Davos. They're all attending the World Economic Forum. Hurry! The conference ends soon."

I don't budge. "You think your *pensées de Frank* will fit into the Davos discussions?"

He struggles to comprehend my stupidity. Out of his deep pocket he pulls a news photo of rioters fighting heavily-padded Swiss policemen.

"Why, *Madame*, it's obvious that there is a difference of opinion raging in the streets not a day's drive from where we stand, from the hushed dining rooms of the world's privileged to the hordes behind these barricades of barbed wire surrounding that town."

"Yes, I know, about the W.T.O. and the World Bank, that happens every year in Davos, but — "

"And why? An inability to agree on what is good for society! You see, place two men on the earth; they will only call good, virtuous, and just that which is good for both of them. Place four, and there will be nothing virtuous except what is suitable to all four. What I say of these four men must be said of the whole universe! These leaders in Davos cannot go forward without any thought for what will be for the good of all."

"Well, Bill Gates will do whatever he wants . . . "

V. loses patience with me, "Now, here, here, take these as well," he says, thrusting a second pile of envelopes so high they slither to the floor.

He throws up his hands. "I should've gone myself. I could have used a 'hotmail' address at the hotel business center."

"Speaking of going — "

"Yes, do. I'm so very busy now . . . "

It's true. He seems to have a hundred irons burning away in that feverish brain of his.

In fact, just yesterday, he got one of the biggest thrills of his after-life. The *Neue Zürcher Zeitung* reported in a two-inch squib that the Arnheim Provincial City Archives' Edwin van Meerkerk had unveiled a lost fragment of V.'s sci-fi hit, *Micromégas*, that tale featuring two intergalactic spacemen. The absurdities of war, the vanities of intellectual elites, the ignorant superstitions of V.'s time, are artfully satirized.

Is it my imagination, or has V. abandoned his frothy verses and his scientific apparatus for something new? His fables like *Micromégas* are more political, almost philosophical, and (if I may say so out of his earshot), a lot more readable than his notes on Leibniz's monads.

V. fondles the tiny N.Z.Z. clipping for the fiftieth time. "They could have included my portrait," he comments.

"Of what, your bones?"

"Tsk, well, maybe that painting by de Largillière that I had done for that actress, what was her name?"

"Suzanne something."

Really, I think the guy's getting on.

With or without the mug shot, this posthumous publicity pleases him. One of his latest ideas is to produce more fragments – which I will conveniently unearth somewhere under Peter's wine bottles in the bike room.

Another phone bill arrives, demanding two hundred francs just for calls to Pakistan.

"It's about Pakistan," I say the next morning. V. looks like he hasn't slept for days. The desk is covered with print-outs and drafts of letters.

"I used the fax. There's so much to do — "

"Yes, I know, but even if you stayed here for another two hundred years, you couldn't remake the world now, any more than you did then. These calls to Pakistan — "

"Ahh, but I did remake the world once, you see," he says, black circles under his eyes.

"They call me the Father of the French Revolution, and it was those very calls for liberty, fraternity, etc., that inspired your American Founding Fathers, or so Mr. Franklin told me when he visited me in Paris. If it hadn't been for me — "

"What do you think you can do, when no one but me can see you or hear you?"

He looks at me dismayed. "You don't need to 'see' or 'hear' something to know that it is part of a sequence of cause and effect. But if you want to be so tediously literal about it, well, today I've devoted myself to the question of slavery in Sudan."

"Oh?"

"I've put a call out on my web site, L'Infâme.org, for *manifestations* at all the Sudanese embassies next month." He giggles wickedly, "I got the idea from those Falun Gong people. They mobilize thousands of people within days without warning."

"Monsieur Voltaire — "

"Speaking of the Chinese, I've made a cyber-link to the Tiananmen Mothers campaign. But you know," he sighs, totally distracted now by his own train of thought, "overall, I'm rather disappointed by the Chinese . . ."

"These phone calls to Pakistan?"

"Faxes, not calls," he corrects me.

"They still cost two — "

He thrusts a clipboard in my face. "Could you sign this petition demanding the Communists tell the truth about Tiananmen?"

"It's a deal, if you lay off the fax machine."

His eyes fill with incredulity. "And how do I send this in after you sign? Or – or – these briefing papers to the Washington lobby against capital punishment? I've got lots of experience with wrongful executions that's coming in useful here!"

"Monsieur Voltaire — "

"You can't cut me off like this! You can't! Just last week, I learned that people actually want to stop inoculating their children against disease. Unbelievable, isn't it, after the trouble I took to introduce smallpox inoculation to France! It was one of my Letters from London!"

"Monsieur Voltaire! Frank!"

"Look, look, I've had – *un instant*," he pecks frantically with two fingers at my keyboard, "*voilà!* Four hundred and seventy-two hits on my Sudan page since Monday. Timed for a Congressional hearing on oil companies evading the embargo on trading with the Khartoum regime. I shall use your Real Player to regard it on C-Span!"

I pause to take this in. "Four hundred and seventy-two people visited your web site?"

"The Dalai Lama gives cyber-blessings online. Why shouldn't I have a few hundred disciples? You look pale, *Madame*. Are you unwell?"

I sink into a chair. "Four hundred and seventy-two people think you're real?"

Voltaire groans. "*Madame*, I exist in the minds of generation after generation. I exist every time someone says, 'I disagree with what you say, but I'll defend to the death your right to say it,' even if he's never heard of Voltaire. I was so wrong to despair. My spirit is not dead at all! Now! The B.B.C. broadcasts a program called 'Talking Point'. Let us call in. You will do the talking so I can make the point."

"Monsieur Voltaire, I'm trying to make a point right now — "

"*Please, Madame*, there'll be some technical problems if I try alone," he pleads. "The faxes to Pakistan are something else. It's a support hot-line for Dr. Shaikh. I'm part of a global letter-writing campaign to save his life."

"Oh, God. Who's Dr. Shaikh?"

"Ah, so little has changed! Dr. Younus Shaikh is a physiology teacher in Islamabad and a member of the International

Humanist and Ethical Union. You've never heard of him?"

"No," I whimper.

"He spoke at the World Humanist Congress in 1999!"

"I missed it."

"Well," V. shrugs, perplexed, "Dr. Shaikh now stands condemned to death because students at the Capital Homeopathic Medical College allege he taught that before Mohammed became the Prophet, he was uncircumcised, with unshaven armpits and," V. gestures below his waist, "et cetera."

Now I can't believe my ears. "They want to execute a profesor for saying that Mohammed had body hair?"

"Well, of course Mohammed had body hair. Mohammed adopted the ritual of circumcision and shaving only after he became the Prophet. Will it never end? Those who believe absurdities are bound to commit atrocities. I parodied these religious wars between turbaned fanatics and warmongering Europeans two centuries ago. I'm adding a cyber-link between L'Infâme.org and Dr. Shaikh's campaign before the Movement for the Finality of the Prophet can have him killed."

"Well, Monsieur Voltaire, that's very worthy, but we can't go on with these incredible bills!"

"Oh, in that regard, I've got good news. Here's a letter with an offer from some fruit vendors. Perhaps it will help to pay my website costs."

"This is an offer to appear in an Apple computer ad. How did it find you?"

"My web site. I don't approve of their grammatical style."

"Don't tell me. I can guess."

He holds his quill up to his brow, his aquiline nose quivering with energy, and his eyes shining with life. With mock gravitas, he intones, "Think Different."

Later that day, I try again, heading for the office with fresh determination. V. jumps up, covering the screen with his hands.

"What's this? Another letter to Kofi Annan?"

I lean over the laptop, but he quickly tilts the screen away. Amidst his frantic attempts to close the "window," I read aloud:

"'Eh, mon Dieu, my dear child, what are your legs and mine trying to say? If they were together they would be well . . . Those lovely thighs so soon to be kissed are now shamefully treated . . . I shall be coming only for you, if my miserable condition permits, I will throw myself at your knees and kiss all your beauties — '"

"*Madame!*" he shouts, "That is private!"

"I'll say! Wooooooa, what is this?"

I continue reading, trying hard not to laugh with the shock of catching him *in flagrante delicto*, "Stop pushing me!"

"'In the meantime, I press a thousand kisses on your round breasts, on your ravishing cunt, on all your person, which has so often given me erections and plunged me into a flood of delight — '"

"*Madame*, you've no right to read my letters!"

"Are you blushing?" I'm laughing hard now.

"Reading other people's letters is a despicable, shameful thing! Frederick the Great lowered himself in my eyes, that monster, by doing just that in Potsdam."

"Madame du Châtelet read other people's letters and you didn't stop her."

"She had a right to know what was being said by her guests!"

His bony face is perspiring with embarrassment. He's pulled a thread on one of his lacy cuffs, and his cap is askew. I've injured his ageing masculine pride.

"You said you retired from the sex game. Who's the lucky lady?"

He straightens his cap. "Madame Denis. I'm revising some of my letters to her in case there should be a reissue of our correspondence."

"Let me see," I read a letter open on the desk. "'My dear

enfant, I shall not see you today. My days are not all happy ones. I can neither go out, work, rest, digest my diet or sleep . . . I've had not two good hours since I saw you last . . . I don't know yet when my affairs will allow me to leave a place I abhor.' Oh, thank you very much, Monsieur Voltaire. You abhor it here . . . "

"These weren't about now, *Madame*, these were written while I was laboring away in that rat-hole in Versailles. I'll hide them under the floor and you'll come upon them — "

"Wait a minute – Madame Denis – is she the lady who came to visit Émilie and you in Cirey?"

"*Oui.*"

"Monsieur Voltaire! That woman is your own niece, your sister's daughter! That's incest! Aren't you the guy thrown in the Bastille for writing that the Regent was sleeping with his daughter?"

"He *was* sleeping with his daughter. But this is different. Latin cultures do not consider it incest to sleep with your niece. In my day, a man could marry his niece by dispensation from the Pope for 40,000 ecus." He smirks, "But I hear the satirist Marmontel got his niece between the sheets for only 80,000 francs."

"Well, times have changed!"

His expression looks almost satyr-like. "Humph! Not necessarily for the better. Now the Pope's too busy covering up for his own priests to worry about nieces. Anyway, you shouldn't act so superior. It just proves my theory that other people's weaknesses brought to light give pleasure only to the spiteful."

"I'm not spiteful, just . . . just disgusted. How long did this go on?"

"Well, let's see, we all went to Paris in 1744. Richelieu asked Rameau and me to write that play for the wedding of the Dauphin to the Infanta of Spain. Things took off about then."

He smiles the most self-satisfied, dirty-old-man leer ever seen.

"That was only two years after you left Émilie's bed, five years before Émilie died! I thought you said Madame Denis was fat and stupid. Then you fell in love with her?"

V. pulls his weedy frame upright.

"*Madame*, you understand nothing! Love is a canvas furnished by Nature and embroidered by imagination, of which I, at least, have a great deal. For the last two centuries, Madame Denis has enjoyed her reputation as an honorable widow, a warm hostess, and besides," he hesitates, "besides, she had such a delicious derrière, really *mignon* — "

"Oh, YUK! All she cared for was your money. You think she changed once you made a fortune selling war supplies with those crooked Pâris brothers? I know what your niece was after!"

His eyes flare up indignantly.

"It wasn't just physical. Sensual pleasure passes in the twinkling of an eye. The friendship between us, the mutual confidence, the delights of the heart, the enchantment of the soul, these things do not perish and can never be destroyed. I loved her until I – well, anyway, nobody knew about my passion for Madame Denis. It was a great secret from history and you wouldn't have known about it if you weren't such an aggressive, inquisitive – American!"

"Oh, stop being an old fool. She was greedy as — "

His frosty expression tells me I'm wasting my breath. "Well, I certainly don't begrudge deserving people who share in my good fortune. And at least *she* doesn't *nag!*"

Blood floods my cheeks. Exhaustion from over-exposure to the kids' homework problems, the frustration of publishing rejections, the burden of ever-mounting housework, all wash over me. V.'s bills and insults are the last straw.

"You're calling me a nag? You boney, old, snuff-sniffing has-been? Your ninety volumes are crumbling into dust! Look at this mess, these brochures, these posters, these leaflets. The only people reading you are a bunch of French lit majors and –

and – and web geeks. Your histories are all outdated. Nobody stages your plays! And if we get any more bills like these, I'll tell Peter exactly who's the house guest from Hell and he'll call an exterminator or, yeah! Even better! A priest! An exorcist to flush you out, you horny old insect — "

I stop yelling at him, shaking too hard to go on.

His eyes turn mean.

"You? Threaten me? With priests? I came here to help you. You know nobody, you are nobody. You should have stayed in New York, kept your career and stopped slobbering over those three – WHO'S A HAS-BEEN?"

I whisper viciously in his face, "You're jealous you never had any children."

He can sink just as low. "You envy me my fame, my success, my – my – my *GLOIRE!*"

"Which is nothing but glorious DUST!"

That turns him whiter than usual. His trembling hands slam down the lid of my laptop. He grabs his walking stick and raises it in the air, struggling for breath. His eyes are wild and he collapses in my chair, choking out, "I'm speechless."

"HAH. For once! Well, I'm not. I seem to recall a certain Enlightened Philosopher once said" – I mimic his French accent cruelly – "'The necessity of saying something, the perplexity of having nothing to say, and a desire to be witty are three circumstances which could make even the greatest writer ridiculous.' Ridiculous! So there!"

"*Madame*, you are excused!"

Really, it's too much. When he was young and attractive, his ribald side had its eighteenth-century charm. I enjoyed his double-entendres. I understood his passion for the mercurial, mathematical Marquise Émilie. Am I jealous? No, lechery in a great man of his advanced age for his fat, money-grubbing niece is just not endearing.

I admit I'd started to avoid V., his eternal rivalries with that Maupertuis and all the others, and the back-biting over his only "real friend" Frederick. The sheer vanity of the man has come to outweigh any fun we've had.

I'm too proud to let him think I'm pre-occupied with our fight. I attack the Tibet novel, lost cause or no. I throw Eva-Marie's birthday party at a bowling alley. Theo must be driven to orchestra rehearsals. Alexander's backpack needs cleaning out. I have to polish my mother's silver. Really.

Peter's sixtieth birthday approaches. Desperate to escape the claustrophobia of St-Cergue or the sterility of a dinner in Geneva, I arrange a very special night away for the two of us in Lyon, over the border in France, ninety minutes' away.

We drive through heavy rain towards an industrial city wrapped in white sales and late winter fog off the Saône and Rhône Rivers. I feel I haven't really had a chance to enjoy my husband since we moved to Switzerland. We check into a luxury hotel and soak in a bubbly jacuzzi for two, sharing foot massages. We dress up and eat a four-star meal at Léon de Lyon that consists mostly of truffles and *réductions de veau*.

Peter is relaxed, passionate, and tender. He doesn't say a single philosophical or archly witty thing all weekend. It's great. It brings back our happy times in Hong Kong, before house restoration, school confusions, and Swiss taxes cut into our *joie de vivre*.

I reflect over a glass of fine wine. Who needs the Big Wig? Haven't I adjusted well to Switzerland? I no longer mail order my clothes from the States or save that last ounce of special hair rinse from the York Avenue pharmacy. Do I still need the so-called solace of V.'s wacky faxes, dirty letters, and egotistical poetry readings?

I ride home Sunday night, braced all over again to evict the Greatest Mind of the Eighteenth Century from my corner of the twenty-first century. If he clears out, I might start a new novel.

While Peter carries our bags in from the car, I march upstairs to my office, girded for what will be a difficult scene.

The corner of my office is stacked with boxes spilling over with V.'s stuff. The oil portraits of his buddies Cathy and Fred "the Greats" are rolled up. I find a note on my desk, written in the elegant hand of the greatest letter-writer of the eighteenth century, a man famous for penning more than fifty thousand letters in his lifetime.

To me the master of correspondence can only manage one word: "*Ciao.*"

Ciao?

Les Délices

I survive three whole weeks without him.

The house is silent. I finish a morning's stint of half-hearted revision, and tackle the housework with ill-humored ferocity. Peter is thrilled with the near-Swiss quality of our domestic life. When I catch myself dusting the North Korean Red Cross medals in Peter's cabinet, I crack.

Twice I reach for the phone, but whom do I call? How do you hunt for a phantom? Where would he go? What would he haunt? The Académie Française? The Globe Theatre? Berlin whorehouses?

Letters for "Frank Arouet" overflow our mail box. The Tiananmen Mothers' rally in New York comes and goes without his petition. The invitation from the American Anti-Slavery Group to a conference in Washington D.C. sits un-answered.

Then Mr. Mustapha telephones.

"Please, very kind lady," he says, "may I speak to Mr. Arouet?"

"Well, I can honestly say that Frank's not here anymore. He left no forwarding number or address."

"It is very important I get in touch with him, dear lady. A letter from Mr. Arouet at this time would be most useful, most necessary, indeed."

"I wouldn't count on any more letters for the moment. He's really out of contact with me."

"Oh, that is most unfortunate, most unfortunate. We have a situation of extreme delicacy, involving a certain Dr. Shaikh."

"You're referring to the capital punishment case in Islamabad? The disagreement about Mohammed's, um, uh, personal grooming?"

"That is the case, dear lady. Peace be upon the Prophet." I have the impression that his last utterance is to wipe out any contamination caused by my irreverent summing up of the Islamic circumcision dilemma.

V.'s caller continues, "The arguments are in the balance. The mullahs from Bahawal Nagar have tried to reason with the mullahs from Islamabad that no blasphemy can be committed if issues are raised about the period before the Holy Prophet declared his prophethood. The mullahs in Islamabad are almost convinced, but they don't want to lose face. Dr. Shaikh's life hangs by a slender thread, slender indeed. The pen of Mr. Arouet could find a way around this, I am very sure."

"Well, I'm sorry, I've no idea where Frank went. Have you checked his web site?"

"Yes, lady. We have sent Mr. Frank Arouet many e-mails, but to no avail."

I take down Mr. Mustapha's telefax number which looks painfully familiar. I promise to let him know if Frank gets in touch.

Frank doesn't get in touch.

Finally, I turn for help to the only French literature expert I know. It's a little hard to get Christine by phone. I haven't seen her, the "Duchess of Richelieu," since our New Year's Eve party, where she so charmed V. with her *sagesse* and smiling blue eyes. Jean is always travelling to distant parts on behalf of children with AIDS, and Christine teaches full-time in Lausanne. I have to try at least three times before she answers the phone.

"Christine, I'm doing a little research. I need some information on Voltaire."

"His stories? I can lend them to you, in French of course."

"No, not his stories."

I've certainly heard enough of his stories.

"Well, how can I help?" I hear little Charlotte singing in the background.

"If you were Voltaire today, where would you go?"

Christine laughs, a little confused. "*Pardon?*"

"I mean, if you were Voltaire around here, where would you spend your time?"

"At the theater?"

"Yes . . . Any other ideas?"

"Maybe at home? He had a house in Geneva called Les Délices, on the Rue des Délices. He used to insulate the flooring with books he'd already read. I take my students there."

I find Rue des Délices on a Geneva city map. I can't believe I'm doing this. I spent weeks hinting to the man that he should clear out. Then I can't endure the silence without him. His old-fashioned science collection heaped in a cardboard printer box is starting to fade into invisibility. His leather-bound books are shedding little piles of dust at each corner. Any minute now, I reckon, the rest of his belongings might be collected by one of his po-faced secretarial wraiths, like Longchamp or Wagnière.

"You don't seem very happy these days," Peter observes, and orders me up his cure-all – new bras from Victoria's Secret.

The April skies pour with rain. As I set off from St-Cergue, angry curtains of water obscure Geneva from my view. Even in good weather, I'm a lousy driver. I drove rarely in Hong Kong and New York. Usually I only drive to and from schools and music lessons along well-memorized routes.

My car pushes down the curves of our mountain against a virtual cloud of flying raindrops, as if Lac Léman has risen up and is throwing itself against the Jura. The weather lets up for a few minutes as I round a hairpin curve into a blanket of steam, drifting in wisps through the tall pines.

"Rousseau would love this," I complain, then realize there's nobody at my side to share the laugh.

I reach the expressway on-ramp by nine in the morning, my hands clenching the wheel, headlights beaming against the fog. My car is caught up in a pack of commuters taking lane-changes at 140 kilometres an hour. The wake of their speeding fenders splashes against my wheels. I'm pulled along by their reckless momentum into the suburbs of Geneva, elegant villas hiding behind manicured hedges.

Ordinarily, I would take the right hand turn up the Avenue de la Paix, to the International Committee of the Red Cross. Instead, I plunge along a river of commuter traffic, winding down narrow lanes never meant for impatient cars, past the overcrowded train station, sidewalks spilling over with people under umbrellas pushing against the lights.

"Not the left lane," I warn myself, as that would shoot me over one of the bridges to the Old Town of Geneva, with its stolid bank buildings lining the *quai*. "Lemme over, you turkey," I curse the truck blocking my shift into the right lane mounting the Rue de Lyon. I sail on with no way of reading the street signs, slowing down or pulling over to consult my map. Cars honk and screech their wheels around me.

Where am I? Rue de Benjamin Franklin whizzes by, and then Rue de Tronchin.

"If they're naming streets after your friends, you must be around here somewhere," I address the empty passenger seat.

Nothing eighteenth century catches my eye. I pass an Ethiopian restaurant, second-hand shops, and boarded-up store-fronts. I can hardly imagine V. strolling this neighborhood in his red velvet coat with its satin piping and grosgrain-covered buttons on each cuff. I can't recall – did he take his rain cloak?

At one point, I reach a corner of Rue des Délices, but a traffic warden waves me off in the opposite direction. Sweating in my plastic mac, I lurch desperately into a loading dock and yank off my driving glasses to read the map. North African youths shout at me to back out of the path of a departing van.

White-knuckled, I finally work the car into a tiny space along the Rue de Poterie. I'm probably parked illegally and I no longer care. I'm tossed by blustering spring winds down the Rue de Lyon, past Rue de Tronchin. The wet map slaps into my face.

Ugly signs raise my hopes: Video Voltaire, Voltaire Pressing, Voltaire Pharmacie, and Bibliothèque Voltaire. My feet turn into the Rue des Délices. Finally, I stand before stately gates and peer through the whipping gusts to read a sizable bronze plaque engraved, Musée Voltaire.

I squeeze past the gate into a garden of hedges set out in a formal maze and then, what a house! Two stories high, of classical dimensions, with a little round window peeking out from the attic floor through the roof, a stately entrance up a few steps, V.'s own stately home. Well, why *wouldn't* he prefer this elegant dwelling to my crooked farmhouse with its low-ceilings and bat-eating cats? Even in the rain, his garden is immaculate compared to my mountain *potager* with its torn plastic tunnels collapsing on to weedy seedlings.

I adjust my soggy appearance. Inside the tall double doors sits a Cerberus of a man, his beard cut into an artificial curve along his chin, his broad face as sun-burnt as a sailor's. He gives only a hint of a smile.

The house is dead silent. My shoes squeak.

"Put your umbrella in the stand at the head of the stairs, then go around these rooms, starting on the right," the man states without any introduction on my part.

"Then go upstairs," he adds.

I dutifully shake the water off my umbrella before putting it in the stand. Like a schoolgirl, I obediently enter a long gallery decorated in panels of light blue and yellow. Display cases filled with documents and letters from Voltaire, Madame du Châtelet, and Frederick the Great line the center of the room.

How strange to see their handwriting – so human, so real!

I know V.'s hand – large-lettered, rounded and full. Émilie's handwriting is sharp and urgent, her letters like rows of anxious rose thorns, her words full of constant anxiety for V.'s safety. Frederick's letters look the strangest of all, for someone coming down through history as so "great": teeny-tiny letters, the meek presentation of a boy thoroughly bullied by his ogre father. I am startled to see that I can read every word of the Prussian's epistle to his mentor, his calligraphy is so polite and modestly unaffected.

Here is V.'s pension from Marie Leszczynska, the Queen of France! Just a simple piece of paper, noting the size of V.'s portion, 1500 francs, in the corner, almost as an afterthought. No royal seal, no majestic flourish below the simple, "Marie." Here is a girl who knows that had she not been miraculously located in a stable by her dethroned father King Stanislaus as he fled Poland, she would have been raised as a foundling. She knows who she is, this girl who relies only on "Marie."

Now here's a landscape of Les Délices as it was during V.'s time. No Voltaire Video shops then. Not even a hedge. Just grass and trees and bucolic estates in the distance.

There is a stale quiet inside this place, while the Geneva traffic pounds away through the storm outside the curtained windows.

I move to the next room, painted pistachio and vanilla. My eyes fall on a portrait of Émilie. She's a bit pudgy around the chin and her nose is a little too long. The whole effect comes embarrassingly close to a friendly weasel with highly-colored complexion and sharp, intelligent brown eyes. Her dress of green velvet has a deep décolleté lined in fur. Around her throat is a necklace of feathers. I recognize the sensual spirit in her smiling portrait. Everything in the painting is touchable, from the abundant curls and white skin to the fluffy adornments.

Voltaire is nowhere to be found, unless you count the smiling portrait hanging not far from Émilie's, the oil painting by Largillière. Well, here he is, with all the good looks and bright hopes of his youth, a shadow of dark beard giving lie to the flamboyantly curled white wig, his thin lips still rosy with *bon mots* to come, his brown eyes shining with life.

This is how I remember him looking that first night in Theo's room.

"He had dashing looks in those days, didn't he?" says a deep voice behind me.

I turn to face a fantastic creature dressed in a gold vest covered with an ermine coat splashed with wine stains. Jewels twisted around his neck can't hide the stubble of a bad shave. A dramatic turban set with rubies can't distract me completely from his red-rimmed, watery eyes and pudgy complexion.

"Lekain, at your service, *Madame*."

"Of course, the actor," I nod, a little nonplussed.

"The world-renowned *artiste*."

"Yes, I beg your pardon. Is Monsieur Voltaire here?"

"I haven't seen him since our little performance, *Madame*. As you can see, I haven't had time to change out of my costume as Orosmane, the good Muslim sultan."

"Yes, *Monsieur* says you were fabulous in all the parts he wrote for you."

"I still am fabulous." Lekain cocks a displeased eyebrow at me. "*Monsieur* is devoted to my talent," he says, preening himself. "But I must say, his own performances these last few weeks have left something to be desired."

"He's here then! Is he unwell?"

"Is he ever well? That man will insist on getting up and playing parts which no longer suit him, no matter what we say," Lekain toys with his chain of paste jewels.

"Where is he? I mean, is he receiving today?"

"I haven't the slightest idea. You know how he hides himself away until he needs an audience. The last thing I heard, he was holding court upstairs, soaking up praise for his portrayal of Lusignan."

Lekain makes it clear he has better things to do. Making a final turn around the ground floor, I finally spot Voltaire sitting at his desk.

"Monsieur Voltaire," I say. He doesn't respond. Nor does the right hand clutching a pen even budge.

"Monsieur Voltaire?"

My friend doesn't acknowledge my voice. Head bent over his beautiful escritoire, he doesn't move at all. I'm addressing a museum dummy, dressed in V.'s own white brocade damask three-piece-suit with the flowered embroidery around the coat lapels, lace fluffing out around his craggy neck above the long waistcoat. A cheap wig sits on its head.

I've thought often in the last few months that I'm losing my mind, but there's something especially weird about this place. The dead actors talk to you and the liveliest of companions turns out to be wood.

I emerge back into the foyer. The man behind the reception desk hasn't shifted a muscle.

"What's upstairs?" I ask politely.

"The rest," he says, with that sly smile unchanging.

"Thanks so very much."

I trudge upstairs. Here there is no eighteenth-century restoration. A huge plaster monument to V. occupies a whitewashed entry hall. A card identifies it as a copy of the famous statue by Houdon that sits in the Pantheon in Paris. There's no sign of my friend.

I thread my way through two more rooms of display tables, full of his letters and documents, even a housekeeping list sent to Wagnière:

"Bring the papers from the desk drawers of my bedroom. Keep all the contracts which are in the drawer and all the outstanding bills and send me a memorandum. Take ten rolls of fifty gold louis each out of the bag in the lower left drawer in the library and send them to Monsieur S. for paying my debts . . ."

Here are his silver pots for ink and powder engraved with his coat-of-arms, the three golden flames held by two grey-hounds . . .

"Those are very valuable, of course," says a haughty English voice behind me. A tall, thin man brushes at his nose with a delicate handkerchief. He sports stiff satin breeches and a matching tail coat. He's sitting, knees crossed rather daintily, on a tiny antique chair.

"Have you seen Monsieur Voltaire?" I ask, forgetting to introduce myself or ask his name.

"Oh! You just missed his performance? His appearance and costume were the most preposterous to conceive! That gaunt figure with its sword constantly getting in between his legs, that coat left over from Louis XIV's day, that ridiculous little matching tie-wig, the whole surmounted by a huge pasteboard helmet. Oh! I think it was all in the most absurd and ridiculous taste! I could hardly keep from tittering!"

He leans back, arms folded across his chest and scrutinizes me. "Tell me, what do you think of him?"

"Well, I – I didn't catch the show, but I'm sure he acquitted himself well. Monsieur Voltaire can be a wonderful actor — "

The Englishman brushes away my praise.

"He's past it. You must've seen him in the old days, not now. I can't believe I traveled all this way to see *that*. It was quite an exertion to smother the urge to have a good laugh."

"I suppose you'll tell everybody?"

"Well, I did right here, you see? Here's my letter back to England." He joins me in the middle of the room and points through the glass of a display table at a faded letter.

The signature reads, "James Callander of Craigforth, July 1765."

"Do you think I could see him, Mr. Callander?"

"Humpf . . . The question is, can you get away from him? It seems to be a point of indispensable etiquette for everyone to administer a *quantum sufficit* of adulation on the histrionic talents of the man; in fact, he's much more sensitive on his acting of Lusignan than on the poetical merits of the play itself. I'll be slipping out while I can."

"Mr. Callander?"

"Yes?"

"What was the name of the play?"

"Why, *Zaïre*, of course."

What else? The first thing V. would do when he got home would be to stage his favorite play. I return to the reception desk.

"Do you have a copy of Monsieur Voltaire's play, *Zaïre?*"

The bearded Cerberus smiles again, and points me towards a small door on the side of the first gallery.

"Wait there," he dictates. I hear the small clicks of hidden locks and, at a nod from Cerberus, I turn the knob.

Like Alice in Wonderland, I've fallen into another world. The skies outside have cleared and the sun streams into a gallery lined with tall windows, illuminating walls lined with hundreds! thousands! of books by Voltaire or about Voltaire. Leather bindings with gold lettering gleam in the fresh light. The center of the room is flanked by two rows of reading tables.

A tiny woman emerges from a glass office at the back, and scurries towards me. As far as I can tell, she is as real as the furniture and the books. She has bright eyes and brown hair but manners so timid! She leans around from behind chairs and tables as we talk, like a pretty mouse thrusting its nose forward to sniff the air.

"I am Madame Walser. May I help you?" she whispers.

I dare not accuse this kind stranger of hiding Voltaire, so I ad-lib, "Um, I've come to see a copy of *Zaïre*."

"In French? English?"

Within seconds, I have editions of *Zaïre* and collections of Voltaire's plays neatly arranged in front of me, piled according to various originals, translations, editions and typeface. Before

I've turned over the first few, Madame Walser has slipped away to the safety of her office.

I flip through the volumes, skipping from verse to verse, play to play. I read exquisitely turned phrases, poetic flights of ecstasy and violent passion. There isn't a blunt word or abrupt breath in sight. Good grief, I think to myself, reading the archaic rhythms of eighteenth-century rhetorical neo-classical style with embarrassment. V.'s characters are incapable of something so simple as a declarative sentence.

"Where're you going?" reads, "Whither do you carry your steps?" "Let's go!" is rendered fussily, "Let us take ourselves hence from these places!"

No wonder nobody's reviving Voltaire anymore. I think of Mr. Callander's scathing critique of V.'s clanking performance with less indignation. It's beautiful to read, but I'm not sure I could sit through more than a few scenes myself.

"You mock, *Madame*, but a little revision and it might hold up," a familiar voice interjects.

"There you are!"

I blush with delight to see my friend at last. He's wearing a new embroidered dressing gown buttoned tight across his scrawny frame, but underneath the splendor, he looks exhausted. A trace of flesh-toned grease-paint sits in deep wrinkles collecting around his neck. His wig and face are covered in a light film of dust.

"I've been unearthing all my versions of that play. You know, I rewrote it so many times that the actors got fed up and refused to learn new lines. Finally, I sent the lead actor a pie with live pigeons hidden inside, each bird holding a roll of correct verse in its bill. The final version was an enormous success. There were even two parodies of it —"

"I can well believe that —"

"But they were both failures —"

"I can believe that, too," I say, relieved to shut the edition, even if it leaves me coughing. "Oh, I'm glad to see you! Well, what I can see of you under all that library dust!"

"Ah, you know what they say. From dust we come and to dust we shall return . . . So . . . you missed me?"

"Yes."

He grins that self-satisfied, simian smile of sheepish vanity. He trips over his dressing gown as he seats himself at the long table. I notice a slight palsy in his hands as they rest on a pile of books with cracked bindings.

"Does *Monsieur* miss me?"

"Don't press your luck. Having a good time here?"

"Of course," he nods. "We produced *Zaïre*. Heard anything about my performance?" He glances sideways at me, hope dancing in his eyes.

I skirt this dangerous territory. "The reviews aren't in yet. Any plans for more performances?"

He shifts in his seat. "Not at the moment."

"Many visitors? I mean, to the museum?"

"Oh, yes, yes. We had a school visit a few weeks ago . . ." His voice fades off.

"And I bet things'll really pick up when the summer begins. American tourists, Japanese groups . . . Remember Christine from the New Year's Eve Party? She'll bring her students. Who could resist those gardens outside?"

"Hmm." He picks absentmindedly at a first edition's priceless binding.

"Oh, you've got a lot of mail up at the farmhouse, *Frank*. I suppose I should bring it down here and leave it with Madame Walser?"

His eyebrows lift at the idea. I can see he's biting his tongue. I drift the lure a little longer across the shifting waters of his pride.

"And you got a call from a Mr. Mustapha. He wants you to write a letter to the Mullahs of Islamabad, or was it something Nagal, or Nagar? Oh, I can't remember. Anyway, it's probably too late —"

"Well —"

" — besides, I can see you're too busy to bother with all that now that you're, um, home."

There is a pregnant silence. I glance briefly to see how V. reacts. Our sideways glances meet and we chuckle, a little embarrassed.

"When did he call?"

"Yesterday morning. I took a message."

"They might miss me here if I left," he sighs. "And the museum curator, Monsieur Wirtz, is testifying right now in an important copyright case."

"Needs your advice?"

"Well, I keep an eye on things. It's a hearing over my reprint rights in a Parisian tribunal next Friday. The Musée Voltaire versus the Voltaire Foundation in England."

I laugh at the irony of it. "Still battling with the printers and rights people! Remember your school pal Thieriot pocketing your royalties? Well, that should make you feel wanted, just like old times, eh?"

I look around at shelf after shelf of what must be at least a thousand volumes of his writings and centuries of Voltairean research.

"Still . . ."

"You said something, *Madame*?"

"Oh, nothing."

"Well . . ."

"They've got more than enough of you here, I must say. Not to mention that mummy at your desk."

"Very unflattering likeness," V. sniffs. "Children are well, I hope? Eva-Marie doing her leg exercises? Theo using his scarf without fail?"

"They're fine. I've had more time to help them with homework since you left."

"Oh, that's good, of course. How is Alexander's subjunctive coming?"

"Better than mine. Everything's fine. A little quiet, maybe . . ."

"Quieter than here?"

"Well, maybe not. Excuse me for saying so, but this place is pretty dead."

"I know what you mean," he sighs.

"You can't live in the past, you know."

"I thought that was what I was supposed to be teaching you," he shakes his head. "And all I've done is make you think of your past – California, London, Hong Kong, Peking . . ."

I can't deny the irony of this. No words come to mind, so I shrug and stand up, reluctantly heading towards the door.

"Where are you going?" he cries, pushing himself clumsily up from the table.

In an inspired second, I wheel around and strike my best Comédie-Française dramatic pose. I thunder out those ponderous lines, "Don't you mean, 'Whither do I carry my steps?' '*Où portez-vous vos pas?*'"

He recognizes my mockery and takes a deep swallow of his pride, while I go on, in full Voltairean flow, "'Let us take ourselves hence from these places!' '*Ôtons nous de ces lieux!*'"

Luckily, Madame Walser can't see me from her office.

Voltaire heaves a deep groan, grabs his walking stick, and beats me to the door, muttering, "Oh, to hell with it, hurry up. They lock us in here at five!"

Grief

The homework and music practices are done for the day. The house is tidy. The writing is picking up. The uneasiness I carry about with me is temporarily quieted. There's a voice inside me that constantly nags that I should be somewhere else – Hong Kong, New York, London – doing something different, something *more* – but it's silent tonight, I confide to Voltaire.

V. shakes his head, "Beware. Think of the man who is falling from a church steeple and, finding the air soft, sighs to himself, 'Long may this last.'"

"That's a rather pessimistic image. Why shouldn't I adjust to this tranquil Swiss life?"

"Thank God for that," V. mutters. "You know, I've never seen anyone who didn't have more desires than real needs, and more needs than possibilities of satisfaction."

"On an evening like this, you could almost pretend that everything is as it should be. There must be some sense to it all."

"I once believed that," V. corrects me sharply. "Madame du Châtelet was already preaching her dear Leibniz's theodicy at me, the justice of God."

I can't account for the sudden mockery in V.'s voice as he sneers, "The justice of God! If everything is as it should be, how can you reconcile earthly evil with divine goodness?"

I'm not interested in his philosophical barbs. "Everything

seems so peaceful tonight . . . " I sigh. The simple good of a
kitchen floor swept clear of Corn Puffs floods me with a silly
degree of satisfaction. V. seems intent on deeper musings.

"How can we believe in God if he creates a world sullied by
genocides, corruption, famines, poverty, human cruelty — "

"Don't forget earthquakes," I add, not perhaps as seriously as
V. would like, ". . . thousands buried alive in India, or Sal-
vador, or Japan. I know about tectonic plates and all that, but
there's a whimsical God for you."

"I thought you believed God was perfect," he says slyly.

"Maybe good and evil are just human terms?" I argue, "and
life needs imperfections for the whole to be as perfect as God
intended? Sin is an evil, but isn't sin part of man's having a free
will?"

"And the afflictions of men? Earthquakes, plagues, acci-
dents?"

"Well, if a better world were possible, then God would have
created it!" I protest petulantly. He's drawing me into a serious
discussion, when all I wanted to do was serve dinner. I know
life isn't just. How did he back me into this one?

"No!" he bursts out, so suddenly that I drop the butter dish
on the floor.

"What the — ?"

"Those who go about preaching the rightness of things as
they are are charlatans! Lord Shaftesbury, Leibniz, the whole
lot of them! Imagine telling my poor friend Alexander Pope
that God could not have made him without that painful hump
on his back! What would you say to the thousands of faithful
who went to church one Sunday morning in Lisbon and were
crushed or burned alive – the entire city perished, *Madame*, in
the earthquake on November 1st, 1755?"

I'm on my knees, sweeping up porcelain slivers before small
bare feet reach the kitchen. My evening's serenity lies shattered
with the butter dish.

Voltaire looks deeply upset. "When I heard about the

devastation in Lisbon, I wrote –

> Dangers and difficulties man surround,
> Doubts and perplexities his mind confound
> To nature we apply for truth in vain
> God should His will to human kind explain
> He can only illume the human soul,
> Instruct the wise man, and the weak console . . . ''

That night, while Peter is reading a story to the boys and Eva-Marie is splashing in her bath, V. hauls his weightless frame off for one of his regular evening walks along the cow trails above the house.

I take advantage of his absence to check my e-mail.

Immediately I sense something amiss. I have a message from Judy, the widow of that brilliant journalist David who intoned "shame" at the Foreign Office officials. Or rather, Judy, happily resettled in Africa with her second husband, *seems* to have sent me a message. Strangely, the title of the message is a reply to an e-mail I sent her more than six months ago.

I realize it is from her husband who had hurriedly used a very old message of mine to instantly contact me by reply mail. I feel an icy, forboding hand reaching for me as I read, "I must inform you we have been involved in a terrible car accident. Judy is alive but . . . '' he gives no more details, but asks us to wait for more news.

The dizziness and fear that floods me has a sickening finality to it. I fumble at my computer, mis-sending, then losing the message, flailing at the wrong keys. I realize that my old friend and I have communicated so regularly by e-mail since her move to Africa, I have never had the telephone number of her new residence. A blank nausea washes over me.

I reach someone at their office who is diplomatically reticent. "Here is the home number, but I'm afraid I am really not in a position to give you the details."

I suddenly flash on a memory of Judy in Hong Kong in 1992. She's laughing as she carries serving dishes to the table at which are seated various of my girlfriends. She's throwing a farewell dinner before my departure from Hong Kong for my new life in New York with Peter and the boys.

I look at the time. I've lost half an hour in fumbling. I finally reach Judy's husband.

"What's happened?"

"Yes," I hear him swallow his resignation to something so ghastly, he must gird himself to merely say the words.

"We were driving outside town . . . a truck didn't see us. It swerved and smashed into the side of the car where Judy was sitting. The car was completely destroyed —"

My friend —

"And when I came to, there was my wife, bleeding all over. They wanted to give her a blood transfusion in the local clinic —"

"Oh, no," I blurt out, thinking of H.I.V. contamination of blood supplies.

"Well, I refused that, of course, and luckily we got a doctor in an ambulance to come out from Harare . . ."

Another memory of Judy sitting on a sunny terrace in August, gold earrings shining in the late evening light. We're laughing and reminiscing, talking about mutual friends and loves and long ago in Hong Kong . . .

" . . . she was dying from loss of blood."

Judy takes my history with her. My laughs, my links to so much. I'm listening like a robot, taking notes by force of habit like a reporter. When you are unable to think, write it down.

"The arm was very damaged, the left arm. They had to cut."

It takes me a full three seconds to take in what he's said.

They have cut off her left arm.

"I see," I say, steadying myself, to listen to more? That wall of fear that had been teetering over me since the e-mail on my screen appeared, comes down. An arm or a leg or an eye. All the hints, the reticence lay there, like lentils down a terrible trail.

A few more seconds of this. I ask, is he whole, unharmed? I put down the phone and run into the depths of my clothes closet where the kids can't hear me. No, no, no, no, and already life is moving on, seconds are ticking by, and Judy is lying in a hospital bed with only one arm.

One grieves and does the chores at the same time. With the simplest movement of hairbrush, broom, or saucepan, I ask myself, "How will she do this from here on?" I hear her happy voice saying so recently, "I'm so happy to be driving again. I couldn't really drive in South America, but now, I can just get in the car and go where I want. I feel so independent again."

Independent.

I crazily review the one-armed people in my catalogue of experience, but try as I might to connect the dots, none of this relates to my friend.

Sympathy is of no concrete use. Through her haze of pain and medications, I hear, Judy has learned the worst.

For once, V. stays discreetly in the background. "Courage is of some use. It flatters self-love and it lessens misfortune," he says gently. "I can't conceive that what is, ought to be. In this each doctor knows as much as me."

Judy needs more help, more examination. There are other injuries, to the face, the ear. She will be flown up in an emergency medical plane to Geneva. The hours for me become manageable as a count-down until the moment I can see her. We talk on the phone. She's determined, brave. After a few days, I can send a worried mutual friend a message:

"I wasn't allowed to see Judy until today. Her indomitable spirits were (finally?) slumping a little . . . She says she's mostly worried about the recovery of facial movement, 'I can manage over the arm, but if I can't get my face back to normal, well, I just can't function . . . ' I think the first visit from the prosthetics man was discouraging, and she

understands that anything she has won't be as useful as it is cosmetic, 'to at least give me a little balance.' Only a few days ago, she was expecting to have something that worked, goddamit.

"Judy's private room is on the ninth floor, sun-filled and clean . . . Seeing her in her cotton hospital gown, standing up bravely to greet me with that shocking empty sleeve, like a frail bird with a broken wing, broke my heart. She really held up, so God knows, I had no choice but to do the same . . . "

The next Thursday, I dress up and drive to Geneva again. V. stays at home — respectful, silent. Messages of sympathy and encouragement pour into my computer to deliver to Judy at the hospital. I am thankful for something to do.

On this second visit, I find her shaky, self-conscious. She sets herself on the edge of a chair by the window, but on a slant, literally putting her best face forward. We chat of whatever we can, bouncing from the doctors' opinions, to gossip about friends and then back to whatever adjustments she's come to contemplate about being one-handed. She is less determined than a few days before. She's skipped her morning shower and all its exertions, letting the nurses wash and care for her.

And why the hell not, I say to myself.

We talk daily and sometimes the phone conversations are easier than face-to-face ones. These conversations with my friend are a privilege, like looking through a window into her soul. Her speech is slightly slurred, but her thoughts are crystal clear.

"Gosh," she says in her slightly breathless Australian accent, "you think life is going to be a smooth path, unexciting then wham, you get a new challenge like this. Well, this is just the way it's going to be from now on."

After a successful five-hour operation, the doctors tell her it will take up to a year to recover the lost facial movement. Being Judy, she's convinced things are already better. Her husband and she check into a hotel to sit out a week of healing. I drive down again, through a miserable foggy cloud encircling the lake, to meet them at the reception desk.

My friend takes my breath away as she emerges from the elevator. She is extraordinary. Is it possible the accident was only two weeks ago? She crosses the lobby, empty sleeve swinging from under an elegant cashmere wrap. A hospital plastic eye-patch has been replaced with a more flattering one. She greets me ebulliently. We embrace. These are the first steps of yet another chapter in my friend's life. I hesitate to take her remaining arm. Will she feel pinned down?

We set off for a place to have a coffee and chat, weaving clumsily between parked cars. I want her to lean on me, and at the same time, I feel her struggling for her balance, searching for a new equilibrium, determined to keep her independence.

Seated at the table, she ruminates. "My twenties were fun. Then the thirties were all right, but David had his breakdowns and that was difficult. The forties were interesting, but David's death was so hard. Now the fifties and this," she nods towards the space below her shoulder.

We gossip about the dismissal of an acerbic and well-connected China-watcher from the *South China Morning Post*. We cluck over the less-than-credible disavowals of the *Post*'s editor-in-chief as he defends the decision to put a Communist Party hack in charge of China coverage.

Our time together is so short. And with that, the truth slams into me – *life* is so short. A sequence of swift scenes – some of us get one act, some last for three, Voltaire *insisted* on no fewer than five full acts plus encores. Sooner or later, the curtain drops on us all.

It seems only minutes, not days, before her bright and breathless voice over the phone announces, "Well, we're going back to Africa! We've reserved the seats. I must say, I'm a bit stunned. The plane leaves in a few hours."

I am flabbergasted, although I struggle to understand her eagerness to leave. "You must be anxious to get home," I stammer.

"Well, I must say I'm looking forward to, well, digesting all that's happened. I saw the doctor this afternoon and he said my ear is going to be all right."

"Well, I know it isn't much of a consolation, but when the alternative is not being here at all – that's what I remind myself each day. Just to hear your voice makes me feel better."

"I just wanted to thank you for everything you've done —"

"Oh, Judy —"

"I'll e-mail you when I get back, and thanks again, lots of love and big hug to Peter and the kids."

I'm feeling so bereft. I put the phone down as tears rush to my eyes. The Flying Doctors got her here two weeks ago, but now she sets off to resume "normal" life. I think of her as she boards the commercial flight at Cointrin Airport amid the curious stares of strangers. She's a trouper, opening her next act with unmatchable style.

Within thirty-six hours, there is an e-mail from Africa.

"It's so good to be home, to be with the dogs, to enjoy the garden and warm weather, and to sleep in one's own bed!! Our maid cried for over an hour upon seeing me; I was very touched but it didn't do a lot for my morale. I'm feeling fine but exhausted – but as you see, I'm managing to type to you!!"

Outside the bedroom window, spring's thin daylight is fading. I abandon my ironing and sit on the end of the bed and sob out nothing but anger.

Nothing that has happened to Judy makes any sense or can arguably be for any purpose. No one can persuade me that this hideous accident fits into any larger picture of goodness or rightness. I will always be angry at God for this. And in the silent solitude, I fight off the selfish loneliness that her unexpected arrival – with all our shared laughter and rueful sighs – temporarily interrupted.

There is a polite cough from V. in the bedroom doorway.

"A cup of tea?" he offers.

"Oh, it's you."

"Only *moi.*" he shrugs. "You're not alone, remember."

"But you're DEAD!" I burst out resentfully. "I haven't met one person like Judy since I got here. You're not real. You talk to me with clever quotations and epitaphs and aphorisms, and parables and – and – anecdotes and essays and biographies. You have absolutely no sentimental feelings whatsoever!"

"Even the dead had feelings once," he says. "And not always with such good reason. My best friend Thieriot acted as my literary agent, all the time betrayed me, stole from me, lived off my reputation. He never once thanked me. But he was my friend. I loved him from our schoolboy days at Louis-Le-Grand until the end. That never changed. Believe it or not, I still miss that rogue."

He holds out an exquisite square of cambric edged in hand-crocheted lace. Too fragile to stand up to earthly grief.

"Thanks, I'll stick with Kleenex. You wouldn't want to see that thing in shreds, would you?"

"This piece of frippery?" He flips it into a breast pocket and sits gently at my side. After a few moments, he sighs, "You're luckier in your friends than I was. What was that Chinese saying Jane said while visiting us?"

I sputter out the Chinese tones, "*Ren sheng, lao, si, Tian di wu qing.*"

"Yes, yes, I overheard her recite it. 'Man is born, ages and dies, the gods in heaven don't care.'"

"Nothing is as it should be," I despair.

V. whispers to himself, "Thirty churches filled with the faithful attending All Saints' Day Mass . . . Forty thousand innocents buried or burned, crying to God for mercy as they died. I wrote,

> Mysteries like these, no man can penetrate,
> Hid from his view remains the book of fate.
> Man his own nature never yet could sound,
> He knows not whence he is, nor whither bound."

Grief

I spend the rest of the afternoon starching the hell out of
pillowcases. It's all I'm good for. My fury over what has
happened surges and subsides in heaves. This stream of anguish
cannot be stopped up, but will have to dry, as all streams do,
only when the season changes.

Casanova's Advice

Presents, letters and various requests fill up our mailbox for the outspoken "Frank Arouet" who has flooded L'Infâme.org and the editorial columns with his acid wit. The volume of correspondence keeps on growing, even as the man himself shrinks before my eyes. I can believe that his writings fill ninety volumes; he's running a second epistolary marathon right under my nose.

We work on his correspondence together each morning. He works in a whirlwind of paper scattered all over a desktop suspended on ropes over his bed. It's his own invention, hauled up out of sight only when he collapses into sleep.

Not everyone is thrilled at the resuscitation of the spirit of Voltaire. He actually gets a death threat from a fanatic Christian evangelist in Alabama, threatening to "burn down his house."

Even fans are hard to please, like the man who demands that Mr. Arouet urgently tell him, by registered return mail no less, whether there is a God, and whether man has an immortal soul.

"I thought we settled that one two centuries ago," he says to me, tossing it on a towering pile one Monday morning.

More gratifying, a female minister for humanitarian affairs sends him flowers, which has perhaps prompted his outburst this fine spring Saturday morning.

"*Madame*, you must cultivate your garden!"

"Isn't that a quote? From *Candide*? Something about how work fends off boredom, vice and, um, and — "

" — need. Yes, well, you must excuse me for repeating myself. A man can have only a certain number of teeth, hair, and ideas. There comes a time when he necessarily loses all his teeth, his hair, and repeats his ideas."

I put aside the morning paper and squint down at V. from my comfortable seat on the shady balcony.

He's certainly lost all his teeth somewhere along the line. What's left of the hair is covered by an immense wig topped with a bonnet of black velvet. There's just enough flesh to cover his bones.

He must be getting old to start repeating one of his most famous lines. Even I've heard this one before, something about making the most of the day, not trying to remake the world, or seek fame and wealth in vain. One should just build as much of a paradise in one's own yard as possible.

Isn't that what Candide was singing by the end of Bernstein's show? Isn't that exactly what I'm doing now? Enjoying my paradise?

And I deserve a rest more than ever. Last week, I caught my Swiss neighbors looking askance at my bare-faced house and took their cue. Now I fully intend to bask in self-satisfaction at having installed window boxes the length of the balcony rail. Send the Geranium Inspectors. This Swiss housewife is ready.

Now isn't it just like the Un-idle Idol to pick on me during a few languid moments? This morning will pass fast enough without his nagging. The last light fixture was installed three weeks ago, only nine months behind schedule. The long winter of repairing, restoring, economizing, and worry may be coming to an end.

"I've done the best I can, *Monsieur*! I suppose you want me to go into that office again. It's not my fault the Tibet novel hasn't sold." I won't tell him that my erstwhile agent recently sent her biannual e-mail to remind me, with all the sincerity of a Weather Channel girl, of my shortcomings in the editorial marketplace.

"No, no, no," V. shouts at me, hitting his walking stick imperiously along the worn stone path down to the *potager*. "I meant, you must start weeding your damned vegetable garden! Come down here, now!"

The Swiss cultivate each square of workable soil with the passion of any over-crowded people. Flower beds are shifted from tulip gardens to geranium dormitories with the regularity of Buckingham Palace guards. A day's descent to the warmer suburbs reveals a dazzling epidemic of spring gardening.

I drive once a week to the mall in Nyon and compare these self-satisfied little corn and sunflower fields, cossetted apple trees in netting hats, fenced and be-rosed vegetable plots with plantings I've seen around the world. I recall the splendid formal gardens of the Chelsea flower show in England, soggy rice terraces carved out of the Balinese hillsides, the greedy squares of wheat sprawling across northern China, the shaved green lawns of California, the desperate plastic tunnels and parched irrigation ditches on the Himalayan plateau outside Lhasa.

All my life, I've been a botanical Peeping-Tom, so I hoped my first garden would be a combination of influences, a satiation of my Lust for Leaves.

I join V. at the edge of the lawn and cast a glance down the steps leading to my vegetable beds. Planted with such enthusiasm after our arrival last autumn, the winter spinach and early lettuce are sprouting alongside a frightening crop of mountain thistle and poison ivy.

"Where did that stuff come from? I pulled those things out last September."

"Have you never gardened before?" V. chomps his gums at me.

"C'mon! Did I have a chance in London, Hong Kong, or New York?"

"Weeds need regular removal," he scolds me. "And you should shelter the lettuce from the sun before it bolts, and tie those beans to the fence."

"I know, I know. I don't need a city boy like you to lecture me about agriculture."

He certainly doesn't look like a gardener this morning, all muffled up in a flower-patterned dressing gown.

"Hmmph! I was no mere gardener, *Madame*, I was a *patriarch*." He takes my arm and leans on me as we descend to the leafy beds. He pokes his stick under the weeds to make sure the spinach is still there.

"In Ferney, I had four hundred beehives, pasture land, forest and flower gardens, three miles in circuit. We raised fifty cows, dozens of oxen and horses, poultry, and sheep. I had fruit trees, grapevines, wine presses, and hothouses for my seedlings. We got permission to install pipes through the Widow Dutil's fields and had pure water running straight into the kitchen – when Parisians still had to pay for the polluted waters of the Seine carried upstairs by porters!"

"You did all that?"

"*Madame*, I was prouder of my ability as a builder, a farmer and a gardener than I was of my philosophy!"

"You don't dress like the Martha-Stewart-in-Mudboots type. You had help."

"I reserved one field which only I could touch."

"Sure, how many workers did you have for the rest of your estate?"

"Up to eight hundred, but I supervised every one in person."

"You obviously formed a bad habit. I never asked you to supervise me!"

"Stop arguing and start weeding here. These dandelions blew over from the lawn above. They're choking your red cabbage."

And to my astonishment, V. arranges a thick pillow of newly-cut grass from Peter's compost heap, kneels down on those serviceable stockings, and starts yanking weeds.

"My people never complained. I fought off the vicious tax-farming that kept them poor. I petitioned to end the serfdom that bound their neighbors to the land. The feudal laws cost those poor souls their houses and property if a son so much as dared to move his family away from his father's home."

"The state could confiscate their property?"

"It was the Church's idea, of course! *L'infâme* strikes again! Lying behind your very house, *Madame*, are two valleys that were tyrannized by the Benedictine monks that ran this whole area on a fistful of forged documents dated from the twelfth century! Their rights were transferred to the prebendaries of Saint-Claude in 1742, but things got no better, I tell you."

I wrest out root after root, and feel a guilty pleasure wash over me, as the destructive pessimisms of the winter's hibernation find an outlet in virtuous cultivation. V. rattles on without taking a breath – about local bondage, church abuse, slavery and sin – but the speedy progress he is making down the line of *épinards d'hiver* is astonishing for a man his age.

"I will give you just one example," he says, waving a bouquet of dirty white roots in my face. "A surgeon in Morez applied to the local monks to pay his fee for treating their sick slaves. 'Instead of paying you, we should punish you,' whined the monks. 'Last year you cured two serfs by whose deaths we would have profited by a thousand francs!' You see, when the poor serfs died, their property reverted to the monks' greedy pockets."

"That's detestable. Ow! I need gloves. These thistles leave welts."

"But not unusual by any means. These prebendaries robbed a woman named Jeanne Marie Mermet of her entire inheritance from her father on the simple grounds that she left her childhood home to spend her wedding night under her husband's roof."

"How medieval."

V. brushes crumbling dirt off his fingers with relish. "I

exposed it all – the fraud, the theft, the abuse. The last petition was just a year before I died. You wonder why some people here are shy and deferential to you? Why they don't raise their hands at teacher's meetings? Why they obediently fill out application forms merely to take their children to the dentist? Why only foreign mothers joined your Lunch Club?"

I sit back on my haunches, and rest an arm on the concrete of the vegetable bed and reflect for a moment.

"Because they're descendants of serfs?"

He nods. "That's your neighborhood, *Madame* . . . Les Rousses, Morez, Belle-Fontaine . . . all those little French border towns behind this village."

"Les Rousses was full of serfs?" I ponder this astonishing picture, and reflect on the vague air of depression and lack of initiative that hangs over nearby French villages like a melancholic miasma.

"*Oui*, there were twelve thousand serfs in these parts during my lifetime. Not so in Ferney. I built my peasants houses, gave them employment, lent them money — "

"At eight percent, no doubt."

" — only four, only four. You have missed some weeds over there. My aristocratic friends paid six percent, and even that rascal Richelieu only paid back a third. My village of forty peasants grew to a town of twelve hundred under my care. I converted my theater into a silkworm house. Pretty soon, Catherine the Great was wearing silk stockings made by the son of Jean Calas at my estate. Our watches and jewelry were shipped to Holland, Italy, Spain, Portugal, Morocco, Russia, China and Ameri— "

"Hold on. We're sitting at eleven hundred meters' altitude. You're not suggesting I raise silkworms!"

"You've never heard of hothouses, *Madame*? We can always try. The severity of Ferney's climate was very discouraging."

"Look at this poor plant – all shriveled up – and you talk about discouraging." I smooth some dirt over the roots of my struggling eggplant shivering in the spring breeze. This is not eggplant country.

"Oh, I had my failures," he laughs, "even though I consulted no less than the head gardener of the tree nurseries of France, Moreau de la Rochette. But I had asparagus and artichokes from my greenhouse in winter. And all summer – peaches, apricots, apples – what the devil are these blue pebbles?"

"Snail poison pellets."

"Interesting . . . the exact color Pompadour chose for her porcelains from Sèvres . . . what was I saying?"

"Tree nurseries." He hikes his coat-tails to straddle rows of early *Reine de Mai* lettuce.

"Oh, yes. I planted twenty thousand chestnut trees specially ordered from Savoy. All died. Four times I set out nut trees along the main road and three-quarters perished or were torn up by the peasants. I wrote to Moreau and asked him to ship me two hundred elms and one hundred mountain ash, and six weeks later, I tried again with fifty maples and another fifty plane trees. I never gave up."

"How old were you when you did all this?"

He shrugs. "Seventy-three."

We finish the weeding and I make lunch for the family. Monsieur Voltaire now takes a nap at midday, although he won't admit to it. He finds me later folding duvets that have been airing in the sun.

"Am I expecting visitors to my wing?" he inquires.

"I thought we might have some of Peter's family this weekend, but they cancelled."

"Just as well," he nods, relieved. "I would have been able to do more at Ferney, had it not been for all the infernal house guests. Fourteen bedrooms, always filled! Madame Denis longed for Paris society and was an excellent hostess, but whew! – sometimes it was too much for me."

"I hope we have more house guests soon. Not that you aren't company enough."

"Well, don't invite that chatty Boswell! That eager Scot will invite himself and never leave! And even after he goes, he writes you a letter saying he hasn't finished, comes right back and tries to convert you to Christianity! Don't have anybody as long as I'm revising *La Princesse de Babylone*, please."

I give him my most indulgent smile. "Anyone else we should snub?"

"Well, Casanova can come back. I always found him amusing."

"The famous lover?"

"No doubt, given his habits, there are now a lot of little Casanovas running around. Yes, the Italian who came to see me after he had visited the scientist Albrecht von Haller in Bern, the most important Swiss of his time – the biggest religious bore that ever lived. Haller was so devout! When I set up shop in Switzerland, he told everyone Satan had arrived!" V. chuckles to himself at his old wickednesses.

"What did Casanova say?"

"That meeting me made it the proudest day of his life."

I nod, "Yes, yes, of course, and — ?"

"He told me he had been to see that religious stick, Haller."

"Yes, and what else?"

"I asked Casanova politely whether he was pleased with Haller? He said he had spent three of the happiest days of his life with that man. I congratulated him. Casanova said he was sorry that Haller was not so fair towards me. You know what I answered?" V. asks me, eyes twinkling. "Aha! Perhaps both Haller and I are mistaken!"

"Why did Haller malign you?"

"My attacks on the Church, of course. He told Casanova that 'contrary to the laws of perspective, many people have found Voltaire greater viewed from a distance!'"

I have to laugh, and after a moment of feigning irritation, so does V.

"Yes, Haller was a clever devil. But you want to know more

313

about Casanova, eh? He told me that superstition was necessary to govern, for the people would never give a mere man the right to rule them, while I argued for a sovereign ruling over a free people, bound to them by reciprocal conditions."

"I had no idea intercourse with Casanova could be so intellectual," I respond.

V. shields his eyes from the sun's glare with one spidery hand. "You know, I found Casanova a little sad, his arguments a little cynical. He seemed to have a bad opinion of his fellow creatures. He told me, 'Your master passion is love of humanity, Monsieur Voltaire. This love blinds you. Love humanity, but love it as it is.'"

"He said that? A bit like the old 'cultivate your garden,' and let the rest go, isn't it?"

V. looks at me out of those old, foxy brown eyes, and waits for my reflections. It goes deep with me, for some reason, and V. knows it.

"Love humanity as it is," he repeats.

I break a long silence at last. "You think I'm impatient with everything and everyone, don't you?"

He repeats to me, intently, "All of my clever words haven't sunk in as much as poor old Casanova's, have they? The simple advice given to me by a backstage brat, abandoned by his parents, living a life of chicanery, tricks and stolen affection. He saw a great deal, *Madame*. If we take his advice, we will both be much happier. 'Love humanity, but love it *as it is*.' —Who in God's name is that?"

"Who, what?"

"*Mon Dieu*, a midget priest has come to call?"

I Believe in God

I see only my first-born son talking to his father in the distance, and I laugh. "That's Alexander. He's trying out his First Communion robe. Have you forgotten? Mass tomorrow at eleven?"

V. struggles to his feet and screeches like a banshee across the lawn, waving his stick at Alexander.

"Take that thing off at once! You're not going to let our clever boy undergo that superstitious ritual? Don't you remember what La Barre died for? To avoid worshiping a 'God of Dough?'"

"Let's not start arguing again," I plead.

Voltaire can be witty, courteous, and charming, but on the subject of the Church, he is so embittered, I don't want him spoiling this for Alexander. Amidst the rough and tumble of his classes, the petty torments of classmates, and misunderstandings with teachers, nothing has been such a balm for Alexander's homesick soul as the uncomplicated welcome offered by the catechism teachers.

"Leave him alone. You can see the excitement all over his face —"

" — I will not be a —"

" — Just be nice and come with us to Mass. You don't have to pray if you don't want to."

"Well, what would be the point of that? You treat your God like a pasha, or like a sultan whom one may provoke and appease! If your prayers match up to his wishes, it's useless to ask Him to do what he's already resolved to do. If you pray that He does the contrary, you're praying for him to be weak, inconstant, you're practically mocking Him."

"I don't pray to a HIM. Even Eva-Marie calls God a HER."

Rebuffed, V. pulls his dressing gown tighter around his rake of a body. "Well, I'm glad to hear it. All I'm saying is that everybody prays to God, but wise men resign themselves and simply obey Him."

"Point taken. And as far as superstition goes, you're lucky I'm not like half the modern world, worshiping crystals or proselytizing about the health benefits of green tea."

He winces, "Oh, it's all so discouraging. *Bien*. When is this superstition-addled ceremony?"

"Eleven. Be there."

"Well, if it must be, let us pray with the people and resign ourselves with the wise men."

"Let us." I press my lips together, resolved not to let this argument go any further.

The next morning, Peter drives Alexander into the village ahead of us to prepare for the First Communion Procession with the rest of his class.

My husband shakes his head as he returns to the house. "First Communion must be a really big deal around here. The village is teeming with cars," he says, settling down in the kitchen for a last coffee before we return to the village to witness Alexander's procession up the hillock to the chapel.

Half an hour later, Peter, Eva-Marie, Theo and I find ourselves facing a very Manhattan-like experience in our own little village – hunting for a parking place. The small church parking lot is filled. All the spaces around the tourist kiosk are taken. We try the side street leading past the Ancienne École and the train station parking lot. Full up. *Complet*.

I shrug my shoulders. "Well, St-Cergue has the chapel and the saint, and even the fountain that cured leprosy back in the

Middle Ages, so the catechism classes of Arzier and Les Muids haven't any choice but to come up here."

"Leprosy cure? That can't be it," Peter argues. "How many kids are receiving First Communion this morning. Five hundred?"

More curiously, the owners of these vehicles are nowhere to be seen in front of the Reymond's grocery, the prime spot from which to view the Communion Procession. At five to eleven, a handful of other families from the lower villages straggle up to join us from distant parking places, their cameras in hand. We exchange a few handshakes.

"Do you think the people who parked around here are already warming seats in church?" I worry, knowing that even if he had a corporal presence, V. would be too thin to do us much good saving a pew.

The door of the *Commune* office swings open and out comes our African missionary beaming widely in the sun. He is followed by a parade of shy, embarrassed kids, loping along in white robes of various hemlines and droopiness. This is not New York or Paris. Under their robes, all but Alexander are wearing their every-day high-soled sneakers. They're holding their palms self-consciously pressed together, some under their chins, others at waist level.

The column halts while a few speeding French drivers shooting through town from across the border whiz across the junction. More than a dozen Sunday motorcyclists crowd the outdoor café tables of the Restaurant du Jura on the opposite corner. Like great beetles in their black leather, with helmets in hand, they stop chatting and smoking to gape at the black cleric and his cavalcade of home-grown cherubs.

The priest finally signals his charges to cross the hazardous street. Cameras and camcorders start whizzing and clicking away.

"What's that?" Peter asks.

I stop filming. "Thanks a lot. Now I've got you asking,

'Wazzat' on video."

"I hear it too," Theo pipes up.

Hundreds of voices are singing a French hymn. A long procession of solemn people, led by six pallbearers carrying a simple coffin, appears around the corner of the butcher's shop. Their path is heading straight for our First Communicants.

"So that's what all the cars are here for. It's a funeral! Who died?"

Peter dodges into the *tabac* for a word with the ever-informed Mrs. Weber and returns with some startling news.

"It's old Berner, remember him?"

"The guy who drove his truck into our rain gutter?"

Peter nods. "He collided with a motorcyclist on the Route d'Arzier."

I hardly have time to express some kind of polite regret when I hear V. mutter, "Here comes another collision now."

He doesn't fool me. His expression is all innocence, as he holds his large, festive hat, with its gorgeous lavender plume politely across his breast out of respect for the passing dead. But the old goat's eyes twinkling out from under that outdated cloud of a wig can't disguise his growing delight as the two columns of pious – one joyful, one mournful – now only a block apart, proceed head-on towards each other.

The short, bearded Protestant pastor leading the funeral column sings louder to fortify his mourners for the coming test of wills as his right hand furtively signals his troops to tighten their formation to let the children pass. Their chant grows louder, more resolute.

The procession of Catholic children falters in their sunny little First Communion ditty as they look up from their clasped hands to see a herd of grown-ups heading straight at them. Their straight line starts to fray. The priest, following an enormous crucifix brandished by the post lady's chubby child, resumes the cheerful rhymes about "Spring lambs and Baby Jesus" in a breath-taking baritone, but he can scarcely be heard above the much more numerous Calvinists laboring away at their gloomy dirge.

Pomp and Ceremony are giving way to the battling forces of Death and Rebirth. The mass of funeral attendants gives the impression that everyone in St-Cergue has turned out to send off the old woodcutter. The carpenter who "works to live," and the painter who lost his lover last autumn, the teacher who scolded us for speaking English, the mothers who let the Lunch Club down, the crossing-guards, the walrus-moustached postman, the Reymonds, the dry-cleaning lady, the *Commune* official with his hunting dog on a tight leash, the cowherd couple with the flame-embossed jeep – all are marching toward us, along with hundreds I've never seen before.

My entire first year in St-Cergue is parading past me, a line-up of Fellini casting rejects.

As the space separating the two flocks narrows, it's becoming clear to worried onlookers that the priest, with his substantial belly leading the faithful, is not about to lead his twenty-odd lambs off the only curb at this junction into the dangers of the Sunday tourist traffic rounding the bend from France.

Nor can the bearded little Protestant – his neat dark jacket and collar pinching in the spring heat – control or reduce his hundreds spilling over the sidewalk. I've given up hope of videotaping Alexander from where we stand.

"I can't watch. Tell me when it's over," I tell Peter.

"I love this," Voltaire giggles.

The spirit of Ecumenism compels our two village shepherds to acknowledge each other's flock with a slight bow, dance from left to right for a few seconds, the heavy crosses on their chests swaying in time, and then, ruthlessly signal the charge.

Before our eyes, the two processions merge into a roiling sea of rather sodden adults with funereal faces red from tears and alcohol, being jostled and poked by the happy, determined Catholic kids in their baggy robes.

Amidst flashes of white linen, the heavy Crucifix teeters and tips in the air over the heads of the mob, threatening to kybosh a very old, hunched woman sobbing heavily into a handkerchief.

People are dodging and twisting sideways, pushing in both directions, fighting for their place on the sidewalk, yelling a little too loudly for a solemn occasion, *"Pardonnez-moi, Monsieur, Excusez-moi, Madame, Attention, mon gars! Après-vous, ma belle."*

Alexander is utterly lost from sight. Someone yells at the kids, "Show some respect!" and followed by, "OW! Who did that?"

I train my eyes on the clearing below the hillock leading up to the chapel, the first possible space to spot Alexander again. It's like some old-fashioned science film showing the division of cells in slow-motion. The amoeba of the religious appears to be moving, blob-like, into a re-establishment of their competing forces. Two ends bulge and bob before, with a sudden pull, the pushing, shoving procession with two heads becomes two separate columns, two separate faiths, once again.

The sobbing old lady has survived the scrum, but is now heading in the wrong direction, inadvertently swept up in the column of First Communicants.

V. and I watch this distraught woman, her face blinded by tears, jostled by the kids towards the wrong church.

"I hope that isn't the Widow Berner. She'll miss her own husband's burial."

"She'll see a more cheering show," V. suggests.

"Last autumn's 'Descent of the Cows Festival' was more organized than this," I comment dryly to Peter as we finally reach the door of the chapel. We are so far at the back of the crowd, we can barely make out the altar at the head of the nave. As he is indifferent to the ceremony on principle, no number of silencing glares from me can stop V.'s chatty reminiscences.

"Nothing like my triumphant return to Paris in the spring of 1778! I'd been away, now let's see, twenty-eight years. And what if the clergy should attack me in their pulpits? Who cared? What if the new King wanted to send me to the Bastille? Paris had become the capital of the Enlightenment, thanks to me!"

"You had a few helpers," I whisper.

"Oh, yes," he chuckles, "There I was at long last, arrived at the gates of Paris. The customs men demanded, 'Is there any contraband to declare?' 'By my faith, gentlemen,' I chirped, 'I believe there is nothing here contraband but *myself*!'"

V. laughs at his little jest and the subsequent irony of the Parisian officials scouring their old records for warrants for the old *philosophe's* arrest and, after so many years, finding nothing. Decades of exile hung on the old King's word, nothing more.

"Shhuush, I think the kids are about to come in."

"Oh, that was a procession!" V. giggles, whispering to me behind that plumed hat. "Would you believe three hundred people filed into my rooms at the Rue de Beaune in only the first day! Benjamin Franklin brought his grandson for me to bless. Cheering throngs held up my carriage on my way to the Louvre for a special meeting of the Académie Française. I had finally got in as a member, you see."

I whisper, "Tell me later."

Everyone inside the Chapel rises to their feet.

"Oh, oh, oh," his old man's memories are unstoppable. "Just like the standing ovation when I arrived at the Théâtre-Français to see my play *Irène*, an ovation that lasted twenty minutes!" He sighs.

"Look, I think I see the kids now over in the door of the sachristy," Peter says.

The organ is revving up with a bouncy ecclesiastical tune.

"They were yelling, 'Hail Voltaire! Honor to the philosopher who teaches us to think! Glory to the defender of Calas!'" V. strains to look over the heads of the strangers in front of us and pokes me in the shoulder. "Hey, we could rouse them with a few shouts, don't you think? What would that grinning buffoon of a priest do if you yelled from back here, 'Hail Voltaire! Death to *l'infâme!*'"

"Shush! I'm trying to follow the ceremony, despite your nostalgic driveling."

Peter pulls me through the crowded foyer and squeezes us into a space at the back of the church. The congregation stays on its feet as the children prepare to enter the chapel in a giggling jumble.

V. shrugs, happy to entertain himself. "Even the Queen rose to greet me. And then, the performance of *Irène*, after which one of the actors came to me, and put a laurel wreath on my head. Can you imagine? I had to drink twenty-five cups of coffee a day to keep up with the excitement. They rechristened the Quai des Theátins, the Quai Voltaire."

He sighs with pleasure.

"Can you get that feather out of my nose? I can't see anything from here. I told Peter we should have gotten here earlier."

"Old Dr. Tronchin, you know what he said to me in Paris? He warned me, 'You're living on your capital, Monsieur Voltaire, not your interest!'" V.'s wheedling breath is like a faint spring breeze at my ear, "It was worth it, to see d'Argental, my old schoolmate from Louis-le-Grand! What an old man he looked! Hee, hee!"

"Let us pray," intones the priest, stretching his two enormous arms out to embrace the congregation in spirit.

I finally make out Alexander's round face, smiling out at the whole congregation, unable to spot us.

"Then I spoke at the Académie Française, proposed we revise the dictionary, adding hundreds of new words and new ideas! Each of us would take a letter. I would take the letter A. And the Marquis de Chastellux thanked me in the name of 'letters.' Not bad, eh? I went incognito to see a performance of *Alzire*, but of course, someone recognized me – forty-five minutes of applause!"

He is grinning a toothless old man's smirk. His bony joints press through his worn finery. His silk stockings are unrolling down his knees and his plume has broken in the struggle to squeeze himself between Eva-Marie and me.

He starts coughing and brings one of his lace-edged handkerchiefs to his mouth. I am shocked to see blood stains.

"You're not well! Go sit in the car."

"*Non, non, non.* I bled like this in Paris and they called in a priest. Oh ho! That was the night I made a sort of confession! Let's see, what did I say to that abbé?" His frail form hunches over as he retreats into his memories.

Up at the altar, the children begin reciting the Act of Contrition, "*Je confesse à Dieu tout-puissant que j'ai péché en pensée, en parole, par action* . . . I confess to God Almighty that I have sinned in thought, word, and deed . . . I ask the Virgin Mary, the angels and all the saints, to pray to the Lord . . ." My first-born speaks in French the familiar phrases I can follow only in English.

V.'s rasping breath breaks in, "Confession! Hah! I confessed to that old hypocrite exactly as much as I thought would win me a warm, decent grave; that if God disposes of me, I die in the Catholic religion in which I was born, hoping in the Divine Mercy that will pardon all my faults; and that if I had ever scandalized the Church, I ask pardon of God and her."

"After eighty years of ferocious attacks on Mother Church, did they buy it?"

"No." V. shrugs.

The sun is shining through stained-glass windows along the side of the chapel on to the white robes of the children, delighting them with the rainbow colors glancing across their laps and hands, turning their hair bright purple or blue.

Soon it is time for the Credo. The childish chorus chants, "*Je crois en Dieu, le Père tout-puissant, Créateur du ciel et de la terre* . . . I believe in God, the Father Almighty, Creator of heaven and earth . . . And Christ shall come again, to judge the living and the dead, to sit at the right of the Father . . ."

V. mutters, "Rubbish!" He shouts out over the heads of all the proud parents, "And what's holding Him up from descending in a cloud to establish this Kingdom of God? What's the delay? Thick fog over Mont Blanc?"

Not a head turns, of course, to burst his gleeful bubble. The old man leans back with a mischievous grin.

The children file into the pews at the front of the church. The priest descends from the altar to stand right in front of the first pew.

"What does God intend by giving us the sacrament of Communion?" he asks, smiling over them.

There are nervous titters. Finally a little red-headed girl pipes up, "To communicate?"

"*Oui*, to be one with Him. And what do we feel when we take Communion with our Lord?"

"We feel joyful," says another dutiful little girl.

"*Bien, bien*," he says. "And why are we on earth?" he barks out at the children.

There is a long silence. The children fidget nervously. This is a theological curve ball, not anticipated by the volunteer mothers on Tuesday afternoons.

"Why did God make us?" The priest raises an eyebrow and leans threateningly over the row of ten-year-olds, who cover their mouths with their hands to suppress their giggles.

The priest, clearly amused at wrong-footing the candidates, turns his gaze to the teachers themselves. They shift nervously at the ends of the pews, poking their charges to answer.

"WHY DID GOD PUT US HERE ON EARTH?" the African booms up at the gallery. The organist's elbow accidentally hits the keyboard, and a single amplified note shocks the entire congregation out of its composure. More titters.

One arm finally goes up. It is thin and white and the heavy robe falls away to reveal my inadequate job of ironing the Oxford Boy's Shirt (size ten) mail-ordered from Land's End.

"Yes?" The enormous priest lowers his arms and beams greedily over his victim.

A weedy voice with an American accent reaches our ears at the back.

"TO KNOW, LOVE, AND SERVE GOD IN THIS LIFE AND THE NEXT!"

The priest raises his eyebrows, leans back, and looks Alexander up and down. There seems to be a finality to this exchange which flummoxes any further interrogation. The priest gazes at Alexander one instant longer, nods, and mounts the altar to finish the Mass.

I am not so surprised, because I know exactly who has infiltrated his Deist prejudices in my unsuspecting son's unconscious, God only knows by what telepathy.

"It's the best answer," V. sputters as we move slowly out of the church. "Deism is an ordered consensus among reasonable people tempered by mythology to keep the majority in check. At least Alexander didn't mention all that Trinity and Communication nonsense."

We're pressed in on all sides by cooing parents and grandparents. Nobody notices a bouquet of daffodils tangled in V.'s hat, and when he finally extracts himself from the crowd, one flower is comically twisted around his broken plume.

Once home, the First Communicant, still flush with "Grace," offers to help set the table. We're going to have his favorite Chinese chicken in orange sauce. He had to return the robe, but he wears his crucifix all day. I think wistfully of the big family lunch we might have had for him, were we still in the U.S. It's at times like these that I'm the loneliest, knowing all the while that romantic visions of huge family banquets peopled by happy generations around a big ham are best left to Norman Rockwell paintings.

"I wish he'd take off that cross," Peter grumbles. "The boy's acting a little too 'illuminated' for my taste."

"It won't last more than a few hours," I reassure him. And

for better or worse, while still wearing the crucifix, Alexander fights with Theo over some Lego piece before the evening is out.

I shiver as I clean up the kitchen that night. It's close to eight o'clock and Peter has already gone upstairs to take a bath. Although we had a warm day, spring departs from the mountains rather reluctantly. Friends tell me that New York temperatures have hit the upper seventies. Down in Nyon, roses are smothering stone walls hiding old villas. Up here, the humid chill of thousands of pine trees wraps its evening cool around the house.

V. is trembling, sitting over the heater under the dining room window, wrapped in a plaid blanket. He says he wants to watch the last sunrays fall over Mont Blanc while he sips his hot chocolate.

"Well, perhaps it wasn't such a good idea. I can no longer see so well."

For a moment, he closes his eyes and sways a little. I run to his side and he opens his eyes and looks at me a little dizzily.

"What was that?"

"Nothing, nothing," he smiles. "Just one of those little moments I've been having lately. I call them God's *petits avertissements*. I'll be all right."

He coughs slightly.

"I haven't long to go," he mumbles.

"Stop it! Every time you say that, I find out you've got decades to go. You don't look a day over seventy," I joke. "You're just the same old humbug who turned up here un-invited last November. You do look a little tired. Go up to bed."

"*Non, non*," he says. He drops his precious Chinese cup with a dangerous clink, splashing a drop. "*Mon Dieu*, what I would give for a good cup of coffee, but I can't drink it anymore. If I have to go to the bathroom one more time for no reason, it'll kill me."

"Maybe you've been taking too many baths," I suggest, as cheerfully as I can muster. "You've always been the cleanest guy of your century, or for that matter, of any century."

V. allows himself a little laughing retort, "Regimen is superior medicine," but I notice his hand is trembling as he straightens his floppy knitted cap. How slight he's become!

"If only a doctor could see you. Come to think of it, that's how all of this started. Remember? I mistook you for the doctor!"

He sighs, "As far as doctors go, I only trusted Tronchin in Geneva. He was six foot tall, wise as Aesculapius and as handsome as Apollo. His charity, his disinterestedness, his affection and care for his wife, all of him inspired me with boundless respect and regard —"

"How lovely —"

"Yes, especially as his wife was the sulkiest, most unendurable woman in existence!"

He cackles at his own joke, but starts coughing blood again.

"No." He twists Émilie's ring around and around his middle finger. He is deep in thought, avoiding my affectionate gaze.

"*Chère Madame*, it has been a pleasure staying with you but, I think, it is time for me to go."

"You're tired. You'll feel ready for action after a good night's sleep."

"Yes, I'm just fatigued. Nothing gives me more life than the work I see ahead. But I've been worried since that death threat came that it might be you or the family who get burned down, not my little ghostly office upstairs."

"Don't be silly. Now, go to bed. You worry about all these causes, these infamies so much, it's wearing you out."

Waving a sort of apology, he struggles up the office stairs, leaning heavily on his ornate cane. It hasn't occurred to me until now, having had this fancy stick thrust in my face during our little rows, that the cane is more than just a cherished prop of his theater days.

He stops to catch his breath. "Funny, I've often been sick in my day, but rarely so feeble. It reminds me of that last night in Paris."

"Last night? What last night?" I ask.

"Yes, my old *ami* Richelieu heard I'd been coughing up blood for weeks. He sent me a vial of opium. I don't like to discuss such private matters, but the coughing wasn't the only malady. My urination was becoming painful, almost impossible."

"You love to talk about your maladies, you old hypochondriac," I chide. "I don't know how many times I've heard about your pissing problems. I never knew a man so fascinated by his own bladder."

"Then, if you know me so well, *Madame*, you can imagine I was anxious to get better! I was only eighty-four, for God's sake! I had lived this long with a very weak constitution and only care saved me, but now, I'd been so busy during those weeks of my homecoming to Paris . . ."

He labors up a few more steps, then looks down at me with an expression of indignation and frustration. "I even bought a house and was intending to stay in Paris, never to return to Ferney! Paris was so much fun!"

"Dr. Tronchin warned you to take it easy."

"If I'd listened to my doctors, I would have died the week I was born! But I misunderstood Richelieu's instructions and drank all the opium in one go. It put me into a delirium, or it must have been a dream, because I remember some priests turning up and saying my confession had been inadequate!"

The hunched craggy figure clings to the railing and gazes up at the rest of the stairs to be navigated. He turns to me with a disgusted expression. "Would you believe they wanted me to profess belief in the Divinity of Christ! Me! Voltaire!"

"Thanks for coming to church with us. Now, go to bed."

"Believe in Christ, hah! In God's name, don't talk to me of that man! That's exactly what I yelled with the last breath of my body at them!"

"Goodnight. Sleep well." I say. "Remember to snuff out your candle."

He shuffles up the rest of the flight of stairs, mumbling to himself, "Yes, let me go in peace, I'm really very tired."

His words worry me, and his appearance even more. I know that look, that shadow of death. I saw it in my father's face two nights before he succumbed, a grayish pallor coming over his skin as he lay in the hospital bed, his mind muffled by morphine. He rambled out memories of jungle warfare in the Pacific. I saw it in my mother's face her last night too, as the cicadas sang her to sleep in her bungalow on that April night in L.A., nearly twenty-five years later.

Did I think that by making friends with the dead, I could defy death itself? I sense shadows moving towards me. I can sleep only fitfully, my dreams mixing the church ceremony with visions of V.'s blood-stained handkerchief and graveyards full of applauding villagers from St-Cergue.

The Patriarch

On Monday, after everyone else in the house has sailed off to their regular ports of call, I glance at the stairs leading up to my office. V. is late for our promised debate about moving the archery target to make way for a hen house. He proposes selling fresh eggs to pay for his book buys. I relish all our recent arguments, and not for the first time, am so happy to have someone to enliven the silent hours.

With relief I hear him inching down the stairway, humming a little tune, broken by fits of coughing. The buttons of his damask dressing gown are fastened to the wrong buttonholes.

I pass him his mail – an appeal against female circumcision – but he leaves it unread. His skeletal hand is lying on the kitchen table. His soft white cap flops over one ear. He smells of lavender soap, but some foam lurks behind one ear where his razor missed.

He raises his head from his reverie and repeats, in the gentlest of tones, almost a whisper, "You know, I meant what I said last night. It's high time I go home."

To my surprise, he lifts my hand and gallantly brushes a kiss over it. His own hand looks frail and – I catch his eye as we both notice – a little transparent around the knuckles.

There is an embarrassed pause, so unlike our usual morning banter. There must be something I can do to fend off this melancholy mood.

"I think your batteries are running low," I joke. "I'll get you a lobster from the fish market. You ridiculed people who said it was good for their blood, but hey, it's worth a try."

He doesn't answer his own old joke about lobsters feeding the blood and eels curing paralysis. I start to panic. Is my best friend going to leave just like this, fade out on me, go all see-through, and vanish into a steam cloud?

"You know, I didn't really mean what I said about you being the house guest from Hell." I clench my teeth to keep from making some kind of whimper, that awful whine of loneliness that his arrival had erased from my heart.

His face brightens a little, "You know, it's time to tend to my estate."

"That mausoleum in Geneva? C'mon! It's okay for school tours and visiting scholars, but you tried that once. You wouldn't be happy there, watching Lekain play Orosmane over and over again. Then you'd have to listen to the snide comments of that Englishman – what's his name? – Callander?"

He wags his head. "No, I mean we're going to Ferney."

"*We're* going?"

"Of course! It's still standing, *non*?"

"We can go to Ferney, just like that? Yes, yes – of course we can. Why didn't we think of it before?"

"It's not far from here. The private owners finally sold it back to the town. It was in the local paper, which you're too much of a snob to peruse. They're turning it into a center for free speech, a sanctuary to showcase the works of persecuted writers and artists. I can go home now. In fact, I'd better return before they make it some tourist nightmare or mummified library, *n'est-ce pas?* Besides, there's something I want to find out, something I couldn't learn at Les Délices."

"This is wonderful! The greatest house guest of the eighteenth century is finally inviting me to his château?"

"Well, somebody has to drive me," he says testily.

"Oh! Oh!" I cry with undisguised delight. "Wait a minute –

oh – what about the kids? Theo and Eva-Marie come home for lunch at eleven-thirty. Damned that school! I can't go!"

"*Madame*, you will leave them a note. You haven't noticed, but I have. Your children are growing up. They will make themselves a little *goûter* of peanut butter *tartines* and watch appalling *Wishbone* videos. They won't miss you for hours."

And so for the very first time, I write a note to my children, grab my driving glasses and passport, and the two of us set off to play hookey.

As the sun hits my face, I realize it is the last day of spring. The brilliant, dry day makes anything seem possible. We exit the back end of the village, and cross the higher plateau of La Givrine, heading towards the French border, formerly Voltaire's Serf Central.

I can hardly imagine what I'm doing – just driving toward a part of France I've never visited, no phone call to Peter, no conception of how long it will take and what we will find, just speeding along with V., his lanks of white hair wafting in the draft of the open window.

Why has it taken the old journalist warhorse in me so long to throw off the yoke of maternal routine? Why has a creeping fear of dislocation and alienation kept me hiding in my house? I feel like breaking into song. We are "Crosby and Hope," we are "Thelma and Louise," we are "V. and Me."

Over the last few weeks, V. has been visibly suffering from age. The cane is now his faithful third leg. He's given up the wigs altogether for his floppy nightcap. His brown eyes have lost a great deal of their fire, although none of their sparkle. Now our getaway gives him energy I haven't seen during the final, bleak months of our long, stubborn winter together.

Seven minutes later, I slow the car to pass the customs kiosk and inch around the German shepherds of the Swiss drug narcs and the lackadaisical French *douaniers* chatting over their coffees. Then turning sharp left, we drive along the ridge of the Jura mountains.

"Can't we cut down to the highway?" he says, scanning the map spread across his tail-coat of black damask. I haven't seen that garment in ages.

"Why would you want to take a road that didn't exist in your day? I chose the old road for your sake."

I am such a misguided Romantic! Of course, Rousseau would have taken the forest road. Voltaire is the modern man of Science. My choice of the scenic route adds a quarter of an hour to our drive, but I gasp at the untouched forests and steep crevasses.

I'm thankful he didn't get the homing urge last January. Warnings for winter drivers dot the roadway, "Check your brakes," "Drive carefully," and other hints as we swerve through the pines. Running below our two-lane tarmacked road is a rutted dirt track at the bottom of the valley.

"The old carriage road!" V. exclaims. And of course, I realize now, before the ski industry invaded these backwoods, there was no reason to cut a road halfway up the mountains, when the refreshing streams and fertile little valleys offered security below.

V. drums his thin fingers on his cadaverous thigh. "Can't you go faster?" he grumbles.

"Don't get cranky. This was your idea." I grip the steering wheel a little too tightly around another sharp curve with an unpleasant thought. He seems to be in a hurry. For what?

After twenty minutes, we start a steep descent down the mountains back to the lakeside plateau and civilization again. We're still in France, but within ten minutes of Geneva, too.

At the bottom of the long plunge, we pass through Gex, which my friend built into the watchmaking capital of Europe. Gex has fallen on seedy times as an antique center, surrounded by do-it-yourself malls named things like Bricorama. We pass the Buffalo Grill, Shalimar Restaurant, the Dragon of Saigon, and the Mai Thai. God help me if Voltaire's beloved Ferney has turned into suburban sprawl.

With one last swing through a round-about, there we are, driving toward the center of Ferney. The streets are overhung with shade trees, the shops and low-rise office complexes are genteel and prosperous-looking. It looks good to me.

"I don't recognize a thing," V. complains.

I spy a statue; surely, I think, of V. himself. To please him, I point the car straight towards the beckoning stone figure, its wing-like appurtenances on either side an ominous signal, but my eyesight is not that much better than V.'s. Our faces fall. It is a statue of V. but V. as in the *Virgin Mary*, here in the center of *his* town!

He groans. We take another turn, and there, thank goodness, we see facing us a second statue, this one – yes! – it is of my V., smiling benevolently over an inscription "*A nôtre patriarche, Voltaire.*"

It takes us only a few more minutes of looking for a parking space to realize that every other corner of the village is punctuated by a small sign, pointing towards a facsimile silhouette in black and white of Voltaire's château and a rather commercial rendition of his face. Considering how bad-tempered he's been during the drive, I'm amused to see that the Historical Voltaire is condemned to an eternity of serene smiling down from every lamp post and bus stop.

I watch my own Voltaire steady himself on his two pins and walking stick and admonish him, "I think you had better pull up your stockings."

"Let's see, where are we?" he asks, gazing around the parking lot. "Ah, there's the hill and if I'm not mistaken, my house is above that school yard."

We head up the steep path. He leans on my arm, no weight at all, considering everything. We see children frolicking in a steel and concrete playground. He shakes his stick in warning, "If this school is named after some wretched saint — "

" — or Jean-Jacques Rousseau — ?"

" — we're heading right back to your house," he threatens,

breathing heavily. He marches us over to the plaque over the school entrance.

"École Jean Calas," I read aloud.

Visibly relieved, V. nods, "That poor, tortured soul. How good of them."

We pass a graveyard, the tall gray stones basking in the sun. "Are you — ?" The question is so ominous, I haven't the heart to finish it.

"We shall see, we shall see," he says. A grim expression crosses his face.

The weather is so warm as we skirt the outer walls of V.'s château, I am relieved when we reach a cool, dark little gatehouse. There isn't much here, just a few book-shelves and a reception counter. A desultory pair of French girls chitchat, smoking into each other's faces, twisting their hair through their fingers. You'd think I was as invisible as V.

Finally, one downs her cigarette and sells me an entrance ticket. She tells me to wait for another forty minutes before the next "*grope*" is taken through the gate.

I glance around me and there is only V. We wait in vain for more arrivals to join our "*grope*."

The gatehouse is sufficient proof to me that the worst excesses of the international tourist industry have yet to discover my good friend. There are no: "*Écrasez l'infâme*" T-shirts, no "Cultivate Your Garden" kiddie tool-kits (8–12 years), no carrier bags with "I ♥ Voltaire," no mouse pads covered with Newtonian calculations, no "Madame Denis Cookbooks for Entertaining Hungry House Guests," no Louis XV puppets or books of Madame de Pompadour paper dolls.

In short, no Voltairiana Crap in sight.

Our "*grope*," still only us two, is taken in hand by a well-fed blonde student named Sonya.

Just outside the gatehouse, she points out a substantial chapel built by the previous Swiss proprietor, a Monsieur de Budé, but re-designed by Voltaire. Engraved over the chapel door, I see

---

DEO EREXIT

VOLTAIRE

---

that is, "Voltaire erects this to God."

V. whispers to me, "This is the only Catholic church I know erected to God alone: all the others are consecrated to saints. I preferred to build a church to the Lord than to His servants."

"The letters spelling 'Voltaire' are a lot bigger than God's," I comment. V. smiles impishly.

"Please pay attention, *Madame*." Sonya scolds. "When Monsieur Voltaire reconstructed the chapel, he added a pyramid along the side, half inside, half outside, meant to be *Monsieur*'s final resting place —"

"Half inside the church and half outside, like me!" V. crows.

"Monsieur Voltaire wrote to Pope Benedict for relics for his church and received a piece of hair shirt belonging to St. Francis of Assisi. There were two bell towers for Monsieur Voltaire and Madame Denis, who was his niece and house-keeper —"

"And so very much more," he winks at me,

" — but in the end these burial places were not used," Sonya concludes.

V. shoots a look of alarm at the girl.

The chapel is closed to the public, like most of the house. I realize that not only are there no knickknack sales, V.'s house hasn't been fully restored. Visitors' rules are no impediment, however, to the master of the house, who is wobbling ahead of me on his cane to inspect his property.

"When he arrived in Ferney, Monsieur Voltaire described some forty shoeless savages and a dilapidated house which he rebuilt in stone and expanded with sixteen bedrooms. Soon so many famous celebrities came to pay their respects, he would come to be known as the Innkeeper of Europe," she recites to me. "One of the first things he did was to chop down the trees that grew along the line you see there, facing east, to open the view to the Alps."

"That blasted beautiful panoramic view of Mont Blanc. I cut down the trees to make way for it, and then I tired of it," he mutters back at me.

"He drained marshes, constructed houses, paved streets, installed a public fountain, and built the village a new Catholic church."

"With NO Virgin Mary," he stipulates.

I turn to take in for the first time the full breadth of V.'s château.

I gasp, "It's beautiful!"

"*Mais oui*," he sighs. "You expected a goat shed?"

The château stands three stories high, with a main hall and two wings extending on either side, one wing for V. and one for Madame Denis. I hold my breath as Sonya leads me towards the front steps, but V. is too fast for her, struggling on his cane to extend to me a proper welcome to his last abode, the supreme host and gentleman to the last. He holds the door open with a "Ladies, please," and then jumps up with a strangled, "AIIIGH!" His eyes are like two boiled eggs with shock.

"Here we see two statues greeting us as we enter this historic residence," Sonya announces. "On the right, of course, a statue of Voltaire himself, and on the left —"

But I'm already staring, like V., at the statue on the left, as elegant and finely wrought as the one of my friend.

" — a statue of Jean-Jacques Rousseau!" Sonya concludes.

I stammer, "B– b– but Voltaire *hated* Jean-Jacques Rousseau. Who put this thing in his own foyer?"

"NOT ME!" he shouts in Sonya's face.

Unperturbed, the girl explains, "The house was inherited from Voltaire by the Marquise de Villette, the child whom he adopted in his later years and whom he nicknamed La Belle-et-Bonne. Many years later, La Belle-et-Bonne sold it. It fell to the Lambert-David family who kept it until quite recently, when the *Commune*, which became Ferney-Voltaire in 1890, assumed ownership."

"Not Lamberts descended from Madame du Châtelet's lover?"

"No relation," she assures me. V. follows us, but not before giving the Rousseau statue a vengeful kick with his soft shoe.

V. leans on my arm, recovering from the shock of the Rousseau statue. He gestures out of the bay windows over the grounds and points out the Lyon tapestry depicting a Chinese scene. I can almost ignore our guide pratling on about Catherine the Great's purchase of V.'s books after his death, the family disputes over the house, the demolition of the original bed chamber, and the restoration that will be done on the floors above.

"You noticed the heating works I installed near the front door? Did you see the matching *trompe-l'oeil* wall on the other side? I thought that was very clever," he boasts.

"A turquoise and yellow color scheme?" I cringe at the garish lacquer on the walls.

"Very authentic, *Madame*," says Sonya.

"Terribly chic at the time," V. butts in, then jokes, "I wasn't born into a *beige* age. Ah! There is the chair upholstered by Madame Denis herself!"

I lean over to examine the less than masterful greenish brown threads. "Was needlework her thing?"

"Hardly, but it distracted her from insisting I produce any more of her dreadful plays," he replied.

"*Madame,* please pay attention," the girl orders me. "Monsieur Voltaire built himself a hot-water bathhouse, one of the first of his time."

"I feared too much hygiene was weakening me, so then I tore it out," he adds.

". . . And here we see a portrait of La Belle-et-Bonne, or La Marquise de Villette, whom Monsieur Voltaire adopted from a poor, but respectable family when she was about to be sent off to a convent to become a nun — "

"You bet I stopped that!" he crows.

" — and whom he married off to the Marquis de Villette, the son of his old friend, Suzanne de Villette."

"Not a bad boy, but he always cherished the vain and wrongful notion that he was my bastard son," adds V.

" — and some say was Voltaire's illegitimate son," Sonya adds – to a groan of protest from V.

Sonya crosses the room and gestures, "Here at the foot of Monsieur Voltaire's bed, we see the portrait of Marie Thérèse, Queen of Austria. Monsieur Voltaire liked to joke that — "

I finish it for her, " — it was so pleasant to wake up with an empress at his feet."

Sonya looks startled. "Why, yes! That's exactly what he used to say! And over here is the shawl La Belle-et-Bonne wore to Monsieur Voltaire's funeral."

Before I know it, V. has stretched himself out on the slim blue bed and closed his eyes.

"Now here," she says, gesturing at a small oil painting, "is a painting of the actor Lekain of the Comédie-Française. He performed at the château many times. And here, of course, we have a portrait — "

I find myself looking up into V.'s youthful roguish eyes twinkling down at me from an oil painting.

"He looks so . . ." I struggle for words.

"Handsome, is the word you're looking for, *Madame*," says the crotchety old man from the bed. "Snappy, debonair, brilliant and — "

"So much like him," I falter, to V.'s disgust.

"Humph! I'm going for a walk!"

I ask our guide for directions to the ladies room.

"There is nothing working in the house, but some temporary facilities are outside," she says.

"Some restoration!" he grumbles on his way out of the door.

A very up-to-date blue plastic toilet cabinet sits inside the shady flank of the house. I find V. a few minutes later, gazing down from the terrace.

"Yes, yes," he murmurs to himself, stopping now and then to measure by eye the acreage of flattened grassland below.

"Let's see . . . over there were the vineyards," he explains. I try to imagine him striding the fields at sixty-five years old, laying them out with his workers. What optimism to lay grapevines when most people are lining up for pensions!

A dappled pathway beyond is packed hard by his own repeated use two centuries ago, so hard that still nothing much can sink a root here. Sonya has told us that after his death, vengeful interests of Church and State tried to eradicate much of what he had built up but this long worn footpath resists time.

Neglect hangs over the place. The beech trees have lined both sides of the path long enough to form a dense canopy of leaves only a few feet above my head. The effect is protective rather than tunnel-like; my friend made a retreat for himself inside his retreat and now he is sharing it with me.

I have never felt closer to V. than in this "*cabinet de verdure,*" where neither one of us is surrounded by the trappings of our separate centuries – the distractions of my children and kitchen, nor that garish aqua and egg-yolk decor of V.'s house.

What is two hundred and twelve years, after all? Figure that my hardy Swiss mother-in-law lived ninety-five years and V. himself lived eighty-four, then add one more life as long, and suddenly V. and I seem separated by so little, we two who tread his favorite path, me in my mail-order driving moccasins and he in his wooden-heeled, hand-crafted shoes.

There is no sound around us but the twittering of birds. Time has totally stopped for me here in V.'s garden. No wonder Boswell pleaded by letter to Voltaire to stay over for one night. If I hear anything beside the birds, it is the murmurings of grateful souls whose lives V. changed for the better, including mine.

To Dust Even Voltaire Shalt Return

A farm truck jounces its way across V.'s former vineyard. And it jolts us back to the present.

"I think that well-rehearsed child is waiting for us," V. sighs.

But Sonya has run out of things to tell me. We've finished the tour of V.'s study filled with souvenirs of his triumphant procession to Paris and volumes in crumbling leather bindings under glass.

She waits for more questions and I have so many, my heart is full as I stand before this girl with her fresh face, neat summaries, and memorized anecdotes. She knows a great deal about the historic Voltaire, but so little of my friend, V. – his disappointments in love, the betrayals of his friends, his terror of failure, his political humiliations. Does she see him, bankrupt in exile in England writing to his faithless friend Thieriot for emergency funds? Can she picture him arguing from the footlights with the booing audience at *Artémire*? Does she pity him, sobbing with sorrow at Cirey, where Madame du Châtelet's corpse lies warm on her bed? Does Sonya follow him on his solitary carriage rides by night across Europe, fleeing torture and *l'infâme* for the sake of a few pointed stanzas of truth?

V. has taught me to understand all the small forks and turnings that anybody's half-century would bring. Perhaps this is all I share with him – not his fame, talent, wealth or royal friends. I know my friend as the companion of every day of my difficult, lonely first year in Switzerland. It is more than a twenty-year-old could have time to know. And as I stand before this sincere young woman, I cannot speak.

Bereft of more tourist patter, Sonya translates for me a motto painted over a large black cenotaph standing against the wall of his bedroom, "My heart is here."

"Where's the rest of me?" V. whispers. His quavering voice speaks of the terror with which his generation feared an unmarked grave. Hadn't he reeled with shock at the hasty burial without rites of Molière's corpse under cover of night? Hadn't he boasted that one of his finest hours was his protest at Adrienne Lecouvreur's body being tossed like a dog into an unmarked heap of quicklime? Hadn't he envied Newton's funeral procession marked by tributes of English dukes and earls? His earlier elation has disappeared.

Trembling, he turns his back on my bewildered expression. He is reciting to himself the poem he wrote memorializing Adrienne, ". . . *Celle qui dans la Grèce aurait eu des autels, je les ai vus soumis, autour d'elles empressés; sitôt qu'elle n'est plus, elle est donc criminelle! Elle a charmé le monde, et vous l'en punissez!*"* He practically spits out the words, then turns to me, his expression furious.

So this was behind his impatience all morning.

"Sonya, I do have one more question, maybe the most important question of all. Where exactly does Monsieur Voltaire lie now?"

"I actually allowed a priest to sit at my deathbed," he says, quivering with tension, pleading in his eyes. "I've got to know."

She nods, smiling. "Oh, yes, I forgot. The religious authorities in Paris refused a burial, so Voltaire's nephew, the Abbé Mignot, smuggled the corpse, propped up in a carriage seat, to his own abbey in Scellières in the province of Champagne. But

---

* "They deprived her of burial, she who in Greece would have had altars. I have seen them adoring her, crowding about her; hardly is she dead than she becomes a criminal! She charmed the world and you punish her!"

not before La Belle-et-Bonne's husband, the Marquis de Villette, had himself removed Monsieur Voltaire's heart during the embalming."

"Is the abbey grave well-kept?"

Sonya looks embarrassed. "Well, no, they buried the corpse in a hurry under two feet of lime in the basement before any Church orders from Paris could stop them."

I cannot bear to look at my friend, who mutters, "At least it was a burial."

Sonya adds, "But he was honored during the French Revolution when the National Assembly moved his remains to the Pantheon in Paris!"

I hear a soft "Ah," behind me.

"An oak wreath was put around the head and the body was moved to a sarcophagus, but not before an admirer had stolen the heel bone for the Museum of Troyes."

"Relics of me, like a saint!" he remarks in ironic wonder, smacking his toothless gums.

Sonya now paints a glorious return to Paris for my old pal. "On July 6th, 1791 a squadron of revolutionary cavalry, followed by infantry, set off with his sepulchral coach from Romilly-on-Seine on the five-day journey to Paris. Villages were lit up at night to illuminate his passage. Mothers held their children up to kiss the sarcophagus. His coffin was set down to rest on the site of the Bastille, now torn into a pile of rubble by vengeful revolutionaries."

This is just the beginning of the hero treatment.

Once in Paris, V. gets an eighteenth-century version of a ticker-tape parade – Swiss Guards, flag-carriers, Bastille-wreckers, French Academy members, and all the assembled writers of France bearing volumes of his works – marching past half a million cheering onlookers.

Sonya tells us that his coffin bears the inscription, "He defended Calas, La Barre, Sirven, and Montailli. As a poet, thinker, and historian, he gave mankind the greatest gifts. He has prepared us for liberty."

"Are you quite satisfied?" I signal to V.

He's grinning behind me. "Hush, this is good."

"The procession halted at L'Opéra, where the company sang a song from Monsieur Voltaire's *Samson*, which became, with 'La Marseillaise,' the anthem of the French Revolution."

"Wake ye people. Break your chains!" V. sings in glee around Sonya, who, unmindful of the croaking old monkey, continues, "After L'Opéra, they passed the Tuileries. Every window was filled with spectators, save one. Behind that, closed and barred, sat King Louis and Marie Antoinette, awaiting their doom."

"*Tant pis*," V. quips.

Sonya adds, "The sides of the coffin bore two of his own quotations: 'If man is created free, he must govern himself,' and 'If man has tyrants, he must dethrone them.'"

"Mellifluous, *non*?" V. crows.

I interrupt. "So his body lies in the Pantheon?"

My blunt question startles Sonya out of her dramatic re-creation of Voltaire's glory.

"Oh, no," she says, matter-of-factly and starts towards the exit gate.

V. and I give a start, and chase after her, panting a little in surprise.

"Why not? Why can't we visit his body in the Pantheon?"

"Because Monsieur Voltaire's bones were stolen with those of Jean-Jacques Rousseau by reactionary fanatics in 1814."

"How?"

"Orders from the director of the mint, a Monsieur de Puymorin," she answers with the complacency of youth contemplating dead history. I hear a shuddering choking next to me.

Sonya blithely finishes her tale. To this young woman, it is all one – the Pantheon, the pit, the parade, the guillotine. "The thieves drove by night to a city dump at the Barrière de la Gare. Some accomplices had already dug a big hole and —"

"The city dump? There's no grave at all?"

"Well, no," Sonya shrugs. "Monsieur Voltaire's remains were lost forever."

Taken out with the garbage. With Rousseau, of all people.

She adds, "Of course you can go to see the statue of him by Houdon at the Théâtre-Français."

I steel myself to face the crumpled, crestfallen old man, merely a bundle of bones in his homecoming wrappings of linen and damask. It saddens me to see the once-elegant figure of theatrical gaiety, who danced with a toy sword across the narrow width of my office, reduced to this. Those wise old eyes start filling with tears, his expression pleading with me to change history itself.

Then he stumbles blindly out of the French doors opened to the garden, a low wail piercing the air, his despairing form limping jerkily away on his stick.

I thank Sonya for the tour, but she lingers, sensing that she has failed me in some way.

"You seem more interested than most of the American tourists we get here," she says. "Maybe you'd like to meet the curator some time?"

"Yes, yes, I'll do that," I say, glancing out of the French doors for a sign of V. The sunlight warms the wooden floor, but the story of Voltaire's bones has chilled me. Sonya jabbers on about how soon, the "*cyber-chocolaterie*" will be offering coffee, hot chocolate, and internet access, in memory of Voltaire.

I shake her hand and excuse myself. When I reach the steps, I scan the whole vista – the broad path leading to the house, the grove of trees where his theater of three hundred seats once stood.

Then I hear a familiar chuckle escalating into a hoarse shout of laughter coming from his "green office." I spot him standing in the middle of the verdant corridor, waving his cane, wildly gesticulating for me to join him. I dash over to find that he is not collapsing, but merely gathering his breath, shaking his head as if at some enormous joke.

"Oh, what does it matter?" he cries to me, pointing at the skies. "What did it ever matter? HE has had the last laugh. From dust I cam'st and to dust I shalt return! What does it matter now, if I'm here again, and we can stroll together? Why did I care so much? Why? Why?"

"Because . . . because you're the great Voltaire, the true king of your time, *La — La Lumière*," I stutter, near tears. "I'm so, so sorry."

He looks at me, blows his nose, and shakes himself like a bony old dog. We stand for a minute staring at Mont Blanc.

Then with a clawlike grip, he takes my arm. "We never talked about my efforts to clear the name of Admiral Byng who lost the sea battle at Minorca to my friend Richelieu. The vanity of England was so hurt by this defeat, they court-martialed and shot their own man in 1757 — 'to encourage the others,' they claimed."

My heart is still thudding from the fear that his soul has been swallowed into some unreachable place along with his useless, despised carcass. I can't take that risk again.

"Do you mind if I jot down some of the things we've talked about?"

"For some little book *philosophique*?"

"Something like that."

"Why not?" he says. "Frederick always said that any companion of mine with nothing more than a good memory could make a brilliant book out of the good things I said just at random."

Clearly mere old age will not dim his ego, nor time wither his courtier's vanity.

He wags an arthritic finger in my face. "Just remember that history is a form of playing tricks with the dead. It's gross charlatanry to pretend to paint the portrait of a man with whom you've never lived!"

"Oh, I've lived with you all right. And now I want to write down what's happened this first year, how you've kept me company, all the stories you've told me – something fictional, but at the same time —"

"Fiction is nothing but truth in disguise," he states, tapping his stick on the beaten path.

"Yes, that's what I mean – truthful fiction – that's the idea, although," I hesitate, not a little embarrassed, "at the end of the day, I'm not sure what it all means."

He chuckles and sucks at his gums, "Oh, I wouldn't worry. The most useful books are those in which the readers supply half the meaning. That was the point of *Zadig*."

With that settled, we set off to walk the shady length of his "green office" together under the last rays of early summer.

"You'll come to visit me often?"

"Are you sure you'll be here?"

"I don't think I'll take any more trips to Paris. The last one proved so fatal," he jokes. "This house needs work. That Rousseau statue goes first. I can use those computers in the coffeeshop to run my web site. And God knows what the *Commune* intends as a center for writers. If I can't persuade this bunch to revive at least one of my plays, I might as well give up the ghost."

"So to speak," I respond, smiling.

V. wipes a little dribble off his old man's chin. "Persecuted writers, humph! Let's hope the quality of their writing is worthy of the persecution. I won't stand for any second-raters on my lawn."

He grins defiantly through his withered gums.

"Oh," I interject, "The B.B.C. reported that a Professor Holgate in Southampton has just discovered the asthma gene. You remember the night you arrived? Theo's asthma attack? They hope for a cure within ten years —"

"You mean gene therapy might work better than two hundred pints of lemonade? Hah!"

We laugh so hard, we break our stride. Then he collects his breath, and resumes his careful steps.

"You've learned a little from me, *non?*"

"*Oui*. Except how to speak French."

"You know what I've learned from talking to you, *Madame?*"

"From me?"

He nods. "That I had the best of all possible lives. Yes," he sighs, "most men die without having even lived. Not me. I'm contented now. You know, the news broke only days before I died, how my appeals had finally cleared the name of General de Lally, executed for treason in 1766 because he lost our Indian colony of Pondichéry. That dear girl La Belle-et-Bonne pinned the news to my deathbed curtains, written in huge letters so that I . . . Well, anyway, it was kind of a French version of the Byng outrage, you see . . . ."

I notice that half way up the leafy glade, he slips on Peter's sunglasses to protect his wrinkled eyes against the bright haze. Well, what's a pair of Armani sunglasses between old friends?

Acknowledgements

Inspiration from Voltaire's spirit was substantially assisted by past and present Voltairean scholars. I hereby acknowledge my gratitude to the authors of these two works:

The Life of Voltaire, vol. I and II, James Parton, Houghton Mifflin, Boston, 1882

Voltaire, Georg Brandes, Tudor Publishing Company, New York, 1936 (especially useful on the mystery surrounding Adrienne Lecouvreur's death, although the deductions are my own)

I am most grateful to the following authors and publishers for granting me permission to quote Voltaire directly or indirectly, or make reference to translations from their works:

Candide and Other Stories, Voltaire, The World's Classics, Oxford University Press, translation Roger Pearson, 1998

Letters Concerning the English Nation, Voltaire, The World's Classics, Oxford University Press, 1999

The Portable Voltaire, Penguin Books, 1977, edited by Ben Ray Redman, including: *Candide*, *Micromégas*, *Zadig*, *L'Ingénue*, *The White Bull*, *The Philosophical Dictionary*, and *Miscellaneous letters*

Thanks also to Simon and Schuster for permission to reproduce in part historical narrative related in:

The Age of Louis XIV, vol. VIII, Will Durant
The Age of Voltaire, Will and Ariel Durant, vol. IX
Rousseau and Revolution, Will and Ariel Durant, vol. X, from *The Story of Civilization*, Simon and Schuster, New York, 1961

Thanks to Sony Music Entertainment for permission to quote notes by Didier C. Deutsch accompanying:

Candide, book by Lillian Hellman, music by Leonard Bernstein, lyrics by Richard Wilbur, additional lyrics by John LaTouche and Dorothy Parker. Original Broadway Cast Recording 1956, Sony Broadway, Sony Music Entertainment Inc., reissued 1991.

With special thanks to M. Charles Wirz, director, and Madame Catherine Walser, librarian, Le Musée Voltaire, Les Délices, Geneva for their help in locating the following background reading:

Correspondance, Grimm, Diderot, Raynal, Meister, etc. vol. IX, Garnier Frères, Libraires-éditeurs, 1879

Épître CVIII

L'Orphelin de la Chine

Zaïre

Essai sur les Moeurs

The Works of Voltaire, A Contemporary Version, Dingwall-Rock Ltd., translations by William F. Fleming, 1927

Lettere d'Amore al Nipote, Sellerio edizione Palermo, 1993

On Tolerance on the Occasion of the Death of Jean Calas

Voltaire et la Chine, Meng Hua, *Thèse de doctorat ès lettres*, University of Paris, Sorbonne, 1988

The French Image of China Before and After Voltaire by Basil Guy, *Studies on Voltaire and the Eighteenth Century*, vol. XXI

Also useful for background were:

The Age of Louis XIV, Voltaire, Everyman's Library, Dutton, New York, translation Martyn P. Pollack, 1969

Voltaire and Enlightenment, The Great Philosophers, John Gray, Phoenix/Orion Publishing Group Ltd. 1998

Voltaire in Love, Nancy Mitford, Carroll and Graf, 1957

Madame de Pompadour, Nancy Mitford, Hamish Hamilton, 1954

"Voltaire and Frederick the Great," from *Books and Characters, French and English* by Lytton Strachey, 1915 edited by Geoffrey Sauer

"A Village Mobilizes To Save Voltaire's House," by Marlise Simons, *The New York Times*, June 9, 1996

Voltaire à table, Christiane Mervaud, Éditions Desjonquères, 1998

Madame Voltaire, Gilbert Mercier, Éditions de Fallois, Paris, 2001

Larousse Gastronomique, Prosper Montagné, Crown, New York, 1966

Afterword

The democracy activist Xu Wenli was released from prison by the Chinese authorities for health reasons on Christmas Eve, 2002. He and his wife He Xintong immediately joined their daughter Xu Jin in the U.S.